Coolton Ascent

Rebecca J Cunningham

"… As workers fell ill, the land ravaged by flood, its poisonous skin a toxic history, New Britain remained suspended above it all, untainted.

Elsewhere, there were plenty who planned beyond the politics, those who were populating their own new and wholesome kingdom. And while storms lashed the coast, homes abandoned, histories swallowed, Coolton Ascent thrived and grew. A sanctuary, an archive for the forsaken.

It was said, by those who watched, that there were riches beyond the wildest up there, untold wealth sacked from all sorts of privileged places. An old man and woman who ran the place pretended they could bring the dead back. Yes, imagine! See spirits and watch them fly out of the body. Some people could catch them. And if you knew how, you could do it yourself – catch a soul. If you knew how. If you believed it..."

After its days as a sanatorium, Coolton Ascent lay empty. It was not until 2013 that the old vicarage was finally restored to its former glory, this time offering asylum to a different kind of exile.

Twenty years on, in one of its upper rooms, an old woman's life draws to its close. She recounts her passion for the house, the politics surrounding its demise: floods, riots, the souls…

Behind Coolton Ascent a procession of worshippers emerges from a small church and filing past, they look up to an open window.

'The meek are promised the earth,' they have been told. An inheritance.

They're still waiting.

Acknowledgments

Beatrice and Kim: the quantum leap.
Samuel Palmer: the enduring inspiration.
Tony Hibbett: the learning curve.
John B Cairns
Special thanks to Julia and Biddy: a new view on blue.

Coolton Ascent

Rebecca J Cunningham

Blujah Books

Coolton Ascent

Blujah Books: ISBN: 0-9542616-2-3
First published in Great Britain

Printed and bound in Great Britain by
Basingstoke Press Ltd, Wade Rd, Basingstoke, Hants RG24 8QW.

Published by Blujah Books,
440, London Road, TW7 5AD

Impression number 1

Dorothy Eileen Cunningham
June 1918 – September 1964

Wrapped in silence

Contents

Part I

Flower

2023

Christmas Rose

A boy ran across the sea.

"Foddly! Your son, he's here!"

She wasn't listening.

Bug Itin stopped calling. A vast cloak soaked him up, his life unwrapping from the velvet and mud beneath. Lying face upwards – a small man, hair sticking to the blades of grass, eyes closed. He could see a sky stained with red, amber, then green, like old traffic lights.

Time to go, he thought.

No one was waving to the cameras now; they were fleeing across the field – pushing that great fat thing in a wheelchair. Where do they think they'll get to? The world is the size of a handkerchief.

A few feet away from him a young man, also fallen – golden hair spreading out like serpents – tried to climb back, and failed. His stomach split open, gutless.

"Did that to yourself. No guts," Bug murmured, floating above. "You were a friend once, a beautiful traitor. Perfect treachery. Quite remarkable. There was a reason, I suppose – the most absurd nothings pivot on that."

Bug had been watching himself as well for a while, but that too must cease. She was here, the boy with her at last – mother and son rocking gently as he drifted in and out, an old man beside.

"Made a mistake there," whispered Bug, fading from his review.

She was bending over now. He couldn't explain. It would take too long to explain – another lifetime. How many of those do you get to the second? Hardly seemed to matter what he had to tell her yet she had taken up the whole of his existence. She must know by now.

The sun expanded, filling the sky, spilling over the high iron gates of the Factory. He was leaving that behind. Let somebody else find the words to describe the colours of a body emptying under sunset.

But names, give me names . . . Foddly! Come here, Foddly. The whole show is infinitesimal; if you understood that . . . you would . . . understand. That's why I'll never leave you. I can't. There's not enough space to get lost. To be honest, sweetheart, I knew it would happen, what they've done. The end has helped me see that. So in a way, I'm as cowardly as you.

Still here?

The earth has a very lovely curve. Pity it has taken this for me to see it. Why did I ever worry about you tipping off? It will be a privilege to be intimate with that arc. We can make one ourselves.

But I keep going back. Don't go, Foddly.

"What about the rainbows?" he asked the old man, as he had asked him years ago.

Glastonbury leaned nearer, his answer the last. "Bug, you're a very lucky fellow."

From the rim of the earth, a dark figure was directing it all.

2039
Coolton Ascent

Lilac

A boy ran past with his dream.

What was that?

I made mistakes. Can't think what they are now. D'you think I've been pardoned, or will people carry on measuring my shortcomings and judging me . . . afterwards?

I don't suppose any of it matters any more, all caught up with itself. You are a testament to that.

It's a beautiful day. Open the window and let some air in. The fragrance from that lilac is as soothing as ever – reminds me of so much. I wonder if the garden I return to will have lilacs or any flowers at all. There is another season, you know, that is without scent. But I've done my gardening, had a long and interesting journey and now have you, my final companion; what more could an old woman want? Come here and let me look at your lovely face.

Just one more thing . . . I'm not afraid, you do understand that, but I've taken to worrying . . . if a spirit can really travel through glass. Rather silly. Nonetheless, don't close the window, my dear.

*

A boy ran past with his dream, couldn't see us, his eyes were so full. And we laughed at how a child can cut out the unpleasant, spring up from the pain and fly right away.

We watched him running on, weaving in and out of his dreams, riding on the backs of dragons, of monsters, visions lifting him above the treacherous paving stones, the dismal earth, his heart as high as heaven.

One day the dreams would stop, the whisperings to his invisible companions cease. He would grow up and away from himself.

Childhood is a season we slip out of. It withers on the sleeve of a winter coat, a summer shirt.

One day it's forgotten. Heat and chill.

We bound our early friendship on the veranda of that run down café.

It was a bleak winter dawn, not long after she'd gone, from herself. I think it was that which brought us together and ultimately took us apart.

I had never seen it before, what they did. A surge of electrical current into the brain and a past was severed, everything with it.

I decided to keep the son she had abandoned, until it was his time, whenever that might be.

Glastonbury didn't agree. He said it would take too long for us to return to the house where those wretched doctors carried out that barbaric treatment.

It did. About fifty years. A lot can happen but against lifetimes, half a century is as nothing.

Leaving the terrace opposite the sea, we walked along the beach. Glastonbury took my arm and guided me around to his left side, away from the shore. His hand tugged my waist like a catch of wind. A breathless tug. And for a moment, I felt like a child myself, abandoned to the surge of joy.

He had this effect, almost like a father playing with his favourite girl, her knowing there would be no one else like him; that she must hold him down in her belly like a breath, as long as she could because somehow he was the reason for everything. Even breathing.

Glastonbury had eyes like no one I have ever met. Even afterwards, people knew who he was.

Looking down, a green that goes on forever in autumn and winter – no matter how far one wanders, always in his sight. Just like a father, sometimes.

I think we did love each other – for a while at least. This is all you can expect. Nothing lasts, you know. We had our passion – most certainly. I could pull the colours out even now – an intense frequency of colour rising from our skin, all about us the canopy of differing seasons. Childhoods.

Of course we were young ourselves then. Well, I was. Never quite sure about him. I was a nurse from Ireland and he was training to be a doctor. I knew from the moment I saw him he'd understand my ideas. It was the right time for us.

His skin, that freezing morning, told me so. The smell from the sea, the searching and finding of each of our pulses, the fragments of hymns weaving in and out like the dreams of a child running past. It was like going to church, but beyond the parochial coercion of religion, mystical, a moment illuminated – how I imagine the painter Samuel Palmer and his *Ancients* may have felt in the woods of Shoreham a century before, with their exaltations of bread and honeyed fervour.

A radiant newness.

Glastonbury tugged my waist and looked down.

I wanted to tell him everything, empty my life before him there and then, remove every garment of artifice and fall naked into the air. Become an angel like him. Yes, I'm sure he was that.

"You will live to be a hundred, Sonjia," he'd said.

A magical man from a place in Somerset, with eyes that went on forever being green. I would have given my soul to him that day, if he'd asked.

Decades later, after the Floods, he became quite a collector: William Blake, Turner, Pre-Raphaelites. Early works too: Dürer, Artemisia Gentileschi, Caravaggio . . . had no scruples about taking those, but he didn't want . . . *me.*

Not even for safekeeping.

1962
Coolton Ascent

Pansy

What was the last thought I had?

"Heard the one about the dying man and the narcissist, matron?"

"No, sir." The matron shifted on her seat and brushed a doily with a plump hand.

"Think I'll save that one for our new fellow. By the way, he's very impressed with our *home*."

"I'm glad he's settling in," replied the woman blandly, and slid the doily to the centre of the table, like an offering to the gods.

"Yes, we are so fortunate to have this house, matron. Gardens, palatial rooms, panoramic vistas. More like a hotel than a hospital."

"Yes, sir. I'm told it has that . . . informal atmosphere."

"All down to you of course, the way you run it. Marvellous staff." The consultant, effusing momentarily, twirled a fleshy hand to indicate the overall splendour of the drawing room, leaned back in his winged armchair and stretched his legs beneath the long walnut table. "We're a big family, don't you think?"

The matron looked doubtful and offered the man a tray of powdered Turkish Delight.

"Yummy!" And taking one, he winked absurdly at the table.

"Talking of new staff," she continued, riding the upward mood of this normally flaccid man. "We have an enthusiastic young nurse joining us, in outpatients at the moment. Clever girl. And she's very keen to see the treatment. I wonder . . . of course, it's not procedure . . . but my staff nurse has no objections."

"Oh, the more the merrier."

The matron raised an eyebrow and felt at the iron-like cladding of her hair with its new permanent wave. "I do appreciate that, sir."

"Not at all. I'm rather evangelical about my work. As you know, psychiatrists can listen all day, but there are instances in which a patient is resistant to that kind of therapy or analysis of *any* creed. It just doesn't work! I'm only too glad to have a chance to show the *proof of the pudding* . . ." He wriggled forward, prised up another slab of Turkish Delight and popped it into his mouth. "*Is in the eating*," he concluded, cheeks bulging, and sank back once more in his chair.

And the matron was glad she'd broached the subject when she had, although for the life of her, had no idea why she should petition for the young Irish nurse who had only worked in the place five minutes. "And of course we have the refurbishment of the west wing to consider," she pressed affably.

But the consultant had slipped from conversation and was gazing at a fob watch. He had an appointment at six.

*

"Can you tell me why you're here?"

"We have ten minutes left."

"I don't know why I come."

"Maybe you wanted to talk about . . . how you're feeing?"

"There's a new nurse. I haven't seen her before."

"It is time."

"Now I have to go all the way home on that train. I wish I'd wake up. Can't live in this dream. Those nurses look at me. And that scent: lilacs all the time, even in winter. His clothes are too small for me. I've tried, you know. Can't stretch a child's vest . . . But I keep his shirt in here – in my bag. Oh,

for God's sake, you fool! How can you know what it's like not being a mother anymore? You've never been one."

"We can talk about this next time."

"*I can't come here again. Talking does no good. Get rid of that damn clock. I can't find him in that, in this wretched room with a clock! I hate this place, an old house, broken into pieces by doctors and nurses who know nothing about . . . anything. It should have stayed as a vicarage, all garden fetes and inane chatter. I'd like to burn down that miserable church – this house! He's not here, my little boy . . . Doesn't he know what he's done?*"

"We must finish now."

"*I don't want to go into nothing again. Let me stay. Please. I've got nowhere to go to, not anymore. There isn't a place safe enough.*"

Sweet pea

"Why did you come here, to Glastonbury?"

"I wanted to see what the place was like. Not that interested in rambling, I can assure you. Heard the area was special, possessed a magical quality, ley-lines, something about energy and life forces. Of course, my companions know nothing of *those*."

"Does it live up to your expectation?"

"Not quite sure what I expected, to be honest. But it does feel different. So do I. Didn't you say you've lived here all your life? So, what makes this part of Somerset so different from roundabout?"

"A history, ancient memory, perhaps. Some say it goes back to King Arthur. It is even suggested that part of the cross . . ."

"Yes I know. And about Holman Hunt's *The Light of the World*."

"And He, the *Light,* was passing through."

"Thought it was Joseph. D'you believe that?"

"As you say, I've lived here all my life. Possibly I'm not the one to ask."

"There's that hill. Druids . . . Have you ever seen the fairies?"

"Can't say I have. I'll take you there, if you wish."

"I don't really know. Seems like an exciting idea – to search for the unlikely with a strange man. Very daring. I'll do it. Only because . . . you have the most *impossible* green eyes."

"And you're improbably direct, with your raven curls and alabaster skin."

"It's the Irish. My name is Sonjia, with an 'i' *and* a 'j'."

"I'm James, with an '*a*' and an '*e*'. It's the English."

"Far too proper. Think I'll call *you* Glastonbury because you seem to belong to all this special-ness. What do you do for work, when you're not being a guide?"

"I don't at the moment. I'm training to be a doctor. And you?"

"Coincidence, I'm a nurse – just moved to Kent. Not that you'd know the place. It's a sanatorium. Psychiatric. I'm still settling in."

"Another coincidence, Psychiatry is my field. I've been applying for a post – registrar. As you can imagine, there's not much scope around here."

"I can't say there's much there either. The treatment they use is utterly primitive."

"Can you manage, Sonjia? Nimble with gates too. Glad to see you're wearing sensible shoes; if the farmer sees us . . ."

"Not worried about him. I come from a family of farmers. And it's not just my shoes that are tough – I'm very determined. Glad we've left the others, I wanted to have your full attention."

"I see. Why do you say the sanatorium you work at is primitive?"

"I didn't. You weren't listening, Glastonbury, too busy looking at my legs. I said the *treatment* is primitive – barbaric, actually. Which school do you subscribe to, Freud or Jung?"

"Can't say I *subscribe* to either, but I would consider Jung the more advanced."

"Knew you would. Pity the people at the sanatorium aren't advanced – they don't believe in anything at all. You wouldn't think we were living in a civilized country. If patients don't find the talking works, they're zapped!"

"Zapped? Ah. You mean . . ."

"So you know it. Torture!"

"Rather dramatic. Anyway, why are you working there if you think it so dreadful?"

"I'm not dramatic, I'm passionate and I have other ideas, Glastonbury. Have you seen what they do?"

"Yes. I've worked with men who suffered during the war. Shell-shock."

"Shell-shock? Which war? How old *are* you?"

"The effects of events don't go away, Sonjia. Victims can suffer the rest of their lives. The body, the *soul* can store up memories for . . . lifetimes."

"You mean, you agree with that kind of treatment?"

"No. I think like you. We should find ways to outlive our history, apart from obliteration. But there are some who cannot face their life as it has become and I don't know whether we have a right to force them."

"But it's brutal, Glastonbury – there must be other ways."

"Are we ready? Can we bear to witness the suffering of others when we have the power to take away that suffering?"

"And the remnants of their life, the good memories, children, lovers . . . what happens to those? Have you thought about *that*?"

"I have. It's a problem."

"Not if we could save them, Glastonbury. Imagine if we were able to . . . No, I won't tell you."

"We can't be keepers of lives. We can only walk with them for a while."

"Would that be enough? There's a woman, an outpatient at Coolton Ascent, where I work – her young son drowned – I know *she* wants obliteration. I see her wandering off at the end of the day as if her own life has gone."

"What about her husband?"

"She's a widow. It was almost as if she depended on him, her son. Now there's no one. If you could meet her, Glastonbury, make a difference. Walk . . ."

"Expect I will meet her."

"What do you mean?"

"Coincidences, Sonjia, if you believe in those: Coolton Ascent – used to be a vicarage? The consultant is a clown but like you I believe there's work to be done."

The young woman with the raven curls and pale skin stared in amazement at the tall man who had walked silently beside her.

"What happens to them when they go?" she asked out loud.

"They become missing – but you know that."

"But it is a wonderful house, don't you think, Glastonbury? As this is a wonderful moment, and you . . . I wish this conversation would keep forever."

"It has."

She wanted to touch him, yet couldn't. Everything fitted together but that wasn't quite right. "The consultant – does he know what he's doing?"

"I doubt if any of them do."

"I'm just worried, Glastonbury. What will happen? You said something about lifetimes . . ."

"We have a lot more to talk about."

They both turned. A group of young people were calling and waving.

The two stood waiting for the group to join them.

Coolton Ascent

Touch Me Not

"There is no way out. Why do you call it that?"

"An amnesty possibly, from this war, escape from pain."

"It is a war, a battle for peace. I still dream of him, my son. Everything could have been different. Can't you change the way it happened? You're the one with the words, in control of the story."

"What happened is not the story."

"I keep remembering . . . that day. If only I'd known . . ."

"But you didn't and you're here now. Some things are beyond our control. We cannot accept responsibility for all the terrible events in our lives."

"But a mother must never look away – an instinct should make her aware of danger. All that remains now is the edge of it: a small crevice in a rock, a thin line, distinguishing the past from now. It's so very, very slight, and yet the difference is incalculable. Wasn't a question of turning right or left, you know. I didn't make a decision, just didn't see."

"Are you torturing yourself?"

'He tortures me. Calling, always from the sea. I can't reach him, but I still want to swoop down like a bird at that edge, that line, and snatch him back, rescue the instant. But you can't bring him back either, can you? Talking, dreams, I can't find my son in here."

'No, but if we talk about him, it's a way of finding again."

"You're better than that consultant – more understanding. I wish I could forget it all, go to sleep and . . ."

"Yes? Go to sleep and . . ?"

"Wake up and it's all over. Everything gone."

"A fresh start – is that what you mean?"

"I want none of this to ever have happened, existed, not even him. Is that betrayal?"

1963
Coolton Ascent

Hawthorn

"They know each other – that new nurse and the trainee doctor."

"She looks like Katherine Hepburn."

"Wrong colour hair and age."

"Oh, you know what I mean. Eyes and cheekbones, straight as a broom."

"Don't you mean *Audrey*? Anyway, it's *him* I'm interested in."

A thin sun slid onto the two young women tucked into the cool embrace of a wide bay. Stiffened by uniforms and cold, the nurses talked between mouthfuls of white bread scraped with margarine. A solitary yellow apple wobbled on a low table, its fall from the shiny oak arrested by an ashtray.

A nurse with cropped hair and thick wrists, flipped up her starched apron. It fell like an oversize meringue over her arm. Tutting, she fanned it down and reached for the top pocket of her blue-check uniform.

Her companion, shaking a head of shiny blonde curls, frowned sententiously. "You don't keep your fags up there, do you? Matron'll have your guts for garters."

The short-haired nurse flicked open the packet, pushed up a cigarette, put the tip to her mouth and snatched the packet away, a cursory offering to her colleague on the journey down. "Shit! Where're my matches? Go and ask someone on the ward."

"No! You can't keep asking for lights. Go to your locker, you've got time."

The other nurse pulled out the packet again and replaced the unlit cigarette. "Shame that posh one's not here. She never stops, always got one on the go."

"She's being admitted this afternoon. I've got the wonderful task of greeting her," sighed the blonde.

"Should be a bundle of laughs."

"And then I'm off. Two whole days away from this bloody place."

"Going to miss your gorgeous doctor *James*. He'll be doing the *electric bed treatment,"* giggled the shorthaired girl, shaking her head wildly, tongue loose and eyes staring. "Our patient won't be looking very glamorous after a few of bolts of lightning."

The blonde nurse shrieked with laughter, banging her head on the wooden shutters of the window. "I wouldn't mind a bit of the bed treatment myself – thrash about with him all day."

"You're kinky. Go and get me a light, you peroxide tart."

"You wait! I'm going to spring up on you in the west wing one day – hide in one of those rooms to see what you get up to with that orderly."

The shorthaired nurse placed a middle finger and thumb around a thick wrist, eyebrows raised. "The linen cupboard – a very tight squeeze."

"Dirty cow!" exploded her friend. "We're supposed to be psychiatric nurses, interested in the mental thing."

"Drives you mental, all this misery. I'll be taking the sweeties myself soon. And now we've got 'superior' Sonjia. Won't be able to get away with anything, bossy little witch. Only been here five minutes."

"And how come she knows everything? Very funny."

"Jesus, they're all bloody funny – it's a farm for *funny* people."

Winter Jasmine

A red bus came close to the curb. A spray of filthy rain splashed her shoes. Overwhelmed by an alien scent, a woman in cashmere coat, her hair flicked up, dark glasses, two lines gathered like pencil marks above the bridge, stepped out onto the road. Could have been anywhere – in the country, in the Town, by the sea.

Soon by the sea: the rush of salt. Couldn't help her there, either.

Stepping from the curb, she heard him shout. It was a man, someone else calling from behind the blast of a horn.

As smooth as a ribbon fluttering across chaos, twisting between the sheets of wet, she crossed a road thick with traffic.

"What the bloody hell are you doing? Look where you're going!"

She reached the other side. Knew the station, could find it with her eyes closed. More colours this time, not so dark.

Platform 3.

Weaving through the straggling crowd. Yes, just like a ribbon, catching up the stray ends of hair, untidy floatings that irritated the skin, feed through the silken ends then gather all the wriggles and tidy them away.

This might be her last journey to the seaside. Today may be the final time she would make her way across Victoria Station, feeling this way. Maybe she ought to mark the occasion with a cup of tea, or some flowers, a tribute to her life, everything, but before she went. Like a premonition – some people have that, a vision of their end. And if you drown, apparently, life unravels before you.

But a child would not have that much to unravel. So what would they see? A future? Not theirs. Wouldn't have one. Their mother's future without . . .

The woman stopped suddenly.

Still had time. In those meetings they always talked about how much time was left, had that huge clock on the wall. Hadn't done any good, talking. Hours. You can't talk out this kind of pain because nothing goes on forever being nothing. There are no signals or signposts in eternity. A clock doesn't chime out there. The big hand does not meet the little hand.

She leaned against the glass of the ticket collector's booth.

"All right, missus?"

"Platform three."

"Where you goin', missus?"

"The seaside."

"Which bit? Let's have a look at your ticket then. Foreign, are we?"

"Not really." She handed the man her ticket.

"Bit nippy now. Relatives, is it?"

"No."

"Platform three, quarter past. First class, front carriage. Change at Gillingham. Mind your step," he said, clipping the ticket.

That had ruined the flowers and the tea. She turned back towards the man at his box. "Will they have refreshments on the train?" But her words flew away – like ribbons not secured by pins or hair, rippling across the noise, the people, up in the air, their colours disappearing in the black and the smoke, the fog falling on the thin shiny platform.

"Let me help you, madam. Does this go in the luggage compartment?"

"Do I know you?"

"Er, sorry. I thought you might need a hand. Of course if you're making a change early on, better keep your case with you."

That was rude; he was only trying to help.

Choosing an empty compartment the woman settled down, undid her coat, smoothed down her skirt and slipping stockinged feet from high pointed shoes, curled up against the seat, clutching her large leather handbag. She clicked open the brass catch and drew from the capacious velvet throat a silver cigarette case. Rummaging amongst keys, lipstick, compacts and squares of silk, she produced a gold lighter, slid a cigarette from the silver case, secured it between tangerine lips, lit it and sank back. With one world rocking between two slender fingers, another tipping from her lap, she was almost complete.

The woman heard her handbag fall, the whistle blow, felt the brakes release and the train ease out of the station, chugging, wheezing and panting, gathering a shaky speed yet still hanging on, reluctant to let go; tugging at the grey of the arched canopies, the platform, its carriages rattling past depots and other trains, past the points of no return, her body and mind converging with every tremor of its departure.

A tall man went by in the corridor. He pressed against the glass of the compartment for a moment then withdrew. "Won't disturb you," he said, even though it was impossible to hear or see him – her eyes were shut. He walked on.

She wouldn't change at Gillingham, in country, city or seaside. She would change somewhere so remote, no one would interrupt her thoughts again with silence and nothingness. More than change, she would transform. A big house on a hill would help her do that – take away all the stations before this one, the carriage, tickets, eliminate the shadow of trains on tracks in freezing sun, the naked platforms, the empty buffets, rub out the lonely greetings of nurses. On her final way to somewhere quite different.

Was she afraid? Yes. And opened her eyes.

Other people would see yet it would remain private, a concealed conversion to a separate way. Rather like an excursion, she mused wryly. Public, but the view would be a very private affair, exclusive. "It has to be like this," she told the off-white antimacassar of the seat opposite.

Above, in the mirror she could see the reflection of the empty luggage rack. She was going all the way but her case was too heavy to lift up there.

And dropping her head against the back of the seat, slept.

Coolton Ascent.

Forget-Me-Not

"I think I've wet myself."

"You're disgusting."

"Shouldn't make me laugh so much."

"Stuff a towel between your legs. We've got to stay put till she goes past."

"How long's that going to be?"

"Shut up! Listen, she's got him with her. I'm going to open the door. Jesus, hope she doesn't want bloody sheets!"

"They're going to smell the smoke. If we get caught . . ."

The two nurses huddled in the linen cupboard on the second floor landing. Once a dressing room, the cupboard was now layered with white, its walls clothed in aertex blankets and linen counterpanes. Sheets, laundered into trays on racks, served up the irredeemable scent of carbolic and cigarettes.

A very tall man in a white coat wafted up the corridor. A young woman, impeccable in starched cap and uniform, walked silently next to him.

The man stopped for a moment and glanced at his companion.

Sonjia shrugged, she hadn't time for games. "You know, doctor," she said loudly, "I utterly loathe the smell of cigarettes. One day they'll ban smoking."

The occupants of the linen cupboard sought each other's eyes.

"*Witch*!" And spluttered into their hands.

* * *

The matron at Coolton Ascent had summoned the shorthaired nurse to her office.

It was a narrow room with thin mean windows, and those compelled to view its sombre walls would focus on a crack just beneath the coving. It was safer than looking at the matron because when roused to ire, her cap twirled like a weathervane on hair which looked hilariously like a corrugated iron roof.

The sanatorium had started life as a vicarage. Its original, magnificent church had been lost in a fire. The replacement, an unprepossessing dumpy stone building set just behind the house, was still kept in flowers by a few devoted parishioners.

The house retained a benign if somewhat eccentric aspect. Vast rooms, although now lined with pristine beds and tables, were still imposing, their history bridling within the hasty conversion from private home to hospital.

Built in the Gothic style, on three floors, it was set in ample grounds with orchards and a small pond. The gardens had been well laid out, and a hill beyond a wicket gate had been allowed to roll uncontrived to a little glade – or *fairy glen,* as the locals called the spinney. Even a folly graced its gardens.

Private patients attended the sanatorium as well as those sent by the larger hospitals under the National Health system, and despite the consultant's accolade, the place could have both afforded and benefited from a more elegant transition.

Coolton Ascent was regarded as *avant-garde,* and favoured by what some cynically called the 'new breed of quacks,' encouraging this *nouvelle hystérie.*

The resident consultant, a pragmatic man, was trying to dispel this reputation for indulgence. He liked results; proven or otherwise, but even back in the days of vicarage the incumbents had sought those. And, as church failed to offer solace to the spiritually destitute, those serving this modern conviction were as hapless as their predecessors.

"How is your patient?"

The nurse, itching to flee the bizarre figure, fidgeted nervously. "She's comfortable, Matron."

The woman repositioned her cap and smoothed down the ample folds of her navy-blue dress. "What's this about her having visitors?"

"What visitors? I don't know. I thought that new girl was looking after . . . I've been on the east wing with the *other* patients."

"On treatment days, we all work together. The new nurse has been on her own, with no support from either of you older girls."

"What about the other doctor?" enquired the girl petulantly. "She hasn't been on her *own* at all, Matron."

A flash of colour rushed to the woman's face. "I've received certain *reports* about you, young lady."

The girl rolled her eyes. "Oh, we've got a squealer . . ." she muttered recklessly.

"I beg your pardon! Do not tittle-tattle to me about other members of my staff. I am not one of your acquaintances, nurse – if you can call yourself that."

Sonjia appeared in the doorway, a flash of eyes and smile. "May I stay on with our private lady, Matron?"

"No, nurse, you go. You've been here since seven."

"I feel perfectly fine, Matron."

The other nurse looked on in disgust.

"Did I see you going to the church this afternoon?" asked the matron, so altered from frost, the other nurse wondered if this was the time to slip away, all misdemeanours melting in the rush of summer.

"In my break," replied Sonjia. "I need to be with my thoughts sometimes, in a quiet place."

The other nurse was beginning to feel sick. "Matron, can I go?"

"Yes, of course, if Sonjia's staying on. Write up your notes and we'll see you tomorrow."

Sonjia smiled radiantly at the departing nurse, who in a new moment had forgotten why she hated her.

* * *

"What is your name?"

"*You know . . .*"

"What is your name?"

"*I've told you . . .*"

*

"I have a headache."

"Lie still and I'll get you something."

"Where am I?"

"Where would you like to be?" asked the visitor, crossing his legs and brushing down his spotless moleskin trousers.

"I don't know . . . on a beach in the Mediterranean, the sun beating down."

"Can't help you there. What about your husband – family?"

"Husband? My family? Lovely of you to visit . . . whoever you are," the woman murmured, her eyelids drooping.

A nurse with raven curls and sharp eyes had been studying the visitor. She shook her head. "The patient needs to rest."

The man, a quiver to his soft pink lips, nodded. "Of course. Doesn't she have anyone?"

"No, not anymore."

The stranger stood, his body *bas-relief*, as though he had been superimposed upon the room. "Shame. Pity when it ends like this. Someone go?"

"Why do you ask?"

"Curious: a beautiful woman, alone in the world; doesn't seem quite right. I like to be of help."

"And you think *you* can help?" Sonjia, her face for a second pinched by grey, stepped back, moving over to the marble fireplace, as if to mark her distance from the man who had arrived unannounced at the patient's bedside.

"I doubt it," he said brightly. "Nonetheless, I pop in from time to time to see the *frail.* Not everyone enjoys good fortune in life. When you think that any one of us could be struck by . . . malady. But I'm glad she's over it – for now, at least. Marvellous what modern medicine can do."

"Hardly, it's medieval."

"Does the trick."

"And what *trick* is that?" enquired Sonjia briskly.

"To remove the unpleasant, wipe away the misery. Don't have to face it anymore – the endless days, the waking to mornings that have no hope."

"You sound as if you have some understanding."

"Oh I do! Indeed, I know the condition *intimately*."

"And yet you are spared the malady, almost as if the despair is not your own, sir."

"Mmm. I see you've taken down the photographs, the reminders – mother and son – very wise. Would be like her waking up to someone else's room, or life."

"I can't let you have the child, you do know that," Sonjia told him.

"Is he *yours* to bargain with? Surely, if he's been left, abandoned?"

"He hasn't. Is that why you're here?"

"Your patient has a headache. Why don't you find her something for the pain instead of cross-examining me? You should be carrying out your proper duties, nurse," the man reproached, inching back over to the bed.

The patient, now sleeping, turned, her dark hair wriggling across the pillow. On a locker next to the bed a large leather handbag lay open, a silver cigarette case glinting from its muddled contents.

Sonjia folded her arms and watched carefully.

The man lifted the case from the bag, inspected the engraving, flicked it open and drew out a long cigarette. "*Du Maurier*," he said without breathing and putting the cigarette to his lips, pocketed the case and strolled to the French windows. Opening the doors, he stepped out onto an ornate balcony and turned to look at the nurse, then plucking something from the pocket of his dark suit, lit the cigarette.

Through a cloud of smoke Sonjia could see his face: sharp, well-proportioned features, brilliant azure eyes, an even mouth with its flickering beacon.

"This place has undergone a bit of butchery itself," he observed. "Appalling what they do with a building these days. People, yes, but architecture . . . sacrilege. Ah well, no doubt there'll be worse to see on my return travels," he tittered. "A good choice this, I must admit. Be interesting to see what you make of it." He motioned his cigarette to the patient: "A fruitless exercise – she won't have learned anything, and if you think you can re-unite them at a later stage . . . Oh dear. Your *young* friend should know better. At his age! *Glastonbury,* indeed! What have you done to the poor fellow?"

Sonjia couldn't reply. Her mouth was drenched in singing, the tongues flying into her throat, and choking from the stench of cigarettes, left the room.

* * *

"I took the photographs, Glastonbury. They're in the church."

On the beach the two walked, Sonjia and her consort, their limbs bumping like the wind brings together the branches of an old tree, brushing up, leaf against leaf, close as sun on colour.

But there were no trees here, no sun, just a bitter morning unfolding across a distant sea.

"Our patient discharged herself yesterday. She's a new person, can you believe that?"

"If that's what she felt, Sonjia. You brought her down here?"

"Yes. We walked right along. The tide was coming in – not a flicker. Nothing. She's cast her life, that boy adrift, Glastonbury. No one to comfort *him* now. His mother can't hear."

"No, but our friend can – which is why he came – and he has a point: mother and son will always be lost to each other. If the boy returns, it will be through another, different pain; and other lives, other children will be caught."

The young woman shook in a gasp of wind, a blast of reasoning snatching her breath, hair about her face like frozen leaves tumbling across ice, and cried, a final frailty dwelling on the threshold. "Glastonbury, what have I done?"

He'd twisted around, tugging at her waist, submitting to her like a father to an errant child, her supplication too tender to refuse.

"But they must meet again, Glastonbury. A chance at least. I can't leave that poor child out there. And it's the closest . . . to you." Her hand reached up to his face, then their arms were together, as unlikely as flowers entwining around the wind.

She smelt him, tasted him and even though her senses were swept away on freezing tides, felt she had returned from somewhere with him, from another season. "I've made you human," she murmured.

Impossible as lilacs on winter sand.

1992

Wisteria

A boy ran past with his dream. His eyes so full, he couldn't see us.

What was that?

"Did you catch sight of him, Glastonbury? And in a public place! He almost tipped me over, the riot of a fellow."

But Glastonbury had already jumped to his feet, knocking the table on the deserted terrace. "That was young Bug. What's he doing so far from home?"

"And what on earth did he land on?"

"A skateboard, Sonjia – they all have those. Which direction?"

"That-a-way," she pointed. "Somewhere west, over the rainbow I think. So the tornado has a name?"

"A name *and* a destination."

"So what location will be hit by *skate*-boy next? Sit down, Glastonbury; you've lost half your drink."

"It's not a location, Sonjia, although that comes into it. A new girl – the family came last spring, moved to that private estate backing onto the woods." The man sat down again, picking up a glass dripping with beer.

His companion offered him a serviette. "Moneyed, then. Sounds as if you know them . . . Any connections?"

"Maybe."

"The boy's struck. Must be all of eight!"

"Nearer ten – small for his age." Glastonbury mopped the edge of his burgundy velvet jacket then set to inspecting a small darn around the last buttonhole. "Her name's Fodellah."

"Mouthful."

"A combination of Finian and Odella, I presume – the grandparents."

"Oh you don't need to explain to me, Glastonbury. As long as there's one good Irish . . . *Who* did you say?" The woman, her sharp eyes shielded by the brim of a wide hat, scrutinised her companion from the privacy of darkness. "So she married again."

"Hardly surprising. The family moved from the coast. Bereavement."

Sonjia's eyes still fixed on the man. "Close?"

"The girl's grandfather. The parents are divorced."

She lowered her gaze. "Aren't they always? Mind you, wouldn't need much of an excuse to move from here. Even more desolate than thirty years ago. How old? The girl, I mean."

"Four or five. A baby."

"A ruffian like him, smitten by an *infant*?" She traced a long grimy nail around her own glass. "So there is a link . . . that boy's receptive."

"What does that make the *infant* . . . a vessel?"

But Sonjia wasn't listening. "We better go back to your garden, Glastonbury. We've yet to finish the rest of the bedding-out. I want be gone by the weekend." Rising from her chair, she tightened a scarf and with a lilywhite hand, adjusted a large cameo brooch on her mandarin jacket. "Approve of the yellow shirt, my dear. Goes well with the plum. But you've grown old." She pulled a tapestry purse from her rucksack. "I'll pay the man, although the miserable article doesn't deserve it. Margate! Alas, I knew you well."

And crossed the terrace.

* * *

A boy lifted the black iron griffin then let it fall into the smooth dent set in a sun-hot door.

And again.

"Is Foddly in?"

"No. Well, she *is,* but having an afternoon nap, upstairs in the main house. Can you call back later?"

"I'll wait."
"Oh . . . Where?"
"Here."

The woman, an elegant beauty compressed into her sixty-odd years, gazed beyond the rigid boy towards a lilac bush overhanging a garden wall, then back to his mud-caked shoes. "I don't think we've met. I'm Odella, Foddly's grandmother. And you are?"

"Bug Itin – her best friend."

"Come far?"

"Not really."

The woman stroked the raised pattern on her blouse, thoughts busy. "Bug, do you like those ice poles?"

"They're OK."

"Because I've got so many in the freezer. Why don't you come in and wait for your friend in *my* flat?"

The boy, who hadn't moved his eyes from the woman, shrugged. "Good."

Smiling, the woman guided him through a carpeted hallway to a door. "This is what they call a *granny flat.* Dreadful description."

The boy followed her into a large lounge with dark furniture and paintings. Where the pictures ceased, lines of books took over along the wall. He looked intently at a print above a walnut secretaire. "What's that?"

"It's called *The Magic Apple Tree.*"

"Is it real?"

"Wish it were! The original is in Oxford, I believe."

"No, the *magic.*"

"Now there you have me – and the artist is long gone. Did his best work not that far from here. I have another Samuel Palmer print, next to my bed: *Coming Home from Church.* I've a catalogue of his paintings, somewhere – if you'd like to see it."

The boy scanned the room for other items of interest. "I like the faces best," he confided unexpectedly. "I'll do a painting one day – of Foddly."

"Wonderful. May I have first refusal?"

"What?"

"May I be the first person you offer it to?"

"Are you joking? I'm keeping it."

The woman laughed. "You are a hoot!"

"I'm going to make the eyes vermillion," he informed her faultlessly.

She was in the kitchen now, opening the lid of the freezer. "Mmm, sounds bright, amber possibly. Yes, just like my granddaughter."

"They're like the colour of leaves when it's autumn, her eyes."

The woman had produced a bouquet of ice and let the freezer lid drop with a thud. "Autumn," she echoed. "Yes, autumn eyes."

The boy sat down on a Hepplewhite chair and studied *The Magic Apple Tree.*

2039

Laburnum

Under a canopy of steel and moon the vehicle drew up, half stopping, half going. The driver was either drunk or approaching the reckless state. How he got away with it concentrated the minds of passengers for a fleeting moment, until they had disembarked, their thoughts claimed once more by the futures of the night.

That night was close, breathless on the stifling air. Rain fastening in, a last shift for the workless.

The preacher descended the steps of the tram. Looking around in the darkness he saw two men talking, and banging his big black book on the window, boarded the tram.

"What d'you reckon they'll do with him?" a voice asked the darkness.

"Dunno, but I wouldn't like to be in his shoes when Tor gets hold of him."

"Won't know much about it after."

"Nah, won't *regale us* with stories no more."

Laughter gurgled like water down a drain.

"Bloody weather."

"Been 'ot till now, mate."

"Too bloody hot. Won't be feeling that no more neither."

"Poor bugger. Not that I feel sorry for him."

*

Arranging her skirt over wet skin, Serene gathered an ample of thigh and squeezed.

A tremble of sighing and release.

The customer manoeuvred his leg, lifted and shoved, hand scratching the wall, years of rain beneath his nails already black with age and tearing.

A shudder across the heat, and both were seamless on the hem of summer; a flash of peace lasting longer than it should, a burst of dancing across the jagged line of glass and brick.

"Up, baby! And out."

"Fifteen." Serene demanded without reference to his face.

"What for? Nothin'?"

Another shadow moved without reference to the possible.

The customer had not felt the ends of deals so sudden. His nails clawed at the air and snapped back, void of course.

"I ain't sortin' out the stuff no more, sis."

"Do what yer like, I ain't keeping the others off. There's another bastard like you, going down today."

"If I go down, Serene, so do you."

"That's what you think."

A thin sliver slipped across her face, a crescent of a steel-cold reckoning, colliding with conscience, slicing loyalties as pointless as streamers on a Dutch ship.

"Where d'you get that, Wit? Goin' on yer friggin' travels again? Dreamin' are you, boy? We bin there, done that. I agreed you another lifeline, but you're going daft again."

"I'm giving myself up."

"To what, you fluff? Tor? You fancy that? I know what he'll do after, strangle yer. That's what we should've done, at birth. You ain't no brother of mine."

The shadow was fading.

She kicked at the lump on the sodden ground. "What am I gonna do with *this* bastard now?"

***

A haze of sun rose from the teak deck. Shivering in the pool of rain, yellow filled the faces gathered on that early morn.

The wind had dropped.

This observation might have been received with the macabre humour of the recently reprieved, if there had been any. Something else had dropped. From the rigging. Or someone.

So it was up to the recently dead to note wryly that, after an appalling night the wind had dropped, the sun flickering for just a second, its heat blocked on the journey down, shone bright as forgiveness.

The captain dismissed the men. "Take one hour."

They filtered across the deck, down the steps to the galley, to private bunks and regret, the sun pressing down, singing for play.

Tor scratched his red beard and, calling the first mate, proceeded up the rigging to cut down the body.

*

Wit Daley had been here before. He wasn't afraid, nothing to lose, not now.

The smell of the sea, the salt in his throat, the sun on his skin, he wished he'd been around in the days when the Coast was a place to visit, a space of joy. When did he last have that? Never, possibly.

He stopped to survey the ships, barques and clippers; saw the yardarms. That's where they strung you up.

Tor was not a civilised man, he decided. He was a brute. But like many whom Wit had encountered, had the magic in his soul. The quicksilver thinking that can change bad to good, or freedom to rope around a neck. Not to be trusted in this life, yet in another, an honourable man.

Wit had decided to come from another life. Someone had told him that beyond, *out there,* was a safer bet, no boundaries, no judgment, even fear would slip away to indifference. There was no way of calculating crimes in such vastness. They would be forgotten in the sheer numberless weight of other views. Someone else had said that. He hadn't had the words himself, but he understood perfectly.

He climbed the slimy ramp, slipping occasionally and wondered if this was a sign to go no further. It was too late. A great man with a red beard frowned upon him, eyes as vicious as words, blue and hard, unblinking.

A bad idea.

"The wanderer returns."

Wit, unable to speak for thumping heart, sought beyond – *out there*. It wouldn't come. Edges, borders shot forward like arrows from a crossbow, mortality creeping like a jester shaking his rattle.

"Given up at last – the idea of freedom too much? It won't help coming here. I know all about it."

Wit dropped to his knees, his legs shaking so much he could no longer stand, mouth vanished with terror, the whole of his body cold with the white of abandonment, his brothers, his sisters, the whole of his family, a sweet serenade of memory. Safe from reality, safe from now.

The captain laughed. "Get up, you scoundrel. Follow me."

And Wit did. Staggering to his feet, he clambered up the ramp and trudged after the man.

The decks were clear. He was thankful for that.

Tor stopped, beckoning furiously. Wit reached him, mouth parched, a weight clamped upon his shoulder. Ice or steel – didn't know which.

"You know, young man, I've been waiting a long time for you. I'm glad you've come. Just like your friend – always alone."

Convolvulus

Claudia Shell, rivulets of sweat gathering across the narrow ledge of her mouth, folded paper. One after another, sheet on sheet.

Her eldest boy, Speak, sat rocking in a canvas chair beside her on a derelict smack, watching, counting. "Done a lot of invites there, gonna be a good rumpus, ma," he remarked listlessly.

"And it's *commemoration,*" reminded the woman. "That'll help as well."

"What's *that,* anyway?" another voice stabbed at the heat.

"The war!"

"Which one?"

"How many *wars* you know about, Petrol?" needled his brother. "The *world* war. The one they're all on about. We ain't 'ad no more like that. That's what we're *commemorating.*"

"I ain't 'eard about no war," Petrol continued, as if this ignorance sealed the matter from further discussion.

Speak stood and surveyed the harbour, fondling the polished stock of an old rifle. "Nah, you wouldn't. It's like you don't know nothin'. If you did, you'd see it was a waste of bloody time, 'cause we got sod all out of any of it."

Claudia shook her large head. "We got something now, boy. We got a ship of our own. Who'd have imagined that? What's your dad got? Tuf can't touch us now. We've done better than any of them *deserters.*" She flopped forward. "Where's that girl? I want her here to help."

"Serene's down Harbour Lane, clocking up the business, ma," advised Speak sardonically.

"Well, you'd think they'd a forgot a war so long back," offered Petrol at last, after much thought. Flicking a plait down his collar and stroking the silken strands of hair, he sashayed over to his mother and lowered himself gingerly onto a pile of chain.

"Should get Petrol to fly some yats 'iself," lisped his brother slyly, catching his mother's eye. "Or he can push – likes the men."

Claudia winked, casting an appreciative gaze over her bumbling offspring, a mild tussle between mother and entrepreneur. "Ever thought of that, boy?" she asked, entrepreneur triumphant.

"What?"

Speak sniggered and turned to face the sea. "It's just you got looks, bruv. Ma don't like stuff goin' to waste."

Petrol was confused, but certain there was a compliment behind the barbs, grinned. "I don't like that neither. Stuff goin' to waste, like."

"Yeah. Petrol don't like it that bad, he'd do it for nothin'." A girl in her mid-twenties appeared in the sun. Serene, hair abundant with unlikely blonde, skin tanned, her eyes blackened, mouth smeared and pursed with genetic malice, produced some notes from an inside pocket of her long coat. She plonked her backside on the deck, lifted a split skirt, spread her legs and unzipped a velvet bag hanging from a thick, pink thigh. Bending forward, she grappled with the Cuban heel of her leather boot. "Give us a pull, you dope," she said, nodding to Petrol.

"What? Don't trust *me* not to give a pull?" Speak smirked.

Petrol tugged at the boot. A large vivid coloured stone rolled across the teak. "What's that you got there?"

"Dunno. One couldn't pay, so got this off him."

Claudia eyed the jewel. "Ain't got nothing attached has it, girl? I don't like it when it's got stuff connected."

"How do I know? But one thing's for sure, since that little bastard Wit's been gone, I ain't doin' bad at all."

"Stop your tongue! I don't want no looseness round here," rasped her mother. "He's still my boy."

"Bit late now, innit?"

A sharp slap from her brother brought blood to her lips. "Don't talk to your ma like that. You just spread your cheek somewhere else, not round me."

"Bastard! Speak, you bastard! Ever since Tuf's gone, you think you run my life. Well, you ain't our dad."

Claudia eased herself up and handed Speak the paper she'd been folding. "Claudia's getting very disturbed by all this badness, and now being *commemorations,"* she confided loudly, her mouth bubbling, "she'll have to lie down. With all this difficulty, don't know how long she can last."

Petrol, rolling from his coil of chain, slithered to his sister's feet and snatching the stone, offered it to his mother. "'Ere you are, mama."

"Thank you, boy," she said pathetically, the stone sinking into the endless avarice of her palm, and slowly plodding her way across the deck, tottered down the ramp onto the pontoon, the sun around her bulk like custard over a pudding.

Serene, meanwhile, beaten by iniquity, plotted her revenge in bloodied hands and tears, calculating the time she wouldn't need anyone in her rotten family anymore.

*

Speak Daley smirked, a meagre line dribbling across a bulge of cheek. He was gorging on a memory of previous commemorations; they meant rumpus, celebrations, opportunity, when fools ran riot and forgot the danger in everything.

There were already banners all over the place, Loyalty Stores giving away free drink and candy. Even the New Dutch were allowing people to visit their ships – well, some of them – there were still areas unwarmed even in this stifling climate of optimism.

Of course these tributes were specious. Nothing had been learned, peace had not reigned, turmoil and conflict flourished.

When New Britain fell in 2016, the community was at war with itself. There was murder in the streets, brother against brother.

Now, New Island England, divorced from Europe, alienated from the world, was not in harmony and Speak Daley was of the stable that made sure it stayed that way.

He wasn't a warrior fighting for a cause, a foot soldier on a crusade or even a vigilante. He was just a bad man from a bad family. One phenomenon of many left unchecked; a foul litter gathering in the corner of the collective mind and spilling onto the body, its ubiquity permeating the consciousness, a society absorbing its poison to the point of dependency. An immoral craving – mutation.

No world war but a microcosm in combat with itself.

Like the wrecked fishing vessel on which he now stood, Speak had nowhere to go. He'd reached manhood without knowing he'd arrived, and moored at the threshold of his life, owned no vista of new horizons, let alone the prospect of setting sail again.

At almost twenty-nine his features had already begun to sag and spread, his bleached hair thinning, a mouth worn down by a lifetime of resentment. Like his mother, Claudia, his eyes burned out at the world with an irrepressible hatred. It owed him, had treated his family bad. They were victims – always had been, so the world would have to pay.

Respect was Speak's entitlement and he didn't care how he got it or what it looked like when it came. There was no romance in his heart, no forgiveness, nothing to mark the man from the beast, and he dispatched his desires and appetites in the same way he did his opponents. And if a woman, for he did desire women, aroused too much wanting, she would suffer as a result. An introduction to the family would generally suffice. If not, a night in the company of the yat-flying Serene would reduce the object of fleeting admiration to a subject of abiding scorn.

Apart from his mother, Speak held everyone in this withering contempt. His sister, Serene, although she tried, could never match Claudia and was ultimately an *offending* waiting to happen. And just in case the man may not be in the time or place to note the *offending*, he would 'slap her up in advance, like.' He stopped short of any other violation – she was his sister after all. Plus, he didn't want to come up, so to speak, against his numberless enemies who had passed through Serene's ever-open portal.

Speak was fastidious like that.

He had always ruled his younger siblings – it was his job – until Claudia took in the extra boy, Loot, back in 2017. That was her biggest mistake – a dumb freak that had swallowed himself up, and he'd stolen Speak's brother, Wit – put a spell on him, divided everybody and broke the family up. Loot was trouble, the cause of everything bad.

Even his father, Tuf, had fled the nest, deserted because of him. The big ginger man, who once defended the gross obsessions of Claudia, stood by his boys when they had murdered to satisfy her macabre appetite, found one day he'd gone soft. And Claudia had been the worse for Tuf's leaving. Her great body sagged in a way Speak had not thought possible, as if the fight, the zest for evil, had been drained from her, like the blood from a slaughtered cow.

Although the son would never admit to missing the father, he allowed himself the occasional trawl through their sordid history, to seek a mote of hope, a glimpse of a separate existence, a greater malevolence to contain his own diabolical view; someone, something, stronger than himself.

But there was nobody. Not even Claudia, not anymore, and that was the most dreadful view of all.

So where to next? His devotion to his mother was unimpeachable. Without her he would stand alone. And Speak was a man, for all his wickedness, his killing, who could never stand alone.

Letting the rifle fall to his feet, he kicked at a sheet of grey tarpaulin and leaned against the side of the boat. Sometimes he felt like tarpaulin left out in all weathers; summer, winter, slapping about, covering up crap that wasn't worth anything in the first place. That's how he felt, and it was an odd feeling, for him.

In the distance, the rigging of the New Dutch ships. His youngest brother, Wit, was on there, hanging, or waiting to have his neck stretched from the yardarm. Or maybe the gorm was supping with that bastard, Tor. You could never tell – the New Dutch captain was mad. Needed a woman rotten to cool down the heat. Serene should be inching her trade near him.

He saw his mother waddling across the harbour, mingling in the dull of shingle, Petrol mincing beside her, flicking his hair, looking for the men from the tall ships.

No, nothing bigger than Speak. The world was shrinking.

Feeling inside his leather jerkin, he produced a small packet with a wadge of tobacco hanging off like dead spiders. Heaping some strands onto a thin white paper, he threw the rest overboard and proceeded to roll the cigarette with one hand, the other drawing out a metal lighter from his trouser pocket. He wedged the cigarette between thin lips, lit it and breathed deeply.

Returning the lighter to his trousers, he lifted the rifle.

Above, the gulls crying, sun burning yellow, the coil of chain glistening through its rust, the moments drifting on in a summer that could be endless if it stopped there; a perpetual smell of salt and heat, skin sweating sea, a heart beating like waves on rocks, all ended, caught in flight then turned back on itself for eternal retrospect. The memory of a greater vision.

A bright red bubble burst from his nose, watery on his tongue, then chin. A slow arc of crimson danced without time down his chest, across his leather jerkin and over the hand with its rollup. The other shook. The weight of metal and wood too difficult to argue against gravity, fell. Spinning against the coil of chain, the rifle spun, sparking on the hot deck, then sliding, the percussion from its firing late, as if held up in the accumulation of other noises yet to be discharged.

Serene had been watching – a slow passive watch. Stretched, then torn from belief, she screamed.

Her fallen brother face upward, fluttering in the silence of grey and blood, his words as hushed as a pebble skimming a small pond and landing without significance on the far side.

Speak Daley, his own life now dispatched with a laconic efficiency his ma would surely be proud of.

Part II

Rock

1963
Coolton Ascent

Granite

"Nurse, who cleared this room? Half of that patient's stuff is still here."

The nurse, bridling, fresh from boyfriend trouble, sauntered into the room. "Not me, Staff. Been off. What is it, anyway?"

The staff nurse, herself bristling, displayed a drawer. "Paints, books. Cigarettes."

"Oh . . ." The nurse, quickening her pace, moved over to the desk. "Whole packet. God, it's freezing. Can I shut those doors?"

"Yes. Wanted to clear this air." The staff nurse pulled the French windows to. "Still stinks. Are they foreign, those?"

"Got a *Du* on them, probably. What's the book, *Lady Chatterley's Lover*?"

"You'll be lucky." The staff nurse, a sly glance at her colleague. "Don't say anything, but if you want the fags . . . Not a word to anyone. Ah hello, Sonjia."

"Yes, Staff, you wanted to see me."

"This patient discharged herself. Do you know anything?"

"I do not. Is there a problem?"

"She's forgotten some of her belongings. Only a couple of things, but if you can parcel them up."

"No forwarding address on file," Sonjia informed briskly.

"Is there a follow-up appointment?"

"The consultant hasn't made one, as far as I know. I believe the lady went on holiday. Abroad, I think. Find out, if you wish."

"Yes. I know it's not much but Matron doesn't like any of the patients' property to be left."

"May I look? Oh, isn't that book one of ours?" Sonjia queried softly. She picked up a small red, newly-bound edition of *Gulliver's Travels*. "Think this belongs in the library."

The other nurse was at the door, hand over her pocket. "Bed change."

"Try to find an address please, Sonjia." The staff nurse left the room.

Over at an oak desk Sonjia opened the book and read an inscription, then carefully tore out the page, placed the book in the drawer and pushed it closed.

1997

Amber

"No Fodellah again, I'm afraid. She went out early this morning."

"I've brought back the book."

"Thank you, dear."

"What's the matter with you, Odella?"

"I think I feel a bit like this flat today, Bug – a granny."

"Always were . . . It's something else. What happened?"

"You are a funny boy. I met an old . . . acquaintance. I must have seen him all this time and not realised. Extraordinary. Don't keep in touch these days. My granddaughter runs in and out – and you."

"Who was it?"

"You won't know him. A doctor. James, his name was. Did you enjoy that one? Blake wasn't it?"

"No. Allan Ramsey. I might know him, this *James.*" He handed the book to the woman. "Where's that photograph of Foddly? It's gone."

"I showed it to someone. Forgot to take it back," she said quietly.

"Was it James you showed it to?"

"You really are a strange boy."

"You can't go giving photos of Fod to just anybody."

The woman sat on a couch, twisting the catch of her bracelet. "I didn't exactly *give* it. I just let it stay. Anyway, he wasn't just anybody."

"Is he tall?" probed the boy.

"Who?"

"James, the doctor. With eyes, funny eyes?"

"You and your eyes – you have them as well, Bug. Staring all the while – disconcerting, you know, sometimes," she chided faintly, as if remembering she ought.

"And you're very careless, Odella. Glad I didn't give you *my* painting of Fod because you've forgotten a watercolour. It's in that book."

"Who is it of?"

"How would I know?"

"I am very careless, Bug. If you knew how careworn careless can make one. Maybe you do."

He could see the light around her head, shredding like net curtains torn on a branch. And couldn't speak.

Emerald

"He's revolting! Always saying the wickedest things to me. I want him to go away. For good!" A young girl glared up at Glastonbury sitting with her in his garden.

He smiled at his young visitor, the sun in his green eyes, and crossing his legs tipped back the Bentwood rocker. "Loves you, I expect, Fod."

"You mustn't play like this," she warned. "How can he love me and be so disgusting?" She stamped her foot and went to flee his laughter.

Rising from his seat, the man unfolded to his full height and scooped her up. "And why is he so *disgusting,* and you so *precious?* What does he do to set this firecracker alight?"

"Everything. But you don't believe me. Go away, I hate *you* as well!" Disentangling herself, the girl crashed her way to an open door and sat in the gloom of a tiny parlour.

Dismissed, her host made his slow way down the path, tweaking off the dead leaves of roses. He picked up a few stones and embedded them next to the roof slates edging the soil, pulling out a few weeds with his free hand, whistling softly.

He heard the colour of the girl behind him.

"Bug said that granny had . . . left . . . before she was supposed to."

"I see."

"*That* was wicked, wasn't it, Glastonbury?"

"If it was said to hurt, then no, it wasn't kind. But if he was just telling you something, there's no blame in it, Foddly."

The girl's eyes glistened, hands running through a mass of red hair, she wrenched her scalp till her eyes watered. "You're supposed to be on *my* side, not Bug's. He's much older than me and should know better. It's not true, anyway. Granny just left, like everyone leaves. That's all there is to it. I'm not going to see him anymore, if he can't be trusted."

"Sounds as if he can be trusted, in some things at least. But it's up to you. Bug's your friend after all and you must make the decision."

"He said you are a witch, a man witch . . . you know," Foddly said, a final grist to her mill.

Glastonbury nodded. "Yes, Bug certainly knows how to keep your interest alive. But if it wasn't for him, we may never have met. There's one thing we should thank him for."

Foddly looked doubtful. She screwed up her face and peered at the man who hadn't once looked up from his garden. "I don't think *we* should be friends anymore either, Glastonbury," she said solemnly. "I've been coming here for ages. Maybe I'm due for a change."

It was delivered with such gravity, the man once more smiled. He turned at last, lifting up a strand of hair, a long white feather in a nest of black, and shook his head. "Now that would be a shame. Who will I take with me to look for the fairies? There are very few people who know about the spinney at Coolton Ascent."

Foddly sat on the path, smoothed down her dress and began to play with the buckle of her sandals. "I haven't told him about those." She looked up into the man's pale face, his eyes filling her thoughts. "I *was* going to tell you something else Bug said . . . once."

Glastonbury moved on to a box of geraniums on the kitchen windowsill. "Will you bring me the can please, Fod? These are parched. No, better still turn on the hose and we'll give the whole garden a drink."

The girl's thoughts were drifting away. She tugged at her telltale, struggling as if it was a parcel she couldn't unwrap. Wandering to a tap by the wall, she twisted the cold brass. A gush of water on her feet took her breath away. That was it!

"He said you were trying to get that big house," she reported, handing him the dripping hose. "But the people in the Town won't let you. How can you buy that? You don't have any money."

"If they won't sell it to me, I won't need any," he replied with a grin. "But I wouldn't worry. *I'm* not going away, not for a long time."

Forgetting everything in that treacle moment, Foddly lay down on the hot path, head on the prickly lawn, dreams stuck to the roof of a gentle sky, and listened to Glastonbury as he pottered about, showering his plants, crackling leaves, snapping stems, the sounds and smells of him as certain and safe as the day she was in.

It was safe. Even Bug, her young, unruly friend who tormented her with truths she knew, didn't matter now. She had Glastonbury and he wasn't going away.

Maybe that was the worry in the first place. A tickly bother she couldn't find. So Glastonbury had found it for her.

Curling up, the blanket of an Indian summer over her skin, she closed her eyes and slept.

Sapphire

A boy lay face down on a hill.

The day was scorching, the sky drenched in sun, his fair skin burning. Over the crook of his right arm he watched the haze shimmer above the parched earth, a dazzle rising without form. Moving a fraction, he rested his chin on his hand and squinted.

A world full of space waiting to be filled. "Come on, fill it," he challenged the distance.

Rolling over, he snatched a blade of grass and raising his arm let his hand drop till the tip of the grass tickled his mouth. "You wait till you grow up, Fod," and grinned.

Squeezing his eyes shut, he studied the pictures filtering through. A sudden kaleidoscope, colours and shapes trembling, searching for sequence, like the mind does with letters in a game of Scrabble.

Across the indistinct horizon appeared another colour. More than that, a light that made colour possible. Resisting an urge to open his eyes to see who was approaching him, the boy concentrated harder until he could determine the outline from its source. A tall man settled in the picture. He was walking very slowly up the hill, behind where the boy now lay. Frowning, the man flung what looked like a jacket over his shoulder and flicked away a strand of hair from his eyes. Then stopping suddenly, he waved.

Bug sat up and banged his fists on the ground "Damn you, Glastonbury!" he shouted. "Why do you always have to know?"

***

Boy and girl had rolled down the hill, then raced back up again. Breathless, they flopped down on the grass and listened to their thumping hearts.

"You've been telling tales to the old man again," the boy said eventually.

Glastonbury's *my* friend; I can say what I like!"

"Mine first, and I bet you'd like to know what I know about him. It's not his real name, for a start off."

"Oh what a surprise, *Bug* Itin. You *are* a bug. You *bug* me. *Buzz, buzz, buzz.*"

"Try harder, litttlun."

Foddly realised she was on a hiding to nothing by insulting her companion and was leaving herself vulnerable to retaliation. For as much as Bug loved her, war was war, and you did not enter lightly into invective with a boy as wild as him. "What is his name, then?" This was a serious climb-down for the girl and completely spurious because she already knew.

"James. But that's not important – it's how he got it changed."

This was something Foddly had not contemplated. It was interesting but not enough to pursue. She lay down in the heat, staring up at a canopy of leaves.

A horse chestnut shielded both girl and boy from the sun. Head-to-head they lay on the crest of a hill, behind them, in the distance, a large house.

"I think you're too old for me, Bug," she informed him. "You must be at least fifteen and I'm not even ten."

The boy flipped over and grabbed handfuls of her hair, like fire spreading over his long fingers. "Not as ancient as Glastonbury," he whispered. "You would *not* like to know how old *your* friend is."

"I've tried to work that out," responded the girl, matter-of-fact. "He's been in that cottage since I can remember. My mom told me he used to be a doctor."

"So why isn't he one anymore? People just don't *give up* being doctors, not without good reason. He may have been struck off."

Foddly was unsure of this *struck off,* but it had a bad feeling and she pushed it away. "He used to be at that big house where they keep doing all the filming. Why *are* they doing the filming, Bug?"

"I'm too old to tell you and you're too young to hear."

"Oh, go on. Please."

Bug snapped off a blade of grass and chewed at the end. "It's been empty for ages," he said, deciding that silence game enough. "Some outsiders are trying to knock it down but it's got conservation status, or something. Coolton Ascent is the best place roundabout, so we don't want it changed. The Town pretends it doesn't know – and if someone comes along one night with a ball and crane . . . They'll get good money for the land, that's all they want. All anybody seems to care about is money. Glastonbury should try harder."

His voice, already soft against the air, disappeared for a while. Beyond the woods, the distant hum of planes taking off from behind the Factory, then the birds, snapping grass, all replaced him, and she felt sleepy. All about her head, his silence. She was aware he hadn't spoken for what seemed like ages.

Then: "Listen. Listen to the colours, Fod. We're going to live there, you and me. You won't remember this but before you forget we'll have these years together."

Foddly could hear – his words had rainbows in them, for a moment, then just the usual clipped ring of his voice, the playfulness edging spite.

He was standing now, pulling her legs, dragging her from sleep. "You're going down that hill. No mercy this time; over the top."

"Bug Itin, I hate you! You haven't told me *anything* yet!" She shrieked with terror and delight and noticed how his eyes were as blue as Glastonbury's were green. Caught up in the struggle and the yielding, she laughed and cried as the boy, who was still like a brother, rolled and pushed her wriggling body hot with September sun, down the steep hill.

Ruby

A dark cloud bruised up the horizon. The lines between land and sky blurred. A smudge of graphite, all edges swallowed in grey.

Away from oysters and beer, truculent landlords and sullen hotels, gone from the shoreline where the sand turns to pebble too soon, beyond esplanades sullied by loud awnings and abandoned shops – the two had returned home but as yet hadn't quite arrived.

"Here at last, Glastonbury. Can't believe it. Always smaller, aren't they, places, when you see them again? Never quite the same." Sonjia scrunged up the massive coat, folded her arms and settled her sharp chin in the depths of the collar.

"And you've avoided seeing this one."

"Couldn't bear to, in case it was swept away from me. What a mess, an absolute travesty. Garden's in a shocking state." She turned away from the main drive and strode through a wicket gate. "Wonders will never cease! The folly's still here. But if that lot get their filthy hands on it . . ."

"The Council's broke, the land's worth a fortune."

"What, even now? I thought we were in a recession."

"The developers will sit on it, for years if necessary, and then there'll be the usual wrangling with the planners."

"Lie fallow, you mean? Isn't this a conservation area?"

"They may convert – build on the surrounding land."

"Should stick to dumps like the Factory. That airstrip is bigger, and more suitable for *that* kind of housing."

Glastonbury smiled, creases spreading around his mouth. A strange, lean man in a long overcoat, cropped hair streaked with white, his pale face turned in contemplation toward the old vicarage.

And still Sonjia could not help but stare at him. Compelled to that angled face in a perpetual, if perverse devotion, as if she may still find an answer in the drawn flesh or across his eyes. Or simply that if she turned away he would be gone and would never look at her again.

"What kind of housing?" he asked mischievously.

"You know damn well what I mean, Glastonbury. Don't start that social equality nonsense with me. Actually I am very surprised *and* disappointed we've not made more of an impact. Don't you know the auctioneers?"

"London firm – although it'll be the local boys who'll play the games."

"Do something, then. Get your friend, that little rapscallion, Bug, whatever he's called, installed in there. He can threaten to *candle* it!" The woman struggled with her collar. It caught a row of amber beads, making her look like a bad tempered queen with an orange ruff.

Glastonbury fell back laughing. "*Torch,* you mean. Fiendish in your old age, and that would play right into the developer's hands. Anyway, if Bug Itin got in here, he'd never leave and he'd have you *buried.* The boy's not without discernment."

Sonjia shrugged. "I may have done well with Ireland, but I still have only limited funds."

"Have faith, woman."

"Be just as well if the council do hang onto it. I'm not clear about this Town's politics, but if we could persuade them it was for *local* use . . . Don't they go in for *rehabilitation*? Lost causes?" She stopped.

The man began to move up the drive.

"*That's* what we have to focus on, Glastonbury: *the community.* Get a petition going – they love all that befoolery!" She wandered down the gravel way and stood by the large iron gates.

Her friend had reached the porch by now and was climbing the broken steps. He stood captured in an instant of light, stretching up to the coloured glass above the panelled door.

"Shall we go to the church?" she asked from the distance.

He had bent down now and was grappling with the letter box.

"No, not yet," she heard him say.

"I hope your Bug will behave like a gentleman, if he's so keen on that girl," she muttered.

“Oh yes, *he’ll* be alright, oddly enough. Although not *too* much of a gentleman.”

“No, not like *some* I know, Glastonbury. But as I’ve already waited almost forty years, why stop now?” She waved a flamboyant hand and disappeared down the hill.

Glastonbury placed his foot on an iron boot scraper and nodded.

2003

Bloodstone

"The noise, Bug! I don't know how they can keep going like that, up and down."

"It's not the sound of crickets, I'll grant you, but this is the South Bank. Stop being so sensitive. Can't you see the skill involved?"

"Preferred the National Gallery."

"This is Art, of sorts. Look at that kid, Fod. See him? He's cracked up the curb, bounced off that wall, now he's going to . . . Well, he *could* have done it – should have stuck with the arc instead of trying to impress everybody. It's all about timing and understanding form, the body. I love the way they grab the board, marching off with it, just like soldiers with their rifles." Bug grinned, his slight body arched forward in the gloom, catching the ends and beginnings of movements, of wheels crashing and sparking on the dank Portland stone.

A loose circle of spectators had gathered under the arches where the boarders flipped and turned.

The sun in the future, the battle in the dark and the stench of now.

The pair walked out from the war. Foddly, her nose wrinkled, Bug, his eyes filled with dreams. By the National Film Theatre then onto the shiny bridge, with its taut glinting cat's-cradle-threads wrenched down by an invisible fist in the Thames, and over to St Paul's and the City.

Foddly was tired and wanted to eat.

"There're all sorts of secret alleys round here, Fod. Don't dawdle. Come on, I'll show you. Then we'll get the ferry to the docks. London's so old – people forget that, you know."

But she sat on a stone bench outside a church and refused to move. "Have you got any money, Bug?"

"Why d'you want that?"

"I'm hungry! You seem to forget that I'm human. You're always doing what you want, *assuming* I'll be interested."

"You liked the paintings. You could not help but like the paintings."

"Yes, of course, but now . . . Oh, come on! Something for me."

Bug narrowed his eyes. They burned with temper, the girl thought. It passed quickly, nonetheless she sensed the bully, a cruelty, and afraid, found she was making calculations to survive the spite, employing an artifice. Winsome.

"*Something for me,*" he mocked. His light chestnut hair, shivering under a sudden breeze, blew across his mouth. He shook his head, flipped back the hair and grinned. It was a horrible shape. It lifted his thin jewel eyes and made him look like a wolf.

She didn't like him, not anymore – if she ever had – and longed for the country again.

"Missing the old boy, are we? Well it was Glastonbury who suggested you come. You try going round a gallery with *him* – or worse, an auction. Lecture? He knows everything. Ah, that's what you like, isn't it? Someone who knows *everything*."

"I think you respect Glastonbury more than you let on, Bug," the girl returned carefully. "He told me you'd make a collector, one day. Could even have your own business."

"Not with competition like him around. Anyway, the bottom's out of the market at the moment."

Foddly gathered a lock of hair, twisting it round a finger, wasn't really interested. She looked down at his boots, then at his green velvet jacket and trousers. In *this* weather. And why was he carrying that funny walking stick? Bug was becoming very odd, dressing like an old man. Can only be . . . Nineteen? Twenty?

"I reckon nearer twenty-one," informed the boy.

Foddly shivered. He was doing it again. She saw a woman coming down the steps of the church, the quietness spreading like shadows. A heavy gate dragged, squeaking across the silence. The woman passed, smiling. A laugh lodged somewhere else. Sunk in the time it took her to acknowledge him, Foddly heard Bug talking.

Was it to her?

Then he was moving away.

She stood and called. Then, alarmed, sat back down again and crossed her legs.

He spun round on his heel. "If you want victuals, fair damsel, there be a tavern nearby."

"I can't. I'll follow you later. In a minute."

Bug stopped. Perplexed, he returned to where she sat. "What's the matter, Fod? Come on, I'm only playing."

But the girl was biting her lip, face collapsed, her eyes like autumn swimming with rain. She was rubbing at the freckles of her arm. A confused schoolgirl out with an older, callow friend.

Bug stroked his chin, long fingers twisting his mouth until it was ripe as cherries. "It's not far," and offered his hand.

She shook her head. "Leave me alone . . . please."

He jerked at her elbow. She fell forward on her feet, spinning in confusion, and putting her hands on her pale lemon jeans, covered herself.

Laughing out loud, Bug, put his head back and roared. Grabbing her shoulders he kissed the top of her head: "Baby Fod! At last! You're not a baby anymore," and removing his jacket he tied the sleeves round her waist, the velvet muffling the bright red shrieks of womanhood.

*

On the train home, Bug leafed through a catalogue.

After her leakings, he'd sat Foddly on a chair outside a pub, and then sprinted to the nearest shop. On his return he'd presented her with a cheese and mustard sandwich and a packet of sanitary towels. "Could've got tampons, but who wants a rival of cardboard and cotton wool," he'd whispered.

"I don't like mustard!" Already overpowered by crimson, Foddly had slipped into the pub to find the toilet, and cried.

Even after this and despite her discomfort, Bug had insisted on a visit to Bond Street where he dragged her through the auction houses.

He could be such a cruel boy.

Now, curled up against the window of speeding landscapes, he studied the form. "Paintings are the thing to collect, Fod," he advised. "And oak, of course – country stuff. But painting's the one – new artists. Start buying." Glancing up, he tapped her foot with the toe of his boot. "Listen! Think of colour. If you had no money or furniture at all, what could you fill your home with?"

"You couldn't. You'd just have the walls," Foddly drifted airily. "And a table, have to have that . . . Oh, and a settee. Couldn't not have a sofa. What would you sit on?"

"No furniture or money, I said."

"Oh, I don't know. Just the bare walls. O.K, paintings."

"*Paint.* You're trying to please but not giving pleasure. Colour is a *thing,* an object all its own, Fod. It has an energy, an identity. You have colours – apart from your knickers."

Foddly switched her head away.

"They pour from you, all of us. Artists work, move within it. Just think, handling all that chaotic energy."

"I wish I was old enough to understand what you're talking about, Bug."

"You stop yourself, and age has nothing to do with it. If we're going to work together, you'll have to stop limiting your senses like this. You, Fodellah Shaw, own the same knowledge now as you will ever possess. You were born with it – back and forth it, spins on its axis. Future, past . . ."

"Glastonbury's the one you should speak to. I don't think I'm the one to have knowledge."

"I can see I'll have to wait. A few more years of your redcurrant moons, a score or more of bloodied cups to spill. *That'll* be the way we meet, biblical – *knowing,* meeting as if for the first time."

Foddly eyed him suspiciously. "You can be really dirty and crude. I don't want a boyfriend and if I did, it wouldn't be one as crazy as you."

Bug returned to his catalogue.

The ticket inspector hummed by. He cast a cursory glance at the tickets lying on the table. Halfway down the gangway, he spun round and shimmied back to the seat. "How old are you?"

"Who? *Me*?" Foddly blushed. "Fourteen. I'm not fifteen till October."

"Any I.D., young lady?"

Foddly looked at Bug.

"She's under fifteen, on a child's fare. What's the problem?"

"No problem. Except if she isn't a child, we do have a penalty fare."

Foddly rummaged in her bag. "What sort of I.D.?"

"Passport or birth certificate."

"What? You expect her to be carrying around a birth certificate on the off chance . . ?" Bug said, mouth curling.

The inspector, eyebrows arched in an expression of endless victories, fiddled around in his leather bag, and lifting out a pad began to punch numbers on a metal machine.

Bug twisted forward and peered up at the man who continued to punch out a ticket.

"That'll be thirteen pounds, *plus* . . ." The man didn't finish.

Foddly saw the inspector stop halfway, his face empty for a second, stubby finger poised above the numbers and letters on the machine. Returning the pad to his bag, he sighed and wandered off.

Bug closed his eyes and sank back in his seat. He looked pale and ill, exhausted, his face drawn, once more sucked into its lupine state.

"What happened there?" asked Foddly.

He didn't answer. He said nothing at all for the remainder of the journey, not even when they left the train, just walked on, a little distance between them, in silence. He was thinking.

It was the deepest, strongest thinking she'd ever known anyone have – worse than Glastonbury. At least he'd throw her the odd word when he was angry. The girl had no idea how she could understand such things as how strong a mood could be, but her young friend had crossed to some other place and she daren't try to follow.

At the bus stop, a car passed them and sounded its horn. Someone leaned out of the back window. "*Hi, Fod!*" The voice was carried off, a trail of noisy dust.

Foddly glanced up, knowing Bug would be asking. Her heart shook. He was staring at her, his eyes the hardest things she'd ever seen; stones, precious things, like sapphires – too valuable to wear or have in your pocket. So what were they doing on someone like him?

"That was Sedge Beat," she said, trying to laugh as if she was guilty and making a joke of it. "He's even *older* than *you*, Bug."

"I know how old he is, and the trouble with *Sedge Beat*," he said violently, "is he won't get much older!"

Foddly sickened, remembered the ticket inspector, the thoughts Bug had picked out of her mind.

"I don't want to be your friend anymore," she said slowly. "You'll have to see Glastonbury. I won't say anything, but I am not going to see you until you've talked to him, because there is something very wicked in you."

* * *

The cottage sat deep in the woods and unless you knew it was there, you could easily miss it.

The tiny house was surrounded by other properties; none inhabited – an area of forgottenness, careful abandonment and contrived neglect, as if the owner wished to discourage new visitors.

The place was accessed by a dirt track, unsuitable for cars or large vehicles and, considering it was a good three miles from the Factory or transport to the nearest Town, it was a wonder Glastonbury had any visitors at all.

But he did. They found his little home, sat with him in his garden, helped cultivate his allotment, bed down his plants, dig up his vegetables, worked in silent talk enjoying the time spent soaking up the rain or the sun as they walked across the seasons, the scent of lilacs never far away.

Bug was not interested in horticulture. This young man was not going to be arriving rake in hand or heaving manure on a shovel. Glastonbury had something more for him, and it was buried deeper than earth.

He sat in the parlour, a gentle rain splashing against the open door, listening to his friend scraping and clattering around in the shed.

The door banged. "I've got something to show you, son." Glastonbury rustled in, weather clinging to his smile, and shrugging off a raincoat, stepped into the tiny kitchen.

Bug got to his feet, clicking his boots loudly on the tiles and followed the man to an adjoining room.

The cottage was a cornucopia, a time machine piled with books and prints; every inch saturated with all manner of antiquary. Bug wanted to own what Glastonbury owned, have the knowledge that enabled him to acquire such things. Wealth was in that knowledge, and Glastonbury was the richest man he knew. The boy was as jealous of him as he was of Foddly, of the people who seemed in possession of a quality he ached for. Yet it had nothing to do with money, he knew that. It was certainty, fulfilment he found unattainable.

Glastonbury perused a tall oak bookcase and carefully inched out an embossed book. Removing a marker, he flipped it open, offering an illustrated page to Bug.

"An engraving. 19th century?" was the young man's response.

"And by whom?"

"What is it?" Bug turned the page and scanned a line or two of verse.

"Milton," advised Glastonbury softly.

"Did he . . . Palmer, illustrate Milton?"

"Oh yes, late in the piece of course, commissioned by a fellow called Valpy."

Bug examined the plate then returned the book to the man. "What chance do I have, with you around?"

Glastonbury grinned, placing it back on the shelf. "Guessed you'd like it. Call me a custodian. Anyway, what brings you here today?"

"Something more prosaic. Can I see that photograph, on the side?"

"Help yourself, son."

Over at a shelf, Bug slid out a picture of Foddly and blew dust from the glass. "She can't have been more than eight when this was taken. It's as if she's been talking to me for years, all the way down the line."

Glastonbury raised his eyes sharply. "And what line is that?"

"Like a telegraph wire. You should know – or have you already become disconnected?"

"From what, exactly?"

The boy shrugged. "It's just she reminds me of something, a situation. Takes me somewhere or pulls me back. Whatever you did there, at that house . . . There will be trouble," he concluded portentously.

"Are you asking me or telling me?" murmured Glastonbury with a wry smile.

"I'm asking *why* I know. The reason I come here. It's probably the same one as hers, although she doesn't know it."

"Like you and I, Bug, we have out little chats, explore our thoughts."

"But *who* encouraged her here in the first place? What led her to you?"

"*You.* Brought her to the cottage. Remember? Made her sit on the back of your mother's bike. A first treasure?"

Bug laughed, suddenly flustered. He turned away, his face smarting. "I'll be the custodian of this," he said, as if a trophy should salve embarrassment.

"Be my guest, although she won't want to be reminded of those carroty locks."

"We've had a split," the boy informed him briskly. "Says she's too young, or I'm too wicked. But I don't want anything from her, not in that way."

"Not yet, at least."

"She's like a sister, Glast, a *little* sister. I just joke."

"I see. And you have self-knowledge, boy – with your *memento*?"

"She was my friend, so I thought – as you are. There doesn't seem to be . . ." His face began to tremble. He clenched his jaw but the thin blue eyes were brimming with pain.

Glastonbury heard him cry on the scent of the room, the colours fighting for expression. "When you're ready, son. We'll say nothing of this," promised the man, "until you're ready."

"Ready or not, there's no one, is there? On your own forever. I frightened her, Glastonbury. I was too strong. I can't stop it. She has it too but she bottles everything up."

"Bug, these skills must be learned, respected. You shouldn't despise those who cling to the main track any more than you should be applauded for choosing the hard one."

"I didn't choose anything!" Bug, his face cleared of tears, stared up at the man. "And *they* despise – people who have no knowledge. They're the ones making judgements."

Glastonbury guided his friend back to the parlour. "A sample of my new batch? Some food, perhaps?" he tempted, *en-route* to a dresser.

Bug sat in a bentwood rocker, watching the man pour two glasses of damson wine. "Forget the food, Glastonbury, I like to drink on an empty stomach."

The man shook his head and set the glasses on a low table. "An absolute hedonist, Bug, that's what you are."

"Working on it. And no matter what I say or do in the future, I'll come back, you know."

Glastonbury eased into the creaking of his leather armchair, sipping his wine and listening to the colour around the young man's hands.

***

"How long has Glastonbury been in that place, Freda?"

"Seems like he's always lived there. He worked at Coolton Ascent when it was a hospital. You know that. Can't remember when it stopped being one. Must have moved to the cottage then, although to be honest, I hadn't set eyes on him until you and Fod became friends . . ."

Bug sat with his mother in their front room. She held a delicate teacup in her hand, tipping it to the light to see the pattern on the bone china. She placed it on the table with the rest of the service and picked up a book.

Freda and her husband Sal had lived in the three-bedroom terraced house long before Bug was born. The couple were not adventurous, had no interest in foreign holidays or improving their small home. It didn't belong to them anyway. The house was tied, along with all the others in the street, to the Factory, a quarter of a mile away.

Sal never said what he did at the Factory and Bug had given up asking him.

All the money they made was put into savings and investments for when Sal retired. An American by birth, he had a bit of story, a bit of a past, but now he was a quiet man and any expression of his history was manifested through the unpredictable nature of his son.

Sal allowed Bug latitude. His boy was good with money and most of the furniture in their home had come from country auctions. And even if the man was never sure from one day to the next on which chair he might sit, or at which table they might eat, as long as the marital bed endured, Bug could buy and sell and fill the house as much as he wanted. Their son, though eccentric, he assured his wife, would always make something out of nothing and one day that something would turn their lives around. He was convinced of it.

So despite their overt conventionalism, they lived an odd existence.

"I'm sure Glastonbury told me the moon was a sixpence falling from a sailor's pocket," mused Bug whimsically.

"Certainly sounds like him. I'll have a wee ponder on that. He's a very nice man. Trust him with your life. Well, Mrs Shaw has, with little Foddly. He's been like a father to that lass."

Bug folded his arms and coughed irritably.

"How did your trip to London go?" asked Freda, hot on the trail.

"Those handles aren't right on that bureau. By the way, did you leave out the camphor chest? It's got to be polished. Might have a buyer lined up."

"Yes. Pa brought that down. He's put it on the truck. You are a clever boy, the way you find things. No Fod this week, love?"

That was reckless.

In fury, Bug smashed his hands down, splitting the walnut coffee table he'd repaired the day before, cups and plates crashing to the floor.

His mother raised her eyebrows, put down her book and got up to prepare the supper.

In the order of her kitchen with its gleaming surfaces, Freda felt a little safer. But her hands were shaking. Wiping her eyes with a tea towel, she turned on the taps.

She felt him, standing by the door. Like a child again, always the unruly boy who didn't know his own strength, awkward, out of shape, at odds with the world around him, not unlike Sal when they first met, but she'd softened her husband in a way they'd both hoped Foddly would soften him.

"Doesn't matter how I try to fit in the box, Freda, my elbows and knees just keep sticking out. So I'm getting out of the box altogether."

His mother acknowledged what he'd said with a wave of her hand. Couldn't make any comment. He always picked up her thoughts and arranged them like a row of neat tomatoes on a salad dish. She had no idea what he meant, not really. Yet somehow it made sense. "Is this a box, here? Are we the box, love?" she asked, voice hovering above the sink.

"No." He came over and kissed her.

Somehow Freda felt worse.

* * *

"We'll probably get a television if Bug's gone long," Freda told the girl when she arrived looking for him.

Foddly glanced around the room. Why had she never noticed? Then she realised, angrily, the place would have been so full of Bug, so crammed with his selfish activities, all eyes would have been on him. His parents would not have been able to retreat into another world, their own or anyone else's. Now he had just gone, left them without an explanation of why or where he was going.

And her.

"Are you sure he's not living in somebody's garage or shed? He's done that before," Foddly said, a little panic edging her voice.

"No, he's taken the car. Quite a bit of his stuff's gone." Sal put an arm around her shoulder. "Don't worry, he's old enough and ugly enough . . . He thinks the world of you, just don't see anything except for his own self."

The girl surveyed the couple through a screen of hair. They looked perfectly normal: his mother, hair set in its little bubbles, floral dress, a pale cardigan over her shoulders; his father, small and stocky, neatly dressed, gazing out benignly from steady blue eyes. The only resemblance between father and son was the sharp nose and bad-tempered nostrils, and of course the secrecy. Both Sal and his son could hold a confidence.

Foddly contemplated these two people as if they were the last link with him, wondering how someone like Bug could have ever come from them.

They walked her to the door. Freda pressed a twenty-pound note into her hand. "Go get yourself a wee present, sweetheart."

The girl felt confused. "I don't need . . . You mustn't. Thank you."

Sal patted her hand and winked. "So long. Don't forget to come and see us. And if his lordship makes contact . . ."

Her bike was leaning against the drainpipe, a pedal wet from an overflow. She wheeled it to the front of the house, half expecting Bug to spring from behind his father's truck. But he didn't. "Bye, Freda, Sal!" she called. "Thanks."

Cycling down the narrow road the sun red in the sky, she saw the small planes taking off from behind the Factory and was flooded with a sense of liberation. No more foul temper and bad words. No more feeling embarrassed for the simplicity of her ideas. Bug was gone, his wicked unpredictability vanished, and that was as predictable as he could get.

On she cycled the crimson spilling over the gates of the Factory, up the lane flanked by wire. Pausing for a moment she clung onto the mesh. What *did* they do in that place? The airstrip had once belonged to the military but now only private planes and helicopters used the space. Why all this security? Foddly stared ahead. Nobody about. The day was done yet she didn't want to go home, still the thinking about Bug to work out, and continued cycling. After a couple of miles she stopped and pushed the bike up a steep hill. Reaching the top she sat for a while.

Coolton Ascent was the road that led up to the old vicarage, and as the house was the most notable thereabouts, had assumed the name.

In its own way, Coolton Ascent was as strange as the Factory, yet beautiful in that oddness. Turrets and pinnacles were covered in moss, patterned bricks smothered with ivy, huge bay windows blind with boards, even with that crumbling porch and broken steps the house was appealing. Seemed to be calling out for her.

Today the high wrought iron gates were open, the chain that had secured them hung loose. The estate agents' signs were also gone. Some hawthorn had been cut back and the place seemed tidier. Something had changed.

Pulling her bike upright she wheeled it up the road.

Not quite fifteen, sunset hair, her body lithe in clinging jeans and the softest curve of new breasts nudging the cotton of a skinny top, Foddly stood, a late flowering.

And somebody driving slowly behind her.

A silver Range Rover drew up and a head popped out. "Hi, Fod! Thinking of buying, are we?"

Foddly blushed. No Bug to be jealous now. "Yes, of course. I have all of twenty pounds in my pocket."

"That rich?" A young man in his mid-twenties, wearing a linen suit and soft leather sandals, eased out of the car. Slamming the door, he ambled towards her, cradling a tiny phone. He flashed a smile, patted his white shirt and gestured expansively at the house. "Care for a tour, madam?"

"You? Have you got it, Sedge?"

"In a manner of speaking – and as a student of the law, only a manner – but I do have a set of keys."

Maybe Bug's departure had released the girl to a new perspective because Foddly was taking note again. He was strongly tall and thick set compared to Bug. His sleek black hair fell in a shiny fan over his forehead; skin dusky and smooth, was almost like a woman's; eyes sunk in deep brown, set perfectly in the easiest face she'd allowed herself to study. His mouth? Not sure. "Are you working at your dad's?"

"Not at the mo – articled."

"Oh. So how come you've got the keys?"

"*I'm* the lawyer. *Because*. Come on." Sedge pushed at the gate and ushered Foddly onto the gravel driveway. "Stick the boneshaker over there," he said, pointing to some bushes. "In case anyone comes past – might wonder which century they're in."

Her bike hidden in the gorse Foddly joined the man fiddling with a set of keys and saw the porch had mosaic tiles with narrow seats at either side.

Struggling with the lock Sedge glanced nervously behind him then placing his shoulder against the door, shoved.

Foddly peered down at his watch. "Can't stay long – got to be back by nine."

Sedge screwed up his face. "Got wings, this pile – east and west. Oh, and church comes with . . ," he said, jerking his head to the left. "Sort of *en suite* salvation."

They entered the house. The hallway, a vast expanse of marble, was littered with leaves and twigs. The side window had a pane smashed and a branch was poking through.

Foddly couldn't go any further – smothered in scent and dust. The staircase was so big. A frightening sweep twisting up to an unfathomably dark space, and it made her dizzy trying to see it. The walls were dripping with something. Paper? Wallpaper flaps, not drips, she told herself.

"Bloody stinks," said her companion. "The staircase is safe, but I'll go up first."

That was kind. Bug would never have thought of that. "Can I go in here, Sedge? Must be the sitting room. I just want to see what the windows look like on the inside."

Sedge shrugged and began tapping the buttons on his phone.

The girl had not seen a room so big: dark panelled walls, dados above, roses on the ceiling and, across the vast floor, shapes of furniture under blankets and sheets. "Who guards it?" she asked the shadow leaning in the doorway.

"A man pops round from time to time – and this is a *withdrawing* room, Fod," he said, arching his eyebrows. "I want to check upstairs, so if you're finished deciding where to put the *Steinway* . . ."

She followed him up the stairs at last, its iron balusters held in place by a sweep of mahogany, steps creaking and moaning, talking, telling her of things she should already know.

They reached the first landing. There was furniture here too, and carpets rolled up in alcoves. They passed a long side window overlooking a cascade of leaves, then a room with a deep tub in the middle; up to the second floor – another washroom. Foddly began to feel sick. "You don't smoke, do you? I can smell cigarettes."

Sedge was banging the wall with the side of his hand and rattling doors. "Certainly not! Now, what's this?" Turning a handle, he squeezed into what appeared to be a linen cupboard. "Come here! It's still got the sheets in it." And pulled out a white counterpane. "Smell it. That, young lady, in case you've never suffered a private education, is carbolic. Vile."

Foddly sniffed. "It's gone, that smoke. Was really strong." She peeped inside. There were racks of sheets and towels, linen still in paper wrappers. 'Hardworth's Laundry', she read on one. "There's a Hardworth's in Town. Must be the same." For some reason she felt very tired. Maybe it was being alone with Sedge. He was a sort of friend, knew the family, but he was a grown man and she harboured the impression that neither of them should really be here.

His phone rang, very loud against the sleeping rooms.

She wandered over to a set of doors facing each other. "I'm in here if you want me."

Sedge lifted his eyes, a sudden glimmer, and smiled to himself.

The room, even in that warm summer evening, seemed cold to Foddly. It had an irregular shape, didn't seem to possess a centre. There was a lovely green marble fireplace over on the far wall and French windows leading onto a balcony, the curtains were half-drawn so she couldn't see out properly.

That smoke again, as if someone had passed by with a lighted cigarette. Then gone. Strange.

Sedge was still talking on his mobile. He came in nodding and beckoning to her. "Shit!" He raised a hand, a gesture of apology to his young companion. "Hang on," he said to someone.

That was considerate too.

"Sorry, Fod. Big resignation," he whispered. "This is *so* important. – stuff going down," and returned to his conversation. "I'm coming up tomorrow. If we don't make our move now, we never will. They'll have to recall . . . You still there? *Hello*?" He swung round. "Fuck!" Raising his eyes at the ceiling, he slipped the phone into a top pocket, smoothed back his hair, a quick review and glanced to the side. "Fod, we've got to go."

She had a red book in her hand. "I found this on that desk. It's a copy of *Gulliver's Travels*. I know somebody who collects old books. Can I take it?"

Sedge frowned. "Better not. There's bound to be an inventory."

"I thought *you* were the . . ."

"Dad's just put in an offer. Doesn't work like that. As the agents, we're not really supposed . . ." He stopped. She was still only a kid, and although he could see the girl had the makings of a stunner, it was clear she'd never be a predatory one. "Some woman has her eye on this dump. It's not a done deal. In business, Fod, nothing's a done deal – until you wish it wasn't."

"And you have got the Factory, *and* the airstrip."

"And *that* really *is* a done deal."

Halfway down the stairs the mobile rang again.

"Hi! Yes, I'm there now. Got young Fod with me – *Fodellah.* The Shaws, y'know. She was *desperate* to look over the place – couldn't refuse." He winked at the girl, whose steps were slowing to a heavy tread. "Something about a local history project for school, and as I had the keys . . . Tell mother, I'm up early tomorrow." A pause. He blew Foddly a kiss. "I agree, Dad, too much on our plate . . . and to be honest, it wouldn't suit." He clicked his phone off.

Back in the hallway now. Foddly, heart laden with doubts, thoughts drifting back to Bug.

"Thanks for that, Fod – got me out of trouble there. You don't mind, do you? Good girl." And ruffled her hair. He pulled at the door. Glancing at his watch, the sun sinking behind the hill, Sedge was lost in dark for a while. "Got half an hour before you turn into a . . ."

Foddly was walking away, pride uppermost. She grabbed her bike from the hedge and stood waiting for him to lock the door, naked twilight flitting across the grounds

Then a glimpse of movement, a shape edging from the dusk. A woman was striding from beside the house – must have come from that church. Dressed in a long oriental silk coat, she trudged towards Foddly and came to a halt, stamping a pair of muddy Wellington boots on the gravel. She wasn't old exactly; it was impossible to count her age in years. Her hair, snatched up in a tight bun, was almost striped, like a zebra and despite the fading light, a pair of heavy sunglasses wobbled on an up-turned nose. "Take no notice of him, my dear. I'm glad you like the *House*," she beamed. "We'll soon have these gardens in order. In the meantime, I'm afraid, a few heads must roll."

Sedge was ambling down the driveway. Seeing the woman, he raised a hand, rubbing the other across his stomach, as if drying his palm.

But she too was leaving. "Park your *tractor* more considerately next time you come foraging!" she bellowed.

Despite herself, Foddly caught the young man's eye and giggled.

"Bloody barmy," he suggested, his own pride tweaked. "Did you see what she was wearing? A kimono and gardening boots!"

The girl slid out of the gates and onto the road. "Is that the woman . . ?"

Sedge still rattled. "She's welcome to it. This heap's a bloody liability. It's going to take years, absolute *years* to sort out this Gothick horror! You'd *have* to be barmy to put all that amount of effort and money for absolute sweet F.A. at the end of it. Sorry." He snapped open the door of the Range Rover. "*Tractor*." and slipped inside. He leaned from the window. "Got lights on your bike?"

The girl, one hand on her saddle, the other twisting the handle grip round and round.

"A little kiss?" he ventured, eyebrows quivering.

She wouldn't look up.

He started the engine and glanced in the wing mirror. "Drive carefully, Fod. And mind that *saddle*."

She watched him reverse, zigzagging down the hill.

Apart from Glastonbury, maybe all men were like that.

2039
Coolton Ascent

Agate

"Is that you, Loot?"

Foddly? Who is it? Can't see. I'm marooned in flesh and marrow, an old woman – you'll have to make yourself known.

I can't smell anything, except the noise. There's a lot of riotous activity downstairs. I hope no one comes in here, haven't changed the curtains for . . . unless . . . Would you mind? There's a very good set of brocade. I think young Foddly keeps them on the second landing. What a treasure she is. Shouldn't have been so hard on her. You learn that about people. Too late then, of course. Like wisdom and ancient bones. Wouldn't care, but my thoughts are so light, as agile as when I was twenty.

Years make fools of us all, my dear.

Best get it all out, while you're young and beautiful.

What was that awful racket? The builders must be doing work on the east wing.

Smoke! Glastonbury! Those wretched nurses have set light to the linen cupboard. We'll never get this place now. Where are we going to keep our baby?

Jet

The sky was like a mussel shell. Inky black. Then Wit remembered he was looking at the inside of an umbrella, a very large old one with a wooden handle.

His mother, Claudia, was covered by one as well. They all were. All about him, the shiny shells of mussels. Or the wings of bats.

Wit couldn't make up his mind. His thoughts were jumping about and wouldn't settle. Free ideas set from chains, liberated under the canopy of shiny black shells. A gust of change lifting the tops off things. Lids off coffins. Yes, he would like that lid to be lifted. Just to make sure.

Claudia stood at the front of the mourners, a large polythene cape stretched across her defiantly broad back. Serene was beside her, high-heeled boots, a short skirt cutting into the bubbly fat of her thighs. She kept turning round to look at him, he thought, but her eyes were glazed and soft with hungry pulling, and he realised it was a message for the man behind.

Other semaphore – a little shift here, a sideward glance there, a hand raised, a tap of a shoe. Imperceptible flags at the end of a marathon. Or a race already won. And it wasn't by him. His brother, enemy and tormentor, had put himself in the lead, had won it for him – so how did Wit feel about that?

He didn't know.

A soft sludge of shovel on earth and stone.

So Speak had gone into the ground. Few got buried these days. Claudia had wielded her last influence.

A discordant sound rose from throats, hovered about the mussel shells, and died.

Claudia was levered from the wedge of mourners and shifted, like a compressed serving of seaweed, out into the road.

"Everyone's going to Harbour Lane," someone expressed without enthusiasm. Or maybe that was the labour of grief.

Wit held back, letting Serene and Petrol move ahead. They'd invited him, or assumed his number to the ranks, so he presumed they expected him to follow.

He turned, aware there were others straggling around the little plot. And saw his father. After all those years, here he was.

Tuf was swallowed up in a long dark coat. He was thinner, his ginger face creased and hard. Wit noted the young woman by his side. Hair tied up, she wore a purple cape that was too big for her. Neither of the pair had an umbrella and were drenched through.

He raised his in offering.

Tuf shook his head and was about to move away, when the girl pulled at his arm. The man stopped, stricken by feeling, put his face in his hands and wept.

An afternoon of rain and mussel shells, of a coffin going into the sodden ground. And now tears. An illegal occupation of alien territory. Feeling.

Everyone was guilty, outcasts in their own land.

"We didn't see you, Wit," the young woman said, her voice shaking. "I'm Brenda, your sister! Don't you know me? My brother . . . You gone thin, boy. Very thin." She held her father's hand.

So remote from memory was that gesture, so foreign from all experience of his family, Wit himself felt the heave and fell upon Tuf, salt and hurt buried in this incomprehensible day.

"Done it to 'iself," mumbled the young woman, wiping her nose with the edge of her cape. "Who'd've thought it? I wouldn't. Dad didn't believe it neither. Just don't make sense, someone like Speak. He was the one what done it to everybody else . . ." She hesitated catching their father's eye. "Well, I'm just shocked, that's all."

"You going to this wake thing, Dad?" enquired Wit, steering away from his own memory of the brother.

Tuf sniffed and composed himself. "I ain't got nothing to say to nobody there. We've moved on now, lad. Got a place in deep country, a smallholding. *She's* doing alright, for a daft'un," he said, jerking his head towards Brenda. "Ain't you, girl?"

Brenda smiled. Not a pretty girl. Not entirely ugly either – somewhere in the middle. A bland yet sustainable parcel for some undemanding man to graze on.

"Got a fella an' all, ain't you?"

The girl blushed in the rain and turned her face away, giggling with private delight, a squirmy, secret pudding thought.

Wit was reminded of how, like him, his sister could sometimes be that way when they all lived together in the Town and that was exactly what his family had punished them for – daftness. Simple, foolish enjoyment.

"So what you doing now, boy?" Tuf narrowed his eyes, his body stiffening as if bracing for another blow.

"On the ships."

"Tor, is it?"

"Yes, Dad." A sheet of white, paper-like in its speed, passed under the freckles.

"Don't they do 'angin'?" asked his sister, eyes wide. "What you doin' *there*?"

Wit, besieged by feeling again. "There's been none since I've been on board. Some people say he's gone really mad. I don't want to be on there, but there's nothing else."

"Got caught up in the bad again, I suppose," assessed his father ruefully. "Why don't you let things move on? What are you now – twenty-odd?"

"He's only eighteen months younger than me, intya, Wit?" offered the girl, a mix of pride at herself and admonishment at her brother.

"I don't know what 'appened back then, Dad. It's not really me, what I'm like."

"It's alright, boy. Don't talk about it." The man stretched to his full height, reaching up for a memory it was time to reclaim. "We did come for you, Wit," he said roughly. "I never forgot you, son. It was Claudia what took the offence at you going with that kid, Loot, not me. It was all her." He shook his head. "Doing it again."

Brenda was inspecting the puddles of rain. Words were breaking through. She couldn't help it. "What happened to him, Wit? You don't still see that Loot, do you, bruv?"

Her brother's heart sank. There are some places where people don't change at all.

Except: Tuf spoke. "We got the Church now, son. You should try that. You can forget the lot with the Church, don't matter what it is you done." A zeal, a vibration of fervour radiated from his eyes. A tiny beacon lodged behind the sandstorm sky, almost as if it had fallen there by accident, but had taken hold. It didn't really belong to Tuf, any more than the judgment of her brother belonged to Brenda.

But it was there and for want of anything better, must stay.

A voice rang across the graveyard. "*You comin' or what? Ma needs support, Tuf. She's in terrible shock, but she says to tell you the war's over, it's commemorations and she's prepared to overlook the difficulties of past times.*" Serene, message duly proclaimed, dripped her way over to the three. She eyed Brenda for a second, then let it go. "*Everyone's* welcome," she announced, almost sweetly. "It's for ma – and Speak, of course." Shaking the rain from her hair and flicking up her leather jacket, she walked ahead, sashaying between the slabs of concrete and flowers, and then paused dramatically at a mound of freshly dug earth. "Stopped rainin' now it's friggin over. Didn't do that right neither. Bastard!" she spat, flouncing from her brother's plot.

*

The square yellow structure in Harbour Lane was part of a recent building programme instigated by the Policy Makers. Its purpose: 'To reinstate a displaced community and provide it with a Function Space.'

Harbour Lane was part of the hard standing formed at the tram terminus, offering direct access to the Coast and the New Dutch ships.

As far as they were able, Policy Makers had decided to reclaim the coast. The New Dutch had held political sway since the floods of 2016 and were 'getting beyond themselves'. They had been useful, with their prison ships and their regime, but the time had come for their captain, Tor, to start abiding by the laws of New Island England.

The ferocious storms that once battered the coastline and low-lying areas had abated. The summers were hotter and drier and the shoreline was once more returning to the seaside of some fifty years before. No one knew how long this would carry on, but the more popular the coast became, the less powerful the New Dutch were.

Yet, if a traveller had passed by Harbour Lane this summer's day in 2039, with the slate skies, torrential rain and the wind ripping across the tall ships, they may have wondered if this might not presage the beginning of yet another deluge. And once inside the square yellow building, being witness to those riotous activities in celebration of Speak Daley's life, they may have wondered if anything had changed at all, *post-diluvium.*

Maybe it never would.

"Got a fella have we, *Belly*?"

Brenda let the blow fall, her stomach a cushion she'd been told to make when faced with an attack.

Serene pushed nearer, a drift of scent tickling a memory, the pain of blows uncushioned.

"I'm not called that no more, not for a long time," countered Brenda, resisting the desire to apologise.

"Oh, so what's this fella call you, then?"

"Just the normal, Serene, y'know." The younger girl trembled, the thinking whisked away by that memory, snapping her back, undoing all the learning and believing she'd clung to.

"*Good,* 'is he?"

"He's nice. What d'you mean?"

Serene pressing her back against the wall opened her legs and moved herself up and down as if scratching an itch on her round fleshy back. "Oh! Ah! Ooh! Yeahsss! *That's* what I mean. Don't call you Brenda then, does he? Call's another name, then." She laughed, a pink tongue wriggling between small uneven teeth. She drew back from the girl and eyed the guests, yelling and falling. "Friggin rumpus. This ain't what I'd call interesting. Losing so much business. You working, girl?"

"I work with Dad."

A dark cloud crossed Serene's round face. "Ma cracked up after you left with him. Broke up real bad. I reckon Speak . . ." She faltered, trying to squeeze a semblance of humanity into her faint blue eyes. "His trouble was caused by all that malarkey." And as if remembering her lines in a macabre play, rushed to the middle of the room and began to wail. "Oh, my brother! My darling bruv. He's gone!"

Tuf caught Brenda's eye and jerked his head towards the door. The girl picked up her bag and made her way to the exit.

They were too late. Claudia and Serene had fallen together in the doorway, a violent barrier of weeping flesh.

Claudia peeped out from a dribbling eye, her mouth lost in a row of bottom teeth. "Don't leave me, big man, my Tuf! Claudia *needs* you. Your little girl can't live without her boy. He's gone and left her and now her big man is going."

She couldn't continue. Petrol had fallen on her, adding his weight to the obstruction, all three howling.

The guests looked on in satisfaction. They were guests, not mourners. None there could ever admit to grieving the loss of someone like Speak Daley, yet anyone who associated with Claudia would know that things can change very quickly in her company. It was entertainment, of sorts, and all promptly switched their attention to Tuf, daring this heartless man, this father, to leave his partner and children beside themselves with awesome grief.

Tuf swayed.

Brenda lowered her head and sat on the side of an upturned chair.

Wit was in the corner, shrinking into the wall.

Three against three, thought Brenda, quicker than she'd ever been. She stood. "I think our ma might need a bit of *privacy,*" she said without falter.

Tuf peered in disbelief through a brush of lashes.

The guests eyed each other reproachfully, noting the empty glasses, the naked tables and empty bowls and made to leave.

Claudia, face now as dry as a bone, lurched forward. "No! You gotta stay."

But guests were murmuring in disarray, their pockets bulging with sodden fare, and Claudia was forced to abandon her disposition.

Serene staggered up and plunged into the departing crowd.

Petrol followed, grabbing at her arm. "Gemme some jelly, sis," he whined.

"Bugger off! This ain't a kiddie party!" Serene snarled, and swaying, collected a glass from the floor and drained its contents. Stomping her way behind a line of metal tables to a raised platform, she kicked at a loose panel, fetched out a small bottle, twisted off the cork and pressed the neck to her lips. Rocking on spindly heels for a moment, her weight braced on trusty calves, she turned to the near empty room. Her father was leaving with that silly bitch. "Come back, you bastards!" she yelled.

Brenda began to shake, her hands trembling.

"Where you goin'? Where you live, *Belly?*" Serene spurted, her mouth twisting from the venomous brew.

"We live in the country," interceded Tuf. "Long way from here, girl."

"We don't live *here*. *This* ain't a friggin' house!" Serene tottered over to her father and sister, breath foul on the air. She narrowed her eyes until they were like flies on meat, her dyed hair held in girly plaits by a scarlet ribbon, face roughened by salt and sun, skin cracked around the space where a mouth should be.

Tuf cast his eyes to the wall where his youngest, Wit, stared out. All skin and fear he was – always the weakest, face still a blizzard of freckles. "You coming with us? Me and Brenda, son?" A rallying call.

"I'm with the ships now, Dad."

"Tor don't own you."

"Yeah, he does," slurred Serene. "He's waiting there for that *Loot*, intya, Wit? He thinks Tor's safer than being with family. All we've done for him . . ."

Over at the table, Petrol was suddenly overwhelmed by sentience and crumbled against the wall. Blinking, his long soft face flooded with tears, he focused on his father and found someone he'd never met before. "Why did Speak do it – kill 'isself? Weren't we no good?" the young man asked, as if this stranger might know.

Serene took another slug of her brew and decided she felt tired. Moving from war, she too began to greet the reality of a dead brother and diminishing dynasty and slumped to the floor.

Only the Shell and Daley family remained in the Function Space now. Together, after almost seven years – only one of theirs missing, but they knew where he was. That was something.

A bang at the outside doors. The wind, maybe. Then a thin rap becoming a thunderous noise of iron on wood. The knocking continued until it reverberated throughout the concrete building. It seemed more than mere noise – a summons. But no one answered within.

Everyone in that room, with its broken chairs and squandered tables, heard the double doors crash open, the footsteps crossing the stone foyer. They searched beyond the shadow that fell across them, a wary searching, just to see whose shadow it was.

It was only the preacher banging his big black book on the walls and doors as he stomped into the hall. "Last tram to the Factory! Last tram!" Twitching back his cloak, he revealed a heavy silver cross inlaid with jewels. "Mrs Shell," the man warned. "*He* knows the hour and day of our coming and the *nature* of our going . . . Praise the Lord." And having delivered his last sermonette of the day, left.

2008

Pearl

Beads of rain hung from the clusters of fennel, shivered, then fell. A damselfly, iridescent on the wing, landed turquoise on a large leaf.

Bent forward, his elbows resting on his knees, Bug's attention was fastened on the colours. The rain fell, sliding across the man's long chestnut hair. It dripped from his nose, dribbled down to his chin and clung in droplets on his short goatee beard. He watched the water slip between his fingers. And looked up.

Some people with umbrellas were wandering down the sloping garden, towards the bench where he sat. Rising, Bug noticed another damselfly, subdued in moss green, hovering nearby.

He walked on, away from the group and made his way to a gate. Clattering briefly with his bicycle, he jumped on the saddle, kicked open the gate and swerved down the road.

"Very dramatic," quipped a female voice. "What does he think he's proving?"

"He's looking for Foddly."

"Think I'll tell Sedge he's had an unwelcome guest."

*

Sedge Beat was not so much charismatic, as easy – easily pleased, easily led, accessible and affable. He was easy to speak to so people felt relaxed in his company, and because he seemed to be interested in them, they were drawn to him. So these engaging vacant ways spread like a mild contagion throughout the area and he became very popular.

Admiration was not new to Sedge; he had been a precious child born to occupy an obsessive place in his parents' ambitions. From childhood it was impressed upon the boy that as a wonderful, special person, he could, and should, achieve great things and after three decades of instruction in this matter, had accepted it as fact. By looks alone he was bound to devastate.

He wasn't a bully – didn't need to be – his was an inherited grace, an inner tranquillity in harmony with its own purpose in life. And despite an often reckless disregard for consequence, he remained charmingly impervious to criticism.

If conscience was thrust upon him, if he was forced to confront his blunders or deal with misunderstandings, he would simply apologise – and with a good audience, Sedge did contrition beautifully. You couldn't help but forgive him.

Since his worshipping parents had moved on, the man had a need to work a greater audience for further affirmation.

Loving a child too much can sometimes be a deeper impediment to its future than not loving it at all.

Today he was hosting a soirée and stood with his wife, Tezzie, on the lawn of the substantial family home. The sky now blue, sun rippling across the grass.

She had been telling him about their visitor. "I don't think Bug likes you. Thinks he's got competition."

"Don't his folks work at the Factory?" returned the man, tactically.

"You like *her*, don't you?"

"Don't be bloody stupid, I've got more things to worry about other than the icy Foddly Shaw. That clown, Bull Somerset, whipping up support for that *Policy Maker* farrago, for instance. He won't get anywhere with that – tantamount to vigilantes. Anyway, I've got Gul and his new MEJA on my side. This flood business is going to work to my benefit."

"How do you *know* she's icy?" persisted the woman, clinging like a limpet to her new obsession.

"Look, if you're bored, go and see to Saprah and dress her up in a few more ribbons and bows."

"If people knew what you were like . . . So popular, aren't you? So democratic! If people knew what your *real* beliefs were!"

Sedge could see figures emerging from the French windows and begin to cross the veranda, picking their way through the tubs of basil. He paled slightly behind olive skin, deep brown eyes flitting across the horizon, mouth twitched into a painful smile. "My gorgeous princess, I adore you and *only* you. But now there's a *gentleman* I must speak to. He's come all the way from the city and it's very, very important, sweetheart."

Tezzie was satisfied and drifted off, acknowledging the man from the city, nodding deferentially a little play of her own, pursed on the luscious lips.

"How old are you now, Foddly?"

"Twenty-one – next year."

"Twenty . . ?" Tezzie, hair piled high, dark eyes narrowed, sat back on the couch and scrutinised the girl's face. She took account of the pale complexion, the cascade of locks subsiding to auburn, the wide space between slanted amber eyes, the high cheekbones; considered the small mouth and concluded, even with its elfin appeal, the face was not beautiful. It did, however, offer another threat, an elusive will-o-the-wisp curiosity and some, namely Sedge, could find that irresistible. "What are you doing, these days?" she probed, tetchily. "Don't most singletons join up?"

"Not all of us are desperate for uniforms, Mrs Beat. I'm doing 'voluntary' for the council."

"Has my husband been helping you there?"

Foddly, forearmed with the knowledge of this woman's inexhaustible jealousy, shook her head firmly. "Not at all; I've been working for the community, for peace."

"And are you interested in this Policy Maker idea?" Tezzie wanted to gauge exactly how close their ideologies lay.

"Bull Somerset is not as ferocious as he looks. I hope your husband considers his suggestion. The way things are going with these floods, if Sedge, Mr Beat, is elected, he'll have to have some local infrastructure. It's been absolute chaos up till now with the other lot."

Tezzie's mouth shrivelled. Infrastructure? The last thing she was interested in was politics.

Foddly tapped her hostess' arm. "Your little girl, she's in her nightie. Isn't she gorgeous?"

A sublime creature of barely five had sauntered into the lounge. Gasps and exclamations at its beauty, cooing and soft words followed the tiny vision, who squirmed with delight. "Where's Daddy?" the child demanded.

"Talking to important people, Saprah," Tezzie replied.

"I'm important."

Everyone laughed.

"Daddy's going to play the piano soon," shooed her mother. "Are you going to be a good girl and sit quietly?"

Foddly sipped at a glass of wine and smiled. Tezzie and little Saprah had a lot in common. She wouldn't get married, or have children. Selfish people just got out of control of themselves when they were forced to feel about others, and as the cool young woman had detached herself from feelings, believed she was one of the selfish.

Through an arch she could see people gathering in a far room. Women with long dresses drifted across the parquet floor.

The room had emptied now, except for an intense looking girl of her own age, teetering on the edge her chair.

The girl had been watching Foddly for some time. At last, with no one looking, she gushed over, as welcome as a vase stuffed with old flowers – falling.

Foddly braced herself.

"Hello! I'm Angel Brown," she gushed. "You're Foddly, aren't you? Seen you here before. D'you think he'll get in?"

"Sedge? Don't know. *He* seems to think so. There're a few more hurdles yet and he'll have to prove that he takes the flood business seriously."

"Dreadful, aren't they, the floods? My mother's been affected, and she's not at all well. So many poor people are suffering."

Foddly nodded. Couldn't make her mind up about this unexpected and effusive compatriot.

"If we can just get some support for the locals," continued Angel breathlessly. "I'm prepared to give *my* time. We really need to build up a sense of community."

Foddly placed her glass on a side table. "Have you ever thought of Coolton Ascent? They have plenty of groups there. It's become a sort of rendezvous for the people who've been affected. Self-help."

Angel wrinkled her moon-like face. "I know the place. Thought that was an alternative community – you know, progressive health types."

"Maybe it is," replied the other girl blandly. "But it doesn't stop them assisting. What do *you* suggest?"

Angel didn't have a chance to answer. A bulky man in his thirties sporting an untidy beard had stumbled into the room. Peering around, he saw Foddly and put a cautionary finger to where his mouth might be. "I'm late," he uttered *sotto*, tiptoeing to where the girls sat.

Foddly glad for a new focus, beamed up at him. "Bull, this is Angel – Angel, this is the *venerable* Bull Somerset, our very own Policy Maker and scourge of The New Britain brigade."

The man saluted. "Pleased to meet . . ." He nodded to Foddly. "Not going to be tinkling the ivories, is he?"

"Any minute," Foddly giggled, turning to the girl. "Bull thinks Sedge should be standing for the *other lot*, considering his background – landed."

"The worst – speculators, developers – they own half the land, the Town, including that pit, the Factory," confirmed the Policy Maker.

Angel shuffled on her seat, a little censorious pucker to her mouth. "His parents did. Sedge can't *help* being privileged and he clearly wants to put something back," she returned tightly.

"You don't live locally?" intervened Foddly.

"No. Can be a bit of a trek from the country, but I have commitments. I really look forward to these new transport ideas New Britain is proposing."

"What, a ruddy tram?" Bull snorted. "You'll be lucky! Not a native myself, but I've been around long enough to see *that* won't last five minutes with the villains in this Town."

Angel sighed. A quiet lamentation for the outcast.

Bull caught Foddly's eye, and winked.

In the distance a murmur of approval, a thickening of air, layers of scent on scent.

Foddly closed her eyes.

Bull began to hum softly.

Angel shuffled and stroked her plump hands.

Just a phrase or two, a chord exquisite as flight, on the wing for a second, a quiver in the air. Silence and then Sedge playing across it. Summoning the air, the moment at his playing.

With a touch like that, surely he'd be forgiven. For anything.

Moonstone

Sedge had been right when he'd told Foddly, all those years before, that there'd be nothing to be made on Coolton Ascent. He meant money of course, but then not all of us were looking for that.

At the close of the first decade of the twenty-first century, the property market in Britain had fallen so low, it had become a standing joke amongst estate agents that this was to the time to begin excavating. But if they were suggesting they might venture to the underworld to find some profit there, they had failed to realise they'd already arrived.

There were plenty who awaited the demise of the demon Capitalism. Nemesis at last for the greedy, for revenue machines destroying the land, profit warriors invading mind territory, retribution for the media fiends creeping subliminal into the thoughts of the young and sappy, sucking thieves, incubi preying on dreams and tickling wishes until thought itself, a product marketed and sold. Money, the great certainty spell, without which, people were told, the world would refuse to turn.

The crash was a good thing for some. Glastonbury was able to tell Sonjia that at last their purchase of the old vicarage was near completion, while the woman herself had snapped up another old pile, deep in the country, threatening to call it her *priory* when 'the time came'. And Bug, not averse to a little free enterprise himself, had returned from his *grand tour* to claim a smallholding, which Glastonbury had acquired on his behalf.

Once back from the continent, Bug had spent time in London, dealing in reliquary from Tibet and China, acquiring paintings, shipping works over from Eastern Europe and North America. In New Britain, fine artists were once more enjoying patronage and there had been plenty of scope to invest in fresh talent. But the young man was losing his appetite for distraction. A couple of significant purchases of eighteenth-century Asian daggers allowed him the excuse to seek the advice of Glastonbury, to go back where he belonged; to where the cause of all those years of distraction remained.

A man can travel the earth and still not see what's in his own back-yard, but in Bug's case it was this knowledge that had driven him to the world in the first instance. He saw Foddly in everything. Within or without, there was no space safe from her influence. Even though she knew nothing, the girl in her innocence had taught him immeasurable pain: longing.

Confused and angry, he attempted to skim the surface of life developing ruthless liaisons, hurting and punishing closeness in the way he felt he had been punished. All the while his body soaking up the fury, his skin sucked ever closer to the bone, eyes burning out like jewels. Repellent to love, Bug not only hungered like a wolf, he was beginning to resemble one.

That is what his mother had noticed on her son's return. Although they loved their boy, were pleased to see him, both parents were relieved he had a place his own. They'd missed him and his strange ways, but in the time he'd been away, they'd rediscovered their own back yard, even though it wasn't they who had left it.

And Foddly?

Over the years, she had kept in touch with Sal and Freda, would call by and talk of the new politics, but as they refused to discuss such things, they were fading in importance. And the girl hoped, as her work with the community increased, Bug himself would recede and finally vanish.

He had written never leaving an address. Foddly couldn't reply, had no voice, her views un-aired, feelings unexpressed. Once more he'd forced her to remain an observer, to concentrate only on him. So at the news of his brooding countenance presenting at various places, she felt only resentment, especially as it had taken him some weeks since his return to arrange a meeting.

Still played his teasing games.

Yet, even irked, Foddly was preoccupied by the thought of seeing her erstwhile friend after so long.

That morning in her room, she brushed her hair until it was like a halo of autumn falling on her wide smooth shoulders, painted green on the lids of her amber eyes, drawn a fine burgundy line around her mouth, lavishing the pout in shiny pink. Finally, rising and dipping, she squeezed into an emerald dress, teasing the silk around her curves until it found verses in her shape even she could not ignore.

Assessing a bank of footwear, she slipped her feet into flat leather pumps. Running downstairs, dragged on a raincoat, grabbed an umbrella, called goodbye to her mother and headed for the Town.

It began to rain, light at first. A bus went past. Might as well walk. Should have chosen more suitable shoes.

She moved swiftly across the road, noting the air thick with grey, everything sodden, a relentless wet saturating the mind with gloom. Crossed the bridge over a swollen river. Someone brushed by, offering tobacco. Beneath her umbrella, she didn't see the faces – wasn't looking anyway.

Why did Bug choose today? It was horrible in Town on Saturdays . . . and these stupid shoes.

A volley of shots sounded over by the estate. Then a lone gun firing. Weekends were always dreadful. She'd cancelled an appointment to meet him, and wished she'd been more circumspect. Canterbury would have been safer – could've joined that big march for New Britain. Yes, a much better idea – a reunion silence camouflaged in other people's noise. Bound to be silence. What can you say to someone you haven't spoken to for years, and the last time you did, were too young to have an answer to their nasty questions? Anyway Bug wouldn't be interested in politics. He hated Sedge Beat, probably jealous, although nothing to be worried about now, the man was gone and married.

Maybe Bug was. He must have found someone by now. Never thought of that. And suddenly felt foolish and overdressed.

It had stopped raining. Shaking her umbrella shut, heard the blast of a horn; saw a dog skidding across the greasy wet.

Must be somewhere round here.

Graffiti had obliterated the street name but this must be the place. The old Town. Dignify this with *old?*

A scent of yellow. Yes, a colour with a scent offered itself to the question, the finest cord of light pulling her senses away from monotone. She had been tipped over an edge from bland mundanity. A bouquet of madness dropped at her feet, tripping her up because she queried why one street, leading off another quite ordinary street, should be called 'old'.

Bug wasn't here anyway.

Then she saw the café. It was set back amongst a row of warehouses, some clearly abandoned. Little tables were scattered outside on the pavement, all very chaotic. The paintwork of the café was purple, its number in aquamarine. The doorway – there wasn't really one of those – was a continuation of the street except at some point it became smothered in yellow. How could you miss that?

There he was. Standing by the bar. And Foddly realised why she had worn flat shoes. He hadn't grown at all – a small slight man. The girl, overwhelmed by self-consciousness of her own height, was suddenly aware of how she had imbued his memory with power, had created Bug into a towering figure of potent authority, whereas he was in fact . . . diminutive. Ineffective.

Then shame at the riches she had been prepared to bestow on that memory. Her careful dressing, her lips, eyes. And yes, Foddly had to be honest – it snapped back to her like elastic does when stretched then released – a blistering shock of honesty recoiling and waking her up. He was a boy she used to play with, and he had made her think she belonged to him. So she had thought it too. There had been no one else. Could have been – Sedge, for instance.

So many ideas, a spinning Catherine wheel, spitting and sparking, in one moment of seeing Bug Itin at the bar of this almost derelict café.

Walking reluctantly, she entered the yellow, scent issuing from her skin, acrid, pungent. Fear and anger. Yellow scent. And he turned.

Bug had heard her approach and, unsure whether he wanted her to see him first, had left the table outside, gone into the bar and ordered a drink. His pulse was racing and he couldn't stop it. He may as well have not been anywhere, for all the distance it had put between him and this fever.

He'd spoken to Glastonbury earlier that day, talked about the market, babbling on, generally trying to cover the tracks of his anxiety.

The old man had known, of course. "You're pouring," he'd warned. "Dark." And advised Bug to either alter his light, or not meet the girl at all.

So Bug had altered. Rhubarb wine altering, staggering through the woods removed from himself until he'd arrived at the Town, sober.

The woman behind the bar took the money, Bug lifted the glass and Foddly stood, waiting.

She'd grown taller than him, but wasn't, as she feared, too tall. Not wearing those shoes could have been embarrassing for her. She'd be thrown by a thing like that – traditionalist. 'Baby Fod,' he heard his thoughts say. 'What *are* you wearing? That green with that hair. I can't look at you like this anymore. I'll have to turn around and see you properly.'

"Hi, Bug." Foddly stood over by a stool, wanting to say, 'I can't stay.'

The man was wandering over, grinning. "Well that's the short and the long of us, then, Fod," he replied to the unspoken. "But for the few moments you are here, let me buy you a drink."

"Er, no thanks," she stammered, confused – had forgotten about that one.

"Even *nuns* like the odd tipple, girl."

"OK, a small glass. You haven't changed, Bug." She didn't look up. "So, are *you* a *monk*?"

"Might as well be, but I wouldn't take my vows in this country. Somewhere in rural France, a decent sized plot with plenty of vineyards. Now go find a seat with a table."

He crossed to the bar and Foddly took the opportunity to squeeze in a critique.

His hair was long and tied in a tail. Surprised to see the short Van Dyke beard made his profile almost noble, certainly better than she dared hope. It actually suited him, but his clothes . . . A long cloak, velvet, as far as she could see, and with those big black boots, he looked like an old highwayman.

She glanced around. There were loads of tables free. Hadn't noticed the place was so empty. And sat down on a cold metal chair.

He returned with a large glass of wine and a straw. Typical!

Eyes now fixed downwards, she noticed how long his fingers were, seemed to take ages for them to move away from the glass, then folding some money into an old leather wallet, he slipped his hands inside his cloak, pulling them out again like a dance. He kicked at a chair and sat.

At last she dared look. Any boyish yield had vanished from his face. Sallow skin was drawn tight over sharp, high cheekbones, the short beard, almost ginger like the moustache, was clipped neatly around a soft mouth bursting with . . . Well, he'd just had some wine. Yes, fruit – glistening from supping fruit. And the eyes still hard, the strongest, loneliest gaze seeing her from somewhere she had never been nor likely to be, except in him. And all this lit by the scent of something that was taking so long to realise. Unravelling like perfumed thread. But from her.

Silly really.

"So, where are you off to now, Fod?"

Her stomach sank. What did *that* mean? "Expect I'll go to a meeting," she said emptily. "Remember Sedge Beat?"

"Surprisingly enough, I do."

"He runs surgeries now."

"What kind, cosmetic or brain? Trepanning, perhaps? They dig up neural pathways as well as roads these days, you know."

Foddly bent her head and blew on her wine. Why? It wasn't hot. "*Politics*! New Britain, actually," she told him loftily, a vain hope it might impress. "There is every chance he'll lead the local party. We've all been working hard."

"Don't hurt your head."

"Sorry?"

"Sedge Beat always reminded me of a swimming pool."

"You're mad!"

"Before you dive off the top board, you have to ensure the water is deep enough to take the plunge. And Sedge Beat, my grown-up Fod, has only the merest dribble of content between you and certain devastation." He smiled, not exactly kind and leaned back, scanning the deserted café bar. "Like it here?"

"Not really. It's one of those *Reprobate Bars*," she returned coldly. "Aren't they *passé*?"

"Are degenerates ever out of fashion? If so, I really am on a losing streak. Anyway, I must go too. Still plenty of things to catch up on."

"Oh . . . Can I finish my drink first?" Foddly's depression deepened. How did *this* happen? How did she start with such confident objectivity, indifference almost, to end up feeling like this? Hadn't wanted to meet him at all, but now she had, why leave straightaway?

"I thought *you* wanted to go," he said quietly.

"I didn't want to come in the first place." Foddly gave up. He had been picking out her thoughts again. It was impossible to separate reason from his nonsense so why bother? He was still a bully, a wicked man.

Her eyes hurt, itchy, burning, hot salt down her cheeks. Even fastening her teeth on her bottom lip didn't stop her chin trembling. Bug was leaving again, standing up, graceful movements with his fingers, gently lifting his cloak, treating it better than he'd ever done her.

Through a blur of tears, she saw his boots were hand-stitched, polished soft leather. The best. His clothes showed discrimination now, care. Vanity? No, more than that. Possession. Bug had achieved that.

An ugly little man with a greed for control.

She watched him turn out of the café, her hands were soaked. She bent down to hide her face, emerald silk taunting from the coat. "Hadn't even seen my dress," she sobbed quietly.

A long cardboard tube, an unexpected shape lay next to her umbrella.

Bug had left something behind.

Then she saw the writing: her name in large runic scrawl, and leaning over, tore at the cardboard. Inside was a thick roll of paper. Sliding it out, she peeped at one end as if it were a telescope, then began carefully unrolling it. A white stone on a fine chain fell out. A small card followed.

'Sorry I missed all those birthdays, Foddly. We have many more pale moons left', it read. Pulling open the scroll, she found a drawing. He'd done it. One of his . . . of her . . . Autumn hair and a green dress.

***

For nothing better to do, Foddly caught the bus to the next town and took the train to Canterbury.

A space, an empty thought. Hope fallen through holes of an otherwise tight weave of a day.

Stepping up to the carriage, she was first hit by the smell of disinfectant. Why do they use that stuff? Cattle. Are we in a cattle truck?

A soldier in moss-green uniform of short trousers and bolero, gun upright, acknowledged Foddly as she passed on her way to the seats.

"Hi, Fod." Eyes pushed to an outermost edge.

"You don't have to be doing this," whispered Foddly to her old school-friend.

"Are you joking? I wanted to get married," her voice wobbled. "There's nothing else. Anyway, how you doing? You were always with that ginger guy. Not settled yourself, then?"

Was he ginger, Bug? Is that how everyone saw him? "No. Expect you'll be off overseas soon."

"Fat chance. They're stopping the big flights now, even talking about quarantine. No, babe, stuck here, shifting sandbags – these floods are chronic. Anyway, you off to the march? Always were poetic, Fod. Get with the New Britain lot, they like the arty stuff." Doors swished open. A winsome look. "See you. Think of me."

"Bye."

Then gone.

Foddly did think of her school friend. All of them. No money, no contacts. The military, a brutal alternative to privilege. Bug could have been like that, but he had his collections – a wily way with other people's desires. He had gone well beyond the game.

She closed her eyes. Water seeping again, then:

"Foddly!"

No. Please no! I'm a hypocrite – let me sleep. "Oh, hello, Angel; you must be going to the march."

"I'm so glad to see you. Knew you wouldn't let the side down. There's been some fantastic news! That gale last night – Saltersea, it's been lost. Complete deluge. Managed to accommodate everybody."

"What?"

"Sedge predicted that. Defences were in a shocking state and the local guys did nothing. We've got the entire ward on our side. We're goin to win!"

"Rather a sad way to achieve success, Angel."

"I know. I'm not gloating. Oh, God! Do I seem gloating? Look, it's just that no one is doing anything except Sedge."

"And what *is* he doing?"

"He's been there all morning. The Forces, everyone. They're all listening, Foddly. It's fantastic."

"Where is Saltersea?"

"Oh, it's a little caravan park – not far from the estuary, pretty much . . . on its own. Quite small, actually." Angel, face upward, round soft features, a smile creased in a mound of love and cake. Foddly didn't want to spoil it for herself or this new-found happy bakery.

"You look piqued, sad," volunteered Angel with a perception Foddly did not anticipate. "Boyfriend, is it?"

Eyes stinging, she nodded.

"You are *so* . . . lovely. How can you have that trouble?"

Foddly gazed through a fog of wonder. What did this soppy pudding say? "What's the point of anything like that?" she stammered defensively. "I've just seen an old school friend who said I was poetic, now this. Everyone understands me so well!"

"I know how you feel about Sedge," offered Angel.

"And how *do I* feel about him?" Foddly hadn't wanted to rage, but this was going too far. All these assumptions.

Angel withdrew into the grey of the window. "Maybe it's *my* expectations of what he can do. There's nothing left, you know, service or devotion. Some people are still with the Church but I was never fooled by that." The girl tilted her head, placid eyes for a second illuminated, compassion flickering, stranded alone. A solitary sapience. "There are people out there *we* can save, Foddly. But control is not the way. Madness, delusion is not an option. I've heard about this woman – calls herself the Abbess – she says the Church is definitely on its way out. Could be mad herself, of course. Surely there's *someone*? Oh, well. I thought about what you said, regarding Coolton Ascent. Went there but it's all shuttered up again. When *will* they sort that place out?" Angel smiled again, almost lovely herself. "Maybe this Abbess woman has the way . . . But you do love him, Sedge, don't you?"

Foddly felt ill. "No, but you do!" Did she really say that? "I'm getting off here. Bye, Angel, I've got to go."

"Oh. You're not coming? Take care, Foddly."

Foddly left the train and caught the bus all the way back. How long the journey took, she had no idea, but the road seemed to talk on for ages. Conversations that had started with direction were going nowhere. Chattering miles, all missing their connection, words blowing like litter.

She wanted to get to Glastonbury. Must get to him.

It was well past dusk when she reached the Factory and felt afraid. The high black gates, the brick building, like some sinister stage set with its looming clock tower. Behind, on the airstrip, the new military planes squatted on the rim of dark.

This darkness could be anywhere. She, Foddly, could be anywhere and her rampant thoughts and sudden scrutiny made her wonder where she'd been before all this.

She'd gone mad since seeing Bug. Crazy.

The woods were dense, alien to most, but attacks had been happening all over. Some might pick the puzzle clean. Find a way in and harm.

And who was this woman, the *Abbess*?

Foddly loved deep country but only because Glastonbury lived there. She remembered the first time she'd visited the cottage. It was Bug's idea – implored her to come. It wasn't cruelty that time, just a desperate need he had, to show her to his friend. She'd sat on the back of his mother's bicycle, hanging on as he'd raced through the woods. When they'd arrived, Glastonbury was standing at the door, tall as a tree, with eyes the colour of summer. Not a word was spoken all that afternoon. Bug gagged up with pride and passion. All three sitting in the garden looking at their feet.

And now he was here again, Glastonbury, wandering through the twilight.

Foddly rubbed her eyes. "Is that you?" she called.

"Or my revenant!" he called back. "And what are you doing stalking the woods? Aren't you supposed to be with Bug?"

"I just fancied a walk, Glast."

"I'm on my way back. You tagging along?"

"Can I?"

"What have you got there, Fod? Gifts already?"

"Oh, just something. Don't want to talk about it."

Glastonbury walking obligingly silent, his long overcoat brown and untidy, his dark plaited hair, straying over the collar, boots hard and cracked under the polish. Tough leather, but worn on worn.

As they both trudged through the broken leaves, she glanced up at his face and found it slipped into an expression the girl had not previously encountered, shocking, yet worthy of respect. Like meeting the newly dead where nothing one remembers of them remains. A gracious acceptance of their secret selves.

Walking with a revenant in another season.

Foddly was neither upset nor surprised now she understood. It was the longest, strangest day, and when they arrived at the little cottage with its door ajar, she walked straight to his private study, dropped her presents on the floor, removed her raincoat and flopped down on the ottoman.

He ambled over and moved a few papers on the desk. "Drink, oh elfin queen in emerald green?"

"What kind?"

"Think we'll try the elderflower."

"Please."

He decanted some wine then brought over two lead crystal glasses placing them on a fretwork table. "Your friend has good taste. What d'you think?"

"I don't know. They're just glasses to me."

"Let's hope this isn't just elderflower."

Sipping slowly, the day's thoughts soaked in wine, Foddly's gaze languished across the room, stretching into dark corners, settling at last on a pile of books. "What's that?" she asked, sitting up.

"A khanjar – pistol-grip dagger. Pretty nasty old cutlery."

The girl crept over. "That blade looks like a crescent moon."

"Culling crescent. The hilt is black chalcedony inset with rubies and diamonds," he murmured.

"Those jewels, they're magnificent, Glast. But all that art and care for a . . . killing thing?"

"Maybe death is glorious to some. There's more – over there, on the wall."

A sword, enamelled in blue and green, decorative beasts clambering to the hilt. "Horrible and wonderful at the same time. Don't tell me . . . Bug?"

"He likes his weaponry." Glastonbury, in shirt and linen trousers, reclaimed the ottoman and swung out his long legs until his bare white feet touched the far wall.

The couch wasn't very big, but he managed to save some room for his guest. She crawled next him against the smell of musk and happiness. Playing with a loose button on his shirt, she felt the heat from his skin, saw his hand lift up the glass and disappear, heard him sip, his throat swallow. He is human then, she told herself. "How old are you, Glastonbury?"

"How old d'you want me to be?"

"My age, then I can marry you. I did, you know, want to marry you, once. And you don't have anyone."

"Who says I don't?"

"Never see you."

Glastonbury smiled.

"You're very handsome, still." She stroked his face, breath covering his skin, her fingers over his eyes, his brow. Tracing the lines around his mouth then landing cool as rain on his lips.

The man lay unperturbed, as though in the hiatus, the girl had merely walked beyond a garden, a child traversing new earth in search of frontiers, only to find light and the tantalising contours of scent. He felt her heart, its steady pace quickening, saw her face fill with misery, and slid the glass to her hand.

She lowered it to the floor. Confused, the girl couldn't decide where the origins of her aching lay. Bug? Sedge? Herself? She fastened onto him. *Appliqué* upon sturdy form. "I love you, Glastonbury," she whispered. "I don't know how. I'm too grown-up, but still feel like a baby. If anyone knew how special you were, they'd take you away, I know it."

The old man said nothing, his eyes closed, watching the dream. He'd heard her before she spoke and was prepared.

"What happened to Grandma Odella?"

"Why do you ask?"

"Years ago, Bug said she'd gone before she was supposed to. I remember telling you, Glastonbury, so clearly."

"Why now?"

"You were a doctor at that house, weren't you, when you were *James*? We've never really talked about. . . Everything else except that."

"Yes I worked there – sort of. They had very strange practices, barbaric in our opinion. We didn't agree with the methods, or the results."

"We?"

"A . . . friend. You'll meet her one day."

Foddly blinked rapidly, her wet lashes on his arm, a column of light penetrating the black. "What practices?"

"To put it simply, administering electrical currents into certain parts of the brain."

"And what was that supposed to do?"

"Offer the patient relief from illness or in certain cases, painful memories."

"And did it?"

"For a while."

"What did Grandma want to forget?"

"You think your grandmother had that treatment?"

"Yes. You know she did, Glastonbury. You were there!" Foddly buried herself in his stomach and listened to his breathing, caught and scratchy. She'd only guessed, but she had to find out.

"Sometimes the sadness of a situation can overwhelm and there seems no way out. If anyone elected to have that treatment, they must have been deeply, inconsolably wretched." The man chose his words carefully, laying them out before his young friend, like beads for threading on a fine string.

"Was anyone forced to have it?" the girl asked.

"Oh, yes."

"Did you give this electrical treatment?"

"I was part of a team who did. When I first started, a very long time ago, there was a woman – I suppose you could say she was my first patient. . ."

"And she was forced?"

"No. It was something she chose. It was utterly wrong. I believed she suffered a *reactive* depression, that is, she could eventually recover, given time."

"Why, what happened?"

"Someone very close had drowned and she, the patient, was becoming increasingly withdrawn, blaming the world, herself. Talking didn't help, medication, nothing alleviated her torment. It was all mixed up with guilt, even anger at the person, as if they had abandoned her. Yet given space and healing, I'm sure we could have reached her."

"This secret *we* is annoying me, Glast. Maybe she didn't want to be reached."

"I think she did but lacked courage," continued the man quietly. "Wanted just to break away, to cut out her old life and start again."

"Break away? No history? She'd have no past. That can't be Grandma. She was sensible, so lovely, always laughing. And Grandpa Finian. He was happy too."

"Well there you are. Case solved." Glastonbury waited for the girl to resume.

"When Grandma went, it was very sudden. Mom didn't say anything really – which isn't unusual. I was about . . . Don't know how old I was. Nine?"

The man shook his head. "Can't recall myself."

Foddly rolled over, separating from the angles of limbs. She focused on a pattern in the rug. "Imagine, just leaving everything behind. You couldn't. There'd be reminders. Photographs! Have to be photographs. You can't just forget it would be impossible. Friends, other relatives . . ."

"If you were alone, if your only relative was the one you'd lost, it might be easier than you think."

"I'm trying very hard to put myself in that position, but I can't. Can you, Glast? I mean, there would be something."

"Oh certainly. There would be something, eventually. A trigger."

"If it was her husband who'd died, well, I suppose she could start anew . . ." Screwing up her eyes, Foddly tried to make the pattern on the carpet disappear into the line of the wall. It wouldn't. "If she'd lost . . . No that would be awful."

"What?"

"A child – because later on if she had more, one of them might look like it. Imagine, Glastonbury, waking up to all that pain again. You'd have to face it then."

"Or not."

"It might be later. A grandchild maybe."

Silence and Glastonbury was counting.

"Am *I* like Grandma Odella?"

"You're like Foddly and there's never been anyone else like her."

She lay on her back and yawned. "Tired. Can I sleep next to you?"

"I'll probably snore."

"Then I definitely won't marry you."

How they slept on that ottoman, the man and the young girl, was a miracle.

Foddly, in her emerald silk, sunset hair spilling over Glastonbury's hands, a little treasure in his custody.

2039
Coolton Ascent

Garnet

Do you remember when we finally achieved this house, Glastonbury? Was an achievement – had taken years. The moment yielded like a fruit. After all that time aching under its bower, it just fell into our hands.

We danced around the drawing room and one of the shutters burst open, the light swimming in, drowning our feet with an old sun. On we danced. Don't know what it was – a jiggerty polka, something we made up.

I can't say what age *you* were but *I* must have been a youngster of sixty-five. So thrilled, could have burst inside-out.

I recall leaping up those stairs and you waiting at the bottom. When I looked down, the dust was a storm on the naked wood, you in it – standing so still in a storm of dust I'd made. Then *that* man's image as strong as yours. *He* had stood by her bed in his own dust. That's why I hate cigarettes, Glastonbury. He came, contaminating our palace of souls with his smoke.

I did love you. Your bold Sonjia, in love with a man she'd never really met. And our little boy was . . . waiting, hiding from the storm. D'you think he knew when we arrived?

Silica

On the tram home from Speak's funeral, Brenda watched the preacher with interest.

She'd never really seen him before. He was the usual one, just that she hadn't taken any notice up till now.

Tuf looked like he was asleep. Her mother sat staring at nothing in particular, while Petrol and Serene mumbled between themselves. Her young brother Wit had returned to the ships.

The first light was streaking across the sky, veins in an ancient stone. Restitution from somewhere. Forgiveness for the unrested. A day had begun and Brenda realised she had not witnessed beginnings either. Her days weeks and years had slipped into habit as she'd poked her legs through overalls, or her thick arms into shirts. Occasionally, like today, she'd wear a dress, but these times were rare.

Behind her, from the back window, a panoramic vista of the dawn, a flood of crimson then lemon, a cascade of breaking light.

She and her family were alone on the last tram. Or was it the first? Couldn't tell. They ended and began at the same time. And as always, the preacher.

Brenda was tired, but couldn't sleep. Had work to do.

The Church owned the land on which she and Tuf worked. The rent for their small home came from the 'payment for toil' also given by the Church. Another cycle. Payment for toil then rent for easement, payment for toil and so on

The evangelicals were not bad landlords, better than most. Their only requirement was the 'proof of toil,' which was evident and devotion, which was not.

Many toilers just went along with the stuff, the singing and chanting, but some preachers could read the language, and doubters were stripped of trust and forced to prove their worth some other place.

Brenda and Tuf had never been found to lack faith. If anything, they were over zealous, always keen to convert the fallen, getting in the way of the preacher whose tongue was silver rather than made of wood.

Father and daughter had a nice home, a good plot and all in all were praising the Lord from dawn till dusk. Hallelujah! And now the fallen were sitting next to them. But were they converting? No, they were not.

The tram was approaching the Factory, except there was no Factory there now – housing units had been built over the site. Many wicked deeds and evil thoughts had traduced that contaminated land: insurrection, murders. In fact, many of those events had been instigated by these very travellers on this last or first tram to the iron gates of its irredeemable history.

Gathering herself, Claudia peered up damply at Tuf and Brenda. "You can come up if you want – both of you," she said without feeling. "But I got some sleep to get out of my head."

"Nah, we've gotta be making tracks," Tuf mumbled, tugging at his coat collar.

Petrol and Serene gathered at the exit, both crammed in its narrow portal, morose, ashen, their souls abandoned to mortality.

Serene wobbled and rubbed her eyes, bleached hair matted, eyes black to their sockets. An animal wearing lipstick. "Give over belly-aching, Petrol. Ma, he's been belly-aching, all the time cry, cry, bloody cry. You ain't gonna bring him back with that racket."

The preacher watched in silence as the group descended the steps, gently bouncing his glistening cross on his vestments.

Tuf raised his hand in acknowledgement: "Thank you, sir," he croaked reverentially. The tram operator was turned away, so Tuf couldn't offer a farewell to him. He called to Claudia and the rest of his family. "You lot are welcome . . ." Then caught Brenda's eye. "To the *Church*, I mean."

"Yeah, thanks, Dad. Think we'll skip it," replied Serene, not without humanity

"I might wanna come," Claudia whined. "I might go, Tuf." Her eyes quivered. "My big man."

Petrol had fallen silent. So full of belly-aching, he could ache no more.

"Which *church* is it you go to?" Claudia asked, surprised she had the energy to ask.

Tuf wondered if this attempt at saving had not been a conversion too far. Bad thought. And told her: "Coolton Ascent. That place on the hill."

"The old vicarage, you mean?"

Brenda bit her fingers hard, eyes burning out at her father. Saving should be for the savable.

"Yeah," Tuf said weakly. "It had a church next to it, remember?"

The others were gaping at Tuf and Brenda. Holy in the moment passing. Salvation.

Serene spoke: "That big house what had all the gear? Don't be daft! The mad Abbess woman was there." Unforgiving eyes scoured her father's face. "We done time for them! That's a wicked place, Dad – you don't wanna go near there. That Loot come from them. You won't wanna meet *him* again. *He* started it all . . . taking our Wit!" she added, failing at righteousness.

"It's a sacred house now," defended Brenda, recklessly.

Her mother, who had been circling the conversation, swooped. "You really got the Coolton place? Oh, Tuf! Little Claudia *will* go to church."

"No, Ma, we ain't actually *got* it," Brenda stammered. "The *House* don't *belong* to us. Some people still live in it."

"Who?" But her mother knew, as did everybody. It was an old dream, one the dreamer knows will burst open to an empty starving bed and have nothing to show for itself.

Just for something to do, Brenda left the group and retraced her steps, waiting for it all to end. What would the preacher say?

In a gesture of supplication, entreating as a child, the young woman approached the steps of the tram. The operator was on his stool, sleeping off the drink till the next run, his chin in a puddle of saliva.

Peeking inside the vehicle, Brenda saw the lump of black with its glistening chain that marked the shape of the holy man. Arms outstretched, head back, he reclined in heavy silence on the rear seat

Then Brenda saw something she hadn't been trained to see. A little something, that's all, but not what she'd expected. It gave her a ripple of excitement. Wouldn't tell Dad. The preacher agreed that.

His face, which the girl was certain belonged in another place and time, would soon be forgotten. They both agreed that too. A glinting of silver, a click and a snap. Not of ecclesiolatry. The slip of white, elegant and discreet, a glow in the deepening gloom, a little beacon for the lost. Then a smell. Pungent, thick. A staining of virgin faith.

All very familiar. And Brenda wondered why she hadn't realised a preacher might smoke.

2008

Diamond

A north-easterly gale had passed the night Foddly slept at the cottage in the woods.

Sweeping along the coast, the sea rose swallowing enfeebled defences, then across the land ripping trees, their roots trammelling futures already promised. They lay there, oaks, beeches and poplars, like warriors on a battlefield, limbs strewn without heritage, slaughtered intestate by the edges of fields, blocking the little lanes they once shielded from the August sun.

Gone in a rush of temper, an appetite for vengeance. The deposition.

Already in the brilliance of a new day resurrection had begun.

In his lofty villa, safe from devastation, smug with conquests and further prospects on the ravaged horizon, Sedge Beat sipped a cocktail of champagne and vodka with a stab of lime.

He was amazed he could drink at all and still hang onto his stomach. He'd had a rough night.

His wife and their daughter, Saprah, had gone to the city for a few days. But for Sedge it seemed the world was just a heralding away.

Eyelids drooping, he noted through long lashes, a gazelle-like shadow flit across the lawn, and sighed. A deep rejoicing in senses not yet jaded. One world at least, had come to him. "Fod! What on earth are you wearing? Must have been blown here après party. Join the club. It's early, or late. Can I get you a drink – breakfast, perhaps?"

Foddly had forgotten about her dress. "No thanks, Sedge. Only came by to congratulate you. Alone? Where is everyone?"

"Been deserted – but to be honest, I've got so much to do, need a clear run. The papers are coming later." He drew a discreet finger across an unjust mouth. "Ah, now, just the person. Do you want a little job?"

"What kind?"

"Sort of *communicator.* You know, I tell you our plans regarding the campaign and you liven it up. A spokesperson, Fod. That is if you *remember* what our policies in *New Britain* are," he mocked gently. "Haven't seen you around much lately."

The girl scanned the steps leading up to the veranda, then through the open French windows. A patch of white was flickering across a wall. She could just make out letters and pictures bursting across it. "Have you got one of those remote viewers?" she asked, folding down on a stone bench next to him.

"Of course. Don't want to go blind, Fod." His eyes grazed on the milky hills only just constrained by the folds of her dress, delighting in a little moonstone pendant nestling in the pale valley. Whatever will fall there next?

"They cost a fortune, we still use a monitor," the girl said. "But no thanks, about the job. All that P.R. stuff went down years ago."

Sedge laughed. "Ah, well, that's a pity." He placed his drink in a marble urn and stretched out a long arm, his hand beckoning. All about him was sinewy length. Sultry, in Egyptian cotton swathed like a toga around his body, the whole of him extending honeyed languor. "Why don't you come and take a nice shower, Foddly? I've a *virgin* white robe somewhere. We could have our own Greek myth by the pool."

"I know who would be a perfect candidate for that job," she returned deftly.

"And?"

"Angel Brown."

The man rolled his eyes and reached for his poisoned chalice. "Hard, hard woman, Fod. Refusal, followed by torture."

"She's *devoted,*" Foddly teased, making to leave.

"Don't go. Stay and talk with me for a while, or have we other *pressing* engagements?"

"Nothing at all, Sedge, and I do want to know what you're going to do with the Factory."

Lowering his eyes, he tried the glass once more. Lassitude creeping back. "You've always had an interest in that place. Unfortunately I can't say, at the mo, what our plans are."

"Well that's just the sort of thing the press will want to know. It's been offering local employment for decades."

"Can't help you, I'm afraid," he murmured distantly. "We have some very serious work to do and the Factory is part of a greater project."

"So you weren't serious about me working for you – broadcasting your policies? Maybe you haven't really got any. The other lot say that. Another *myth*?"

The benign sun under which the girl had basked, vanished. Sedge, the mortal, mouth set tight against his glass, a firm, obdurate line – from god to spoilt child, indignant at having to account for itself. "You don't understand, old girl," he said slowly. "There are ways of telling without saying. Politics is like walking a tightrope. The slightest doubt, one word shifted the wrong way, and the body politic is off balance, haemorrhaging confidence. Look down for a moment and the game is lost, the rest comes tumbling. New Britain is trembling on the wire, Fod. We are here *for* the *people,* believe me! We are on *their* side. The land is for them but it's a transition fraught with peril. To extend the metaphor, it's like a scorpion's dance. We are dancing on a knife-edge. Life or death."

Maybe that was over-egging it, he acknowledged inwardly.

Foddly snapped off a rogue blade of grass in the crimped lawn and put it to her lips. "And what about Bull Somerset? He's interested in the *people.* His Policy Makers are as valid as your community forum."

"Are you mad? That buffoon's not for election, he's a bloody vigilante! Decentralisation, community control, doesn't mean a fucking yokel can run the county from his potting shed in between growing tomatoes and brewing cider!"

Frantically plucking the tufts of grass, Foddly blushed. "I'll tell him that. And the military? Would you keep them?"

Sedge tapped his head in disbelief at the sheer naivety of the question. "No *work,* Fod," he reminded gently; conscious he'd overstepped a mark somewhere. "And there have been civil issues. But I appreciate your concern. We can move beyond that *if* we can nip the cause for dissent in the bud. *We* are for inclusion. Everyone should have a purpose, a home, the right to recreation, the opportunity to fulfil creative potential. True democracy."

Glancing around the spotless lawns, over to the house, Foddly wondered if he would ever share this with the likes of Freda and Sal. She giggled. "And what would you do right now, if one of that lot from the estate vaulted over your wall? Invite them in for an orgy?"

"You're here – unfortunately not for that. But anyone can just walk in." Sedge's eyes, soft with promise. "We're on the same side, you and me, the only one. You mark my words, when we move in, and we will, you'll be only too glad to spread the gospel. Anyway, Fod!" Abandoning poise, he jerked forward, a twist to his narrow mouth. "How's the *boyfriend*?"

His attention was pulled away. "MEJA. Shit! My appointment's arrived. He's early!" Levering himself from the chair he brushed against the girl's arm, ushering her to the side.

"I'll see you, Sedge."

"I've got to . . . Sorry, Fod."

Foddly left the bench and quickly walked across the grass to the path.

A man, possibly in his early twenties, with shiny jet-black curls approached her. Dapper in an unlikely silk suit and leather boxing boots, he raised his eyes in acknowledgment as they passed. The enquiry from the startling blue was not of intimacy, far from that, and as he strolled on his graceful passage to her ambitious friend, Foddly was compelled to look again.

Sedge stood, hands fumbling at his classical attire, a look of apprehension, almost fear, alien to his face. "Gul," she heard him say.

The visitor, Gul, had reached his host, and with a sharp flick of his jacket, removed a silver case.

Sedge waved his hands in protest.

Sensing Foddly's observations, Gul turned – a foppish curl rocking on pale pink lips, a cigarette nestling provocatively between them like a feather in cap.

* * *

"Where did you sleep last night?"

"Glastonbury's."

"And this morning, where did you go?"

"Just . . . nowhere."

"Why don't you . . . '*Come and take a nice shower*?'"

"Are you spying on me?"

"Yes, I am."

"You must be . . . I don't know . . . a magician or something."

So hot. The afternoon demanded sleep, a body to surrender to its scent and rest. The hill, exposed to rays of coarse midsummer, of brassy August with her showy skies. The top of a hill was not the place to hide from such vulgarity.

August, a full blouse of a month. Raucous.

Foddly fanned her raincoat over her face, pulled at the green dress and blew. A blue blow.

"I'm going to throw you down that hill, Fod."

It wasn't worthy of response. She was tired from all the talking and thinking, the belly sun beating down, and wrapped herself up in the raincoat.

She awoke, felt the chill. The sun was sinking, grass itchy. He was still there, on his side, resting on his elbow, twirling a blade of grass. Watching.

"Why is it so cold?" she asked.

"It isn't. The sun's still here. Let me undress you then you can feel how warm it is."

"I'm shivering, really trembling. Feel my legs." Foddly shook, her teeth chattering. The sky blue, itchy, damp grass, it tickled her skin, and so tired, but not for sleep, ascent from torpor into fugue. "Why am I so trembly?"

"Because you're on the brink, Fod."

"Of what? I've had a ridiculous few days, you, and then Glastonbury, talking about Grandma, arguing with Sedge. Peculiar. I don't feel I'm me anymore. And I can't stop shaking."

"A tumble down the hill will cure it, promise. We used to do it all the time. I'll hang onto you in case the armoury falls apart. All that shaking, you could shatter at any moment."

"Why did you go?"

"I didn't."

"Don't be stupid. I mean in the first place. You're always so . . . awkward."

"Fod. Sshh."

They rolled the two of them. One clasped the other, folding over air, hand flowering, grasping onto hair, limbs falling, knocking, heads banging.

Foddly decided to laugh, only because it was so silly, and up the hill they went again.

Her raincoat like an empty body, her flat shoes skimming the surface of the horizon, just above the rim of the hill, as if they were flying, or not part of the scenery at all. What on earth were they doing there?

Her dress was stained, green-on-green, a palimpsest of summers. And mud.

She flopped down. "Your beard's ginger. Didn't realise you were that ginger." Above her head, the sky, then rolling, green then blue. Up then down. "Stop! I'm dizzy. What are those . . . dazzlings? I've got ribbons falling from my stomach!"

And there were. Every colour imaginable. Her stomach fell apart, opened, a yielding of rainbows.

And rain on a flower opening and closing.

"You don't recognise yourself, Fod. In a different country, different time, sweetheart. And it's your *solar plexus*."

Sweetheart? Why? "Oh, I forgot. Thank you for the presents. I've got the stone . . . Here. That painting – how did you know about my dress? The colour and everything. . ."

Bug, his chestnut hair falling across her eyes. Mouth like wine – no, warmer, softer, sweeter. His moustache scratchy. He brushed the hair away, murmuring something she couldn't hear, over and over, in a language she hadn't learned.

Her hands flowering above his head, the trees, a hymn passing through an arch of branches. Going to church on a hill.

Tickling, a happy purr. Up and down, earth and sky.

He was burying himself in the sky, or was it her? Hot, but like a little pup, soft and needy. Gripping, purple as a bruise. Deep to the centre of colour.

Her forehead tickling, right in the centre.

She'd forgotten Bug had a house of his own and had no idea how they'd arrived there. Drunk, possibly. Drunk on summer.

Couldn't really be described as a house. A decorative barn in the Jacobean style. It was really just a long wooden hall. Heavy drapes, dark oak furniture, carvings, paintings everywhere it seemed. Open-plan, a door at one end. Bathroom probably.

The bed was on a dais, a stage set or a sacrificial altar, smothered in rugs, except where she was. Trembling. Her dress sticking to her legs, raincoat on the floor, clinging onto her shoes. Where she lay was a sheet of clean smoothness, not an itch to be felt.

"Something to eat, Fod?"

"No, thank you."

"I've spoken to home. Told your folks where you are."

"Thank you."

"Still got the tremors?"

She didn't say anything. Releasing the grip on her shoes, noticed it was dark. Must be quite a way into the country. Or she'd slept again. "Are we near Glastonbury's?" she asked at last, through her teeth.

"Further out. Take you there, if you want."

Did she want?

Bug was standing beside her. He wore a kimono, a heavy silk thing with dragons embroidered on it, and a wide cummerbund. Had a glass in his hand, hair loose, curling at his shoulders, planes of a face drawn up, hung taut on angles, eyes narrow, thin, like an animal. Yet there was no malice. A curiously patient hunger.

"What brink am I on, Bug?"

"Yours, mine. Maybe not, I could be wrong."

Her spine began to melt, disintegrate. A vapour that once was her. The ceiling had a sky, tessellated light, like sun through leaves. Didn't his house have a roof? He was telling her something, but the pitch was too low. She would have to have her ear to the earth, or be in it. A tree herself, perhaps.

Inside again, solid and nicely round and her nipples beneath that green dress were singing, standing up, proud and shouting. And they wanted him to join in. Extremities in chorus. And light, streaming from her head, or into it.

"It's coming from you as well," he said by way of consolation, and offered the glass.

Taking a gulp, she saw he was undoing her. But not the dress, the choir, beneath.

Or was that the solar plexus too?

"Should be in your crown by now," he answered.

She cupped his hand, though hers unsteady, while he tipped the glass. The liquid spilled. A globule of cold dribbling down her chin and onto her dress.

Glass vanished, his finger soaking up the wet. "Let's take this off, you and me, Fod. Slowly and gently."

"I need to wash."

"Plenty of fluid for that, from both of us."

Unbuttoning, unzipping. A murmur of material, hum of silk. Farewell.

Bug pushing up the dress to her knees, her thighs. It went as far her waist and refused to budge.

Foddly looked up, apologetic, as if she'd forgotten how to make a tent work.

He rolled her over. "You'll have to stand. Pretend you're conducting the orchestra – sure we can find a baton somewhere."

So she did. Not as tall as her, yet he towered above. As she raised her arms, an obedient child, wanted to fly again and chase him.

Her emerald dress in his hands. Silent.

Stomach, breasts luminous as moons.

His fingers slipping like a fine chain, cool, silver sliding.

The stone was cold, implausible ice between the swell of flesh.

She turned her face to him, watching how she spun saw her lips drift onto his, ripe tongue segueing from verse to verse.

"Moons, Fod. Full and pale." He moved quickly and was naked. A lean man, strong, a compression of breath held down for years in thought and deed.

Opening her up, he found the space. They filled it together. All around the room they travelled within unlikely gaps, fingers pulling cords glistening with song, his rigid heat pressed against her in an audacious rhythm she found she knew. The moon and the tide

On his knees, drinking from her until she laughed.

Foddly couldn't see, it happened so quickly, the transition. A chord plucked. Which should it be? Music or rivers?

She wanted to taste his mouth again, hard and soft. Hard on a delicious river. Paddling fast, whipping the water so they could slide.

Back on the stage, lying over her, his breath faster, pushing. Pulled away. Don't!

Down to her thighs, licking like a pup, wriggling his tongue into crevice and petal, biting and riding the smooth of spine and buttock.

Dew from sudden dawn.

Then she began to speak. Onto his mouth, lost in salt. Heard him whimper and cry. Found his back, a sea of vapour itself, and swam. A man like him could be so exquisite, unbearable tumbling from her stomach.

Nothing else but each other, each jewel, clarified by its own fire. Had she always known they would be like this?

"Feel me, baby. Let me inside," he whispered through her hair.

Her legs were around him. She could see them, but didn't recognise them as hers, up there, over his shoulders. And him closing on his prey, oscillating between wolf and boy, his eyes dissolving, then stones on fire. No reason to stop and couldn't wait. Tickles, pain, a ribbon snagged, cutting, a wounding flame, just for a second. Was it red? Redcurrant moons.

Then ease, filling her up. Calmer, orange, yellow, migrations of colour. The supple horizon of skin running, rippling in a sweet undulation of edges. A golden section.

A breath she must have been born with caught on a flag. His body, the thoughts from his skin, all she'd ever known. Wanted. In hers.

Expulsion.

"We're here at last!" The remnants of his voice, a shudder. An echo of what boy and man had said for years. "Let go! Now, sweetheart, now! Flow like a river because I'm going to flow into you."

Their dance subsided, sank behind a horizon.

In greed and need the night was occupied, boy and girl playing till dawn. Acrobat, dancer. Juggler, magician. Rising and twisting whichever route they took, met each other.

Then still.

Contemplative stillness. A milk sky, spilled along the line of narrow windows, burgeoned to noon, then onto shadows thickening corners. The two lay with empty stomachs, hands brimming. Girl and boy transfixed.

Hours and hours, soaked up in staring. Still life on a bed. A tableau on that stage. Meeting over and over, staring stillness under the day passing. Sapphire and amber.

Kissing jewels.

And if their perceptions were flawed, their vision imperfect, it could make no difference now. They had waited, without understanding what they'd waited for.

Yet he saw her as he always had. And for as long as he could, would hold onto her seeing him.

"Don't cry, Bug," she said.

Loneliness, an atavistic foe, once recognised, can never be far from resurrection.

1997

Quartz Crystal

"Close your eyes, Foddly. Now tell me when I leave the room."

"I can't see, Bug."

"That's the point. You have to practice."

"Are you still there? Bug . . ? Can I open my eyes? I really want to open them, they're itching. You *are* here. I can feel your breath. Don't tickle me . . . please."

"You can open your eyes now. I left the room."

"Oh."

"Now let me try, Fod. If you do leave, just stay outside so you can hear what I say."

The girl watched the boy squeeze his eyes shut, and bent over to make sure he wasn't cheating.

"You're still here, Fod."

The girl remained for a while looking at him, then had an idea. She crept silently from the room and sat on the stairs.

"I can see you, Foddly. You're sitting on the stairs. Now you're taking your shoes off . . . hiding them up your jumper. You've got a pink vest on."

She bounced back into the room, shoes in her hand. "You cheated, Bug!"

"No I didn't. You can't always see me, but I'll always know where you are."

"That's horrible! Like spying!"

"You may get lost, Fod. Wouldn't be horrible then."

"I've got Glastonbury for that."

Part III

Fruit

1972

Grape

A blue and white Triumph Herald estate was wedged in a dirt track, headlamps picking out the sepulchral shapes moving across the gate. The lights went off.

Inside on the front seat, Sonjia struggled with the top of a bottle. "Am I going to die an old maid?"

"Better than a young one."

"What difference would it make if I haven't savoured the flesh? Am I not desirable?"

Glastonbury shifting in endless limbs peered through the steamed-up windscreen and wiped the glass with an eloquent hand. "Shall we press on? We'll have to broach that gate; got the torch?" And turned to her.

She had her face tilted, head on the plastic rest, red mouth puckered, eyes swimming, with him. Raising herself slightly, she lifted the bottle and swallowed a mouthful of cider. "Glastonbury, you torment me. I'll scramble over gates, cut my legs on nails, be excoriated by brambles, but it's you I want to pierce and scratch me, *impale* . . ," and burst out laughing at the sheer purple of it all, then shook her head, tipsy-woe. "But I do. And we sleep together in this car thing, travel round the countryside, and you *sleep*. I know you do, actually drift off. I can feel your body sink, literally plummet."

"I see."

"You don't *see* at all. I thought you did."

"These are quiet times, Sonjia, dangerous because of the stillness; we mustn't become distracted, lulled to diversion. And I want to say goodbye to home. It maybe the last time . . ."

"We met here, you know. Almost a decade and we've not . . . well possibly, *once*. And I can't even be sure of that."

White skin, her hair caught up in raven coils, the little ringlets around a fairy-queen face, a Celtic lilt to the pointed features, a soft drum. Piquant. "I'm going home, *James* because you belong to Glastonbury and I can't share you. The man doesn't want me, so the magic may as well be returned to fields and stomped on by women with the breasts showing and men who know how to fondle them!"

He threw back his head and roared until the little car shook with his laughter.

"You'd never get away with it in Ireland," she chastised unmoved by mirth. "This to-ing and fro-ing from soul to earth – you either give it or you don't. Can't mess about with the Green Man."

"Is that so?"

"Yes. I gave this, dedicated this Glastonbury to you. Imbued you with its soul because you belonged to each other. Whatever happened in its history became yours."

"Is this *Ireland* talking or is this *scrumpy?*"

"It's me!"

"Then *you* have a lot to learn."

"I could hit you and hate you."

"You're forgetting something, Sonjia. It's this craving that will weaken the resolve, corrupt the prospect. We have business, promises we've made, and you'd simply like me to tip back the seat lay you out and mount you like a . . ."

"Stallion please, Glastonbury – if you don't mind."

The man grinned. Crooked teeth but it didn't matter, eyes like summer, unbearable season. "You might be disappointed."

"More than not having the opportunity to be? Well at least I have the consolation that no one else will benefit from the disappointment."

"And you? There must be others. Why don't you . . ?"

Sonjia, her expression altered from siren to infant so violently. "What? What did you say? Become one of *those* vapid *creatures?* Just anybody? After everything, you don't know me. Glastonbury, you don't!"

He pushed her back against the seat, twisting her face towards him. She was crying now, furious tears bursting down her skin, her face a diaphanous flower ruined by darkness, it seemed.

She had her hand on her cheesecloth shirt, undoing it. "My womb is starved, hungering for the knowledge. It's a real pain, Glastonbury. This ache really hurts."

His eyes so bleak she couldn't recognise them. "And what about that other *hunger*? Are you forgetting him?" he said.

But she wasn't listening and lifting the hand from her face, placed it on her nipple bursting like a bud.

Then shirt undone, both breasts – unsuckled globes in the summer countryside, stomach – a roll of flawless texture. Light as insects, her nails plucking tiny clips and studs on a yielding skirt.

Lowering his head, he sighed on her skin.

Sonjia clung on to him. "Why do you refuse me? You can see how wretched I am for you."

2039
Coolton Ascent

Lemon

I remember an old print; Bug acquired it – *Coming Home from Church* it was called – tenebrous sky, moon as full as this one is now. Can you see it? Swollen like a breast with milk for suckling, bursting for baby. And of course those ubiquitous cumulus clouds. Samuel Palmer was one for the cumulus cloud.

There they are, the worshippers, sculpted from lead, trudging in a solemn procession. I wouldn't say it was an uplifting image: luminous possibly, portentous, most certainly. A line of people bound by the perfidy of consentience.

Is that what you're looking for, my dear? The procession? The peeling away from ritual? Oh, I shouldn't be so hard. Not after all you've been through.

D'you know, my dear, life itself could be an image, a stamp stuck on a flat surface. One bored flick of the hand and we could peel it away. Endless churchy, childhood images, one under another. But what would be the last?

Ignore me – a wicked centenarian lucid with madness. Glastonbury said I'd live this long. He was right. Blame him.

Oh, I've been too harsh, and you're upset. Which one shouldn't I have mentioned? Bug? Glastonbury? Or all of it?

Sorry, it's just when you look at the postage stamp on the top of the world as often as I do, you want to peel it away.

Still, you arrived. I suppose there must be some purpose to keeping it.

* * *

The House on the brow of Coolton Ascent had grown tired. Various windows were shuttered up, the porch dusty, the gardens choked by brambles and ivy.

A small church behind the building was lit faintly by a small lamp hanging from a nearby tree, its arched doors open.

The few people gathered at the entrance, were talking quietly.

On the second floor of the House, a yellow light slid from a set of opening French windows. It expanded until a figure was silhouetted against the amber glow.

The figure stepped out onto the balcony and peered to the left, then withdrew and closed the doors.

A little while later another light appeared, this time on the ground floor, then in the porch. The front door opened and a woman hugged in a large cloak, ran quickly down the steps and taking a path to the side of the house, walked swiftly to the church.

The woman, however, did not approach it directly, and slipped by the side. Hidden in undergrowth, she crept by a wall and waited.

The lamp on the tree went out. Only the light from the pregnant moon remained, and the people huddled in the doorway were etched on blackness like silver-point.

They were waiting in that moonlit moment, for someone.

The woman by the wall also waited, her breath close.

A crackle of branch and a rustle of leaves. Crunching. Footsteps, too clear to be careful.

Beyond, at the front of the small building, more people had gathered. Must have been them.

A tap on her arm. Then a grip. "Foddly?" The voice was low and weary, hand loosening to a warm, soft apology.

"Angel, what are you doing here?"

"I saw you go out. We need to get some reinforcements, Foddly. You mustn't leave the place. Sorry."

"Who's with her?"

"Saprah."

Foddly searched her companion's puffy face, ashen in the light.

"Nothing you can do, not now. Sshh, Foddly, we'll have to creep low."

The two sidled by the wall, treading quiet as death. The group at the entrance had been absorbed into the church, the doors still slightly ajar.

A layer of noise rising, a loose knot of a hymn unravelling as it passed into the cool air.

Angel tugged at her arm and pointed. "One of them's late. Down here."

The severe outline of a tall man strode towards the path leading to the church. He swept by without turning, a hood covering his head. A cross, its jewels glinting bounced against his thick vestments. He paused for a second like an animal disturbed by scent then resumed his journey.

The doors flung open, the noise freed, thickening in flight, then contained once more, frayed and broke.

The two women made their way back to the House and the chill of a vast drawing room,

Once sumptuous, the room now retained only the remnants of opulence. Faded drapes and carpets, the pile worn down in patches, deep skirting boards, paintwork scuffed and chipped, careful colours between wood and wall un-coupled with age. Yet a potential endured within that place – a resurgence surely imminent, its illustrious history must outlive these ill-fated incumbents.

A bearded man sat on a battered leather chesterfield, a gun across his lap. He looked up without smiling as the two entered the room.

A creak. Shuffling.

Another woman crossed the threshold, walking softly – dark and beautiful, her voice hovering over an old thought. "She made me stay longer than I expected, Bull. I couldn't leave."

Foddly was by the fire, prodding ashes with the toe of her boot. She acknowledged the woman with a nod. "How is she, Saprah?"

"Wandering again. I don't think she knows who I am. Rambles on all the time about Glastonbury and some child – a baby. Did they ever have . . ?"

"No – not theirs at least. What about the cigarettes? Has she mentioned the smoke today?"

Saprah shrugged. "I can't remember *everything*," and turned to Angel. "Anyway, maybe she imagines it all. Always talking about what happened – years ago. I don't think it's real . . . Is it real?"

Foddly crossed to a large bay window and secured it shutters.

Without a word, the small group dispersed to various parts of the House and set up their positions. Rifles, pistols, bricks and rope, piled in unsteady heaps.

Saprah wound her way up the stairs, touching the walls as she went. Cool and damp now. Hearing Foddly stop at the foot of the great sweep, she looked down.

She'd known the woman for years. Never liked her. Hard and difficult to grasp – not really there at all. Even so that cold vaporous presence had altered her life irrevocably and she didn't know if she could ever forgive her. All sorts of people had arrived because of Foddly. Other cold imprints: Loot, Wit. No one had asked them to come. And then there was Bug, but he had long gone, left markings of his passing. Of all of them, he was the one she regretted most. But Saprah knew about other things now. Events were being explained.

One day she'd be called to Sonjia's room, the next, Foddly's turn, then Bull. Even Angel was summoned – she was changing too. No one dare refuse.

Each member of the dwindling household spent time regretting in that dangerous place, the night and day sweeping in at that ever-open window.

Sonjia would say things, upsetting words. Even from her bed, the old woman still had the power to capture, ensnaring everyone in the little stories about what had happened, as if everything had been down to her.

Some used to tell but now on leaving her bedside, fell silent. Anyway, the stories would not agree, just as lives are always disappointingly unconnected – in the light of day the colours to secrets never match.

Reaching the second landing, she heard the old woman talking again. This time to that invisible companion patiently listening, waiting. Drowning words carried on the last breath of lilac. Yes, Sonjia was sinking, plunged in the sea. One day her voice would be washed up, all of their voices would, unlikely as flowers on freezing sand.

Gathering her skirts, Saprah tiptoed up a set of narrow stairs and entered a small attic room. Settling on a small tapestry chair, she lifted a book from a table and held it to the window.

The pages were illuminated like stained glass lit by the moon. "If I have sinned, it's because I didn't recognise him," she said. "But I will next time. I'll know next time. We are waiting for him."

*

In the church, the scriptures had been read, grave warnings issued.

Pews still cool, doors locked, congregation left and made their journey down the steep hill.

All was quiet.

The preacher hung back a while and surveyed his flock as they dispersed to darkness. Straddling the shadows, he breathed deeply. Moon high, a mild breeze. Then, moving lightly down the path and past the arbour, he came to a small bench, and sat, basking in the gentle air.

So many differing fronts: north, east. And this? Just right, a decent wind blowing, a balm compared to some he'd known. Rising, he banged the bible against his leg. "We have some work to do, you and I." Turning, he crept silently along the front of the

House and pausing by a large lilac bush, contemplated the balcony on the second floor. A shaft of light wavered. Directing his attention to the side, he noted the deep bays of the next windows.

A sash was up. Had been for some time.

"Soon, I'd say," he murmured. "Very good. I'm tired and need rest myself, madam."

And plucking a cigarette from the night, watched a coil of smoke drift upwards.

Lime

Wit had decided to return to the ships and the captain for further training, not that he had any choice.

Tor was a brute and Wit lived in fear of brutality. He always had, of everyone's. That was his history thus far. Once, the boy had broken away, made a clean break, but the emptiness had occupied him. The lack of faith had struck and severed his soul in half. One to the dark, the other? He'd hoped it would be to light, so it might pull him back to safety.

Up till now, it hadn't.

Tor sat on the threshold of the day, his red beard like wire, his hard face creased into folds the thin edges like the battered canvas of his vast sails. He scrutinised the sky: fine again, no cloud. His men were tired and bored, itching for travel. He turned.

Wit was bent over some rope, gulls screeching overhead. Tor could see the boy was struggling. "And how was the brother's end?"

"All right," Wit mumbled.

"All right? How can a coward, who had a coward's end, be all right?"

"It wasn't that difficult, sir."

The morning was already blistering hot. No chance of relief.

"There were times when it did nothing but rain around here, fellow," said the Dutchman ruefully. "We had trade, potions, tobacco. We ruled with tobacco."

Wit continued with his rope.

"We traded in the finest artefacts, plundered from all over the world. Had cargo your lot were aching for." Tor's voice called like a siren. "A young devil called Bug Itin, he ached, oh yes, I could feel that hunger."

Wit, a memory refusing seduction.

"Remember him? Like a wolf – but he did know his trade. Used to harvest from calamity until it became his own misfortune. 'Live by the sword,' they say. Not a swordsman yet in other ways so close to being a master. I wonder on those times, young fellow and marvel how they continued for so long."

The young man stared at his bare feet.

"Did you make recompense, boy?" asked the captain.

"I don't know what I did."

"Oh I can see that. There are plenty who confess to ignorance, but I know a man's guilt. I can smell it on him and when he travels upwards, he knows I know it too."

Wit began to shake, uncontrollable shaking, his mouth swallowed up in terror.

"And I know about you. It's not so terrible. If you make recompense we can move on from here and you can be a free man."

"I didn't go with the family, I went with Loot. I didn't mean to go back with them. What happened to me?"

"Doubted. You let it creep in, what followed was hunger, a secret longing. You left the path." Tor scratched his beard and considered the young man. "The devil finds a way in. Should have stuck with the boy."

"I don't know where my friend is, sir. Maybe he'll come back here. I would like to see him again, before . . ."

"Before what? You think I'll let you hang? The rope's too good," he laughed. "You had your salvation in that boy. By saving him you saved yourself – from my knot at least." The captain moved away. "My time is up here. I no longer wish to terrify. I could be hanged myself. Maybe I will." He grinned, a quick mischief. "Would you do that for an old friend? My fall is uncertain. I could topple either way. Do it now, good fellow, while my soul is high."

Wit didn't know what to say, the man confused him more. "Am I free to go?"

"Always were, Wit. I would never have stopped you."

The young man threw down the rope and crossed to the edge of the ship. The sea was calm, a welcome as wide as mercy. "Where is he . . . my friend, Tor? What happened to Loot?"

Fig

Claudia Shell had found bone. Her very own rib cage excavated after years of fat. Wedging her hand beneath a layer of loose dimpled skin, she felt again and was about to call her daughter, when she remembered Serene was at 'business'.

A thunder on the side of their unit summoned her from a filthy mirror propped up between two boxes.

In movements almost dainty and appropriate to her new found waist the woman minced to a tiny window and shoved open the glass. "What is it you want?"

"You coming, woman?"

"Tuf? Did I say . . ? You come up sudden and heavy. What's the matter with you?" Her mood salvaged only by another dig into the springless depth of her stomach, she padded over to a long cupboard and fetched out a long dress. She wriggled the garment about her as a charmless circus performer might grapple with a wily snake. Dissatisfied, she cast the dress aside and left the room to cast around for inspiration.

The thundering continued.

"Give over!" she yelled. "I'll come when I'm ready."

The banging ceased, and the woman padded to her daughter's room

Serene had quite a selection of uniforms for her work. A yat-flyer, unlike the old-fashioned Madam, must be prepared to *push,* herself, show the girls by example, and Serene was very happy so to do. In fact, she preferred the pushing to the flying, to be honest.

But the girls were there and so were the men and currency was to be made real easy.

Harbour Lane had been busy of late, trams bringing people to the Coast. And with commemorations, the Function Space was booked up every weekend until the fall, ensuring trade for the summer months. A nice buy up at the stores and her wardrobe was full to bursting. A few crosses, a couple of nooses, a fluffy dress and she was set.

Now her mother, interrogating that cache of props, fondled a silver silken thing. It pulled to a good size but then snapped back. She explored the girl's other treasures: black and pink, soft and hard, card and plastic – none would fit. Serene had her own mirror, somehow less flattering than hers, and tipping it back Claudia draped the silver gown against that still substantial body.

Dragging the dress over her head, she fought her way through the armholes, wrenched the material across the soggy bulges and stood panting before her reflection.

Behind her, a shawl was folded on Serene's bed – very fine and sparkly. She wafted podgy fingers over it, a little flip over to see. If she was going to church, maybe this should be the thing to wear.

If Tuf Daley was horrified by the spectacle of his estranged partner – a metallic sphere adorned in ravishing silk, he said nothing. Maybe the man was beyond horror, maybe he didn't even notice. But he did give her his long coat to wear. And the two proceeded from the Factory units, through the woods, towards Coolton Ascent.

They reached the horse chestnut tree at the foot of the hill

"You got the book, girl?"

"What book? Oh, *that.* Don't they give you one, then?"

"No, it's summat you have to show willing over. We'll share mine. You gotta behave yourself, girl."

Claudia, glancing askance at her big man, was tempted to turn back, there and then. The notion of there being any instance of deference greater than his to her was laughable. OK, he'd gone off for years, but this was now and she was here, dressed up.

Still, the church was too much an interest to forgo on a detail of pride.

"Long way up this hill. Never realised that place was so high," she muttered, stopping to remove a shoe and shaking it until a pebble fell out. Stuffing her foot back into the cracked plastic, she lowered her gaze to Tuf's feet: big leather shoes, polished with laces done right to the ankles, his trousers, a striped slate colour.

The man kept tightly gathered, his face closed. Grit and sand, lines sliced into his cheeks and under his eyes, protruding jaw, long and stubborn, his hands, bananas without grace or feeling were strapped round a black book.

Tuf was something else these days and the woman couldn't say what that was.

The old vicarage appeared in sight: points and arches, ivy swallowing the bays and porch.

Tuf pushed at the high iron gates.

Claudia, a flicker of greed, a pounding of blood through her slow veins. "We're here, big man."

He raised a flicker himself, a gentle puff around his throat. Bullfrog. "You mean you never tried to get in this special place, my little girl?"

"No. Claudia was fwightened by the big House." She pawed at his arm. "We had terrible difficulties because of this place."

Tuf's levity was snatched back into his grim facia of sand and steel. "You wanted it, though – to get in here – we all did. That's what we're going to learn about."

Pausing by the gates, Claudia's gimlet eyes made their assessment. "You mean we got a history lesson when we get in there?"

"And we're all in it. We *all* had our part to play in history."

"Give over. We won't be held to account no more, not with the suffering we've had. The things that happened here – we were denied, Tuf! Left out in the cold. Since the floods we never had any choice. But *they* did," she concluded emptily, noting the indifference in the man's face. "What *do* you come here for?"

"Salvation – and you can have it too." The man bent down, grey eyes stabbing into her. "*We* can have that House." He pointed to the vicarage, the boards, the ivy, a gloomy vista sunk in twilight. "That is our reward. A Kingdom . . . *The meek shall inherit the* . . ." he stumbled.

"Heard that before. What d'you mean, Tuf . . If I just go to this church, the House . . . mine?"

"You can live here," assured the man "We all can, together. This is what I mean, it's *ours.* An *inheritance!*"

As they crunched down the gravel way, Claudia Shell was glowing in the justice of it all, her eyes swimming with memory, encountered a personal window of eternal opportunity. But . . . "Somebody still lives in it. You said!" she accused, irritated that such logic should interfere with dreaming. "The same lot as were there last time. Come on, big man. No time for ramblings. That lot, the Foddly nun woman and the old . . ."

The two reached a small path and the church was in sight. Tuf put a hand over Claudia's mouth. "Sshh. Don't say nothing."

Worshippers came, some wearing black others in brown, all melancholy in wide-rimmed hats or bonnets. Sombrely they filed, heads bowed, man and woman into the dank, clattering over the stone floor, rustling into pews they stood with their books, untidy spilling over silken pages.

Claudia hot and clenched bent her head squeezing a look to the left then right. Shapes were recognisable, people she was sure she knew.

A low hum: a rapid talking in a language she'd never heard. Scrutinising Tuf's face saw he was doing it too, speaking the language. She kicked him.

He carried on, eyes firmly shut.

A couple of pews down on the right, she saw her daughter, Brenda, in a shawl and bonnet her hand locked onto the coattail of the man next to her, like a great moth.

Sensing her stare, Brenda glanced round – a confusion of emotion. Then smiling meekly returned to her book.

The preacher appeared before his congregation. He raised his hands and looked to the rafters.

A discordant song juddered around from post to nave, to font and derelict organ. A rush of cool air and the congregation turned. Another preacher slipped silently down the aisle, a sweet smell issuing from his vestments. Walking with such grace and elegance one could say he floated. Discreetly bowing to the altar, he slid into the front pew.

Claudia was never quite sure about what happened next. She kept seeing a memory, a nasty bit of thought. It was like a jagged glass of a window she'd broken, but now it was cutting her dangerously near an artery

Her dead son, Speak was there – back as a young boy, fat and grinning – he was trying to dance but his clumsy body wouldn't let him. He had a sparkling dagger in his hands, had jewels and a long curved blade. He loved that dagger it made him so happy.

Then Wit, her youngest, turned up in the memory. He was big too, and stupid. But that was years ago and Claudia wanted to push it back, right away to where it belonged. Gone. Then she saw herself watching a woman with a big cloak, moving her hands over a body.

It was the nun. No one else did what the nun did. Wished she could see what it was.

The nun kneeled down. A person had died, been killed. Maybe Speak had done it, or Petrol. That didn't matter. Claudia really wanted to see that dead body because something was coming out of it. She needed to see that stuff, had to know where they kept it all. And until she'd got this seeing, this power, they'd keep on killing.

She was a in a field now, waving to the cameras, all around her lots of flashing light like when the old MEJA did filming.

There was another body – a boy with golden curls. He'd done it to himself and his stomach was falling out.

Then she saw him: a small man was lying on his big velvet cloak, blood spilling all over the place and Speak jumping about shouting and waving that sparkly dagger, dripping with red.

Her boy should have kept that.

But she was here in the church, Tuf beside her talking fast, people around her panting, falling to their knees. Claudia had fallen too. Then she was fat again. So vast and weighed down in flesh they'd put her in a wheelchair. Now she was being rattled about in this wheelchair, a mountain of blubbering blubber her cheeks squashed right up to her eyes.

Maybe it wasn't so bad being wheeled about like this, speeding through the grass and all running away from that wicked Factory. But they'd had to do it. They had rights. The People are entitled.

Perhaps she'd gone too far with *that* killing. After all, when she thought about it, they could have all waited because here she was and they were going to get the House anyway. But the nun and everybody else, what would happen to them?

About to ask Tuf, when another face loomed into focus. Never really liked this one. It belonged to that Loot. All skin and bone, he was, couldn't say anything. Dumb. She'd like to shake the words out of that Loot. He caused all the trouble. Should never have taken him in.

A rough hand on her arm, felt herself lifted. Everyone was going. She staggered to her feet, wobbling behind Tuf, grabbed his shirt and followed.

Out in the air, the moon looked like it was falling out of the sky.

"Did you get the history, girl?" asked Tuf.

"I was asleep."

Tuf looked hopeful. "You been on a dream, then?"

"You're going daft. Nobody spoke. I thought there'd be preaching."

"On Sundays you get that." He frowned. "You gone thin."

Claudia glanced down, just to make certain, and nodded. "How long do I have to keep coming here?"

"Until he comes."

"Who?"

"Who d'you think?"

"Oh, give over. Tell me properly!" she snapped.

"The *devil*," Tuf returned heavily. "When he comes back we can enter the Palace of Souls."

Palace of souls? Where had she heard that before? Claudia trawled her gaze over him, recalling the man she had lived with for twenty years, the father of her children, ally in war, partner in crime, a strong, violent man who should never have deserted her, except he'd been taken by daftness, no will of his own. So it was down to her now to tame him. This time back to front.

"You had a woman recently?" she enquired, handing back his coat and flomping her way down the path to the front of the House.

A tawdry glint of tin passing the gates and down the hill, she turned round to see him slowly walking. A look of horror arrived at last on his face.

"Don't matter to me," she said. "But your *only* Claudia's here, if you want her."

* * *

"You been at my stuff again?"

"I was going to *church*."

"You supposed to learn holy, intya? No nickin'." Serene lay on the unmade bed, her pink flesh wrapped in aluminium foil, a salmon parcel fresh for the oven. She crackled and raised her head. "Next time you go taking, leave a deposit – you split the friggin' thing! The old man come back, did 'e?"

"No, he's gone daft."

"*He* might have, but the diddery wotsit ain't!" The young woman laughed, a sort of screech bursting from her throat, escaping whilst it could. "What's it like there, anyroad?"

"Like a church. Bit cold." Claudia shoved aside a pile of underwear hanging on a chair and plonked her backside in the hole that was once a seat.

Serene switched away and smirked. "Ain't pulling your fat arse off that, neither. Told you not to sit on it."

"I'm getting thin, girl."

Serene looked doubtful. "You ain't really gonna go there all the time, are you?"

"Might. Why don't you come?"

"What! No business in a church. I'm not changing *my* ways. Too much to lose."

"Only asked." Claudia stroked her lank hair, pulled out a silver strand and held it up to the light.

"How old are you, Ma?" Serene asked promptly.

"I dunno. Depends how old *you* are. Add on sixteen or a bit more. Can't remember."

Her daughter made a quick calculation. "You're well past forty. Should get a burial with that lot. Grab back the old man, you'll never get nobody, now," she sniggered.

Claudia, a sideways glimpse in the mirror, sighed, a long exhalation of wondering. "We lost a lot: Wit, Speak, and Tuf's as good as dead. And what was it for? I can't even remember what it was for."

Unused to conversations that involved listening let alone thinking, the unremitting Serene, repulsed by her mother's introspection, rolled, oven-ready and fell from her bed onto the floor, her own repulsiveness contained in its juices. "Unwrap me, and take it easy. I wanna keep me skin."

Folding back the foil, careful for a woman never alert to others, Claudia peeled away the metallic wrap.

The girl began to smear her doughy flesh, lavishing grease on skin riven with creases and scars. "Rub it in then, Ma." Shaking her body, she roused herself, breasts flat against rolls of flesh, stomach soft, little rivers of silver on the falling buttocks.

"I'm coming with you to the Coast today, girl," said her mother.

"What for? You ain't due for no community until next week."

"Tor. I've got some learning."

Serene screwed up her face. "You taken a turn an' all? What happened up at that church then?"

"We can get that place. That House can be ours. They're just waiting for someone, and I reckon I know who it is."

Snatching a robe, the young woman collected the globules of grease from her stomach and legs. "Oh yeah."

"Remember when we went to the *accidents*, years ago?"

"Murders, you mean. They weren't accidents, Ma. You never saw nothing. I dunno why you bothered."

"Because they used to do things up at that Coolton place, with the bodies. Nobody else could see it. That MEJA used to film it all – the spirit stuff coming out."

Serene was wriggling into a pair of trousers, sucking her stomach in and wrenching the waistband tight. "Gul? He was half dead 'isself. And that nun was sick – the lot of them. You know what Dad said, they'd nick your bleeding soul when you was asleep."

Eyes like buttons on a damp sagging blouse, Claudia turned in exaltation to her daughter. "Exactly! And where did they put them? What they *do* with all those souls?"

"You friggin' Law, or summat? Don't ask me. They didn't do nothing with 'em. You're the one what believed it, not me. I just went with the boys to block the gulleys." She shuddered. "That Factory, all them wicked memories, the things what happened. And to think we live on the stinking shit-hole. Never get away now."

"Forget that! Don't you remember the big book they used when they were doing the talking over the bodies?"

"Last rites." Serene, ever one for knowing, supplied. "It's the same book as that poncy preacher."

"Well I want one. Get me one, will you?"

"I don't actually do a lot of business with the *cloth* and them offering me books, like. Think it'd give the game away." She paused, a swift review. "And who *are* they waiting for?"

"The one that's in the book."

"Which one, you silly cow? There's *two* of the main bastards! And I know which one who'll be after you!" The girl's eyes dark as figs, glistened sticky with rage. "I wish I'd never done the other killing stuff. I got bugger all out of it. Spent years on them ships 'cause of your friggin ideas! You wanna go up there, lookin' for souls? You ain't seen nothing and you never will. Stick the friggin' dead where they belong. No church book can help them or *you* now. For all anybody knows it's that creep Gul what's comin' back. If the bastard ever left!"

Serene felt the sting of flesh against her cheek before she could draw breath. Her mother savage once more.

"You, fat girl, are getting too much on yourself. Get your uniform. We're catching the tram."

Serene clacked sullenly beside her mother as they made their way through the monkey-puzzle of tiny roads separating the blocks of units. Reaching the gates, she poked her head through a gap, waving two fingers behind her.

A man in a small tower overlooking the site, leaned out of the window, returned the gesture to the girl and the large gates swung open.

Claudia stepped onto the road and nodded to the man in respectful submission, while her daughter shoved her backside in the air.

The tram was waiting, blind and hollow.

The operator, knocking back the dregs of a bottle, waved the two women on into the carriage.

At the back on the hard seats, Petrol stretched out, languid and sad, a long pendulum of misery. He rolled over when he saw his mother and sister.

"Whatsa matter, boy?" asked Claudia without interest.

"Nothin'. There ain't nothin' no more, Ma. Me bruv's gone, and me Dad. There ain't nothin'."

Boarding the tram, the preacher shuffling in black and silken grey travelled with his book on the lilt of perfumed air.

Petrol shifted, a small eye like a tadpole darting. The pendulum swung a little to the left then the right. "What's gonna happen to us, Ma, now Speak's gone?"

"Same as always – bugger all, you gorm," informed the ever realistic Serene, and parking her encased buttocks next to him felt in his pocket for currency. "Where you bin all night, Petrol?"

"Weren't talking to you, yat! Looking. I bin lookin' for my bruv."

A rustle in the gangway, the preacher approached the trio, a promise of redemption on each squelching issue of his shoes. Squeaking and padding he sat, a cloud of cleanliness rising from his vestments, and gazing forlornly at Petrol, flipped open the book. "*Where can I go from your spirit?*" he read.

The boy began to sob.

"Oh, shurrup, you fluff!" Serene kicked her legs in the air. "My bruv's a fluh-huff. And you can shurrup, an' all," she told the preacher. "Get out my way. What are *you*? Bastard! You never frigging sleep. Never see the main man with *your* frigging face in the road. Anybody think you was it. Get out my way, you ponce and let me see the main man!" Then, in a strange and silent transition, she produced a needle and thread from her pocket.

For once, Claudia didn't respond, and sank against the seat while the preacher read.

As a rule, nobody actually listened to this 'holy man.' Nobody stopped to look at him either. His words merely filled the air, saturating the space between boarding and leaving. Passengers knew he'd come out with surprises, shocks. A little tickle to make you want to spit, hit. Or cry. If drunk enough, fall and beg him to take you into the everlasting arms of whatever. He never did because he didn't have those kinds of arms.

Promises, promises . . .

Now passengers were inured to the calling and didn't bother to hope.

But this time Claudia was sure she could see him: shiny blue eyes and a pink mouth; convinced he was talking to her, itemising her sins, committing her name to the list, promising. Every person the woman had known called out as if in a register, even the ones she'd tried to forget – there they were again, those who were gone, all the old names, ones that had faded, presumed their colours absorbed into the beige of pasts.

The tram stopped at various places, yet all were blurred. Preacher reading and talking, Petrol asleep, Serene sewing her trousers, passengers boarding.

The Coast came into view, the barques and clippers.

Serene said nothing to her mother as she left the vehicle. Petrol too had disappeared, gone to climb on the wrecked smack and lie in the sun, next to his brother's rifle.

Claudia Shell, her children lost, lighter in body, heavier in spirit, clad in simple dress, a reduced woman thinking of her life in a way she had not done before – making her ponderous journey past the yellow stretch of sand, towards the masts of the tall ships with their commemoration flags.

Alone. Unaided, unsupported.

The preacher, a dark witness from the rim of the tram.

2010

Pomegranate

The summer was so hot the land caught fire and everyone forgot the floods in the face of this new devil.

England had not known such unrelenting fuel, an attrition that made babies scream for days and nights and the old lie down and die.

There was no escape from the torment of summer, and people flocked to the coast, dunking until the sea itself was under threat of being lapped all up, the earth breaking off like a crumbling biscuit, to float away into the stratosphere.

How easy it is for a feast to forget its empty tables, and those who craved these cool baptisms, dismissed from memory the months of deluge and catastrophe.

The heat was here and the rain was not.

Roads began to melt, factories laid off their workers because of the haze of sleep that fell with polluting rays. Tram operators and train drivers refused to carry out their duties in the frenzy.

Sweltering days retained in brickwork and tarmac, in public building and private home, the hell was released into sleepless nights that seemed like years. People were mad for respite, for water and couldn't shake their bodies from the fire.

Yet the heat-wave only lasted the few weeks between August and September.

In deep country, far from ferocious Town and its choking perspiring streets, Bug and Foddly slept outside beneath the trees. With only a thin sheet beneath them, they lay like babes in the wood amongst the leaves and twigs, by the rustle of birds, under the moon slipping in and out of shape.

Since their reunion they had rarely been apart and he claimed her in the broad of the night earth with the same terror as within the tenure of their interior bed. As if even the edges of the world awaited her falling.

Sedge Beat – scion and politician, was elected local Leader of New Britain the day the fire went out.

Celebrations were inundated, marquees and bunting, flags and fireworks drenched in a monsoon. And some mused wryly on the omen.

Sedge, however, so uproarious with success, grinned, dazzled and beamed until his teeth became an omen if not an epidemic all themselves.

It was left to the other side to point out that his victory was an easy one and autonomy was up for grabs, so to speak.

The press came and images of wife, Tezzie, so utterly delectable, daughter, Saprah, sublime beyond belief, were affixed upon the collective retina as slogans are sprayed on the side of a tram. No matter which way he turned, from whatever angle the lens captured him – in repose, in vivid conflict, concentrated upon the plight of unhoused or unworked – Sedge was appealing and desirably righteous. And the people knew they had chosen well.

Over the months and years promises were kept, units built, jobs created, sea defences reinforced, community flourished and Democracy was a word used, felt and lived. For a while.

Then there was Bull Somerset. What was he? A bluebottle that needed swatting. Yet irritating buzzings can be elusive and no matter how hard the new Law Leader came down on thin air, Bull Somerset kept on buzzing.

"What about education? What about schools?" he asked, in the endless meetings at Sedge's villa.

"Oh *those*. Why train the resistant? Force youngsters through seven years of hell, when they can receive instruction for what they're good at? Fit for purpose. Vocation. No one should be made to feel unequal, unworthy. Everyone has a right to a place in society. And education actually creates inequality."

"What about little Saprah?" it was asked. "Is *she* going to be saved, or will the child be forced to endure a private education, be exposed to the rigours of reading and writing and, God forbid, like her daddy, play the piano?"

This was not funny. "If there is predilection, a curious mind, our children will flow towards the source – as it is said: *When the pupil is ready.*"

"The school has disappeared."

Sedge smiled graciously.

Bull Somerset was never crushed and his Policy Makers implemented, within the bounds of conscience, the ideas of New Britain.

The country as a whole was in the midst of a scruples shift. Local governments were at war with each other, boundaries set and this lack of co-operation forced County Councils to become brutally self-sufficient.

The Disunited States of Britain.

And as storm and flood continued, the country became more divided and there was nothing anyone could do.

Sedge Beat felt confidently set apart from other administrations. He had an asset: Media Enterprise Journalist Association, known as MEJA, directed by the urbane journalist, Gul. But in these post-triumphal days, Sedge had to admit to himself, for there was no one else around he could trust, that working with MEJA was a bit of a tightrope in itself. After all, there is only one person more powerful than the most powerful man, and that's his advisor. And Gul, though certainly no ordinary advisor, was so intimately acquainted with Sedge's foibles, it sometimes seemed that the sartorial young man was anticipating his every vain move. Laughing at him.

No image of Sedge could be made public until vetted by Gul, no footage released without first being approved by him. Fastidiously cutting and editing, the journalist combed and preened his client's public face as if he was a poodle in a parlour. Sedge didn't really like that. Not at all. Imagine if their opinions *diverged?* What could he do then? The relationship was grafted onto him. Gul was the man who gave Sedge to the people and he could be the one to take him back. And the Law Leader, despite his presentiments, could do nothing about that either.

Gul also had this nasty habit of smoking and not really caring where he did it. Cigarettes were about to get 'Class A' status. Ironically, it was the journalist who was promoting the bloody idea.

Bug had pursued his career as collector with predatory fervour. There were auctions and house clearances. Many homes, abandoned due to flooding, had been given over to salvage and he took unseemly advantage of that.

But even if Foddly was embarrassed by his savage greed, she had learned and benefited from it, developing her own collection, of sorts.

He taught her about furniture, wood, ceramics, took her to exhibitions and galleries, reviving those early conversations and painful lessons from when he had first tried grooming her. He still did – dressing her up in costumes of velvet capes, bodices, bonnets and dresses that weighed a ton. Days or even weeks of themes, Elizabethan, Victorian, Plantagenet, adhered to with maniacal exactitude.

The man had taken to wearing costumes himself and he'd insist she sit for him while he painted, in character, an image of his lover through the ages he claimed to have known her.

Foddly accepted his ways like a mother accepts the excesses of a child's imagination, without judgment.

Eventually he abandoned normal attire altogether, dressing in whatever era took his fancy – town or country, sixteenth-century buccaneer, twentieth-century soldier or Mogul prince.

"He's Bug," she had told Glastonbury. "And apart from us, who else will understand him?"

Foddly must have friends, even Bug accepted that. Nonetheless, he itemised her every move, storing up the pattern of her visits away: her mother, Sedge, the villa and New Britain meetings, even her outings to Glastonbury, until he had absorbed her leavings and returnings as if they were his own. So when they were finally together, he felt she was his to possess.

That is not to say all this was without consent. Devouring can be as much about the object's need to be devoured as it is of unbridled craving, and Foddly found a vicarious contentment in Bug's appetite – a foil to her own, perhaps.

Theirs was not a totally insular existence. Bug could when he wished, be gregarious, generous with himself, charming even. Throw lavish parties, Bacchanalian feasts, He would hold dances, themed events, celebrations of madness where guests delighted in the company of Bug and his Lady Fodellah, nymph, ethereal hostess.

These days, other women were beginning to notice Bug. Wondering as they looked again, why they had not realised the funny little man was so appealing. Succulent women beguiled by his maverick ways, the lupine sneer and chill indifference, intrigued to the point of indiscretion by the man's obsession with the passionless Foddly.

They would suffer for that, one day, for daring to encroach upon hallowed ground.

But he didn't fascinate all who came across him.

Bull Somerset could not understand how Foddly could stay with such a despicable man. It was his greed he found so distasteful. The endless foraging, preying on the recently vulnerable from flood or bereavement. Thieving it was tantamount to. If Bug Itin wanted, propriety did not stand in his way. "A psychopath," he'd confided to his new friend, Glastonbury. "A ruddy lunatic let loose with our Fod."

Glastonbury would nod. "That's what we'd love to think, but of all of us, he's the one who will do the least harm. Anyway, what's a little lunacy between lovers? The whole thing's insane."

Bull had to agree, suspecting it came from the heart, either from dealings with women or from the old boy being barmy himself.

It was a small gathering of friends in the barn the following Halloween – Foddly's time of year.

Glastonbury neglected to introduce his consort that evening, and the woman, eccentric, in Prussian blue mandarin suit with cerise sash, sat adorning the graceful lines of a French couch, twisting a large amethyst ring on a finger, scrutinising.

Foddly, enveloped in lavender taffeta dress, her hair up, a russet coil captured in a tortoiseshell comb, was busying herself at the table. Settling a bowl of fruit on the table-rug, she smiled at Glastonbury, deftly averting her eyes from the bemused gaze of his companion. She'd met the woman somewhere before. Now where was it? This must be the 'we' Glastonbury referred to, and resented her.

Bug was very quiet, reclining determinedly on an uncomfortable Arts and Crafts settle, peeling apples with a small Indian dagger.

The supper was spread Tudor-style, and Foddly flitted self-consciously from kitchen to table with plates of meat, flat fruit-pies and rough-seeded bread, an occasional exasperated glance at Bug.

He rose from his contrived position and brought candelabra from a buffet. Placing it in the centre of the table, he struck a match and lit the candles. Moving away, he brushed against Foddly and breathed on her neck, blowing up a curl of hair at the nape. "You wait, Fod," she thought he said.

The guest caught Glastonbury's eyes and arched her pencilled eyebrows significantly.

The old man grinned and turned away.

The four gathered round the table and ate in silence for a while, Foddly nervously guzzling wine.

At last Glastonbury raised his glass. "May I and on behalf of my fellow traveller, wish the Lady of the Manor, Many Happy Returns, and praise her for such splendid fare."

"You may," responded Bug waving his drink. "But don't take too long. The Lord of the Manor is planning to praise her himself."

Foddly flashed. "He thinks I can't speak for myself," she declared to the room. Then realised she was the only normal person present. Everyone else was mad. And laughed.

"Pray, what amuses you?" Bug enquired turning to her crimson face.

"Don't speak in that silly way! Can't you be *ordinary,* for once?" And wrung a napkin in her lap.

He unprised her fingers and peered up. "What's wrong, birthday girl?"

"I don't know, I just feel stupid." She sought Glastonbury's eyes but they were lost in the flickering light. Casting round for signs of normality, found none. Even the table was covered in a rug, and that great chesterfield stifled in cushions, everywhere, overpowered with things that didn't really fit together. Disparate pieces disconnected from time. A glance at Bug. He was staring again, like he always did when he was off-guard. She could bewilder him. That was something, at least – a mystification all her own.

"I think I'm ill; can't think straight." Slowly, as if weighed down with scales, she raised her eyelids and found Glastonbury's friend smiling.

"In what *way* ill, my dear?" the woman asked. "I was a nurse, used to fevers, or maybe, we are. . ?" She met Bug's blackest stare, then back to Foddly. "Well, a fecund young girl. I only wondered!"

"No, I feel different. Not faint. Unreal."

"Maybe we ought to leave," suggested Glastonbury

"No, don't go. Please."

"Your light's flecky, my dear."

"Sonjia!" A voice, she thought was Glastonbury's, shot across the table. Foddly decided it was time to confront this woman. "Are you the Abbess?" she asked.

"Have been called that of late. You may call me whatever you wish, but my name is Sonjia. With a j *and* an 'i,'" she offered perfunctorily.

Bug leaned back and stroked his moustache, suspicion curling on his mouth.

In the meantime, Foddly had rallied and was pouring herself a glass of the blackberry wine Glastonbury had brought, then another, and stared at Sonjia, or the Abbess, or whoever she was.

The face wobbling about was pert – not young, but neither old, possessing a raw curiosity, a constant renewal. Could even be a kindred spirit. Hair was furrowed with white and drawn back from features that, at Foddly's age, must have been fine, provocatively androgynous, gamin. Eyes, greenish-blue, speckled like an egg, the mouth still generous, would have spread a sensuous promise across a flawless skin. The woman though peculiar was still unblemished in her embroidered suit. Creased and fallen the face may be, yet there still remained suspended other than by gravity, an essence of self. Spirit.

"You must've been really beautiful once," struggled Foddly clumsily, filled to brimming.

Sonjia glanced at Glastonbury and sighed. "And to think *you* turned down the *once.*"

"What did you mean, my . . . my light's *flecky*?" demanded the girl, noting the glance and not liking it.

"Light? Did I mention . . ? You are a lovely girl yourself, with that abundance of hair. Ah, it was that, I probably meant. A little halo."

"No it wasn't," persisted Foddly, swaying on her seat. "Bug's always talking about lights and centres and floating. He thinks I don't understand, but I do. I can't see it but I can feel it. I can now." She began to cry, little sobs breaking from her throat, her body expelling some vile antibody that had taken hold.

"Sweetheart, come and lie down with me." Bug deftly removed the falling glass. "Come over here."

"Too much of the home-brew." a voice accused. "Your fault."

Then Glastonbury was looming over her – didn't know how, it happened so quick – a snowstorm, blizzard. She had dropped from a freezing ledge and he was scooping her up, his hand on her forehead, scent of lilac, spring, birds, blossom, a child calling. Now summer with ferocious heat. Autumn came, trees on fire, orange skies and winter once more, a bitter biting chill that tore into her flesh, an assault of cold that would not let go. "Which is harder to survive?" she probed the hand. "Winter or summer?" But in answer another season came that had no contour or shape, no clue to its direction, an endless search for scent. If it fled winter or escaped summer, she didn't know.

Foddly was lost, until the sea came. Well that must be it. The sea would, by its very nature, demand its own phase.

"Do you know Coolton Ascent, my dear?" Sonjia spoke from across the room.

Then Foddly remembered. "You know I do. It was there . . . I met you, ages ago."

"Of course. Just making sure. Memory can distort things."

"Memory is memory," responded Foddly with dazzling lucidity. "However you've recorded it, it stays like that. I saw you and you saw me. It's just we're older."

"Wonderful, isn't it?"

"Memory? Depends."

"Coolton Ascent. You went inside, didn't you? With . . . I hope he didn't blemish *that* memory, the experience, because it is a beautiful house. So lucky to have it. You really must come and see us. We've done a lot of work to our little *sanctuary*."

"But you're not really an Abbess, are you? They're in charge of a load of nuns. You don't seem as if you are devout."

"Would *you* like to be a nun?"

Unexpectedly alarmed, Foddly reached for Bug, but he was too far away. "No, I would not! You can see I'd never be chaste."

"Oh, we are born damaged goods, apparently," continued the woman, her voice as soft as new bread. "But you are not *sullied* by union, and if our impish Bug has being playing games, I'm sure it is with the *purest* of motives. The flesh can be a conductor of the spirit as well, you know. Desire is what drives us cowards to frontiers we would not otherwise cross." The old woman turned to a stretch of shadow draped beside her. "*Lust*," she informed it, "can make us very bold to travel. And Foddly, though not the most courageous, is travelling!"

"I don't think you're very nice," the girl said primly. "But I understand this is a dream."

"What you need, Fodellah, is guidance, instruction, and I am prepared to spend time until you are ready to join us. Bug is a clever boy, but even you've already acquired a level."

"Pleased to hear it," replied the young woman, gaining confidence over her impudent dream.

Sonjia came nearer until she stood so close, Foddly could smell her heart beating. "After all, my dear," she sang. "I haven't spoken a word out loud, yet you've heard everything. Excellent!"

Foddly was lying on the bed. The sheets were smooth, untouched, Bug sitting on the edge, order laid out behind him. No evidence of guests. She had a jumbled recollection of behaving stupidly, someone asking a personal question and him being annoyed. "Has that dreadful woman gone, Bug?"

"Nobody here. Just you and me."

"I must have slept, Oh, no! Glastonbury was here and . . . I drank – loads. Was I rude?"

"Unsightly, tipsy-woe, drunk as a strumpet."

"*She* thought I was pregnant, that Sonjia. In a swoon, Bug."

"But you're not."

"No, and I don't think I ever will be . . . I don't really like children anyway."

Rolling to her, he tipped her gently. She felt him rummaging at her buttons, undoing her dress, a cool hand sliding from her back across to her breasts. "But I still want to fill you up, Fod. Turn round."

She eased over and faced him, uncertain ceiling, the dress gaping around her shoulders.

Still nimble at her back, he lowered the top, bent forward and curled his tongue between her breasts. Unpeeling in the dark: velvet trousers, silk shirts, dresses brooches unpinned, jewellery unfastened or gelled by the suction of sweat.

He was licking the bow of her arm now, then his breath in her ear. She felt his body arc and tighten, like an animal about to pounce.

"I'm floating, Bug."

"Hang on to me, I'll bring you down to earth." He rolled his weight, squashing his nipples against hers, easing her legs apart.

"I don't know what to think anymore, Bug."

"Well, don't think at all." His fingers were plucking at her stomach again, the colours unthreading along a seam of black. Discordant colour

"Am I cold, Bug? Unfeeling? I think I am. I do feel, but underneath. I *am* warm, *underneath*."

"And in here, burning. Still, if I ever need to chill a decent Muscadet, I'll choose your cleavage."

Foddly nudged his chin. He looked like a satyr with that beard. "No! This is different. Maybe I am different. There's a fight going on, me and you."

"We'll stop it." Bug drew back and slipped from her.

She could see his eyes in the gloom. His face sunk again, lips glistening. His longing was a beat, a stampede to her. Even in dreams. Maybe it, he, was too . . . His hand was a vice, although he didn't touch her. Just below the ribcage, underneath, as if some creature had plunged in and was trying to rip her stomach out. A threat, a warning, from her instinct or his?

He was drowsing in a cradle of shadows, his fingers falling across her skin. Looked like they were playing a piano, moving with such dexterity.

"Are you practicing limbering up, Bug?"

"Why do you ask?"

"You've got a piano lesson tomorrow. Are you practising, with your fingers?"

Eyes blue and as wide as they could be for ones so narrow. "Always practising, Fod, never stop," he whispered, covering her again, "I don't, for all the wanting, want anything else but this. I love you, sweetheart. May not be any good to you, but it's all I've got."

Pressed down from his rising and falling, each descent forcing the breath from her until, swept into his rhythm, she couldn't separate her pain from his.

Foddly dreamed of the sea, crashing waves. A boy she hadn't met came to greet her then ran away. A woman running back and forth on the beach, she was distraught, mad with distraction, calling and crying. Then another young woman with raven curls, comforting. Glastonbury was there talking gibberish and Foddly wondered why she had ever loved him.

The boy again, this time running into the waves. Infuriating. He must know how upsetting it will be – that woman will never stop crying now. "Don't be so selfish!" Foddly shouted at him. He went, regardless. And now she must look after the woman. "I have to look after myself. I don't have any feelings to spare, Grandma. You've taken all my feelings."

The sheets were soaked and she was shivering, naked. "No one in my family had emotions," she explained to the night. "We didn't hug or talk. Not even . . . What's wrong with me?" she reached out for Bug.

He had a glass of water in his hand, – looked exhausted.

"Thanks." Taking the glass, she saw his hands were blue. "Have you been painting?" and gulped the water down. Tasted foul. Must be awake.

Bug lifted the empty glass from her, resting it in his palms.

"Your hands are *blue*," she whispered.

Placing the glass on a box next to the bed, he climbed in. Around him, a body shape of colour, a faint azure glow.

She closed her eyes firmly shut.

"It's called the light, Fod. Can't turn *that* off."

"Was I a beautiful, bouncing baby, Freda?"

"Bouncing bomb, more like," pronounced his father.

"Sshh, Sal. You were *distinctive,* Bug. A late baby. Precious."

"Oh? Better late, than dead-on-time, you mean."

"Bug! You can be so cruel and unfeeling." In the tea-stained light of their front room, his mother snapped a hard biscuit in half, then didn't know what to do with it.

Sal rose and shuffled to the stairs, shaking his head. "What *is* he wearing today? Pantaloons? I'm going up, Freddie. I'll see you later, son. Just go easy on your mom. No bollocks."

"What, you or me?" sniped the son.

Sal paused and attempted to gather a semblance of humour in the fog. He could never spar with his boy. "Oh, *that's* the problem. Well, it's probably down to me. *She* had a bad time." He jerked his head in the direction of Freda. Coughing, he gripped onto a cupboard door and attempted a laugh, "Then you! Couldn't lose *you.* You never slept for hollering! Only came back to spite us." And spat into his handkerchief.

Bug was over by his father, hand forced on his back.

"Hell! You got some heat there, son. Up the woodens. Let me go now, boy."

Freda nodded. "Let him go."

"Don't want me to give you some more hell-fire?"

"You sent me there already. I don't want the devil's work. Goodnight." And Sal clattered up the stairs.

Freda fidgeted. "Is Fod ok?"

"Anything new at the Factory?"

"Actually I was hoping you might . . ."

"He's really bad, Freda."

"Has nightmares. He thinks *they're* waiting to trap him, and all the trouble at the Factory is a plot. Other days imagines he was raised by North American Indians and they've poisoned him." She tried a smile. "Swears, curses. Once said you came with their curse in your mouth."

"I'll touch him tonight – from a distance."

"Don't know what it is, Bug. Some other people have come down quite bad – rashes. It's a real shame. Foddly . . . Can she find out?"

"No one can. It's old history. The Factory belonged to Beat's father, but whatever allows the place to continue operating in the way it does, if it's violating directives, the Policy Makers should know. What they'll do of course, is another matter." Bug stood by watching Freda do something soggy with that biscuit and a cup.

Thunder above. "Get that bastard outa here! He's a fuckin' monster. I ain't fightin' somebody else's damn war. You can kill me first. I work for that *bastard,* Chief Know-All. He say 'no good come to fucked tongue.' You fucked tongue . . . Bastard!"

Crushed and falling, hand like a drooping flower, Freda was half laughing, half crying. "He'll stop, soon, Bug. I call it twilight fever," and raised her eyebrows, keeping his understanding within her reach.

"How often?"

"Most nights. Just like he was when I first met him, full of temper and disappointment." Freda unaccountably tipped the cold contents of the cup onto its saucer, then moved over to the sideboard. A photograph of her and Bug nestled amongst the china and clocks, especially brought out for his visit. Lifting the picture, she gave it a little polish with her sleeve then placed it back in the nest. "Pa used to joke about you glowing in the dark. But there was disappointment . . . before . . . if that's really what your trouble is."

"How many?"

"I had three before you, darling boy. Lost them . . . All went, not long after."

Her face, a mangle of difficult flesh and tears. "And we thought *you'd* gone. But you came back. So angry you refused to leave. A rage, like a storm it was – right into the room. I was so glad. Happy. We always let you rage, Bug, because that's how you survived."

His hand on the door. "O.K. Let Sal rave now. He won't ever hurt you. In the meantime I'll try to find out. If Sal and the workers have been exposed to . . ." He caught her look. "Well put it this way, if it's been a year it must have been twenty-five."

Freda, fingers on his face, tiptoe to his cheek. "Longer. He's worked there since the seventies." She lowered her head and set to straightening the tassels on a sash he wore around his waist. "This is unusual, love. You've become softer since . . . I'm sorry you've got the trouble like that, but it's not a nice world to bring a wee babe into, Bug, tell her that."

He left the house, small and cramped yet empty of him, collected a bike and pedalled to the deep of the country.

*

When Bug arrived back at the barn that evening there were chairs stacked on the long table, tubes of paint and brushes strewn across the room and Foddly naked, sweeping broken crockery around the floor, her breasts sad, stomach smeared with red.

She turned when he called, but only after he'd called.

Blood trickling onto her thighs. A punishment, he felt.

"I hate these cycles, these *redcurrant moons.* Can't you stop them?" she accused bitterly.

"I don't think I can, sweetheart."

He began to take down the chairs from the table, his face set. "Before you start mourning the unconceived, try thinking how you'd feel if this place was a mortuary for dead babies." Bending down, he picked up a large piece of china. "Hope the floor knew it was Royal Doulton."

Foddly remained still, broom in hand. "I can see what *you* value," she mumbled, half afraid. "As long as it's got a stamp or name on it. You and your sodding *provenance.* Get some of your own!" and threw a long sable paintbrush at him.

Ignoring her, he flicked back his hair and cast around for further damage.

Foddly, feeling more and more the recalcitrant child, wobbled to the dais and banged about with drawers and books.

At the other end of the room, Bug was in the bathroom, filling the iron tub with water. Undressing, he wrapped a sarong around his waist. Snatching two towels from a rack, he dipped the smaller one in the tub then wringing out the excess water, collected a bowl from under the sink, turned off the taps and padded towards Foddly.

Up at the bed he spread out the large towel and gestured for her to lie down. Sitting cross-legged on the mattress, he wiped her stomach then separating her legs, began to mop her thighs and legs with the wet cloth. Carefully he cleaned every smear and trace of blood, wiping the creases and folds. That done he inspected her, felt her stomach and dried her with the other towel.

Reaching over to a low cupboard he pulled out some cotton wool pads, placed them against the seeping petals and closed her legs. "Lose anything unusual?"

"No, just normal. You're turning *me* into a baby."

He smiled briefly. "No cramps?"

"Not really. I'm sorry . . . about the stuff. Things I said. What do you mean, a mortuary?"

"Nothing."

Foddly rolled over and wrapped the towel around her stomach. "Have you been to see Freda?"

He was already by the kitchen area with bowl and towel, and didn't answer.

"I said I'm sorry, Bug!"

"What's your *friend* doing with that toxic hole, the Factory?" he asked, crossing the room.

"I don't know. We understand there are a few issues about the place, but Sedge inherited the problem, he didn't create it."

"*We*, is it? Well, *my* father, I calculated, has had about forty years of contamination. So we've all *inherited* it."

Foddly swallowed hard. "What's happened? *Please* don't close up on me."

"Freda lost three." He sank onto a half-upholstered chair.

"What? You mean full-term?"

"That's right. *Born.* Alive and then they weren't."

"I knew there was something like that. Freda sort of hinted at it, once. But you can't inherit that, can you? It's not a gene. Bug, I think . . ." She attempted a touch. "It's superstition."

"Superstition, politics – which is the deadlier, I wonder?"

She closed her eyes. "Don't still be angry with me. I became upset, that's all."

He left her, returning to the bathroom.

"I'll go around to Sal and Freda's tomorrow," she called.

Foddly saw a small halo of light from a candle appear in the room, heard water run, him splash and squeak into the tub. Night fastening against the windows. It was getting colder, would need some wood chopped for the stove soon.

When she crept up he was lying in the foam, staring up at the ceiling, mouth tight, face hard.

He slid his gaze to her, like broken ice thawing on a lake. "Don't take it to heart, Fod. It just seems to me there are some very odd things happening all at once. Think I will spend some time with Glastonbury, at Coolton Ascent . . ."

Foddly's stomach flooded. A flood of panic. She'd pushed him away and he was going.

He grinned. "You can come too but I'm glad it made you jump."

Kneeling down she kissed him, lips soft in the drift of steam, lowering her hand into the water.

"Looking for something?"

She giggled. "Found it."

"Libidinous in our grief, are we?"

She watched his face melt, a deliquescence of winter. A blush suffused the tip of his nose, his lips ripened, eyes filled and darkened, the pupils pushing colour to the rim. He let his head fall back, a vein rising in the side of his long neck, mouth widening, gaze unfocused. It was a strange, disconnected view of his transformation. The variety of expression from pain to rapture, across a man who a while ago had been almost like a distant father, and for her, unbearable.

His eyes had narrowed to slits, her hand in the water, making him change, in control. He lunged forward and pulled at her neck. "Quick, get in, baby . . . now!"

Wriggling from the bloody pad she squeaked into the tub. Gripping the edges, she slipped into position over him, water rising and lapping over the side, soaking the tiled floor.

Rings of red floated to the surface, empty fish breaking into spirals, amoebic, constant changing patterns of menstrual shed.

The water crashed with each move and she watched his face alter. Immersed in the warm, she felt the rage jockeying for possession, then penetration, a kind of violence, a shock that such a strong thing could come from water.

His face shifting planes, teeth a rim of predatory bone, mouth stretched wide. That was shocking too. The slits that were once his eyes, lowered and aimed at her, ugly and frightening. Sobbing now he jerked and shook, clasping her breasts, thrashing like a fish himself; a little man with his wicked powers yet powerless in this passion for her, every thrust and pull, water cascaded, him defeated by lust.

Then she couldn't see. He'd wrenched her face on his, forcing his tongue to the roof of her mouth, shouting.

She stopped. Didn't mean to but a thought, a clear vision diving, darted into sight. "Coolton Ascent. I'm sure I'm supposed to go there too. You said so, ages ago, now that Abbess woman, Sonjia . . . Or maybe it was a dream."

His heat was still in her. Looking down she was surprised to see him taking *interruptus* so calmly. His face had subsided, mouth a serpentine flow beneath the rough of the moustache, hands relaxed in the water. He wasn't ugly after all, she acknowledged in alarm. He'd slipped from that without her noticing, the gentle line of jaw, sharp nose, delicate nostrils sliced to a fine angle, carved cheekbones, even the slanted eyes had lost their edge, an unexpected compliment of perfect shapes she wished she hadn't seen.

There hadn't been any colours from his fingers this time, she remembered. Their language drowned?

Then a bolt of blue shot across her thighs and yellow followed.

"So that's what you think . . . You just don't know the beast," he whispered, and pulled the breath from her lungs.

She swam with him for a while in the rainbow sea. Other fish, other changing faces she couldn't help seeing, also swam by.

1997

Tomato

"Your grandma went before she was supposed to."

"What does *that* mean? You shouldn't keep saying it, if you don't know what it *means*."

"People have a time to go. She went early."

"You don't know anything, Bug! You're a nasty person who frightens everybody. You'll never have any friends."

"I'll always have you, Foddly Shaw. You'll never get away from me."

"But that's not the same, making someone . . . *forcing* them to be your friend. And I've heard things about you too, Bug Itin."

"And I'll tell you who said them because . . . I can see."

"What? What can you see?"

"Nothing."

"Thought so, Bug. You don't know anything!"

"What's a tomato, then? Fruit or vegetable?"

"Vegetable! You have it with meat or eggs . . . stupid."

"Wrong, Fod!"

"Oh."

"It's starting to snow again. I'm going down that hill before it settles."

"Can I push you, Bug?"

"Yes, but really hard this time. Don't hold back. You always hold back."

Part IV

Metal

1997

Silver

"Don't your parents mind you being out so late, Bug?"

"It doesn't matter."

"Oh, but it does. I wouldn't dream of allowing *my* son . . ."

"Yes?"

"Well, you're not that old."

"Was it a boy, Odella?"

"Are we going to have one of our little *plays*? Or has someone being telling you things? James, perhaps? I think I'm going to sit by that bush, if you don't mind. Bring your drink."

"Glastonbury wouldn't say anything. It's the stuff around you, Odella. It's got a hole in it."

The woman sitting on a bench by the lilac, tidied away a wisp of grey hair, and raising her face to the evening sky, drew out a cigarette from a velvet bag and put it her lips.

"What are you doing, smoking?"

"Oh, I did . . . I do occasionally, but I won't if it bothers you." She returned the cigarette to the bag, a smile trembling. "There. Now, how did you learn about these *holes* and *stuff*?"

"You can't *learn*. I don't want it all that much." A little flicker to his mouth. "Except I can tell things about people." The boy sipped at his drink. "You shouldn't have forgotten like that."

"And what have I forgotten, Bug?"

"You would have got used to it. Now you're old, it's even harder."

"I don't know how you've gathered this information, Bug, it's not very-helpful."

"Just say it. The words. No one's listening. It's ours."

"Alright – although I don't know why I should – I had a son. He . . . went. I wanted not to remember him. Now I can."

"What made you remember?"

"Looks, smell, sounds . . . something. I don't know. A wave crashed over me, I think – washed the forgetting away. Did you say a hole, Bug? Can you really *see*?"

She was still a lovely woman, her face drenched in night. Then just her eyes. Pleading. The tiniest flicker of hope. "What else? He was very young . . . Can you see . . . *him*?"

"Doesn't work like that. It's a gap. An emptiness. Got nothing in it."

She dabbed her face with a triangle of perfumed linen, a little pink monogram at the corner. "I had a dream once. Someone was asking me where he would go if I . . . forgot. I didn't understand. He'd gone already. Where else is there?"

"Maybe they get held up, Odella, if they're forgotten. Nobody comes to claim them so they stay somewhere – unless they get stolen. If they're not guarded, they might just get taken."

"What an imagination! Stolen? Sounds ghastly, like looting in wartime. You wouldn't know, of course . . . about the war."

"But I know plenty about loot, and you can't really blame people for taking something that doesn't belong to anyone anymore."

"Doesn't belong? Do they still. . ?"

"You must never look away, Odella. If you let them out of your sight, even for a minute, they might let go and you've lost them forever."

She lowered her eyelids, swaying slightly. Behind her the moon like a silver sixpence falling from the sky. "We won't speak anymore . . . like this. Our *plays*."

"O.K."

Opening her eyes she stood suddenly, straightening up as if returning once more to her own thoughts. "Bug, I'd like to give you a little present – I think you deserve it." And made her way to the house.

"You don't have to bribe me. I'm not going to say anything."

"Of course not. I decided it was yours the first time we met. Come into the flat."

The boy followed her, head bowed.

When they entered her lounge, she took him to a small mahogany bureau, opened a drawer and slid out a picture smothered in tissue.

Handing it to him, she looked away. "Don't open it now. Wait. You're good at waiting, aren't you?"

Receiving the gift, eyes still cast downwards, the boy stood with the picture as if it were an offering at a harvest festival, his voice lost in sighs beneath his throat.

At the door. "I'll look after her," he said. "In my way."

***

"Where did you get to, son?"

"Nowhere. Out."

"I know *out.* Have you been bothering that Shaw girl?"

"No, her grandma, Sal."

"Why do you call me Sal? That's for your ma and other people to say. I'm your father. Call me Pa. And what've you got there?"

"Something."

"*Something*! Don't accept gifts from them. Folks can turn against you, say things. They can forget they gave you stuff. Give it back."

"Why? What have you had to give back?"

"Plenty. Or rather it was taken. You won't know. For all your staring, you can't see inside every soul, boy."

"Soul?"

"Yeah, even *I* know about them. And guess what? It's your own you'll damn well overlook. Can't see for looking sometimes, Bug."

2013

Radium

The Factory was five kilometres east of the Town. An oppressive Victorian brick building, it was set in an acre of land. The airstrip behind was no longer used, and cars and trucks were piled in rusting heaps, the husks of computers wedged against it like grubby snowdrops at the foot of a hill.

Its politics were Victorian too. The Beats owned the building. The workers were paid by Beat, who also took the rent for their accommodation. The family had provided work for generations: Factory, stores and of course, the land.

The area was poor. The only other living to be made locally was in oysters. Now all that was left for the young, even those awash with academic credits, was away in the city, or the military.

Full employment had become a rare thing in the provinces. Employers, petulant and cunning, were demanding more and offering less. Workers' representatives had withered, and here, New Britain was not about to nourish the soil.

If anything, the politics would contaminate it further. There was perfidy to conceal.

Whatever had gone on in the place for almost half a century was now leaking out, percolating and seeping into the skin and lives, infecting the soul, a disease of neglect. Not just the Factory – the Beat's had been very keen to experiment with crops.

Sedge Beat presided over his legacy with chilling complacency. Yet more disturbing still was that he remained a very popular man. Everyone believed he was 'for the people'.

And there was Gul, constantly attentive, listening, guiding – invoking calming images and mellifluous words, or, snap, snap, flicking and beguiling. Amazing as a magician producing a card from behind his ear – or yours.

How did that get there?

As easy as an actor. Believe him while you can and if one lacks faith, then entertainment will suffice.

Yet despite MEJA, 2013 became a challenging year for New Britain. The Policy Makers had acquired information about the Factory. It was not good.

Long-term workers like Sal, were suffering, young women giving birth to babies who were damaged, deformed. Investigations were being held into unexplained illnesses. Soil was tested, inspections carried out. The Formal Enquires.

But nothing was done. Progress stalled, its back wheels stuck in the toxic mud. How could a man like Sedge Beat, it was asked, so in touch with the people be so remote from such fundamental issues as these? It couldn't be true. So it wasn't. Some other element was at work. Cattle, poultry, the land had turned bad all by itself. The rain, perhaps. So, as workers fell ill, the land ravaged its poisonous skin an untouchable history, Sedge was suspended above it all, untainted.

Elsewhere there were plenty who planned beyond the politics, those who were populating their own new and wholesome kingdom.

At Coolton Ascent, Sonjia saw to it that the old vicarage was restored to its former glory, enlisting local hands to build and renovate.

Bug and Foddly took up the offer to join the strange community, tentatively at first, an occasional retreat becoming more regular. Bug had always seen the potential in the House, if nothing else as a repository for his years of accruing, and claimed their room as soon as he saw it: second floor front with wide bays.

Its panelled walls were cleaned and polished, carpets laid, choice pieces moved in, others moved out – baroque consul table consigned to the hallway, Victorian chesterfield exiled to the drawing room, ormolu-mounted commode could stay – until the room was crammed with his own eclectic array of objects: Fine paintings and tapestries were hung, torchères flanked the marble fireplace its hearth aglow with dried flowers and coloured grasses. Jardinières, embraced in gentle alcoves, sat beneath displays of decorative glass and ceramic. Finally, a low bed in the centre of the room smothered with textiles and the room became a little realm all its own.

And as storms lashed the coast, homes abandoned, histories swallowed, Coolton Ascent thrived and grew. A sanctuary, an archive for the forsaken where gentle people in search of respite, attended meetings and discussed the ways one can move beyond the flesh while revelling in its excesses.

Bull Somerset was drawn. Even the solemn Angel Brown, scrupulous of politic, found herself fascinated and visited occasionally – to see Foddly, she said.

And Glastonbury? He wandered between the little cottage in deep country and the House on the top of a hill. Speaking less, an age of worry gathering in the parchment skin. He and Foddly would visit the spinney at the foot of the grassy slope beyond the gardens, but they had always done that, ever since she was a child, and the fairies still eluded them.

For a while the days were long and filled with sun. People returned to childhood had dreams and dwelled in dreaming – found they could free themselves from the baneful world.

Bug slept with Foddly night after night, moon after moon, kept to her scent, the boundary of flesh never more than a line, sure as graphite on paper. Sometimes like a child on her stomach, other times adrift, lost in unformed fears.

When he first stayed at Coolton Ascent there were dreams, their violent narrative forcing him to endure pointless journeys, punished by violent heat or vicious cold. He saw his father consumed with pain, himself on fire and Foddly running, saw faces swooping down to peck at his thoughts before they were dead. Faces of children who weren't yet born or who were waiting to be reclaimed. One, a boy, watching from a corridor of waves, called – ceaseless calling. Bug knew the child from somewhere. "What's your name?" he called back beneath the rush of sea.

Sometimes the dreams leaked into Foddly. She would hear the same boy as he raced across the waves but she didn't want to know anything about him, and asked him to leave.

The boy, whoever he was, seemed to swim between the two lovers, one accepting the other denying. Finding no concord, went somewhere else and waited there.

The dreams stopped.

So Bug had no warning. Anyway, the worst knowledge can be screened out.

As Sal's health worsened, Bug had been making daily visits to his parents' house. He arrived one morning, the air tight around their home. Cycling to the back garden he parked his bike by the window and opened the door. Could smell it: thick with silence – a stinking weight of ends.

In the front room, Freda sat quiet as a kitten, a cup and saucer on the table next to her. The curtains were drawn. Someone else sitting in the corner. Still.

"There's tea in the pot, love. It may be a bit cold . . . Dear me, you look as white as a sheet."

Bug stuck by the door. "What's happened, Freda? Something's happened to Sal . . ."

"I didn't like to bother the Services. He's so peaceful. I haven't seen him so at rest for a long time. He's a tormented man – I don't know why."

"Was."

His mother looked up. Surprise on the cusp of indignation. "Was?"

"You have to tell me, Freda. You have to say the words."

"I don't know what you mean."

"Sal has gone, Ma. Your husband, my father, Pa, is dead. Look!"

"I know, love. You think I don't know? I've lived with my husband for forty three years. I can tell the difference."

Bug stumbled over, his legs trembling, sickness rising.

Sal, cold and dull. A vessel without a light.

Crumbling to a sofa, Bug lowered his head to his knees, his hand stretched out to Freda.

She stroked his hair. "You called me Ma. You never do that. I'm going to miss him. We both are."

Over a hundred mourners attended Sal's funeral, coming from near and far. There were neighbours, workers from the Factory, relatives from Scotland and America. And friends. He must have had a secret life.

Freda didn't realise so many people loved him and she felt loved too. Vindicated.

Sedge attended with Gul. Eyes cast down, blackened windows on a limousine concealing fevered business within. Binding a wreath of words. A little compensation. An offering. Widow may stay on at the tied house. New Britain cared for the people.

Sal had a glorious wake and one could be forgiven for thinking it was a generous thing he had done, dying. His demise an opportunity for touching and crying, seeing the words, for leaning on the shoulders of strangers and friends alike.

Thank you, Sal, for being born and then dying, even though it wasn't right the way it happened.

"Hello, Saprah. And how are you?"

"Why are you here, Angel? Daddy's away."

"They didn't tell me at the door. I never seem to catch him. Can I ask you to give Sedge a message? Or better still, I'll speak to your mother."

"No. You can't."

"What's the matter?"

The girl had begun to cry, a little heart-shaped face crinkled and creased, red with temper or pain – Angel couldn't be sure, but something had happened – she could be of use at last. Crossing her legs she stretched forward on the sofa, saving with unlikely grace, a small pot of petals. "Saprah, you're not on your own down here, are you?"

The girl shook her head, showering tears over her dress.

"Well who *is* here? Foddly?"

Saprah Beat gazed up, eyes melting in brown, unlit, unseeing. "I can't tell you."

"Oh, dear. Well, if something has happened it's important I know, so I can help. How old are you now?"

"Nine and a half," the girl sobbed.

"Well, even big girls of nine and a half need looking after. You can tell me what's wrong."

"Mommy will get really *mad*."

"You said she's not in and daddy's away . . ." Angel had a vision of burglars, political assassins, inveigling their way into this now fortified villa, and she wanted to snatch the child from its immaculate rooms, speed across the manicured lawns to the . . . Where could you take a girl like Saprah in this Town?

A silken voice, deep in pile, trod beyond on some distant carpet.

The girl looked up. "Mommy's upstairs. Don't say anything. She has to spend a lot of time in her room when her friend comes. She mustn't be disturbed. He needs to rest."

Angel couldn't decide whether to be horrified or enthralled. Was Sedge being cuckolded? She may be of more use than she dared hope. "How often does mommy's friend visit?"

"Depends which one. This is a new person. I haven't seen him before."

Surely the child had been listening to nonsense. This was more like the nasty little scenarios the Town people liked to indulge in. Not that she judged them of course. But what to do now? The girl was clearly distressed.

"Saprah." Tezzie, in diaphanous floatings descended the stairs beyond, withdrawing to some perfumed niche when she saw Angel. "I'm afraid you've missed Sedge. You should have been told," the voice explained coolly from the shadows "You can always make an appointment. You know where to find Gul. Come on, Saprah, get your music ready. You've a lesson this afternoon.

The girl raised her hand to Angel and disappeared.

Angel waved and left the room, careful not to turn around. The front door opened and she walked into the wide portico.

"I'm sorry," the voice said without a trace of regret. "Appointments must be made now. Things have moved on . . . and I do suffer very badly . . . with the light."

The door imperceptibly at first, then inch by inch, deferential in its closing, but shutting nonetheless, and the young woman made her way from the classical façade.

Angel caught the bus. It didn't have a destination on the front. Not promising.

That was a strange turn-up at the villa. Foddly should know of this. Maybe not, she'd tell Bull Somerset and that would fire up all sorts of trouble. He was against Sedge, would make a meal of it. Best not say anything. Maybe everyone knew anyway, Angel tended to be the last one to find out about these things. Hadn't even met this boyfriend of Foddly's; not that he sounded particularly caring. Should keep out of the way of people like that. Of course, one couldn't be entirely certain little Saprah wasn't making it up. She did tend to go in for drama – like the mother in that respect.

The bus rattled its unscheduled way into the store depot and drew up with all the others. Passengers began to shout at the driver, who had jumped from his cab and was striding across to join a group of his colleagues.

"What you doing? We've got to get home."

"Action. We're coming out for the Factory."

"We all feel sorry," a voice protested, "but can't we do it in a less disruptive fashion?"

"No point doin' it, then."

"They'll get the military in."

"Yeah, that's the trouble. Everything's military. They'll work the Factory and do it for fuck-all."

"Sshh, mate."

"Why? I ain't keeping my mouth shut because some bastards don't wanna know the truth."

Angel had heard it all before. The truth was the place was falling apart.

Negotiating the broken curb, she proceeded through an arcade and emerging into the thin sun. She noticed some younger people congregating around the small fountain. Their bulks looked familiar, aggressive. Trouble. Felt them watching her as she passed. Heard them giggling. Someone threw a stone.

Really must talk to Sedge. All this anger was clearly to do with a sense of alienation – people have a need to connect, and decided not to take it personally.

Rounding the corner, the young woman walked swiftly to the end of the road and approached a tall derelict building, its windows behind a grid of iron. The place was smothered in graffiti, offers of guns, tobacco. Yats. "*Yats*?" An intaglio image of a giant phallus penetrating a wobbly ellipse. "Prostitutes?" murmured Angel. "New one."

She banged on the door, a quick glance behind her to make sure none of the fountain mob had followed, and tying back her light hair, straightened her jacket and waited. No response, thumped again. Peeking through the letterbox she could only see wire and blackness.

Maybe MEJA had moved – what were they doing here, anyway? Couldn't they afford better quarters?

A man in a tight-cut dark suit was strolling gracefully towards her. "Angel Brown! Thought it was you," he said, reaching her. "You really must do something about those trousers – be calling them *slacks* soon."

"There is more to life than appearance, Gul," Angel reminded him thinly, while making her own appraisal. She always had the journalist down as her age, mid-twenties, but these days she couldn't say. Puzzling. The brilliant azure eyes glinting mischievously, the curl of the pink mouth rocking on chiselled features, which over the years had stayed curiously unaltered. He was a remarkably good-looking man. Flirtatious, very . . . intimate. Well he could be. No risk between the likes of her and him – that was obvious. A relief really, with that face. Never get over one like that. Fortunate it was safe from her yearning. Mind you, it would help her offset this other longing.

"Your mentor is unavailable and you've come to book his attentions, madam. Right or right?" crushed the man.

Angel was mystified. "I haven't come to book anyone's attentions."

"Oh, not to *brook* it? At last!"

"Shuttup, Gul."

"Certainly, madam, but first I'll *open* up. Follow me." The journalist produced a set of keys, which he manoeuvred and turned around at the lock, then pushed.

She followed him up a flight of filthy stairs, plaster falling in the dust. They reached the first floor and Gul bent down to pick up some papers. "Letters! Don't get many of those these days. An ancient Surrey custom, letter-writing," he said airily.

Up another flight of stairs, another battered door. It opened with surprising ease – a fluid ingress.

Even more unexpected was the cleanliness, the pastel smoothness of the room. Pinks and lilacs, a light oak desk sunk into a pale mauve wool carpet, to the side, reels of film, cameras; a large path of flickering white on the wall.

"Like it, my remote viewer?" He ambled over to the desk, a fluent flourish of his hand.

"Sedge has one of those."

"Had. We're working on this Visicom thing. Heard of it? A visual telephone, like a little old Britain *telly,* except when you switch it on, you can see right into someone else's living room. Wonderfully invasive, Angel. You'll like that."

"Had those ages ago. They didn't work out."

"Old technology is always not working out until we borrow it again." He slid onto a steel and leather chair, tipped it back and rocked. "Really have to sort yourself out, Angel. Can't marry the community, you know. Even they won't want you in that. Let me dress you – get something to match those smouldering eyes. Talking of smouldering . . . cigarette?"

"Gul! What are you doing? *Nobody* smokes."

"Clearly not an accurate statement. You'd be done for that in my trade."

"What *trade*?"

"We get on, you and me, Angel. We'll need each other one day." He stopped rocking, and drawing his seat to the desk, slammed both palms on the surface. Leaning back, he let his right hand slide to the edge, dropped it into an open drawer and lifted up a silver cigarette case. Snapping it open, he threw a cigarette in the air, caught it, then popped it between his lips, all without once taking his eyes off the girl.

Remarkable.

"Old stock," he said, lighting it, somehow. "I roll, normally. Got a good supply," he confided, one eye closed, smoke gathering around that astonishing face.

"I don't want to know, Gul. You're . . . What can I say?"

"Mendacious, is what I'd say. Alas! We have a lot of untruths regarding your friend. Your idol . . ."

"What do you mean by that?" Angel stood a less than vigilant prefect before the head boy. She felt uncomfortably sleepy, weighed down with an unaccountable fatigue.

"My client, our Law Leader, is having a few difficulties, Angel. We need people like you to support him."

"But I do."

"What do you support, exactly?"

"Him. Sedge. Democracy. He works tirelessly for the community. There remain many issues around the Town – people who have been misplaced, due to the floods, but that's not his fault. The Factory . . . Well, once again, he's been far more honest than anyone else . . . in his family."

"Honest, did you say?"

"Yes. We've fought tooth and nail for those workers and for the unemployed. We're desperately trying to set up a . . . erm, community-type organisation to support them."

"*We*? Should you be telling me this?"

Angel was confused. What was she telling him? Nothing really. "You must know." She couldn't see his face through all that smoke. "Foddly knows. A sort of Community Service in which *we* serve . . . the community. Inclusion. We're arranging it."

"Where?"

"Well with Sedge, obviously but . . . erm at Coolton Ascent, actually. It's really very interesting, innovative," she said quickly.

"I bet it is. Who else goes there and creates alternative policies?"

"Oh no! It's not *alternative*. I mean, Foddly would never . . ! No, she'd never do anything against New Britain. We are for the people, most definitely." She searched round for a seat herself or a drink of cool water.

"Behind you and behind you."

Angel found a stool and a jug of water on a shelf. She couldn't be bothered with the water after all, and wiped clammy hands on her trousers.

Gul continued: "MEJA is tactically important, crucial to keeping Sedge looking good as well as good-looking, you know."

"You make him sound so . . . facile, Gul. He's a man with genuine politics."

"Good. I'm glad you are a real ally. Sorry, it's something I had to do."

It all made sense. Yes, that's what the journalist had been doing – testing her. There was serious opposition to Sedge Beat.

She'd been useful.

"How's your mother?"

"No better, Gul, but thanks for asking."

"You do a lot. Always thinking of others."

The girl was touched, a blush to her round face.

"Yes, you and me, in the future, Angel. You'd be amazed how far a friendship goes."

She rose to leave, happier. "I'll see myself out.

"Are you sure?" asked the man, closing his eyes behind a veil of smoke.

Angel had completely forgotten about what had happened at the Villa.

* * *

Bull Somerset had arranged to meet Foddly at Coolton Ascent. She was late. Not wanting to venture in on his own, he waited by the small church – a rather depressing building, he decided – small and squat. Could do with a little love and attention. So much going on in the House, people neglected the church. Very sad. Stained glass windows needed attention. Weren't the originals, of course, late Victorian possibly – bit gloomy, but at least they made an effort in those days. Shame about the hypocrisy.

Yes, that Sonjia may be mad, but she was right, the Church became the biggest blasphemer. Possible always was.

He wandered up a side path, rattled the vestry door and turned the iron ring.

"Bull!" a voice roared behind him.

He jumped. "Good God!"

"Is he, Bull?"

"You frightened the life out of me . . . Mother."

Sonjia smiled, satisfied. The message was getting across. "Can I help you?"

"Not really. I'm waiting for Foddly and thought I'd have a look around here."

"I don't advise it. You'll have a long wait, Foddly's been called to the Town. There's been a fracas or something. Surprised you're here."

Bull was aware of the woman peering up at him, and concentrated on the hem of her velvet coat billowing across tiny feet. He tried hard to avoid close contact with her; Glastonbury was his man. "What fracas?"

"A march or an action of some kind, Bull. Now why don't you come into the House?"

"I'd better go. Bug not here either, I presume."

"Gone to market. Angel is . . . "

"I'm on my way."

Sonjia watched him stride down the path. "Like a bat out of hell," she chuckled. And twisting the iron ring of the vestry door entered the church.

An old truck approached Bull as he made his way down the hill. It braked suddenly, and the window wound down.

He paused reluctantly. "Thought you were at an auction, Bug."

"And who told you that?"

The Policy Maker jerked his head in the direction of the House.

"I'm here as messenger," Bug informed him coldly. "Just dropped Foddly off. There's trouble at the estate and they've shut down communications. Your lot better get down there, I don't want her mixed up in that anymore."

The other man was puzzled. "When did this happen?"

"About half-an-hour ago. Law are on their way."

"Who else here knows?"

Bug leaned out the window. "Nobody, yet." He grinned. "Oh, you mean *Mother*? You've a lot to learn there. They would have burned her at one time – in fact they probably did – a witch and she's come back to crack your feet of clay." He shrank back into the shade of the cab. "Must press on. Just on my way to cheat a little old lady out of her entire collection of seventeenth-century miniatures . . . Cheerio." And still grinning wound up his window and reversed down the hill

Bull looked on in disgust. Nothing touched that man, not even his father's death. All the trouble at the Factory, not a care, except when it came to . . . He pulled at his beard, realising he was becoming vicious himself.

But yes, he thought, ambling down the hill, Bug had a weakness: couldn't stand Foddly's contact with New Britain, even though Sedge Beat wasn't to be seen these days. The ruddy dilettante had meetings everywhere but here, now that slippery Gul was running the show – and it was all show.

Bull once had some very positive plans for his adopted community, but this 'inclusion' nonsense was not one of them – no one had anything to be included in. Policy Makers weren't given any real power – there was promise once, but now they were just there to clean up the mess. Trouble on a daily basis meant the Services were stretched and the military seemed to be mostly the half-trained. Nobody had a clue. Farms had been flooded, livestock killed, the soil infected, plus there was something about the land around the Factory being contaminated. No one was doing anything about that either.

So why the hell was he here, getting involved with *witches* who ran bizarre communities?

Because no one else was listening and Bull needed to be heard, his private grumblings lodged somewhere safe. A man of secret prayers – all fallen, thus far, on stony ground.

Now Glastonbury and this strange Abbess creature were speaking the language of heart and mind, soulful talk.

And there was Foddly. Could see why Glastonbury loved her. Flighty creature though, in her cautious way. Yes, a strong connection to Beat, that was pretty clear – you could almost like the scoundrel, compared to that vindictive little man. Maybe she should have married the politician. Things would have been very different. And that young Saprah, what would she turn out like?

"Things don't always work out," he told himself ruefully. "And you, Bug Itin, sorcerer yourself, have a few lessons to learn. That'll wipe the smirk of your face."

He stopped, shaken by such a thought. Sorcerer? Now why did he say that?

Pyrite

In 2014 Carlos Dean was still only a boy. He had been the area's millennium baby – first of the first – and was celebrated for it. There were other things to celebrate about Carlos: he was like an angel. Golden ringlets cascading over porcelain skin, eyes wide and clear as glass rinsed in sky, features still soft, a mouth unrefined and prone to pouting in girlish sulks.

His was the Botticelli face, the female voice serenading within the male to the male. And it had not gone unnoticed. But as yet Carlos Dean remained the child, and even Gul acceded to some scruple.

Carlos' father worked at the Factory. When Sal died, Carlos and his family were among those who attended the wake.

Like Bug, the boy had the changeling about him, which is possibly why he was so drawn to him.

Alien from his parents, he had a precocious awareness of art and history, and folks wondered, as they probably did of Bug, which line he came from.

Carlos also worked a little at the Factory because that's what you did. It was money and he had plans. He was a bit of a magpie himself. So on learning of Bug's collection, formed an instant attachment to the man, becoming a regular visitor to the barn in deep country – taking to whatever Bug did, agreeing with whatever he said. Idolising him.

But there was something wrong with this golden boy. He was growing tall yet his complexion was unnaturally pale, his skin almost translucent. He barely ate and when he did, fell ill.

It was suggested that he come to Coolton Ascent to take the healing.

So Carlos met Glastonbury and Sonjia and became part of the House where everyone adored him and wanted to make him better.

Gul made a note of that too. He could wait, knew there was no competition for what he wanted. Nonetheless he didn't like distraction, preferred a strong knit, and Bug Itin was muddying the waters, so to speak. The journalist too had plans and they went further than a few banquets or plundering some abandoned museum. He dealt in another kind of possession, a commitment to lifetimes.

So aside from having to calm the waters for Sedge Beat, Gul also had to keep an eye on the progress of his golden boy and make sure he wasn't straying too near the *alternative* camp.

To that end he was forced to impose his presence upon Carlos, offer a promise or two, compete with Bug Itin. Gul resented competition it demeaned him somehow. Why should he sink to the gutter for that revolting little man?

"Carlos, move that spool and come and sit next to me. Been doing anything interesting recently?"

"Yeah, we've been up at Coolton Ascent, I've got my own room now. We're decorating it in the *Rococo* style."

"*We?*"

"You know. . . Bug, Glastonbury, all of them. Why don't you come up there?"

"And what makes you think I haven't been already, Carlos?"

"If you had, you'd never want to leave."

"I don't want you to be influenced by the wrong sort. You'd be amazed how certain people can use someone as delicate as my *Golden Prince*. Wouldn't know it had happened and then it would be too late."

"That's good, coming from you, Mr *Director*! Know what I think? You're jealous." Carlos shook his curls and laughed, revealing a line of perfect teeth behind that succulent mouth.

And Gul counted the years.

In the spring that year, Carlos' father died, the same blisters and fever.

Carlos eschewed the old vicarage for a time, choosing the barn for refuge from whatever feelings he had, sitting there, curled up on the sofa, watching Bug paint or mend.

"Look after your mother," Bug suggested. "You'll find strength that way."

"Did you look after yours?" questioned the boy, without judgement.

"Can't say I did. But don't use me as an example – of anything."

If Carlos sought solace from undesirable quarters, then Gul would make his own inimitable contribution, by allowing the boy to see how revenge is a divine and beautiful game in which he could star.

"I'm going to kill Sedge Beat, you know," Carlos announced to Bug one evening. "He killed my father, and yours. He's destroying everybody."

Bug didn't reply, but Foddly, who had been cutting material on the long table, left and went out for a walk.

So maybe it was Carlos Dean who invoked the whole thing – a young boy fragile in grief, a poignant reminder of how insidious neglect can be. He may be affected too. Look at him: A diaphanous, tragic beauty. How long. . ?

It is a strange and irksome fact that, after navigating treacherous waters, negotiating hostile terrain, surviving outrage and injury, it can be the cracks in the pavement that trip us up. The little things in life that lead to downfall.

Carelessness. Almost an insult, really.

***

The summer of 2014 was marred by a few low-level riots but the storms had ceased. Even so, at headquarters and lofty villa, Sedge was feeling besieged. Gul had not been feeding the usual good tidings to the press. He had a band of stalwart hacks under him at MEJA, and they were not scribbling the best stories these days. Gul had also enlisted some extremely able cameramen, and was developing in that area himself – shooting various scenes around the Town and doing some quite baffling tricks with the footage. 'Creating' he called it. 'Working the paranormal, witchcraft,' was the politician's opinion, and it was doing him no service. Apart from that, there were the domestic issues.

Tezzie had left Saprah to her own devices again, and the girl was becoming clingy, morose. Didn't seem to have any friends her own age. That devoted dumpling, Angel Brown, visited, took her out. Not a bad sort, terrifying loyalty, clung like a limpet to the cause – useful, except she always wore that soppy look.

Sedge had to make a couple of speeches in the city and was preparing a few notes, when the study door was pushed open.

"Daddy, are you busy?"

"Always busy, lovely girl, you know that."

Saprah, dressed in pyjamas, tiptoed over. Her hair was up in a coil on the top of her head, and secured by little bows. She looked startlingly pretty and he found himself affected by her. So vulnerable, his own daughter, he rarely saw her. An instinct to pluck her from the ground and set her firmly on his lap and kiss her. Maybe she was too old for that. Yes, how old *are* you? he wondered.

She folded her hands over his knee and gazed up drinking in his attention, adoring him.

Ten, he calculated. Must be ten by now. "What have you been doing today, princess?"

"Nothing really. I had some lessons, talked to some people."

"Which people, darling?" He turned back to his notes, disentangling himself from her clutch.

"They came to see Mommy."

"Oh, not me then? Your mother's becoming more famous than Daddy. What did they want?"

"About a new house. I think Mommy's got a new house and they want to fix it up."

Sedge swung round so hard the girl tumbled to the floor. "What did you say?" He picked her up, shaking her. "People?

Come on, Saprah! Were they men? What did they look like? Was Gul there?"

"Daddy, don't! You're hurting my arm. Don't be mad. I don't know. They could be the men who take pictures."

Sedge paled, his eyes wild. "Did they . . . take pictures? Of whom? What?" He loosened his grip, the child staring in hopeless bewilderment. "Don't grow up to be like your mother," he heard himself say, and felt instantly disgusted. He scooped her up. "Sorry, my special girl. Daddy's very busy and tired. Not everybody loves him like you do. You are my very special lovely girl and I'm sorry."

Crying and kissing him, Saprah buried her face in his neck, her hands gripping so hard they marked the skin, "I'm going to be like you when I grow up. You care for everybody – that's why you're so busy and sad."

He carried her over to a small sofa and held her in the way she craved. A rare thing. "Daddy can be wrong, sometimes, Saprah. He can make mistakes."

"No you can't. Not you."

"Time for your bed now."

Another rare thing – up the stairs, hand in hand, taking her to the little place filled with squashy softness – feathers and ribbons, toys and trinkets. She slipped under the silky sheets and then giggled. "Guess what?"

"Yes?"

"I haven't brushed my teeth." She jumped up and ran over to the sink, rubbed her finger over her teeth, swilled her mouth with water and then spat into the sink. "That's cheating, but I'll do it twice tomorrow."

He could feel her eyes pinned to his face. She wriggled under the bedclothes and held out her hands. How could he overlook such a treasure? He touched her nails with his lips. "Goodnight, my special princess." Sensed her watching his outline at the door, not wanting him to go, imagined her sitting up, leaning out of the bed to see the top his head as he disappeared down the stairs.

When he let himself look back, she was on the landing stretching over the banister. That heart-shape face beating for him.

"I don't mind Mommy going, because then I'll have you all to myself. Unless Foddly comes," she said.

Steel

A dance and feast had been planned for Foddly's twenty-sixth.

Autumn hung from the sky, branches overhanging like brimming baskets, the hills aflame around Coolton Ascent.

In deep country, light shivered through the trees, the earth a carpet of bronze and scarlet. Trudging through the leaves, Bug looked back at his bolthole. Good job he'd got the barn – thanks Glastonbury. And Foddly was safe, at the moment, but he realised it would be the last celebration in that place; didn't know how – just did. Nothing had happened to him personally, although the events of late were indicating dissolution. Like autumn itself, life would be consumed in the burst of fire before the winter storm. That final dance before the death.

For her present, Bug had designed Foddly an elaborate beaded dress. He'd chosen an elf-green satin for the fabric, and commissioned a costumier to make it up.

Rill was an old aborigine and even with eyes washed out with age, he still created extraordinary clothes – almost by divination as if he already knew the pattern off-by-heart. 'Everything made by heart or hand belongs to somebody,' he had said. 'So be careful what thoughts you form, Bug, they will find their home.'

Even if he liked to dismiss Rill as one of Glastonbury's old retainers, Bug was intrigued by his many skills – the sacred secrets of potions he claimed could alter as quick as truth: Blujah, made from pure alcohol and root sap, the powerful Skenk, drawn from the venom of a viper. The alchemist was always promising to share his wicked secrets with Bug: 'If you would care to sample them," he taunted, "you would understand a lot more, because you don't know very much.'

Bug would warn that he'd show a few tricks of his own, if the old boy didn't watch out.

It was going to be an interesting mix. Bug had invited his contacts in the city: artists, musicians, local dealers. And Sedge Beat. Especially him. There would be aficionados of New Britain and others, like Carlos. The politician would be without MEJA support on this occasion – the dapper journalist, Bug noted with some interest, avoided social scrutiny.

Of course, Sedge may be advised not to attend, yet he felt sure the Law Leader wouldn't be able to resist the promise of certain company. And his wife would be fascinated – Tezzie hadn't been to the lair, as she called the barn.

So Foddly wore the dress Bug had designed. And all thoughts found their home.

That night he couldn't bear to lift his eyes from her. The way she glided, her shape beneath the satin, hair bouncing on her shoulders, he could taste her scent even from across the room.

Everywhere she moved, his longing followed – a pain, a physical assault, like terror knocks words cold into the heart. Anyone trying to draw them out is an abomination, another violation preventing surrender to the worst fears; submission to those destructive thoughts Bug hadn't known he possessed. She would surely go. He had made her his sacrifice without understanding why.

Other eyes were concentrated on Foddly. In between the balloons and streamers, tall flowers, games and the dazzling throng of costumes another hunger pursued her. Sedge, paler than usual, still distracted by difficulties, found he was hypnotised by this welcome respite. Reaching behind him to a trail of drink and food, he snatched up a bottle and filled his glass. Then resting back against the table, settled on the view.

She was wearing the most gorgeous ensemble. That poisonous dwarf no doubt *acquired* it. Mind you, she was looking different, and yes, stunning these days – except on that bloody bike! Maybe he'd been wrong about her being glacial; certainly a development from the querulous little pixie sitting on his lawn those years before. Decent family of course – bit odd. Never saw the mother these days, moved away perhaps. Wise decision. Ah, Fod, what will happen to *you* when the scales fall? Can't believe in this crap much more. And you'd be better off without that rake. Look at him: eyes on sticks. He smirked inwardly. What else, eh? Must keep your interest somehow, old girl . . . So you do have an appetite. The man crossed his legs and shifting his weight against the edge of the table, grabbed his glass, another view burgeoning, and felt suddenly offended by the notion of that creature touching her. He'd known Foddly as long as him. The priapic little shit must have subjugated her will by his demands. Why would anyone like her fall for that? What could Bug Itin offer that he, Sedge Beat, could not? It was a matter of bad timing that was all – she'd been a kid, and how long can you wait for a child to grow up?

He was surprised he felt so indignant, but things domestic and political were not panning out the way he liked. Maybe this was the final blow to his crumbling bastion, an unfulfilled past.

Glancing round, he saw his daughter, Saprah, and waved.

She blew him a kiss

Wasn't in the mood for this – standing here, in a vast shack in the middle of the woods surrounded by bohemians, even if they did make a change from the sycophants in the city. And that crone who gave them the run-around with the Gothick horror on the hill – extraordinary garb she had on – like a nodding mandarin, and snorted into his glass, wine splattering over his shirt. "Shit! I'm pissed."

Still shaking with laughter, he made an appraisal of his own attire: linen and silk trousers drawn in at the calf, loose cotton shirt, excellent shoes. Then realised he must be the only sane person in the fucking place. And his wife, of course – Tezzie as always, securely bound by the corporal.

She was standing by a large oak screen, running a covetous hand across its intricate carving.

Sedge drifted over. "That thing belongs behind a bloody altar – give a dirty little choir boy nightmares – look at it, all judgement and hellfire. Which church did he lift that from? Nothing's sacred to that fucking poser."

"You would not *believe* what that little man has. I don't know how he does it. His father was only at the Factory."

"Don't mention that place, old girl. But I do wonder if that's why we're here – as an offering," he said, pointing to the dais.

Tezzie looked up at a mound of cushions and rugs flanked by silver torchères. "Oh, yes," her mouth quivering on a smile. "And crucifixes . . . delightfully profane. You'll have to speak to your *admirers* at some point, Sedge. Anyway, *I'm* going to mingle. Don't interfere, I need a wide berth."

"Take the fucking harbour."

"I think that altar would do nicely. See you." She tottered across the room, fairly riotous herself, low-backed dress, hair loose, high shoes.

Sedge surveyed her with distaste. "He'd have you standing up if the fancy took him. But you're not his type, as rampant as it might be." He became aware of a dance tune being squeezed out of an accordion. No, a bandoneon. "Bloody *Piazzolla.* Another liberty taker." And went to find Foddly."

"*T* for tango . . . We really must sometime, Bug." Tezzie rocked gently on her heels cradling a virulent cocktail. "Remember out last fleeting contact? We had a little *debate* about those prints I have. Didn't believe me!"

From the French couch, Bug acknowledged her with a nod. He was concentrating on something else.

Tezzie, unused to indifference, lowered her velvet-tight body next to him. "Quite a little treasure trove you've built up here. Intriguing place. I've heard about your collection, but didn't realise how *extensive* it was," she issued silkily. "Don't you ever get *worried?*"

"About what? I'll always know where it is - it takes a thief . . ."

"Yes . . . And how did you get that oak panel?"

"The rere-dorse? Seventeenth-century, a fine example. Carving by Grinling Gibbons, of course."

"Of course! So, how can you tell it's by . . . him? Does it have a signature?"

"*P* for Provenance. Or is it Purity? Have to know where it's *been*, Tezzie. Best pieces are ones that don't get put about. And the amount of interest it's created – they *all* want it."

"And what are you asking?" she returned, carefully obtuse.

"Beyond your reach, Tezzie. And you don't have the setting."

"Oh, I don't know," she countered archly. "I mean, *you* . . ."

He brushed his eyes beyond her to a young girl sitting with Carlos. He was dressing her hair with some tinsel.

"Brought your daughter. Looks like you."

The woman turned reluctantly. "Saprah's eleven, and old enough to come to grown-up parties. On the continent they're not so precious, you know."

"And you wouldn't like to leave her at home, the way things are."

"Now, now, Bug. I am only *married* to the politician," and took a gulp of cocktail. Didn't like the sound of this – leakings from somewhere. "Sedge and I have an agreement – nothing to do with the *politics*. Look . . !" Suddenly seized by a confessional urge, she pressed against him, her perfume heavy on the air, the pulse on her skin, fast. Succulent skin. "I do get anxious. He does have enemies in . . . low places. But we have agreed to separate, on purely internal issues. Maybe you need to see me as separate from Sedge."

"Oh, but I do, Tezzie – see you as separate. Always have, especially in matters such as these." Bug, his tongue a teasing snake around his mouth. "Ever since our last *fleeting* . . . "

"Really?" She paused, lowering her long lashes, thoughts feeding on private banquets. "I noticed *you* then. Obviously one is cautious." And raised limpid eyes. He was sweeping her with the strangest gaze, it was filled with . . . What was it? She noticed his hands – with fingers like those he should play better than Sedge, and so much more . . . What couldn't those hands do?

"One always has to be that," he murmured.

"What?" She'd forgotten.

"Cautious. When dealing with . . . Such things must be handled with care."

The way he said that: so quietly intent.

"Always a risk," she admitted.

"You have to take those sometimes. There may never be another opportunity. If we can come to an arrangement mutually suited," he said, joined as dovetail.

"When? Oh, God!" she uttered, so violently it amazed even her.

"Sorry?"

"When would you . . ? Should we meet, Bug? I can come here."

"Oh, I can collect."

"To the villa? Might be. . . Well, I could arrange it."

"Won't take long. Be in and out in no time."

"No, I'd like to make it last, Bug."

"Why?"

"I am . . ." She dropped her own gaze, demurely. "Slow, and I really want to take a long, long time with you."

"I'm afraid once this beast is roused, there is no . . ." The man placed a provocative finger on his moustache, then lowering the finger to his teeth, rubbed it along the wide grin. "They are first impression, I hope. I'm not interested otherwise."

Tezzie raised her eyes sharply. "First *what*?"

"The prints. We are talking about the prints."

He was laughing at her and she wanted to throw her drink at him, but couldn't, her head was in a muddle and that music driving her mad.

"Not yours to sell? Thought you were an independent woman, Tezzie. Your daughter's looking bored." And rising, he turned in pursuit of poison.

Rill sat in a yew comb-back chair, glass in hand, oblivious to the thicket of limbs bumping against him He stretched out his legs and squeezed his face up until it was as wrinkled as a sultana. "Bug, my friend, I can see you have troubles," he laughed without opening his eyes.

"Don't let it depress you. What have you got in that glass?"

"Drop of the Skenk, boy – viper's poison. You want some? It'll make you see."

"I can see plenty."

"Yes, but make it all seem *prettier*." The old man waved a crooked hand in the direction of the ceiling. "And patterns, Bug, you have to see the shapes. Once you see them, you can take anything."

Bug removed the glass from the man and sniffed. "Grass and coconut." From the corner of his eye, he saw a tall figure closing in on a green beaded dress, and handed back the glass. "I need something stronger," he said and collecting an abandoned bottle, made for the door.

Outside, a sickle moon a scythe in the sky, autumn everywhere – in her eyes. He threw back the drink, didn't know what it was, couldn't taste it, then felt himself slipping.

A hand on his arm. Rill next to him. "Your lady is looking the best yet. Get rid of them worries, can't do nothing for you."

The two walked out awhile then sat on a felled beech. They watched the lights dancing around the narrow windows of the barn, listened to the shouting and singing, saw Glastonbury emerge, Abbess on his arm, then Bull with consort, beckoning them in. A dance maybe.

Next, Foddly in the halo of the door, then someone behind. Whispers. Dark and tall, a flash of white.

"Happy birthday."

"Thanks, Sedge," and they disappeared.

Music. Tango. *Libertango.*

A small girl, stood alone on the small stone yard, pretty and lost, sparkling stars in her hair.

She looked around, frantic, went to the far end of the barn and peeped around the corner, then back. "Daddy!" she called. "It's time for the big dance. You said I'd be your partner. Daddy!"

Nobody answered. She stamped her foot and then, seeing the two figures in the distance, ran over. "Will *you* dance with me?" She asked Bug, her face plucked with hurt. "You're small, that's alright, my arms won't be too far up. I think we'll match OK."

Bug rose and bowed. "Excuse me, sir," he said to Rill. Then, turning to the girl, "Madam, the pleasure is all mine."

Saprah searched up at his face in the opaque light. Satisfied, she took his hand, as proud as a fairy princess and quite as beautiful.

*

"You're hurting. Why can't you just hold me?" Foddly tried not to snap but he was irritating her.

Bug lay on her stomach, lapping the heat and trailed it to her neck, nipping and tweaking as he went.

"It was a good party wasn't it? Thanks." Foddly talked over his squeals. "Where did you get to? Ouch. Stop!" She sat up and pushed him away.

The room was in chaos – chairs upside down, the table buried under plates and dishes, glasses and bottles. "We'll come tomorrow," the guests had promised. "We'll have the place sorted in no time."

That was then, this was now and chaos was not what Foddly was good at. It felt untidy, everything, and Bug was behaving like man possessed, again. He pressed her down, telling her to shut her eyes and it would all go away.

She wished he'd go away, then everything would be in order. Just clean straight lines and order.

"*Who* go away?" asked Bug. "I'm here to stay," and buried himself between her legs. He felt her shudder, and pushed deeper. Then away. Sliding his body up before there could be any lapse in the dance he was inside, the whole of him scorching his breath.

She wriggled. Was she trying to escape? "Why, don't you want me?" he asked. "Found someone better?"

If she answered he didn't hear, pulled into the sensation, the tip of pain digging deeper for relief. Riding the monster, faster they went, but no nearer. Where was he going? What was he trying to reach? Her. But he was driving her away. "You, baby, please. Foddly, don't go!" Felt her crying as he pounded, his feet on fire, raging, but such a tender rage. "Why don't you drown *me*? Take *me* away!"

At the end of this line the fish was caught, then wriggled free. He yelled with fury as it sped from him then screamed as it bit once more. The sea, I'll have the ocean then. A short time of close petals, folding rain, inside smaller worlds, pinheads. Then swimming in her. Fragments of him passing through in impossible porthole thin as air.

Looking down, her hair across the sheet, face closed, in submission, acceptance. No weaving, no entangling or singing tongues. Not now. He occupied her, and she was allowing it – afraid. He stopped, bent down and kissed her mouth, a gentle rhythm, then pulled away to watch the lines ripple, undulating against that circle of shiny curls. Saw his stem fly in and out of grass. Gusting through summer. Rhythm upon dance, feet too quick! "Too quick. Slow, baby, slow." On breasts like hills, falling down, rolling. Neck, shoulders all one landscape to fall from.

Hold me forever in this. Don't fall off. Was he saying this, or thinking it? Too late, gasping for air, for life in expulsion, he pummelled and thrashed, until he was wrecked. Beached on her.

Foddly was so still she must have gone away.

"Sorry, sweetheart," he said. "It's as if I haven't seen you for years, but you've only been away for a party."

"I was *at* the party," she reminded coldly. "It was *my* birthday."

"Ah, yes. I remember. We danced together." He rolled over and stared at the rafters, heart pounding. "Once."

"Yes. We did."

Rage. "When you had time," he whispered, dangerously low.

"You danced with his daughter. That was nice, Bug. Kind." She sidled away.

"Yes, and we know *why*, don't we, Fod? *Daddy* was nowhere to be seen." His heart thumping. Rage. Hold it in. Bury it. White, yellow, blue. Change it.

"It was my party," she repeated weakly, raising her hand and tucking a curl behind her ear. The hand settled back down on her stomach. A cool distant hand in repose. Disconnected from hope, hopelessly out of touch.

"Saprah could have danced with Carlos," she pointed out. "You could have danced with Tezzie."

He clenched his jaw, the colour rising again. "You know they've split, which is why you were with *him, all* the time."

She looked over her shoulder, frightened. He was on his elbow, preying over her. A wolf, a beast. What was he going to do? "I don't think so. Not *all* the time, Bug – and even if I was, which I wasn't – I can't see the harm in it." She found a voice. "You're not going to frighten me into not . . ."

"Into not . . . What?"

"Anything. You upset people, playing those games. You always did. And me, you bullied me. I don't know, something's happened." Curling up, she slotted her hands between her knees. "Oh, it's nothing, Bug. I just feel empty, like tonight." Turning suddenly, she stared, eyes accusing. "What happened, just then? You didn't even ask. I don't actually belong to you. I'm not your possession or some booty from one of your trawls. Anyway," she enquired simply. "If you're so threatened by Sedge, why did you invite him?"

He lay down, the bed falling off the edge of the world.

Didn't know where to put the feeling. He couldn't find any place safe enough.

Mercury

At the beginning of 2015 the worst storm for over sixty years swallowed part of the North Kent coastline. It ravaged low-lying areas, including the tiny hamlets around the Town. The Services couldn't meet demands and people were left to fend largely for themselves, abandoned.

The Church would have offered guidance but the Church was gone. Not that it was ever there in the first place. Another certainty lie. The land sold, quick and cheap, new homes built over more histories. Tombstones crushed. Ah, well . . .

*

Two men walked together on the naked beach, the wind still high. Waves rose and fell with such violence they seemed to be heaving with an ancient loathing for the earth and its abusers, fulminating at the world.

Winter was gripped by its neck and hurled into the record of its own savagery. Here, take a look at that. You started it!

The men stopped suddenly, and faced each other.

"You never met Tor?"

"You've never introduced me, Rill. An enterprising brute from what you say. Dutch isn't he? Sailor, or something."

"*New* Dutch, a *captain*, Bug. Trades on the seas. With his men, he plans to colonise all this," Rill said, a crooked finger sweeping across the chaotic horizon. "Then you'll be an old colonial, just like me," he added with a wink.

"No chance. Nobody makes me anything I don't intend to be. Sounds like he's more of a pirate."

"Builds magic vessels, Bug. Never seen nothing like them, in this century or the last."

"Amazing he can find the timber . . ."

"Amazing everything. You must meet him, boy."

Bug, his face grey, fastened the collar of his cloak and drew the velvet tight. "I'll make do with you and Glastonbury, thanks."

"You got thinner blood than me, son. You should wear something to keep the wind out, not invite it in. Let's sit over there," suggested the old man, pointing to a boarded-up café.

The two made their way to the battered veranda, miraculously still standing after the gale.

Folding down on the floor, Bug looked around, his thin eyes a ribbon of blue in the sandy wind. "Sure I've been here before . . . but don't remember this."

Rill squatted beside him. "Everything's forgot in this weather. Anyway, we got some shelter, at least." He grinned, his wide face as creased as withered apples. "And no tame old Blujah, I brought the best, today."

"Jolly good. I've brought the water."

Rill fumbled in his coat and brought out a small bottle.

"Only the Crown Derby – incomplete set. Sorry, sir," Bug said and produced two cups.

"Very English, my friend."

"I'm not. I doubt if there's any more of that in me than in you. Scots and Yank – and don't forget it."

"How far back can you go?"

"Less chatter, old man, get divining," Bug jibed, shoving him gently with his hand

Rill chuckled. "That's your trouble, can't go back as far as us, we go back lifetimes, boy. I have a long, long view. When you have that, you can be anywhere and you won't be lost."

"Except in that nonsense. If I take enough of the Skenk, expect I'll sound as daft as you." Bug handed the man a cup, keeping the other for himself.

Carefully, Rill uncorked the bottle. "You first. I'll guide."

"As you wish." Bug genteelly offered him the cup, the lightest finger and thumb on the fine handle.

The old man held the bottle aloft. "The viper lives, believe me!" and poured the green liquid into the porcelain cup.

It oozed thickly at the bottom.

From a phial, Bug dropped water over the poison. It hissed and lit.

"Take it back. Now, boy!"

From a nineteenth-century cup with its couth decoration of crinoline and bonnets, Bug knocked back the Skenk.

From his tongue floated the sweet sickly smell of fresh cut grass, the spilling of early blighted seed spreading to his throat, then coconuts and ice shooting out range with the fire of it. Sensation vanished for a second. On the edge of Rill; how long had he been sitting there on this freezing veranda waiting for him?

Somewhere above the sky, cloudless now, his thoughts were lodged – the sea soldered to an idea he'd had, oh, years ago. Then a pool of liquid silver beyond, far away from that thought, another flew. The beach now riven with ideas.

Feeling his feet lift from the wooden floor he drifted over to the sand; heard the old man follow a hand touching his shoulder. Remarkable how he could reach out for miles, that man. An old sorcerer. Better than Glastonbury? No, because *he* was an angel or a revenant. Would have to be, not to ache for Foddly the way he did. Or maybe the dead did crave. Gul for instance . . . Why did he know that? Maybe they were all dead – observing a life already happened. Hanging on. Like when as a boy he used to wait for Foddly, then later, for her to come to him at the end of a day.

He turned. That took a lifetime. So much happened in that moment – it was that, a moment – yet none of it really made much difference. No, what happened reached farther back than even that.

Rill walking slowly beside him, the light from his head was tremendous, a funnel of glorious sun, a numinous cascade. Wanted to run to him and cry but it would take too long.

"I'm right next to you. Follow me, Bug, my friend."

So he did. To the shore, the froth of tides, singing counterpoint. Wished he could sing, have Foddly in his throat forever, breathe in, breathe out, exhale and draw her back in, right to the belly, hold and then out she comes – a sonorous transformation.

"She's going, Rill. I know it."

"From where to where? It's all the same place. Look."

Bug looked – never a boy, a man, to do as he was bid, wished he hadn't.

A child was running across the waves, right along the surface of the sea. A wave picked him up and threw him to another, playing catch. The boy writhed, and freed himself, ran some more then stopped. Very close, considering he wasn't there at all, his eyes like someone Bug had never met. So how could he recognise them?

"I know you," the man said. "You've been in my dreams. What's your name?"

The boy didn't answer. Couldn't. Mute. Or the sound was off.

"How long have you been waiting there, in the sea?" Bug called. It was useless. "I can't help you. I'm sorry," he said. "I can't take you back because she's going. I'm so very, very sorry." And he was. Filled with remorse. A callous thief repenting, wanting to return the precious things, the heirlooms, the tender mementoes he'd wrenched from sequence.

But it wasn't his fault this time, so why should he offer recompense?

The sky had shrunk to cloud. Fingers numb. The beach once more and the café, a tardy remnant imbuing the futile with significance. And he felt sick.

Rill hadn't taken the Skenk, he knew that. "Was this all for my benefit?" he asked, pointing to his empty cup.

The old man had bent down and was choosing pebbles from the sand, skimming them across the water. "There is a point we all meet, Bug. The start of something or the finish of it – unless there's no start or no finish and then we can't meet nowhere."

"That boy. He isn't finished?"

"Can't say. Waiting maybe, to begin or end."

"Does Glastonbury play any part in this, Rill?"

"I would say so, but it ain't just him."

Bug, teetering on the brink of fury again his stomach turning. "It's not up to me to carry other people's business, their chattels!"

Rill laughed out loud. "Hear yourself! When *you* been worried about a thing like that?"

"This is different."

"You sure?" The old man shrugged and turned away. "Shame you don't want to know Tor. A listening man, if you can cut through the language."

"No thanks, I have enough trouble with you. Give me that." Bug took the cup from his friend and hurled it with his own, at the oncoming tide. They bounced. Waving, he swept away. "So long, Rill."

"So long."

"It's that Abbess creature, I suppose." Bug's voice carried on the wind. "She's got a lot to answer for. I'm going to have to play a last game with her."

Cadmium

Sedge lay on the couch, sunk in cushions, a cotton robe over his stomach, exhausted. He'd had endless meetings with the Policy Makers, and no one was ever going to be satisfied.

Wife and daughter were away, gone to relatives again – Saprah no doubt holed up at her aunt's while Tezzie went in search of sustenance. She never used to be like this. Or maybe this was her and he'd failed to notice. It was best they carry on as smoothly as possible, for Saprah's sake as well as his.

Tezzie was the least of his worries. Gul had been distinctly cool over the last months. Had taken a fey young creature by the name of Carlos under his wing – if that's what you called Gul's attention. Pretty clear there was some predatory rumblings there. No doubt the journalist would have his appetite under control. He'd wait, right up to the line. Never catch him out.

This Carlos was a strange one. He would appear sometimes, outside the gates of the villa – as if waiting for Sedge then disappear. Sinister hermaphrodite, when female it could devastate, when male would inveigle its way under some authoritative mantel. It clearly hadn't made up its mind – about that, anyway.

Notes had been posted on the Visicom, onerous messages. No visual of the sender but a background picture, like an old painting he'd seen. Horrible, a man having his head cut off by two women – ghastly image. Had he been loose with someone, or had the wily Gul handed out his address to a faction in the Town? Couldn't ever know with him. What the hell was going on?

Another meeting tomorrow and a big interview with MEJA. Statements about the Factory – a poisoned chalice if ever there was one. The road to hell is paved with good . . . "Pop, you did me no favours."

He let his eyes wander across the expanse of wool and silk to the Broadwood piano. "When did I last sit at that?"

His appraisal took in the rugs, the Meissen figures, the fine paintings and prints. Not that he'd chosen them. Had a reasonable eye, but that was never taken into account. Tezzie employed others to purchase taste, purely for impression. No appreciation except in the value. But what value? Paintings, furniture, all manner of fantastic items were slipping under the hammer these days. Someone recently snapped up a Burne-Jones for next to nothing, apparently. So what was the purpose of hoarding if even the best was worthless? This is what it must have been like during the war – people giving treasures away or selling cheap, benefiting only opportunists, scavengers with an eye to longevity. The Church for instance – they'd never ceased amassing wealth, but for whom? Not the people. Maybe the scavengers are right, take it, no intrinsic value to anything. If you're fighting for your life, what's the fucking use of a seventeenth-century rere-dorse?

He stretched out. A patch of light in the corner, a pink line wriggling across it. No, not now. A quick glance at the photograph of Saprah, then shut his eyes. Why was he here when there was so much to be done? All the shit that went on in the Factory, the farmers demanding compensation . . . Nothing he could do. He'd presided over a dream for himself and ended with a nightmare belonging to others.

Mmm. That was quite good.

A blue flash. The patch of light in the corner was alerting. Or crashing.

He left the couch, draping the robe around him, and padded over to the Visicom. '*Messages: 15,*' it read. "Yes, I know. Why are you telling me now?" he mumbled

The little machine flickered again. "Jeesus! This is crap technology, Wasn't any good first time round." He keyed in a number. "Check security," he said slowly.

Imaging the house: front elevation, back, the gates, the road. "Interior," he instructed.

In a long kitchen, a woman in uniform was making a drink, a man, also in uniform, slumped on a stool, talking to her. "Nothing unusual there," remarked Sedge, resisting the urge to turn on the sound. The woman looked up and waved. The man nodded from his seat. Sedge raised his hand and scrolled on. In the garden, the empty pool. Nothing, no shadows or lurking threats. He clicked off the image.

The Visicom screen turned blush pink. A small white light in its centre. Sleeping.

Glanced at his watch – not even nine. Picking up a small metal case, he crossed to the door and was about to leave the room when he was summoned by the Visicom once more. This time the screen was white, fizzing and crackly. A live line.

Over at the machine again, his first thoughts were the Services, Law, another riot, someone in New Britain had been shot. So when he saw the face, was relieved beyond words, then confused.

"Where are you? You never use these things?"

"I've been at my mother's for the week. Thought I'd call to see how things were." Foddly, features distorted and blotchy, her voice fading, in and out.

Sedge hastily dragged the robe over his body and tied the belt. "Just the same. You've probably heard about the incident in the Town, a lynching – like the middle ages, Fod. Not clear which side they were on . . . and the gale. Your end all right?"

"Yes. I can't stay long on here, Sedge." Foddly squinted blindly. "Can't see you very well. What have you got round your shoulders? Looks like a white sheet. Have I pulled you out of the tub? Sorry."

"Not at all. Pleased to hear from you. But why the Mater? Everything OK?"

Foddly's voice muffled. "Yes, of course. I better go. Maybe I'll pop in tomorrow. Should be back." She glanced to the side.

Something's up, Sedge thought. A vague irritation, had enough worries. Then a window – light on another prospect. "Where exactly are you, old girl?"

"In the Town. I'm in Town. See you . . . "

She looked so worried. "You're not going back to that barn now, are you? The roads are still blocked! You'll never get through and it's freezing." A quiver of panic shot through the man, then an adrenaline spurt. More than that, a full red pulse, lower down, blood rushing. "Fod!" he shouted at the image. "Give me the Visi address, I'll send a car. *Foddly, press the address button before you go! Can you hear me?"*

She went.

The man slammed his hands against his face. "Shit! Shiiitt! I've missed it. Jeesus." Then he saw the numbers at the bottom. He interrogated the screen, memorising as he pressed the disc in the slot. An address came up. "What the hell are you doing there?" He picked up a phone. "I need a vehicle, pronto." And gave the location.

*

When Foddly arrived, the politician was dressed and ready – in charcoal-grey collarless silk shirt worn loose over white judo bottoms, black leather Loafers, a twist of colour on a crimson band around his wrist. He'd had a drink and was relaxed, easy, quite prepared to entertain.

It was just gone ten.

She looked tired, vulnerable. Her coat removed, she wore a short tartan jacket with velvet trousers, narrow hips, red boots to the ankle.

"Thanks Sedge. You didn't have to," and undid her jacket.

"Have to wait till morning," he said. "I've got a nice little room for you, what Saprah calls 'the cuddly one.'"

Foddly glanced up. Yes, she could look up to Sedge because he was so much taller than her. She smiled, wanted to cry really. He looked so young and gentle, hair falling over his eyes. Made such a difference not to be at war when you met someone.

He gestured her to the couch. "Got some big stuff tomorrow, Fod. Hope you don't mind, I'll be leaving early. Ask for whatever you want," he said, handing her a large drink.

Thoughtful. He didn't have to be like this. "Oh, I'll be gone myself. "

He sat on a chair opposite and crossed his legs. Leaning back he turned an empty glass on his palm. "What's happened, old girl?"

"Nothing at all. I've just been at my mother's. She's moved, further in. Wants me to go there. Bug won't . . . I think her long term plan is to move overseas."

Sedge placed the glass on a marble table, folded his arms and began to speak very slowly and firmly, like a teacher. "Why do you stay with that . . . man?"

"He needs me. I don't think he'd let . . . I can't just leave."

"You're afraid of him, aren't you?"

Of course not." She laughed quickly. "Not really. Afraid *for* him, maybe."

Sedge turned down his mouth – small and indistinct in otherwise strong, dark features. Always been disappointing, that mouth, she acknowledged.

"Bug Itin, as far as I can see, looks after himself, Fod. It's you, I'm worried about." The man shifted on his seat, edging forward slightly. "You know, when a bully wants control, they isolate their victims, and you, old girl, are well-and-truly alienated. Don't even work in the community anymore." He tilted his head, as if making a slow appraisal of something the young woman had failed to see in herself, or other people had made her blind to. "I remember years ago, when we went to that Gothick horror of a house, I made an off-colour remark and you were, well, huffy, Fod. I'm talking about pride – righteous indignation. Where is that these days? You would never cower then, as you do now."

Perceptive, if rather brutal, thought the girl. Hadn't realised he had that depth, but he must have been taking notice of her. So it wasn't just at the party. All this time, really taking notice.

"He doesn't do . . . Fod, he hasn't threatened . . ?"

"No, Sedge, you've got him wrong in that respect. His is *psychological.* In fact it isn't even that, more sort of . . . I don't know. He's not bad to me, it's just his devotion's a bit restricting."

Sedge lowered his eyes, a glint of something in the brown, a tightness around the jaw. "Devotion? So why are you roaming around the countryside on your own?" He swept back his fringe. "Well, it's not my business, Fod, but we're friends, you and I – go back a long way." He twisted round, lifting a carafe from the table.

Foddly, easing herself, accepted another copious measure of wine.

Sedge moved across to a shelf and brought over a bottle. "Ever tried this?" he said setting it on the table.

"Not sure. What is it?"

"A sort of brandy."

She wrinkled her nose. "Don't like spirits," then laughed, right from her stomach, shaking with giggles until she had to put her glass on the floor.

"What's so funny?" he asked, watching how the blush spread to her throat and that white stone she wore, swinging like a pendulum over her cleavage. He wanted to snatch off that bloody stone and put his hand where it traversed so incessantly.

"*Spirits*, Sedge. That's all anyone from Coolton Ascent is interested in. Oh, it's pathetic – all their ideas . . . I'm really *not* interested in those. Thank you! At least I know now." She moved around on the sofa. "Think I'm drunk. Sorry. Not very funny, am I?"

"You're lovely . . . and very welcome. I'm going up, Fod. Goodnight." Bending, he brushed his mouth against her cheek.

Her hands on his neck, his fingers on hers, down to her wrists, arms, up to her shoulders. A scent of heat. Visceral, no colours. Nothing magical or hidden songs.

But he did carry her.

His room or was it theirs? Uncluttered, a large bed, a chair, curtains open, low windows. A proper house. She stood by the door and watched the sparks fly from his clothes until he was naked. Long and firm, capable. She should never have had doubts, stood on pride. He was what she wanted.

"I can't believe this is happening, Foddly," he whispered, unbuttoning her shirt.

Helping him, her fingers caught up in breath. Hurry. He'd found a zip, and she heard a thought tear, a memory of a green dress stuck at her waist. Pain. "Oh, no! No, I can't."

"I've got a past too, darling. We have to move back to move on sometimes."

Strange how those boots came off so easy. On the bed, just her knickers, cotton wriggled down over bent knees, manoeuvred round ankles, one foot, then the other. She had her hand between her legs.

He took it away. "I've wanted this for so long, Foddly.

Very simple lines and a background that was uninterrupted. A straightforward canvas.

He unfolded her as if she were a bespoke shirt. Slipping into silk. So much wider the air, uncomplicated space, move around. Freedom.

"Slow, else it'll happen too soon." He arched and they rolled until she was on top, his tongue to her breasts. She eased back and straddled him. His fingers a trembly journey from stomach to lips, underneath, inside. Softer, melting like butter under sun.

Hands on her waist, lifting her up and down. The moonstone, hanging from the silver chain cracked against her teeth.

"Take that off," he barked. "Just take it off. Come here." He scrabbled around her neck, and with both hands, wrenched the chain in half. "I'm sorry, my lovely girl, but I don't need reminders." He rose up, swelling between her thighs. Slipping home. "Yes . . . Quick. Oh, my God!" and stopped, eyes wide. "You are so luscious, bloody luscious, Foddly."

She was on the brink – that's what Bug meant – but it had been the wrong one. Now she really must fall or fly. So near to falling.

Sedge had his eyes full. One more move and they'd empty of her. His fingers on the chord. Of course. He played the piano; he'd know what to do.

She started to rock, the end of him tickling, playing right inside. Harder, firmer, rocking and riding. Smooth as a beach then undulating sands, little sandcastles crushed as she rocked. Over mounds, slow, low, one after the other.

He was lapping, sighing like the sea. "Come with me! I can feel you. You are so *fucking* perfect . . ." He groaned, wind through sail.

On the beach, effortless peaks, salt in her lungs, hot sea seeping through the tiny curls and onto her legs.

His hand slid away and onto his stomach. He closed his eyes.

She was perched on top of him. Alone now. May as well be on a cliff-top, her stomach dripping with cold sweat, the moonstone caught in the clothes she'd discarded.

Moons. Many more pale ones. Redcurrant?

A volt of reason shot from her stomach to her throat. Where was she in moons? Looked down. Sedge was asleep. Sated.

Lifting herself, she peeled away.

He murmured something and turned over, a hand waving for a second then dropping.

Liquid plopping on the carpet, she made her way silently to the bathroom and looked. In the mirror, her breasts were full and heavy. Moons – late or early? She didn't count these days. No point.

Her pubic hair was sticky. Needed a shower. Would she wake him, if she showered? She pulled down a towel and mopped her legs and body, rubbing herself until she stung.

Red coils of sunset hair flew around her forehead, amber eyes stared out from a terrified face. "What have I done?"

Returning to the bedroom, she lowered herself lightly on the edge of bed. If he wasn't disturbed maybe he'd sleep the event off and so could she.

"What's wrong, sugar?" His arms around her, warm and simple. Mustn't cry. He kissed her back. "Beautiful girly. Saprah's going to be very jealous of Daddy's new girl. Best not say anything, eh?"

Yes, Saprah, remembered Foddly. Hadn't thought of that. Just hadn't worked this one through at all. "Goodnight," she said.

"Night, darling. Up early. Sorry I'm so tired." And patted her leg.

Foddly closed her eyes and tried to dream, but could only see the moonstone.

After a while she heard Bug call – knew it was him, because of the howling.

Awful howling, like a wolf.

A face flitted past. That wretched boy. "What do you want? Can't you see I'm in trouble? It's no good you looking like that, I'm not interested. Who *do* you look like? It's Saprah. No, Sedge. Go away, I'm trying to sleep."

Her scurry dreams popping up, then a sweet interlude.

She woke with a start.

On the brink. Of what? Nothing. A void beckoning.

Lying next to a man who was himself in trouble. A world endangered. She'd never sleep again, because of the threat; had abandoned camp, broken the laws of magic, the protection of loyalty.

Talisman, smeared over by the punishment of years.

Foddly could never go back.

That relationship with Bug was ended.

Iron

In certain circumstances it is expedient to cut and run. Excise and move on.

If a future is to be eliminated why prolong the agony in its company?

Survival.

"Hello, Bug. Didn't expect you to be in. Called by at the House to pick up a bike." Foddly was on the wrong side of the table. The eight-foot beech bench had been rescued from an old school kitchen. It stretched widthways across the barn, a dividing line between work and leisure.

She was in the labour territory. "Hungry? Got some vegetables, make soup . . . What d'you think?"

It was ridiculous, making lunch at breakfast time.

On the opposite side of the table Bug was silent, didn't move. He was in his big tweed coat, sitting cross-legged on that half-upholstered chair as if about to pounce – a compression of threat – his profile to her, long sharp nose looking even crueller, hair loose, skin white, eyes sunken.

Had his boots on. The bed was still made.

As quietly as she could, didn't want to rouse the beast, Foddly lifted her bag and put it by the door. Removing her coat, she placed it on the back of a chair and tiptoed over to the sink. Gingerly pulling out a drawer, extricated a sharp knife. It was very sharp. Maybe too . . . She chose another, safer one and placed it on the chopping board. Bending down, once more making as little noise as possible, took some carrots from a box then parsnips and potatoes.

How was she to wash them without the sound of running water? She turned on the tap, the clamour crashed through the room. She scrubbed quickly and turned off the tap. Over at the board picked up the knife and chopped. The silence around her industry was equally unbearable, it made her noises more invasive. Shouldn't be here at all.

He would be listening to her thoughts. He must know. Her mouth was dry, began to tremble. Why doesn't he speak? A sly glance over, still not a murmur. Could be dead, so pale.

His voice, when it came wasn't so much speaking as creaking. A loose floorboard under footfall when no one is there. An empty ghostly step, an empty voice. "Where have you been?" it asked.

"I . . . got held up. Stayed on at mom's." Her own voice shook, hand feeling instinctively for the moonstone. Oh!

"I'm not wearing the necklace . . . the chain broke. I've got the stone here Bug, in my pocket." Chop, chop. Must get out of here, he was building up to something. Would he kill her? He was capable of anything. Heart pounding, she peeled and sliced until there was nothing left to cut. "It's a shame we don't have a Visi, sometimes. I could have called you . . . The road's still blocked – it's been a week . . ."

Fell silent herself.

Footfall, wood groaning. His voice, so dusty and old she didn't recognise it or hear what it said.

"Sorry, Bug. I didn't catch . . ."

"Say the words, Foddly. Say it."

That was clear. She dug her nails into her palm so hard they drew blood. What right did he have to do this, making her suffer? "What words? I don't . . . have anything . . . "

"Say it. Where have you been?"

"Mom's, you know . . . I told you!" Probably best leave now. Go to Glastonbury's, if he'd speak to her. Maybe he loved Bug more and would side with him. This thing, its consequences, spreading like a plague affecting, infecting. Eating into everything. "I stayed at mom's."

"Say it."

"You know anyway!" she blurted. "You always know and you're torturing me for the sake of it. " She picked up her coat, couldn't make her fingers work, bits of potato-peel on her thumb.

"Where did you stay last night, Foddly?"

"I . . . I went to the villa. It was late and dark, so . . . I went. I did go."

"Whose villa?"

"You know, Bug. You do know. Don't make me . . ."

"Say it."

"Sedge. It was Sedge's villa . . . Obviously."

"And who broke the chain?"

"I did . . . Sedge. It was an accident."

"What were you doing when he broke it?"

"Now you're torturing *yourself.* I am not going to say . . . that. I'm not going to say it," Foddly cried, burying her face in her coat. "I'm going. Leave me alone, I'm going!"

"You have to say the words, have to face it, my girl."

"What do you think happened? He tore it off because he didn't want reminders. We . . . *made love.*" Her words spurting up like vomit. "He hates you! I hate you. Everybody does. You haven't got any friends!"

This was so childish. Behaving like a child. Blinking through bubbles, she witnessed a flicker, a movement in the snow. Bug was smiling. Then he wasn't.

Couldn't look. His clothes were full of winter, outside cold. And he wasn't going to do anything, too frozen solid in winter to do anything. "You've been up all night," she said dully. "I'm sorry. Were you waiting for me?"

"No. Not anymore, Foddly."

Standing on the wrong side of the table, coat in her hand, she was lost for a moment, cast out in the bitter world. On the brink.

"I don't really hate you, Bug. It's not *you.* It's that . . . I'd like to be myself, ordinary. I can't remember a time when you haven't been in my life, one way or another. But I can't *be* just for you any longer."

Then comprehension, a dawning beyond herself. She'd inflicted a shocking wound by that simple being. Almost careless in the end, the blow, a power of weakness.

At the door. Bag in her hand. Going. "I don't understand you. I never have, Bug."

He was so quiet. No rage. Nothing.

"Sorry," she said.

Bug heard the door open and shut, colours draining from the room. He reached out to a bowl, picked up an apple and bit it. The piece still in his mouth, he took another bite and again until he had found the core and his mouth was crammed with bites of fruit. He picked up another apple and did the same thing – sitting there cross-legged, his mouth so full, it hurt.

It could have been hours he sat motionless, cheeks bulging like a hamster, his jaw aching – pain leaking acidic salvia on his coat. Apple cores around him.

People came, he was sure of that. A tall man with green eyes touched his shoulder. Another man, small and watchful, stood beside him for a while.

Then Freda, frail yet within those limits strong. She sat on a stool next to her rigid son as he dribbled and stared. Taking a folded handkerchief from her bag, she placed it beneath his chin. "Spit it out, darling boy. You always did that . . . an old trick. Come on, let it all out for Freda."

Whole pieces of apple fell, one by one onto the cotton square.

"Good boy." She kissed his forehead. "Your friend, Glastonbury brought me. We knew . . . Can't stop the world going on the way it does." She pulled him close and was surprised he yielded, another falling – stroking his face as he cried in her arms.

Her boy. Her son.

Is this what must happen, before we can meet each other again?

Saprah noticed how Foddly stayed around the house. Never seemed to go away even when her father did.

She wasn't as kind as Angel, didn't seem to care that much, on the inside.

The girl started to fret, became jealous and began to hate Foddly, especially when she caught them dancing together in the lounge. Why were they doing that? That was her mother's job. Or hers. Nobody danced with her father without Saprah knowing first.

But her mother wasn't here that much. When she was, and Saprah tried telling what had happened, she just raised her eyebrows and said: "Surprise! Surprise!" Then smashed something.

Her parents had a violent row in which Tezzie shouted a lot about money and houses and started taking things off the wall.

Sedge told her to get out and that she had a nerve laying down the law, after years of *her* behaviour.

What behaviour? wondered the girl. Her mother must have done something wicked for him to get mad like that. Then she remembered the men who visited ages ago, and her sitting alone when Angel came.

Now Daddy was having visitors and people were saying terrible things about him, and coming to the house a lot. Her mother had nothing to do with those.

Saprah refused to attribute any significance to Foddly's presence and decided the woman was just one of her father's boring friends. She stayed because he was too kind to tell her to go. Have to eventually. He'd tell her to leave because he'd know his daughter was the most important person, and she was upsetting his special girl.

"Daddy, when's Foddly going?"

"Why? Don't you like her, princess?"

"I just wondered. She been here for weeks. I thought she lived in a barn, with that funny man."

"Did you? Now I've got work to do, Saprah."

"Can I read those things?"

"If you really want to, but I don't think you'd find them very interesting."

"It's about what you believe in. I want to know all about what keeps you so busy."

"Actually, Saprah, talking of busy, it's going to be hectic around here, more so than usual, I think it might be a good idea – you get on with Angel, don't you?"

"You want me to go away."

"There's a lot of work being done on the house, and I couldn't think of a kinder person to take care of my princess. Anyway, you like staying in the country – better than overseas, with all that horrid quarantine."

"It's not because of *her,* is it? I'm not going because of Foddly."

"It's because . . . things change, I'm afraid. I'll take you in the secret car. Just Daddy and his grown-up, special girl."

* * *

Bug had been expecting him.

He'd left Foddly's clothes hung up, hadn't touched anything, and in any case he hadn't been able to move for weeks.

Freda had insisted on staying, Carlos visited, whispering of sinister retribution. But they had since left and now he was on his own, expecting him.

Dressing in loose velvet trousers, he wrapped a wide sash around his waist, and choosing a long shirt, tied it pirate-style, a cutlass to hand.

After shaving, he meticulously snipped the goatee beard, and trimmed his moustache. His face was still drawn, tell-tale blisters, looked like a cadaver.

He was trying to picture the mode of transport, when a rap on the door summoned the small man to action. "Yes?" he smiled, and sauntered across the room.

Rustling, bushes pushed back, scraping. A cough, prickly. "Hello there. Anyone in?"

"Who is it?" enquired Bug blandly, his arms folded, lolling against the wall.

"Sedge Beat . . . I've come for Foddly's possessions."

"Can't she come herself?"

"I have a vehicle . . . Easier for all concerned."

"The door is open."

Sedge should have been more prepared. He had the range car, a large bag, that was all.

He wore a cashmere suit, lemon – not a wise choice – and a necktie. Now that was a silly move.

Breeding possibly. You don't expect it

Pushing the door, Sedge let it ease behind him – heard it slam and stepping into the barn, stood untroubled looking towards the dais. A singular audience waiting for the first act.

"I'm over here," Bug called softly.

In the time it took the politician to adjust to the gloom, Bug somehow had lodged himself in the corner, his body coiled, crouched. And then he sprang.

Like a lynx, Sedge decided from the dark, revolting eyes and fists.

Bug punched him so hard he fell back on the table, blood from his mouth gushing onto his shirt. He hadn't time for thoughts of old school tricks because his necktie was a noose and he was being dragged from his resting place across the bare boards.

A solid leather boot on his chest.

Equipped with public school training, Sedge knew he shouldn't be going down for a dwarf like him. Yet he couldn't move, pinned to the floor, the legs of chairs and tables swimming around him.

"You're a fucking lunatic!" he spluttered to the foot. "Get off me!"

How did the man have the strength? Mad, the power of ten men. They say that.

The boot was lifted. He sat up. "Look, old boy, sort this one out." And scrambled to his feet, palms upwards. "These things happen." He looked at his trousers, ripped. Shit! The little shit. And temper rising, stood swaying.

Bug, fists still raised, expression disfigured by loathing.

Jesus, this bastard can hate, thought the politician and raised his own knuckles.

Then his opponent did a rotten thing, without warning, no sense of fair play.

Bug had leapt at the wall and brought down a sword, the pommel secured in a knuckle-white grip. Like a demented ballerina he pirouetted, transferring his dance from one foot to the other, the long blade whipping around the man's head, then a twist and the point underneath his chin, drawing blood.

Sedge, legs buckling. "Give me a weapon, you fucking madman! Can't you play straight?" And fell. He rolled over, seizing the leg of a chair, and hurled it, rolling back in time to see Bug reach out and catch it.

One hand and he'd caught the bloody thing? Jesus. Dealing with something else here.

Cold steel again, this time on his chest. He punched it up. The sword obliged by falling as if tired of playing. "Don't mess with me, old boy," Sedge's voice breaking. "I can finish you, don't forget that."

The sword lay on the floor, Bug opposite, his mouth curled, skin sucked into his face so hard it was a skull, furnaces for eye sockets. The devil realised Sedge. Didn't believe in it, read from the gospels, that was tradition, but if there ever was a demon . . . "No wonder she left you," he choked. "I don't know how she put up with it for so long – you're an absolute maniac!" He was straightening out but still shaking, blood over the lemon cashmere. "She wants some of her belongings. She has a right. Just show me where they are."

"*She*?"

Bug hadn't spoken for some time. Now that he did, it was worse. "And who is *she?*"

"Foddly wants her . . ."

"You do remember then, her name? Touching, that."

"Do what you fucking like, old boy. Keep them. I'll get her replacements. Everything you gave her, I'll replace."

"Is that so? Replenishment, eh? You really believe it? But you don't know what she had, do you?"

"Whatever she's . . . Foddly's lost . . ." Sedge was tired, wanted to sleep. It was too much, the whole scenario.

Bug was over on the other side of the barn now.

Sedge understood he could just leave and it would be over. "I know what you've taken, old man," he said, Parthenon shot. "Plenty. That's your game isn't it, lifting? If you fancy it you'll just take it." Moving to the door, he felt for the handle but then his arm was pinned against his back

"How in God's name, did you . . ?"

"Is that right? And what have *you* taken, Mr Beat? Something you don't even value. That's the worst kind of thief, unappreciative. Going to contaminate Foddly with your lack of discernment the same way you did my father? You haven't paid for that, yet! Haven't *replaced* that. When can my mother expect some restitution?"

Sedge was horrified. The little bastard had a cutlass in his hand now. 'When will it end?' he thought, mind pleading with his body for strength. 'When will it end?'

"You'll end soon enough, *old boy,"* whispered Bug backing away and assessing his quarry.

"What? I didn't say . . ."

"You never do – say anything. An everlasting vacuum is what you are." Bug threw down the cutlass. "Your people finish me? I don't think so. I could kill you now, easy, but everything has a time. And guess what? When yours comes, I won't feel any satisfaction . . . because the damage will have been done. And there's no restitution."

Sedge could feel his stomach quiver. Schoolboy jelly. "I'm sorry about your father, I truly am, for all of it. If I could . . . And Foddly, it happens . . . I didn't force her."

"You are beyond belief. Get out."

Sedge went.

Bug heard him stagger through the bushes, the car door slam and the engine start. Rumble and screech.

Opening a small cupboard, he removed a bottle. Unstopping the cork, he took a slug. Foul. "Blujah, helps you see, eh? Oh yes, Glastonbury, I'm seeing plenty." Brushing down his shirt, he swung up onto the table, and lying down, folded his hands over his stomach, spine clicking on the stained beech,

And closing his eyes, watched.

***

Bull rarely visited the little cottage, he much preferred to meet with Glastonbury at the House. But there were a few private, secret things he wished to discuss with the old man and here, in the middle of the woods, seemed the best place.

Perching on the edge of a battered leather chair, he studied the layers of books about him. From floor to ceiling they spread, a room lined with history. Quite fantastic.

"Can see why Bug targeted you, Glastonbury; it's an amazing collection you have. Read them all of course."

"Twice, at least," Glastonbury grinned, handing him a tray with a bowl of soup and a thick cut of homemade bread. He produced a spoon from the top pocket of his jacket. "Like the sea, isn't it, Bull? Because it's there we rarely visit."

"Won't need to soon," remarked his guest, sanguine. "It'll come to us. I wanted to talk about the floods and . . ." He paused to take a gulp of soup, mopping up its heat with the bread. "What's going on with Bug?"

"As if you didn't know."

"He comes to Coolton Ascent, straight to that room. I've seen him lying there – like a ruddy corpse. And have you noticed anything else about him?"

"Are you talking about the rash?"

"So it is second generation." Bull tugged at his beard, dislodging crumbs, his violet eyes cast down.

"Or it could be what he's gone through. He's been knocked back, Bull, low on resources. Don't forget he's lost his father as well."

"As well? So Foddly *has* gone? You know, Glastonbury I'd be relieved except . . ."

"What else was there?"

Bull placed his tray on the floor. "OK, I'm poking my nose in here but Foddly was very strong in our community work. We don't see her anymore, and if it's not Bug stopping her . . ."

Glastonbury was at a desk, scrabbling around with a decanter and two beakers. He raised his eyes at his friend. "Been a superb year."

"Go on, then, you old rogue. I'll join you."

The old man poured a generous measure, then another. "Help yourself."

Bull stood, eyes still searching the tiny room he moved across to the desk. Picking up his wine, he noticed a large black book on the stained scriber. Its gilded pages intrigued him and he looked closer. There were old photographs poking out, could just make out half a face, he thought. Yes, there were the eyes. Foddly? Can't be – too old-fashioned the way it was tinted like that. No, it was a boy. "Who's this? Spitting image of our Fod. Sorry, Glast, I shouldn't pry. You know what I'm like."

"No, it's not Foddly. Someone's old family bible. Lovely thing, isn't it?"

"I can't remember the last time I saw one of these. What's happened to us?" Bull lifted his glass, gesturing to the walls of books. "You and Bug must be the only ones around here to have this. We don't even write nowadays, our language has become leached of colour, meaning. It's all Political Esperanto and Demo-speak. Have to watch what you say, protect the evil-doers. We've forsaken the *spirit.*" He tried to find a mote of comfort in the verdant eyes. "I'm afraid, Glast, I mean that. We're totally lost."

"But you don't approve of the Church. It let you down."

"It's not the Church – we know what they were up to! They've proved that and sold out."

"Go on."

"Coolton Ascent, Glastonbury. What happens with the *Abbess,* is not quite worldly but neither is it sacred. I don't entirely approve, yet I stay."

"You're an obedient child, probably because it'd be even more frightening playing by your own rules."

Bull wasn't sure how to take that, and gulped at his drink. "We all need to belong. There's nothing out there for me – the Town is crumbling, soon people won't be able to afford to eat. This *right* to this and that is bogus – nobody has any rights to anything. The strongest ones will win, the thieves, the murderers – like they always have done." He slumped down on the chair, presenting a lugubrious profile. "I want to believe but all about me, I see the evidence for doubt."

"We have to live with a view. Yours might rely too much on other people's . . ."

"Can't we share the same one, sometime? In war, civil unrest – like now – we should be uniting as a spiritual whole. Helping, guiding."

Glastonbury, standing in the shadows, so tall and straight, even at his age. Could see the flash of uneven teeth, and he was laughing at him, or with him. Didn't really mind.

"Having a dark tea-time of the soul, are we, Bull?"

Bull shook his head and grinned, suitably sobered. "It's alright for *you.* Know it off by heart you've done it so many times. Don't you get sick of seeing it over and over?" He heard the silence. It severed the artery of thought, words unstoppable on a past momentum "I keep coming up with nonsense like this, ideas just popping into my head, but I tell you one thing." He handed the man his empty glass. "I love you, Glastonbury. I don't know why. Never met anyone. . ." What was he saying? "I've had this wicked stuff, so make allowances. But I do know Beat's got trouble. If he does give that land to the community and they find it's contaminated . . ." By the door, Glastonbury easing him down the path. Fantastic scent of lilacs, spring? Early! "There's one more thing before we part, this conjurer, Gul. Have you ever had any dealings with him?"

But he was walking through the woods, Glastonbury, a distant figure waving. How long would the old boy stand there waving, he wondered. Until he'd gone? Or would he always be in the old man's sight?

Bull Somerset, a solid man, burdened with forty-four years of searching, felt like a boy, wanting to turn back and make sure

* * *

"Gul, can I get you a drink?"

"Not just yet. You go ahead."

Sedge crossed to a low cabinet and snapped open the glass door. On a silver tray was set out a crystal decanter and two small glasses. He eased the top from the bottle. 'I need this,' he said to himself, and poured. Strolling across to the seated man, noting the impeccable suit, the soft leather shoes, the hand gracefully reaching into a pocket, and sighed in pained helplessness.

Gul brushed his spotless jacket with a foppish palm and glanced up. "Been in the wars, Sedge?"

"What was that? Oh, not exactly." The politician threw back his drink, thoughts busy.

"Don't tell me – you cut yourself shaving. Shave too close, I'd say, Sedge. Nasty, those nippers, aren't they? Especially ones with an axe to grind. Why don't you let me introduce you to a good barber?"

Sedge shook his head in mock disgust. "Think you've been watching too many black-and-whites, old boy."

The journalist inspected his nails. "Talking of black and white, we have to make a statement about your intentions. That better be good and clear."

"You've read the transcript. What d'you think?"

"Wifey going to be present, with that divine daughter of yours?"

"Couldn't we skip the family shot?"

Gul smiled, a dazzling sweep of pink lifting up the softest cheeks, creases as neat as tucks in a hand-finished shirt. "Skip the family being shot, eh? What, just you, then?" he tittered. "Mustn't joke, Sedge. No, it's not bad, as far as it goes but as it happens, it would help with Tezzie and blooming offspring. People don't want to see a fractured front when all about them is chaos, even if they know it's a sham. They like to be fooled, you know, the public. An insatiable appetite for self-deception you would not credit. How's young Foddly?"

"Fine." Sedge levelled his eyes at the man. "She's not involved. I don't want her involved."

"Better hide her away. I don't like tawdry dramas. Make it as clean and fresh as poss." Gul stood and sauntered over to the Broadwood piano. "Play, still?"

"Not for a long while."

"I want you playing. No Scriabin . . . Stick with Chopin. Show a bit of that traditional skill. Adroitness is very appealing, even for someone as inept . . . People forget trivial things like poverty and contamination, lynching, when they see how nimbly fingers can work. They won't believe a man as accomplished as yourself is capable of making mistakes. Amazing what fingers can do."

"Shuttup, Gul. You push it too far."

"Not as far as I could, Sedge."

"I said shuttup! Haven't you sorted out that waif, Carlos yet?"

He sensed the journalist bridling as he looked out onto the lawns. Saw the hand move once more to the pocket, this time drawing out a silver case.

Gul lit the cigarette and twisted in a spiral of smoke. "It's your last chance, Mr Beat. New Britain is falling. I cannot prop up your reputation any more than I can prop up buildings when their foundations crumble. What I *can* do, is present to the public a face they can forgive. It is now a question of penitence, making good."

The politician was reminded of Bug's words. 'Restitution.'

"That's a different matter – he's just a greedy little tea-leaf who doesn't know his Art from his elbow," offered Gul, from the French windows.

"What the *fuck* is going on these days? Do I speak without knowing I'm doing it?"

"No, Sedge, dear boy, just your lack of sentience speaking for itself."

Sedge sat down on the couch, head in hands. "I think I'm going mad. Ever since . . ." Then a need to trust, a reckless surge squandered in a moment. "Do you believe in curses, Gul? You know, someone can think that bad and hard about you . . ."

No, Sedge Beat was not a wise man, and becoming less circumspect by the minute. Unthreading before someone who had other patterns, other weaves.

Gul tweaked the curtain and wandering over to the piano lowered himself onto a satin-upholstered chair beside it. "Paranoia is not a luxury the hunted can afford," he judged mildly. "But if you are going to build on contaminated land, or worse, let them work it and they find out, we're going to have to rearrange the seating in this place."

Over by the cabinet, Sedge poured some more. Armagnac this time. "They'll find out sooner, old boy, none of it's been cleared. The floods have produced a . . . reaction."

"The land *and* the Factory? What a cocktail!"

"We still have people working . . . In fact we've taken more on. If there's employment it soaks up the sense of disassociation . . . I wanted none of this to happen."

Gul tittered. "Dearie me, I don't want *that* to happen. You sound like that born-again psychiatrist."

"That born again *what*?"

"You really are out of touch, Sedge. Drop the language and start playing. Let the fingers do the talking."

"As simple as that? I can survive by playing the fucking piano?"

"In what way, *survive*? People played penny whistles and survived, Sedge. Can you get *away* with it, you mean?" The ineffable journalist, architect of MEJA, cameraman, producer now, it seemed, once more smiled stupendously. "When you've been at the game as long as I, sir, you realise it would be better if you didn't. Survive, I mean."

Sedge wished he could smoke – have a cigarette. But they'd banned tobacco. Another holy idea gone up in . . . So why did Gul? Should ask him. And laughed. Jesus! This was crazy. His wife had gone, his daughter was living in the country with that bloody wet nurse, Angel Brown, and while the shit went down in New Britain, he was fucking the property of a psychopath. Now, to top it all, he could swear this silver-tongued bastard smoking and smirking in front of him telling all manner of bollocks, was the devil. Wasn't Bug Itin after all. It was Gul.

You really cannot judge by appearance.

* * *

When Foddly arrived back at the villa she wanted to sleep. After a difficult and almost bizarre conversation with the Abbess, just wished to retreat.

It had been precarious going to the House and trying to avoid Bug, and even though *his* room was now empty, the young woman was convinced he was still lurking, spying on her. Why couldn't he just speak? Surely they could still talk.

But judging from the incident with Sedge, it was clear Bug was becoming crazier. It didn't help.

The Abbess suggested his rage was necessary and that she, Foddly, must experience her own fury, because separation was all about that.

Foddly had doubts about that woman. Glastonbury was the person who understood those kinds of things, wasn't he? And he didn't talk to her in that way. Anyway, she didn't want to have fury. Didn't really want to be separated either. No feelings. Maybe she was shallow after all, vapid, like Sedge's wife. Then why should Bug be so fixated, so obsessed with losing someone like her? No, Foddly was not the girl, the woman, he thought she had been. He'd fooled himself as well.

Her return to the villa was proving equally disappointing. After a cursory greeting from an unfamiliar aide, she was overpowered by the pungent smell of cigarettes and felt violently sick.

Rushing to a cloakroom, she stood over the sink, breathing deeply. Holding down her stomach she counted: One, two, three. The nausea subsided.

Recovered, she tiptoed to the lounge. Sedge was playing – Beethoven. Standing by the door, she could see Gul sitting in a cloud of smoke, rings of it coiling around his head like a hangman's noose drifting over to the piano.

Sedge didn't seem himself. Even the music stuttered suddenly incoherent. Sensing her, he stopped, and swivelled round on his stool. "Back early, Fod? Look a bit washed out, old girl. Go and have a lie down."

She must have slept long and deep because Sedge was undressing in the corner, unbuttoning his shirt, then fingers twisting at the cuffs. A strange thing happened when he got to his watch. His hand turned dark green then red, and not just his hand, the whole of him shrouded in a muddy light. There were flecks of red there too.

Foddly blinked. The light was still there. She remembered someone talking about her light being flecky, ages ago. What was this light? Of course, it was Sonjia, before she became the Abbess, who'd mentioned that, and . . . Bug! He was here. She shut her eyes tight. But couldn't help it and looked down to her own feet bathed in white. Over to Sedge again grubby and crinkly, the colours fading in and out.

He was sitting on the bed now and, swinging his legs over, he slid down the mattress, resting his head against the pillow.

She knew he was looking at her because the light around him changed, orange then red, his thighs suffused in blood and fire.

Was she naked? Forgotten whether she'd taken her clothes off.

"All right, Fod? I had business to sort out. Sorry, darling."

His fingers on her spine. She *was* naked. His lips.

"What would I do without my beautiful girl?"

She didn't know. What would she do without him? Didn't know that either.

Her breasts were being touched now. Tender. The nipples tickled, his breath in gasps. She was floating again. Come back down! Saw his hand, colourless except for moonlight slipping across his fingers, a tangle of limbs, long grass falling, Japanese somehow, reed banks, grey water, uprights and slatted dawns. Through a mirror, saw the moon, a scythe in the sky.

She felt sick again and breathed over and over. In, out.

"Tired, lovely girl? I'll be quick."

A cool voyage from spine to buttock – metallic, its fashioning from a mixture of alloys, arriving at a disappointing form. A design without integrity, not noble or pure.

Sedge was always gentle, polite. His arm around her waist lifting her to him.

She watched their solid selves rearrange but irrevocably sucked to cohesion, the way he gathered her up, his hand on stomach, easing her legs apart, entering her.

Fell back down to earth.

"You just don't know how much I need this, Foddly. It's the best and simplest thing." It was the nearest to passion he'd been. His moans buried in her back, his hair fanned across her shoulders. "I feel like I'm fucking the world when I'm in you. I can see how people could go mad."

He withdrew and flipping her over, kissed her, tongue, lips, eyes, his stomach dripping with cooling sweat. Sitting up, he stretched her legs over his shoulder, his hands under her knees, and thrust a few long strokes. "It's got to end, Foddly. The whole thing's got to go, everything – this, the lot. But for now . . . I'm going to *fuck* the *world*!"

Her retreat was palpable to him. "Come back! Just let me . . ." He fell shouting into the pillow, heart battering against her skin.

Calm.

Foddly crept silently to the bathroom that morning. When she returned, he was dressing, his face to the window. "What are you up to today? I wouldn't mind some transcribing – and if you can do the Visi watch again . . ." He turned when she didn't answer. "Jesus! You look like a ghost. Better go back to bed, old girl. Those witches are doing you no good."

Foddly lay down, unable to speak.

Sedge began to frantically button and zip. "No stomachy things?"

"No," she whispered.

"Rashes?"

"I'm fine, Sedge. I think that smoke upset me."

"What smoke?"

"Gul. Didn't realise I could be so affected."

Pulling some trousers from a press, he shook his head, lips paling. "MEJA will be around at the weekend, I hope you'll be OK by then."

"Not if he smokes all the time. I don't know why you let him get away with . . . He's only . . ."

"Smoking or not, *you* can't be here, Fod. You know that, sugar. Tezzie and Saprah are coming – family scene, can't avoid it. I've got masses of preparation."

She sat up, colour to her cheeks. "Why are MEJA doing all this now? Is this what the piano was all about? Gul stage-manages everything. Even you . . . I don't like that man."

"You think I do? I have an announcement . . ."

"Not the land, Sedge. You can't! Not after everything."

He was at the door. "Keep out of it, old girl, is my advice. Stick to your own business. I haven't got time for queasy stomachs or morning sickness. That's *your* affair. Deal with it."

What on earth did she ever expect – wandering in on Sedge Beat's life because her own had gone astray? Wouldn't stay here. No point. He was in so much trouble.

'When it comes to it, you have to look after your own life.' That was the only sad thing she could remember Grandma Odella saying. It was true. Sedge was trying to protect his. Everybody for themselves. This was war. "I don't really have a life, you know, Grandma," she told the curtains. "I just seem to be part of everybody else's."

* * *

In Video Mass, on private Visi, they witnessed him playing flawlessly in pastel shades across the screen. Then standing contrite, a tall handsome man with handsome wife and child – more than that, stunning.

He apologised. Himself! A politician! When do they do that? But this is New Britain and the meek shall inherit the earth.

He quoted from a book, hand on the piano – his wife and daughter next to him. Together, solid.

She wasn't deserting him. And look at her. Could have anything she wanted.

They asked questions, MEJA – ones that slid like oil. "What about the roads, Mr Beat?"

"Car-gulleys. That's going according to plan. We dig *into* the roads; leave the surface for trams, pedestrians. Private electric cars will be restricted to the gulleys. We've reclaimed the streets."

"Mr Beat, what about our children?"

"We have Visicom. A world education, via the world. Every child has the same opportunity . . . We are all learning, becoming fit for purpose."

"What purpose, Mr Beat? There are no jobs," a rogue tongue roved.

"Life-long work, madam. We all of us have a role to play. No one is excluded. The principle of right to jobs is gone, but in its place, a new self-determination . . . Inclusion."

"The floods, sir, we've lost homes. The Services are nearing collapse."

"I'm very pleased to announce that I am allocating part of my personal estate, a not inconsiderable amount of land for public use. It is up to *you*, the *people* to decide how you wish to use it. In these times we have to think of each other, live together, unite against the common enemy, exclusion, share *all* our resources, whatever they may be. New Britain has come of age. We are growing up. With maturity comes responsibility! Facing life, whatever it may throw at us."

And sat down to play once more.

The cameras rolled. Not bad – as far as it went. Which wouldn't be much further.

* * *

The attic at the House was freezing, there were no carpets and the casement window had not been repaired, yet to Foddly it seemed the best place to sleep – far above the judging world, and she was grateful for her days there.

Bug was away. Members, as some people were calling themselves these days, were busy continuing the restoration of the west wing. Bull and a few 'decent types' from the Town, worked on the gardens with Glastonbury, the Abbess pottering about in the kitchen.

Foddly drifted about trying to summon up interest, but so often listless, found she was sleeping on chairs covered with dust, in alcoves smothered in sheets.

It couldn't continue like this – life, unformed, without direction. There must be a plan in her somewhere, so in a more elective moment, decided on a visit to the Town.

Arriving at a bank of filthy pink cubicles opposite the Loyalty Store, she propped her bike against the cleanest one. With one end of a long chain connected to the front wheel and the other to her wrist, she keyed in an address on the panel beneath the Visicom and waited.

Yes, flashed across the Perspex

Shoving in a card, she waited again, a quick glance up the street.

To her side, the screen flared. "Foddly!"

"Hello Angel, just wondering how you and Saprah are getting along."

"Oh, how nice. It's been lovely having her here, but she's gone. Didn't you see them? You didn't miss *that?*"

"I haven't been . . . I will, now I'm on this machine."

Angel's fractured face beamed through the blemished screen. "He was very good, I thought. Always comes across so well, and what he's doing is so absolutely in keeping with his principles. Have you been in touch with him lately, Fod?"

Thankfully, Saprah hadn't mentioned anything, Foddly realised. "By the way, how's your mother?"

"Not good. In a way I'm a little relieved Saprah's gone. My mother's completely bed-ridden now. Lots of needy people, you know. We're very fortunate, us. When I get back I'm going to knuckle down and . . ."

"Saprah's not due back, then?"

"She needs her family. That's where she should be, at home, even . . ." Angel cast around. "I'm not judging, you know, but her mother's very cool, I've never really taken to her. Doesn't seem to connect. Fortunate Saprah has such a good bond with *him.* I'm totally amazed you haven't seen the footage. Just to think I *know* Sedge. And you do, of course."

Foddly smiled wryly.

The screen began to speak: Metallic voice. *Sixty seconds.*

"Have to go, Angel."

"Give him my love. Oh, better not." Angel's face creased up. "Regards sounds better. Bye Fod, see you soon, I hope."

The screen blanked out. She noticed the box was daubed in anti New Britain, obscenities, threat, offers of yats, of assassination.

Pushing the door of the cubicle, she unwound the chain and rode away.

*

On his veranda, Sedge sipped at a drink of freshly squeezed orange juice. Swamped in mohair coat and holy with survival, he raised a hand to acknowledge Foddly, and smiled. "We think it went well."

Placing his drink on the wrought-iron table, he lifted the hand again, olive branch. "I was a bit off-colour the other day. Sorry, my lovely girl." And dipping his little finger in the orange, he fished out a pip and flicked it to the ground. "Tezzie's still around though. Got a bee in her bonnet now. It works like that, old girl. She does me a favour and she names the price. Not for long . . . You still staying at the Gothick horror?" Stretching, he tapped his foot against the table legs and squinted at her through a fan of thick lashes. "Sort out the problem, did we?"

"What problem?"

"Good girl. Last thing I want, more complications. We have to be very careful with Saprah."

"Why her?"

"Now, now! She could say the same about you."

"I'm not saying anything about your daughter, I'm just asking why *she* should be protected in particular, from what's clearly *my* problem? Don't my feelings count for anything?"

"Oh dear. We don't seem to be getting along. I think you better take a long, hard look. I can't have jealousies around my family, not the way things are. No time for rivalry in this camp."

Foddly inspected the elaborate brass handle on the door, the moulding on the woodwork, and realised it was excessive. "I only came to see how you were."

The man pushed back his chair and stood. He was thinner, mouth even less substantial in retreat from his other, equable features. "Don't rock this boat anymore, Foddly. Don't be a problem to me, there's a good girl. I've had enough bollocks from your lot, what with the *boyfriend* and that little fluff, Carlos Dean. There's such a thing as protocol, me dear. Best learn the rules before you start playing. I always had you down as a bright one."

"Does Tezzie follow protocol?"

His mouth swallowed in dusk now emerged in twists, wriggling from side to side, chewing on its small thoughts. "Remove that fucking bone-shaker from my stucco." And pulling up the collar of his coat, he brushed past her and disappeared into the house.

Foddly had left the villa that morning without knowing where she would go. Without knowing how she felt. No feelings.

The sky was overcast, an easterly wind cutting her face as she cycled. An aimless, grey stretch of a day. All the days were like this. Could almost envy Angel's misguided purpose, even Sedge, with his preoccupations. Why wasn't she indignant? Because she didn't believe it. None of it was real. Wasn't happening.

Imagine, she mused, living in the Town. She'd never survive, someone like her, completely lacking in nous. A privileged girl squandering resources on . . . And if she knew what she was like, Angel Brown would hate her too. "But there's always someone, isn't there?" Foddly asked herself. Never completely alone.

She'd arrived at The Factory almost by accident, and cycled around to the front by the main gates. Undoing her jacket, she wobbled on her bike, back against the mesh wire. Could see the grim clock-tower where the workers signed on, men like Sal and Carlos' father. How could she have overlooked what went on in this place? Sedge Beat was a man overseeing an iniquitous fraud. So what did that make her?

Hearing footsteps, grabbed the handlebars.

A soldier was coming towards her, rifle high.

Was this patrolled? The Factory was armed!

"Fod! It's been bloody years. Fod, it's *me*. Remember? We met on the train, girl. I'm a sergeant, now."

Foddly surveyed her old school friend. She did remember. "Hello! Sorry, I didn't recognise . . . I suppose I'm trespassing."

"There've been some little shits around here, Fod. Waiting for women. I'll see you off the premises." She wore a peaked hat pulled so low it almost covered her eyes. Foddly noticed how she'd become much broader, her jaw more defined, brutalised, the edge of her coarse thick palm chopping at the stock of the rifle.

"Still not married then?" Foddly asked, wanting to make sure.

"No, babe. This is my life now, and to be honest, men are bastards, the lot of them. I like my job. Mind you," the soldier jerked a rigid thumb Factory-wards, "this is not good. I don't envy the bastard when this blows. Anyway, can't say anything but if you ever fancy a drink . . ." She touched her nose with a grubby spatula finger. "We can talk."

The two women walked down the path, the front wheel of Foddly's bike bumping against the wire fence.

"Bloody old beast, that. What is it, cast-iron or something?"

Foddly smiled. "Or something."

"See you, girl. Don't make it another seven years though. By the way, Fod, from a trained eye, you need toughening up." She laughed. "Join us, babe. We'll give you some backbone!"

How long would this day last? Foddly found she was already in the woods as if going home.

She must tell him. That was her excuse. Maybe pick up some things, at least talk to him. Why? What could she say that he didn't already know? But nothing could be worse than this silence.

It was not a good idea.

Tired again. Her skirt kept catching in the spokes. She stopped and tied the fabric in a thick knot, then continued pedalling. Wheels cracking over stones and branches, wind snapping at her skin, came to where she'd turn off for Glastonbury's, she gave a cursory glance and pressed on.

Outside the barn, Bug's truck was parked untidily, tyre tracks on the small path. The windows were dark. He may not be in. Dismounting, she picked up the bike and walked it around to the side.

A tub of soil against the wall, tiny shoots pushing through. It really looked as if he'd been tending them. Bug, nurturing? Hadn't thought of that. But it had only been weeks and plants grow on their own, don't die straight away through neglect.

Her face was wet, hands clammy. What am I doing? I haven't got anything to say. And turned the handle.

Should have knocked. It wasn't her place anymore.

Nothing had changed. Why should it?

The room was empty of Bug, except in the cleanliness and order. In that sense it overflowed with him, brimming.

Around the long table, chairs had been set, three on either side; beyond, in the middle of the room, two more, back to back.

Over at the sink there were cups and plates, cutlery in a blue-and-white ginger jar arranged on the draining board. Well, he'd still eat.

It was as if she was returning to the scene of a terrible crime just to see if anything had survived: evidence, clues, witness to survival. Guilt.

The bed? A tiny flare, frisson. But it was made, a rug over the top. On the chest-of-drawers some flowers in a vase. That was new, Charlotte Rheade. Oh, and he'd actually finished upholstering the Godwin.

Foddly, born again on the outside of Bug's fastidious and enduring life.

The air in the barn was still, holding its breath; a blanket under which she might sneak and hope never to wake up until the awfulness was over and life had regained another, consuming purpose.

She sat one of the chairs positioned in the centre of the floor. Back to back like in a waiting room.

Should have hidden the bike. He may never come in, never find her if he knew she was here. Realising in the dullest, darkest thud, that she did want him to find her.

Torpor had overwhelmed her not purpose. It was dark when she came to. Slept for hours. Hungry. Her hands were numb with cold even though the wood-burning stove was alight. How? Oh, he must have arrived while she slept.

Leaning forward gently, peered round. No one. Sank back, if you can sink in a chair as hard as this one.

She'd forgotten the other, behind.

Head to head, girl and boy.

The backs of chairs touching, hair mingling with other hair, they each faced their own dark vista, their singular malady.

He had his hands on the arms, his fingers resting on the scroll of honeyed patina, didn't move – weren't travelling anywhere, berthed, or locked in transit.

She could feel the top of his head, the light breathing, and tried to imagine his face. "I wanted to tell you . . . for you to hear it from me first, Bug."

"Carry on."

"I haven't come back because of that."

"Good."

"I know what I've done is thoughtless, stupid. I've been . . . careless."

Bug could hear her struggling, saw the light in her stomach quivering distinct from her own colour, a distant luminosity. Maybe he should reach out and pull her in from the ice, but his hands were welded to the chair, couldn't swim, not now, not yet, in such treacherous waters.

He felt her move away over to a small table, patches of silver and white, a tiny fire within yet alien to her.

Then her own light from her head, snagged and torn like a lace curtain on a branch. "Odella's," he said.

"What is?" Foddly looked down at a small print lying with a few papers in the drawer. "Oh, this was hers."

"She gave it to me."

Foddly returned to the chair. "I wasn't going to take anything that didn't belong to me, Bug," she said, with almost poignant sanctimony. "In fact I don't want anything at all. I don't care that much about *things*. You can keep it all. I don't mind."

Bug smiled beneath his moustache. "I think Odella had the same idea."

Foddly didn't understand, or he was being deliberately cryptic. She perched on the edge of her seat and faced the stove. "How late is it?"

"About ten weeks, I'd say. You should know."

"I meant the time, Bug. I stopped counting *those*. You always know. But it wasn't the reason I went, because we couldn't . . ."

"No, that would be ironic."

"I don't really like children. I'm not very good like that."

"Oh dear, more reckless by the minute."

She swivelled round. "Don't you mind?"

"Not much point."

She put her head between her knees, fingers wrenching her hair. "I'm sorry! Can't you see I am? Just hold me, Bug. I need you to hold me. Please!"

He didn't move.

Stiffening her limbs, hot like a child in a paroxysm of fury she banged her feet on the floorboards, crashing and thumping, hair a blizzard around her face. He wasn't her horizon anymore, wasn't there, the everlasting landscape and she wanted to scream, to holler in pain and rage. Childish undoing out of control. They weren't on a hill about to roll, head to head, about to fall; he wasn't going to push her over an edge let her play in terror and then save her. There were no walls to bang against, it was endless space now; unsafe acres too far from boundaries, a terrible openness for someone unused to travelling without a guide.

Bug had always been there to run to and from, so it was his fault really, she decided, not letting her see the other way.

He sat motionless staring ahead, thinking. A screen of history between them. As inviolable as it was pointless.

"I thought you loved me!" she accused.

"Dear, dear me, Foddly. *That* was not good at all."

"You said . . . you *said* once, I'd never get away from you."

"You won't, but that's not quite the same as me baling you out of a situation you got yourself into."

"So it is simply power. You just want power." She stood, wretched, clothes drenched in acrid scent. "I'm sorry I came."

"Got lights on your bike?" he asked.

"Yes."

"Drive carefully."

Falling to her knees she hammered her fists on the table legs until the dust rose from the floor. "No! No!" She crawled round to his chair and shook those legs, pummelling and pounding his feet, swallowing her breath until she was dizzy. "Don't. Please don't!"

"What?"

"Punish me . . ."

He brushed his fingers against his moustache then folded his hands together. "What did you expect? Me to welcome you back, a woman impregnated by a fool, whose noxious family were responsible for my father's death? Protect you from the indifference of a vainglorious runt? Maybe you understand me a little better now, Foddly."

"You're proud. It is pride, isn't it?"

"Entitled. You should have more. Show some self-respect, girl. Never take risks you can't recover from."

"You have, with me."

He looked at her at last, his eyes shiny blue lines, lids swollen, mouth wet. "I'm just letting you go. Wasn't there something about wanting to be yourself? Well, here you are."

"I don't want to be anything anymore, Bug. Just want to go to bed and lie next to you. Sleep and never wake up until it's all over and it hasn't happened."

"That's not a risk I'm prepared to take."

The light was very low, a candle breathing in the corner, a soft glow from the stove. She could see his skin was glistening, but not from tears. Maybe there were never any. She straightened up. "What's happened to you, Bug?"

"I think your word was *superstition*."

The bed was there, the night had come, and if there was another hunger, it didn't speak. He kept away from her all night, an ocean between them.

In the morning the ocean had gone and he was swept up on her stomach, crossways over, habit washed up by an early sun.

She saw the blisters lashed across his back, his face burning.

He prepared breakfast. "I'm not ill, like Carlos is ill. Not everyone is affected. Some people just come straight through it, apparently."

"I'm sorry. . ." Foddly staggered to the bathroom and just made the sink.

"You need peppermint tea," Bug called. "I take it you don't want this," and removed the tray.

Returning to the bed, Foddly flopped down.

He rolled next to her, wrapping his kimono tight.

She turned over, full, ripe. "Be careful, my breasts are very tender."

"I won't be touching your breasts or any of you."

"Never again, Bug? You won't touch me, ever again?"

Jumping down from the dais, he opened a cupboard beneath the small steps. "I'm getting ready to leave, Foddly. You mustn't be here when I return."

"I'll go first, then." She stumbled into her clothes, everything round the wrong way.

He buttoned up her jacket, gave her some fruit and opened the door.

"Is it really over, Bug? I've made you miserable and ruined everything . . . I'll never see you again?"

"I'm not going to the House, if that's what you mean."

"What will happen to me?"

"I don't know."

"Can't you . . . help? We could be . . . friends, still."

"I'll look after you, Foddly. In my way. You have to go now."

Bug Itin stood alone. A small man with a treasury of powers, but in possession of none.

Gold

Bad things seem to happen all at once without pause for breath, recovery. A purging of habit, belongings ripped up and flung from ownership. Provenance in doubt, value lost.

And that other belonging: connection. A certainty view built over, towers of alien chance rising from a once-familiar plan, shouting obscenities at an old window.

Shut the curtains. Look inside.

Where?

Faces that have changed without apperception of their transformation, appear as they have become, without compromise. A shock, a distinct life, a dissolution of the known to the bewildering array of random shapes – once a father, a lover, a mother.

The sun forgotten in such precipitation.

Reluctant to leave his rage, Bug decided to walk through the woods that afternoon. Thoughts dwelling in the dark place, he kicked at the earth, turning soil over grass as he walked, dislodging stones from their cold home. Implacable cold.

When he arrived at Freda's the sun was low. He pushed open the gate and trod down the path. The door was unlocked.

The air in front room was stained with illness.

Freda lay on a long sofa, a heavy blanket over her. She smiled when she saw him. "Must have been in a dwam, Bug. Just had a visit from your old friend, Glastonbury. We had a lovely talk. He knows how to make you feel real comfy. Brought Pa with him – didn't say a lot."

"Never did, Freda, even when he was here. Are you hungry?"

"It's the wee boy, I feel for, Bug."

"What wee boy?"

"Sorry about your girl, but it's not his fault, bless him."

Bug tucked the blanket around her chin and felt her pulse, its pattern flickering against his finger.

"Can you remember what year I was born, yet, Freda?"

"No, darling boy. Keep asking me that. After the others, we stopped counting. The years were getting mixed up. You came between Christmas and Hogmanay. It was the days, the hours that got us through. We didn't care about your arrival it was your staying we wanted. I never slept, so how you sneaked off, I'll never know."

Bug removed his cloak and rolled up the sleeves of his shirt. Taking her hand, he weighed its fragility and put the cold fingertips to his mouth. "Tell me about Sal."

"You love that story. We lived near Ayrshire. Your grandpa was a tailor, made beautiful stuff. Everybody knew him." She squeezed his hand. "Maybe that's where you get your nimble fingers. I used to deal with the customers. One day, this funny looking American came in to get fitted out. Asked me on a date, there and then. So out-of-the-blue, didn't have time to refuse. Every time we met he'd have this brown parcel under his arm. Every time. Until I asked him what it was. *My past,* he said. *Burn it.* So I took it home. When I opened it up, there was a soldier's uniform inside, all folded neat."

"Vietnam . . . He was a deserter. Good for him."

"Sal didn't want to be a murderer. I couldn't let him go back, not to that. So we took him in. Stuck together."

"You were brave, Freda."

"Daft, more like – we came here!" She caught her breath. "Did you ever learn to play the piano?"

He nodded.

"Play 'Auld Lang Syne.' No singing. I don't want your singing."

Bug moved over and lifted the lid of the old mahogany piano. Dragging out the stool, he sat in front of the keys and spread his fingers, picking out the notes, some flat, others mute. A broken sequence.

Freda seemed to enjoy it and sang herself. Sturdy for a second. That happens sometimes, a sudden burst. And then fell quiet.

He left the piano and sat beside her listening to her sleep.

The night came cramming against the sash windows, greedy for witness. Clocks ticking, the floor a still linoleum, the memory of forty-odd years imprinted on its dull pattern. A yellow light hung from the ceiling, its illumination managing the size of a dinner plate. Beyond in the unlit, Freda's hand, febrile and wavering, beckoned her son.

He bent near and listened. Nothing, just murmurings, the shadows of an old argument.

Before she left, Freda opened her eyes: wide as hope, her face young as sixteen years; history smoothed away, a palimpsest rubbed clean for other concentrations. "You must listen to Glastonbury," she told him. "But you won't. You never do. Good night, son."

"Good night, Ma."

Plumes of white mist rising like smoke from her mouth settled over her body. Then disappeared.

Bug stayed with her until dawn fastened an image of the windows along the wallpaper, a shimmering composite of their once home.

He made the call from a telephone with a coiled wire attached. A strange contraption.

After the Services had taken her, he collected his cloak and went into the garden.

By the side of the house the overflow pipe dripped. In the distance, beyond the rows of fences loomed the Factory its siren tearing for the first shift.

Born alone the day, a clarity that shook perception.

In the small garden frost clung to grass, the narrow path between two patches of lawn wriggled to a quick end, a shed and a gate.

He lay down on the path. The cold from the concrete shot up his back. Stretching out his arms, he pushed one hand to the bricks of the kitchen wall, the other to the frozen earth.

And watched the sky until the stars came back.

1992

Platinum

In a sunny garden, a boy wobbled on the pedals of his mother's old bike. Sliding down he sat in the loop of the frame. "You've got loads of books in there," he said, pointing to the open door of the cottage.

"Books are like friends, Bug – except you don't have to entertain them." Glastonbury grinned, a wide space in his long pale face. The teeth were untidy and crooked.

Bug was surprised by them. He'd have to be human then, to have ordinary teeth like that. "I don't like people either. *You're* ok, I suppose."

"Do you have many books, Bug?"

"No. I know somebody who does – my best friend's grandma."

"Best friend? Good to have people your own age."

Bug blushed and began to twist the handlebars, unscrewing the round top of the chrome bell. "Fod's not . . . she's quite young." He scratched his head then tightened up the bell. "Foddly hasn't got a dad, so I need to look after her."

"Glad to hear it. We all of us need looking after, no matter what age we reach."

Bug eyed him slyly. Almost a confession that. "So you *are* very old?" he confirmed, matter-of-fact.

Glastonbury sat back in his rocking chair, bumping the path with his feet and laughed.

"Freda said, would you like to come for tea?" the boy delivered without enthusiasm.

"Tell your mother, I'd be delighted."

"You don't *have* to."

"Why, are you ashamed of me?"

"No, but . . . I don't like ordinary people, and she might turn you normal."

"And what about Foddly?"

The boy leapt from his bike and began to wave his hands. Up in the air he jumped, twirling like a dancer. He kicked the wall beneath the kitchen window without realising he'd done it, ran into the tiny parlour and re-emerged, his eyes filled with dreaming.

"That good, eh?" Glastonbury acknowledged with a smile.

Bug didn't know where he'd been, and stood in a plot of hazy sun. "Can I bring her here? Can I show her to you, Glastonbury?"

"Better wait until I've met your mother, I think."

"No! It'll take too long!"

"These sorts of things don't wear out, Bug."

"What about the rainbows?"

The old man bent forward, his eyes so strong the boy wondered if he should carry on looking. "If she has those . . . then, Bug, you're a very lucky fellow."

The boy raised his hands, the first two fingers crossed. "I really want you to see her! Will you make her . . ?" He turned, snatched up his bike and jumped on the saddle, jerking up the front wheel.

"I'd say she already does. But women, Bug, they can be very difficult."

From the garden of his cottage, Glastonbury watched the boy weave in and out of sun until all that remained was the sound of his passing.

Part V

Pigment

1962

Sepia

Mother and son kept to the sea wall until they found a sheltered spot. Together they stretched out the blanket. The boy ran to collect some stones, placing one at each corner.

The wind played around them as they sat – sneaking under the tartan square, a pleasant favonian wind and soft spray from the sea.

"We're eating fish and chips in the open air, Mom. They taste so much better in the open air."

"You're right, they do. Must be because the sea air makes you so hungry." The woman screwed up the empty newspaper into a ball and stuffed it into a linen bag. She leaned back in a spoon of sun, a bubble of joy bursting over the chalk, and stroked the boy, tugging at his jumper. "You should have your coat on. This time of year it can change so quickly."

"I wish dad was here. When I grow up, I'll look after you. I'll never leave, so you don't have to worry anymore."

"You are a hoot! But Dad didn't mean to go. It wasn't his fault. And he's still here, in a way."

"But I can't see him." The boy, who had been standing, dropped suddenly to his knees, the sand hard and wet. "Mom?"

"Yes?"

"Don't *you* go . . ."

"Where, you silly sausage? I'm not going anywhere. I'm not going to leave my best present, my only darling autumn-eyes – even if mothers aren't supposed to say that to their seven year old sons!"

The boy squinted seawards. "I think I'll have a paddle. You coming?"

"Ooh, cold. Do I have to?"

"You can't come to the beach and not paddle."

"All right, let me take off my stockings. I'll have to tuck my skirt inside my knickers," she laughed.

"That's O.K," the boy reassured her. "There's nobody here. Just you and me." And wriggling off his shoes and socks, he ran seawards.

Odella rolled down her stockings, and carefully peeling them off, tucked each one at the end of her pointed shoes. Piling her bags and some more stones on the blanket, she began to bunch up her skirt.

The sky was clouding over, thick, heavy grey bulking in, the wind changing. Maybe she should put the raincoat over all this.

He was calling.

She waved. "Just a minute, darling . . ." Rummaging in a basket she brought out a plastic coat and secured it over their picnic place.

Didn't take long, a few minutes at the most.

Brushing back her hair, she looked around for him.

The distance between one moment and the next is incalculable – its journey to difference, a brutality from which some may never recover.

2039
Coolton Ascent

Viridian

I didn't see you there, hiding in the corner. Knew you'd turn up sooner or later, although I have no idea what we'll talk about. Expect you want to give me a ticking off, berate me for my feckless ways. Go ahead.

Know how old I am, Glastonbury? One hundred years in a few days they tell me. But you never know . . . the treachery of spring. Might finish me off early!

It's raining again. Foddly wanted to close the window. What for? You'd think they were all afraid of losing me.

I have a feeling she lost something, or am I thinking of somebody else? Oh, we're all bereft, either by never having or by casting aside . . . Did I cast aside?

I can't always remember. I find the memory difficult. Things seem very different now, Glastonbury. Unburdened. History is that, you know – a great weight.

You look very well. How old are *you*? Go on, tell Sonjia. You are a naughty boy leading me on all that time, pretending. I didn't, though, pretend. No artifice in me. That's the awfulness of it all. I really did . . . commit. Maybe like the fools who came here – Bull, Angel, I had nothing else to do but fall.

I haven't seen him recently, that boy, Loot. They're fixated on his return. All out there talking about it. I can't take responsibility for that anymore than you. We have our destinies, don't we? But there are certain elements which have to be dealt with. I suppose that's why you've come. Unless . . . Is it for me, your Sonjia? As wicked as she is . . .

Oh, no! That smoke again. I can't breathe, Glastonbury. I'm . . suffocating. The window . . .

*

Angel sat with Saprah in the kitchen, the only light offered from candles.

"In that book, Angel, it says it will happen like this. You can't stop it. Nobody can."

"I don't believe, Saprah. Never did. I'm not a believer. Anyway, it's always been open to interpretation, that book. But if it gives you some sort of comfort, then . . . "

"It's not a comfort. You're wrong, there's nothing consoling in it. The inevitable is not a friend." Saprah lifted her arms and tied back her hair. Her skin and eyes, an uninterrupted confections. She looked more like her father with every year, except the mouth, that was stronger, firmer.

"Are we going to do anything for her?" Angel enquired, rubbing her hand across the table.

"You can, if you like. Ask Foddly to arrange it." The young woman crossed to the sink and stretched over, peeping through the window. "There's lights on again . . . Somebody's in the church. It's not their day . . .Quick! Come over here."

Angel padded over and duly looked. There were lights, but not from the church. Lanterns bobbing up and down, a voyage of flickering lights illuminating the way. "Go and get Bull. Do something with the doors and windows."

Saprah, hand over her mouth. "It's not my fault, Angel, you know that. What my father did, it's not my fault, please! You believe me. I know . . . the other thing . . . with Bug – you forgive me, don't you?"

The other woman couldn't understand how a past so far back could still exert such vicious influence. "There's nothing *to* forgive. Don't be such a silly girl. It wasn't you . . . There were . . . others . . more culpable."

"I did it out of revenge."

"You didn't understand, Saprah."

"But I do now . . . and it's worse."

Through the windows, Angel could see the procession of lights receding. "Anyway, they're going, panic over. You have to watch Sonjia this evening. Ask her if she wants a cake, although I don't know where we'll find the candles."

2015

Coral

"I haven't seen him for a while, Glastonbury. He's gone." Sonjia walked beside her friend. The day had fled, the beach a stretch of shiny cold beneath an early moon. "I came down here yesterday and nothing then. Our little boy has found a home."

"A temporary reprieve, maybe."

"Don't be like that. It's liberation." The woman banged her arms on the side of her coat. "Yes, we have to keep our wits about us. That girl has been looking very peaky. I suppose I'm a sort of mother now!"

The man walked ahead, coat whipping his legs. The wind was from the east, bitter, March.

"You've become so old of late," she said resentfully at the receding figure.

"I think you'll outlive me this time," was his distant reply.

Sonjia stopped, and bending down scooped out a shell, the coil of sand a satisfying chill. "How many times have you been washed up, along with all the others?" She let the shell rest in her palm. "Glastonbury!" she called. "Glastonbury! I hope we've collected the right one!"

Foddly hadn't mentioned anything to her mother about Bug, or her pregnancy. She decided to wait.

When she returned to Coolton Ascent and heard of Freda's going, she was surprised how this seemed the most devastating of all. The last link, and she hadn't even said farewell. Not daring to return to the barn, sent Bug a note via Glastonbury.

The House was taking shape at last, and with the allotments to the side of the building providing food their tiny community was becoming almost self-sufficient.

Bug's room had remained as it was but nobody mentioned him. The room was his and that was all there was to it. He'd come back, eventually.

Not wanting to speak to anyone, Foddly had taken to the attic and its ascetic chill. With her tell-tale stomach rounding, breasts pushing against the buttons of her shirt, she couldn't stay here for much longer.

She was surprised to receive a message from Sedge. He sounded desperate. Tezzie had been behaving outrageously, he wrote, had taken all the paintings. The piano would be the next to go.

What gall! Why should she be interested in his domestic drama? But that wasn't it. Sedge didn't want the news of his dalliance and subsequent spurning to leak out. But did he really think she'd say anything?

This is about as deep as politics seemed to get these days.

Then there was Carlos Dean. He'd heard about her and Sedge. She'd have to have a careful word with him. He could be very destructive for an angel, and since Gul had secured him, he'd become even more affected. It was an unfortunate union and Foddly could see the workings behind the journalist's jealous mind. Bug remained Carlos' obsession and his eidola had been wounded by Sedge, a man he already despised. With his influence and splicing, Gul could exact a deadly revenge. He would do almost anything to please his Golden Prince.

The second communication from Sedge was to the Abbess. It came with a promise, a peace offering. The Law Leader would support the community. A generous grant from New Britain for such an organisation was wholly appropriate in these times.

Chuckling, Sonjia made her way to the top floor. "Foddly, sorry to butt in . . . Mr Beat has become profligate! It'll mean the east wing and the roof will be done by the autumn," she beamed. "This is going to set us up for a long while. But it does make me wonder . . . would there be *conditions*? I think it's time we had a little chat."

They had a little chat. Foddly, cool and reserved, muddling her words, the Abbess, raising her eyes and shaking her head. "Foddly, my dear, you must do what is most comfortable, but I'm glad we're in the picture now. What about your family?"

"I don't want my mother to know."

"Well, she'll find out in the end, surely?"

"Why should she?"

"We will have to be very discreet, Foddly. Lucky we have Glastonbury to fall back on."

The old woman could be so duplicitous.

The Abbess, once Sonjia, once nurse helped Foddly pack, a guiding hand on the steps of the porch.

The sun was up high, so bright, summer near. How Foddly yearned for hills and blue skies that went on forever being blue, ached for a childhood simple and easy, sun on grass, hair in the eyes, light sliding through like a Japanese print or a Venetian blind facing south. Hands that could talk. Bug.

How a moment can slip from grasp its transition a devastating chance.

But this was not a preoccupation with a blanket on a desolate beach where a child disappears from thought in the complacency of a second. No. This was a conscious choice.

The distance between one moment and the next, immeasurable, but in those following moments, months, Foddly was counting. Looking and seeing.

She could have changed it herself, outlived history.

Raw Umber

What made Claudia Shell such a nasty person?

Like many of her generation, she was obese – punishingly big. Was it the soil, perhaps, that made her eat so much, or was she just greedy?

Maybe the young woman was really a slender lovely suffocating under an avalanche of blubber, her gluttony a mask for self-loathing – resentment amassing weight to give itself authority? Difficult to tell which came first, anger or fat. Could have been a union made in hell. Claudia's hell

But she did take up an awful lot of space, and filled it with an unrelenting sullen demand. And her armoury of children, they were sulky too, all five of them.

Claudia, her partner, Tuf Daley and their riotous family, occupied a two-bed-roomed apartment on a concrete wilderness just beyond the Town. A river slipped down the middle of the estate, a putrid conduit from Factory, separating the bad from the hopeless.

The family occupied the hopeless end. Which came first?

Like everywhere else, the estate was doomed. What would replace it was not quite clear, but the Policy Makers were making some suggestions. It may be a good idea if those wishing to progress to better things kept their noses clean.

There was little to do these days but listen, watch for signs of threat and alien influence. Video Mass wasn't up to much either. Gul and MEJA promised all kinds of new stuff; as yet it hadn't turned up. So there was nothing except the extra-systolic beat of a heart knowing its healthy rhythm had failed for good.

True, there were remnants of the old guard clinging to power, ones who maintained the rights of the former council, legal teams set up to ensure certain schedules within old contracts were adhered to. Can't just abandon the law – what was the point of having one? But the old guard was dying, had no fight left, and those who once maligned and spat at its tendentiousness now grieved the failing ire, as one does a bad-tempered Alsatian when its teeth fall out.

Claudia was one of many who had abused the former system. To her, it had become like the oft-absent parent, to punish and test. Having received no direction herself she was never certain when to stop, and pushing was as much an affliction of her soul as it was of that inflating body.

But there had been rules. And if you broke them? Someone would defend your right so to do, because they were nasty, oppressive people who enforced such draconian regulation.

Surely all wise parents know not to show division? The child becomes confused, plays one end off against the other. The old council should not have been a parent, it wasn't equipped, lacked instinct. Can't parent by committee. Spoil the child and you'll suffer. My, will we suffer!

Despite the evidence, knowledge wasn't prosecuted and the desire to salve and placate was ever pressing. Had to tread on eggshells, the Town was alight now, the beginning of many lightings. Righteous indignation. The 'people' were suffering. No money, no jobs. And the damaged were a race apart, clinging to a personal territory of suffering.

And Claudia was part of the damaged: poor, afflicted. Look at her size. You couldn't ignore it. She'll need a wheelchair soon.

Not her fault.

In the spring of 2015, Claudia and Tuf's youngest issue, Wit, was being squeezed into little trouser pants ready to take in some serious distance between him and his less than loving parents. Wit was not an appealing child. Red and blotchy, fiery like his father, he staggered about their small apartment, like a one-year-old drunk, falling into walls, crashing into doors, landing up at the end of the day with a bottle stuffed in his mouth to sleep off the excesses of an unbounded life. If the child came back for more, Claudia would scoop him up with one great hand and offer him to his father or to Speak, their eldest boy. “Go play with your brother,” she’d bark. So he did, and they were horrible games, torture, and ‘kill the Leader.’ Even at five-years old, Speak Daley had an inexhaustible armoury of punishments. At his age?

So what made a boy like this? Surely there must be something? You can’t just be . . . horrible.

Angel Brown was a woman pursuing questions such as these, interrogating the limits of her own compassion, analysing reasons and causes. The source of wickedness can be traced, an influence stemmed. A life can be restored to balance to forgiveness. Harmony.

Angel was never a person to allow an axiomatic truth to get in the way of her road to good intent; and she simply refused to acknowledge the incontrovertible evidence that some people are just bad.

‘Surely badness is a perceived reality,’ she would argue, ‘a prejudice. The excluded sense it, and it compounds the problem. How can there ever be recovery from pain and alienation, if people are branded? Help. They need help.’ Love? She may not go so far as to say that. This might echo too closely her private needs.

Claudia knew all about the likes of Angel Brown and was working her. New Britain was letting the fat young woman down, bad, and social conscience was a good earner.

Bull Somerset, however, didn’t agree with Angel. His social conscience was so slight it barely existed.

So when the Policy Maker called upon the family, Claudia was suspicious.

“What you want?”

“I’d like a word with your partner, Mrs Shell.”

“Haven’t got one. I got rid of him. I’m a singleton now.”

“Whose is that van parked in the front, then? And aren’t you earning points for accommodation? Won’t get anywhere if you’re a singleton.”

“Tuf!”

Tuf, his face ablaze with freckles, eyed the bearded man, and folding his slabs of ginger meat arms stuck out his massive chest. "What is it you want, Mr Somerset?"

"Tuf, we understand you have a meeting set for this Saturday."

"Yep."

"We can't let that happen, Tuf. No meetings, you know that. There's a ban on meetings until further notice."

"You can't stop it though, can you? It's inclusion – what you lot stand for. We're walking for the Factory, and our kids. There's nothing you can do, Mr Somerset!"

"It's *democratic*," reiterated Claudia. "What this lot stands for. We got to fight for our kids. "

Tuf Daley leaned in the doorway of their shambolic home and squinted at the Policy Maker through a stub of lashes. Dodgy, big bloke. And decided he couldn't be bothered.

"So, Tuf," Bull said in mock surprise. "Does this mean you will continue with the meeting regardless of my *request?* Be prepared to jeopardise your children's future for the sake of a bit of camaraderie? Whip up the *anti*, for something you don't even believe in?"

Bull was a hard man himself.

"Yeah, s'pose it does." Tuf leered down at Claudia. "Yeah, does mean that don't it, my little girl? And if any of us gets a difficulty, we know where to look."

Claudia squirmed in delight, and with a final withering glance at the Policy Maker, turned to her partner. "Come on, my big man, let's go and exercise our democratic right," she gurgled hideously.

Bull Somerset trudged from the estate. "As long as it doesn't result in any more of those revolting specimens," he muttered, and went to make his report.

* * *

Claudia had gathered her brood by the fountain. There was no water cascading from the iron fishes' mouths. The fish didn't have mouths. They didn't have heads either. Only the tails were mounted on steel pipes. It was symbolic.

The fountain was a sensitive gesture of late twentieth-century urban regeneration. The fact that its symbolism had outlived its representational form was – lost.

Tuf parked his ample backside on the steps leading up to the structure. A woman, dishevelled in tight sparkly dress, came up and began to talk to him. He jerked his head in Claudia's direction.

The woman wobbled over and talked to her.

A grey seeping of a man sauntered to the fountain and whistled. The woman turned, stuck her middle finger up in the air and resumed her conversation.

The man went away, looking back every so often and curling his lip.

"Can't treat your clients that way, Kite – you'll lose 'em, girl," cautioned Claudia

"Never lose him, a regular. Just have to tell them who's boss. I'm not his mother, at his beck and call. Anyway, I'm thinking of flying now."

A few feet away Tuf was listening. He eyed the woman through the shade of his light lashes. Kite wasn't bad as yats went, but where did she think she was going to find the girls to fly? "What, you trying to raise business with my Claudia?"

"No, Tuf," she simpered. "Mind you, if there was ever anybody who could work it, your missus would be the one – knows how to handle people. Wouldn't lose any business with her as boss! Hah! Only joking. But you gotta live. Nothing else I can do. And there's this . . ." She scratched her hand, disturbing a new layer of skin over a wound.

Claudia shifted her weight and nodded to her partner. "We're the *damaged*. Look how bad she is. Show him your neck, Kite."

The yat showed Tuf her neck.

He wasn't interested and noted the ridge of pink flesh beneath.

"Everybody helps everybody else, Tuf," Kite leered. "New Britain says that." And grabbing her breasts with both hands, weighed them as if they were produce in a market.

"You'll be at the meeting, then?" interrupted Claudia sharply.

"Try and stop me," Kite cackled, twisting her face slyly towards her friend. "Have you heard about that *other* place, with the church?"

Claudia hadn't.

Kite sighed with satisfaction. "Coolton Ascent. It's up on that big hill, belonged to the church – was a madhouse once. The Council was going to pull it down but kept on changing their minds."

"Oh *that* one," interjected Claudia tartly. "I know all about Coolton Ascent. The daft lot go there. We should have got that ourselves. The old council was in then. They promised us that." She switched to Tuf "Do you remember the old Council? We could have had that big house. They were going to turn it into flats once." She shook her head, another bitter memory of betrayal. "There's not many of the old Council left. When you think about it, we've done really bad out of this lot."

"It's nice up there," continued Kite, feeling the simmer.

"How do you know?"

"Somebody that worked on the inside – bit of painting and stuff – they told me. An old woman runs it. And where do you think they got the money to do it up?"

Tuf stretched and yawned. "I'm hungry," and went to assemble his offspring, running riot around the place.

Kicking up the brake of the pram chair, Claudia also raised herself.

"Wit's grown. Looks like Tuf," offered Kite, teasing out the last threads of contact.

Claudia couldn't resist. "Where did they get it, then – the money?"

"That bastard, Beat."

"Oh, I knew *that*," Claudia lied. "See you at the meeting. And," she added with grim piety, "keep your mouth clean round my family."

Carmine

Here was a situation Tezzie Beat wished to avoid, the one she had always dreaded: a public showdown – her husband was going to be disgraced. Something about that Factory and poison. Very unpleasant. All those years of building up a reputation, kudos, fantastic parties, holidays, nice conversations with intelligent men, fine collections – all gone. For her, that is.

Why? Is there anybody else?

A ravishing creature, she had imbued her daughter with some semblance of self-assurance – if not by coaching and nurture then by heredity, and Saprah was becoming quite the little star in her own right – the same luxuriant locks, exquisite skin, although that came from Sedge too, of course. He had skin. But it was Tezzie who'd started it all. She was the source: almond eyes, cupid mouth, the determined little chin.

Mothers have to hang onto that awareness, their origins. A self too readily subsumed in the drab nothingness of cardiganed maternity – condemned to endure endless years of people addressing baby first, and then coming round to Mom.

'Gorgeous, isn't she, Tezzie? Oh, isn't she lovely? How are you, my dear . . ? Oh look at that little poppet!'

Christ! Stuck out there with pram and toys, nothing for oneself. The husband also a sacrifice on the altar of genealogy.

Where did Sedge go? He was a wonderful man, once. So gracefully clever and stylishly wealthy – that was very appealing. And a lover you could only dream of. Well, everybody else did. O.K, there were certain things regarding longevity but if one squeezed and panted, remembering this was because he found one so unbearably desirable, it sort of made up for it. A frenzy of desire, and Tezzie did invoke that in men.

But she had given up the men. They no longer interested her, except this odd one who had caught her eye. Very odd.

And since this affair of Sedge's, with the flame-haired Foddly, Tezzie hadn't been quite the same.

Of all the creatures he could have picked, she was about the most unsuited. Pathetic. No gumption whatsoever. Her people were well-heeled, the mother a cold cod, who knitted and did things for the old guard. Foddly Shaw was as streak of lightning that had only the right to strike once, but she'd left the scorched-earth effect. Was that the same as frenzied?

Tezzie was thinking all this whilst clearing out Saprah's room. The girl was helping her. "Mommy, there's a nice picture of you."

"Let me see. No, it's ghastly. Throw it away."

"I'm going to keep it. You've got your arm around me."

"Do what you like, but I don't want you showing it to anyone. Cut me out of it."

"But then it wouldn't have your arm."

"Then leave the damn arm, you silly girl."

"No one will know it's you."

"Do they have to know? You can be such an irritating, whining child. I don't actually care *what* you do with it."

The girl sat on the edge of the bed.

"Look, I'm sorry, Saprah. Oh, for God's sake, don't you start! I have enough with your bloody father."

"It's not that. I don't want to leave Daddy. He's very sad."

"Oh, we're all very *sad,* darling. Life is sad." Tezzie flopped down next to her daughter. "Mommy's tired of all these problems, I want you to go to auntie."

"Again? She's overseas. I hate that quarantine place. I'd rather go to Angel's."

"Are you crazy? Angel Brown – a twaddly, tweedy thing like her? Anyway, you'll be much safer out of here altogether. I'd rather you went right away."

The girl bent forward and peered up at her mother. "Safer? Why, what's going to happen?"

Tezzie turned away, her chin unexpectedly quivering, eyes overflowing. She began to swing her leg as if was a lever on a pump, and if she swung hard enough, the flow would cease. Felt her daughter's hand on her arm. Wanted to flick it away but realised she couldn't. Something had stuck. A little bit of the mother nothingness had rubbed itself in, or her out. "Nothing's going to *happen,* Saprah. It's just that I would rather you went . . . away. . . If you don't want to . . ."

"I'll go. I always do. What about you?"

"Oh, mommy's got things . . . I have to do things." A swift scan of her daughter's face. A total stranger. She'd made her that. Had all the signposts to familiarity, like a walk in the park, but you don't need to feel, to be anybody, when you walk in the park. "I don't honestly think I'm very good for you, Saprah. I just don't seem to be able to learn how to take care of baby."

Perhaps this was not the sort of conversation a mother should have with her child, a girl of twelve.

Yet, if it's the last one they have, each word should be weighed like gold.

* * *

Bug had taken Freda's body back to Scotland.

Even though she had never said directly, Sal knew his wife would want to be buried at home, and for years he'd confided to his son that's where she should be. Sal had been a watchful man after all, Freda a quietly independent spirit. And they could always visit, it's no distance.

Life's the long haul.

Bug was feeling stronger. Rill had given him some care. He knew Foddly was away for a while and could come and go around the House.

It wasn't a question of avoidance, more a fear of making contact.

Ignoring the Abbess as she prepared lunch, he perched on the kitchen table and ate a sandwich. When he'd finished, he gathered the crumbs in his hand, threw them in the bin, jumped down and left the room.

Sonjia heard his truck start up, and shook her head. "I sometimes wonder, Glastonbury . . ."

* * *

Of all the moves Tezzie could have made that day, this was the worst, and the best. Lessons are exhilarating if you can learn, a total humiliation if you can't. Irony is an acquired taste and those bent on acquiring, in the material sense, should realise that the fun of the game is in the losing – everything.

Hilarious.

A car had brought her to the barn. She'd have to call it back, wasn't sure when this would be.

The driver helped her take the paintings from the boot and popped a small case on the path.

She gave him first a hand-written note and arranged a meeting for the next day, then some keys. "I may be in contact," she said. "If not, I'll see you tomorrow."

The driver nodded. The car bumped along the dirt track.

Struggling with her packages, Tezzie glanced around. The barn was deserted. What, in Christ's name, possessed her to come here? The pretext was so obvious as to be laughable.

What time was it? Five-to. The sort to be punctual. Clearly obsessive.

She heard the truck swerving with adroit determination, competent handling. Brakes.

Bang on the dot.

Heard the door slam, footsteps clicking. She busied herself over the case, settling her hair.

Bug didn't say anything. He went to the front door, kicked it open and held it back for her to pass. With one boot on the wood, he swiftly scooped up the paintings and deposited them noiselessly on the floor of the barn. Ushering her in, he disappeared to the far end of the room. Sound of water.

She stood by the door, barely breathing, taking it all in. Bridget Riley, Rousseau, a Waterhouse. And a bloody stained glass window. Robbing cathedrals now! Well, eclectic is not the word, she decided. Random blitz, call it what you like he was a thieving magpie – furniture, carpets, no order it seemed, collection for collection's sake – a Moorcroft vase stuffed with flowers, plants trailing healthily from garish jardinière, shelves laden with books. Those too.

He emerged from the bathroom. "Seat," he suggested without concern.

She selected an ordinary chair.

"Drink?"

"That would be nice. What do you have?" she said, slipping off her coat.

Sylph-like in a pencil-sharp dress, its deep crimson clinging to creamy skin, Tezzie crossed her legs, a judicious slit in the satin. Well, it was spring.

"What do you like?" he asked.

"Er . . . vodka, brandy, whatever."

Brushing past her, a rush of cool air, intimately distant, he reached down and pulled out a bottle from a rack beneath the table. "Can do better than that. The old man had a good year – damson." And set down two glasses.

"Is that Glastonbury, the old man I met at the dance?" The name rolled like marbles from her tongue.

Bug smiled, a twitch beneath his moustache. "Yes," and handed her a large glass. "Well, what have you brought for me?"

"I wasn't going to bring them at all – the little game you played with me the last time we met, at the party – remember?" She sipped the wine, full of fruit, and again, powerful, then placed her glass on the long table.

Bug smiled once more, charming and without scruple.

Unwrapping the packaging, she became flustered. Her host came to the rescue, a flurry of proficient fingers as the canvases were exposed.

Her turn to smile, a little fix of certainty midst the doubtful artefacts.

He picked up a painting and squinted, then put it to one side, plucked another from the pile and sat down with it.

She noted his skin, different from the last time; blemished. Yet there was still the hint of boyishness, a gingery face, with that beard. Looked very young with his hair loose, the nose slightly aquiline, flared nostrils. Temper?

He turned, as if knowing she was staring. Eyes blue, penetrating, just for a fraction, but they had the whole measure of her.

"Ah, is that the Paul Klee?" she queried, winsome.

"Is it? If so, gives new meaning to his comment: '*Taking a line for a walk . . .* '"

She looked blank.

"I presume these are your husband's."

She folded her arms. Cheeky little . . . "Actually, they're mine. All of them. I bought them, chose them."

"What, *all*? Oh dear."

"What do you mean, 'oh dear'? If you're not interested, Bug, just say so. I'll take them back."

"I'm not interested. In *those*."

Her stomach stirred just below the rib cage. "Don't play with me."

"I'm not. It was you who arranged the meeting. There's always a risk of disappointment, from both sides. We know that. I simply said I'm not interested – in those."

Tezzie tilted her head, face soft in the harsh interrogation of the room with it halogen lights "I am a woman," she issued slowly, "who speaks her mind, Bug."

"Well, that won't take long, will it, Tezzie?"

The plate was close to hand. It shattered on the side of an enamelled stove.

He just sat there and said nothing. So she threw another. Madness. He was a stranger really, and she was doing this. Dish after cup after vase. Good names and mediocre, all cracking and breaking. So that's what he thought. "Who the fucking hell are you to cast off my possessions, dismiss me? How dare you insult me. You've done this before! So fucking superior, you little . . . worm. What are you? How come you own so much? Know about so many things, with your snivelling little upbringing? You're a nobody!" she shrieked. "Nobody! A short-arsed . . . stunted growth freak . . . Arrested development. Well, you and your witchy little tartlet . . "

Then aware he wasn't responding was lost for insults. "All these people you know," she rallied weakly, "I know people too. You are nothing – give me some more wine, nothing!"

Bug pointed to a bottle on the table.

Grabbing it with as much dignity a grab can muster, she poured heavily into her glass and slumped down. "What is it with you? What is it with *me*, for that matter?" she admitted with surprising candour. "My husband is finished. Do you have any music in this place? A piano? What would be the point? You couldn't play like Sedge."

"No," Bug assured her. "I couldn't play like him."

"You should have killed the bastard when you had the chance."

"I probably did, after you'd done it, of course. So when he finally gets his deserts, he'll have been killed . . . three times, at the very least," he gauged brightly.

Tezzie laughed, a gush of relief, and spilled her drink.

"Go on, have some more," offered her host gently. "How about that music?"

Time seemed to elapse, minutes soaked up by dusk. He was looking at her and her stomach was melting. His face and eyes, those high cheekbones, a mouth oozing from beneath that moustache, made her want to throw things again, and then realised it was excitement, adolescent fever. "I don't want to play, not anymore. I've had enough of games . . . I just want . . ." Couldn't say it, bring herself to ask.

Bug was over by the dais, lighting candles, halogen lamps off. "What do you like? Blues. . . No? Shostakovich?"

"Oh, God, not him."

"Nina Simone – heard of her?"

"Vaguely."

"I'll choose for you, something *especially* for Tezzie."

Tears just sprang from her. That's how Sedge would say it.

Piano, singing, a voice she didn't recognise, deep, rich. It was very fast . . . Made her want to dance.

Love me or leave me, let me be lonely . . . You won't believe it but I love you only . . . I'd rather be lonely than happy with somebody else . . .

She rose. Bug had his coat off, wore strange trousers, the velvet voluminous at the leg, tight at the hips. She took his hand. He took her wrist, his fingers gripping till they marked her skin. It was the narrow gold ring on his left hand, digging into her.

Then quick and loose they moved. And Bug so lissom, like a ballet dancer, swinging her round.

She was taller than him and slipped off her shoes. No more singing for a while, a long stretch of piano, twizzling around close then far.

And: *Have it today to give back tomorrow . . . my love is your love . . . your love is my love . . . no love for nobody else.*

Quiet. Something else.

"Astor Piazzolla . . . 'We really must sometime,' Tezzie."

Ghastly, ghostly, step, step. Pause. Heard this before. Screeching from what must be an accordion, or a sick violin – a hollow aching call – longing syncopated, scattered, shattered chords cast adrift on a blazing beach. Step, step. His soothing hand on her back, an inferno. Cool fingers rippling down her pebble spine, collecting breath quenching as spray. Pause.

But she was here and wearing a dress, wasn't she? What was it? The crimson satin. Looked down. The sleeves were hanging off in ribbons, her shoulders bare.

In a gasp of air the sound was split, hair fraying then split again, a column of pain, a follicle shredded until it was showers of red and gold – this time maddeningly pleasurable.

"Tango? *Libertango*."

Tezzie hadn't noticed it happened so quickly. He had his shirt off. When did that happen? He drew away, unravelling what seemed like sheets of colour. Unfurling clothes like flags. A spinning sound magician unspinning her – horrible and wonderful, determined tearings.

Silence. He was completely naked himself now and in a different rhythm. His mouth on her neck, flipping her back until she was as loose as silk on his wrist, dragging her by that fabulous hair, onto the table, up she went and over. Spread out like a banquet on a hard cold table.

He had sprung up crouching over her, an incubus. "Not interested in you, either," he whispered through his eyes, the aurora an icy remnant of blue. "But I am hungry. We'll eat slowly. You like that, want it to last . . ."

He was hungry, greedy. Music back. Piano? A ravenous wolf, playing the piano in the sea, the worst of her most diabolical nightmares and she welcomed him – incredible as an underwater tango.

Dancing down her, he bit and scratched, his mouth filled with revenge, feasting on reprisal, a crime against the heart – himself. A wriggly shrieking voyage down her stomach, clamouring above a violin dashed across waves.

Lifting her up, he sank his teeth on her thigh tongue slithering upwards, burrowing out the hidden sense and paring it. Knew all about the serpent, how to tease and lunged at its tail, watching it writhe and squirm until the colour of its venom screamed. Heard it burn as he entered, travelling from coccyx to pituitary

Cruel and pointless punishment, why didn't he stop?

Tezzie focused on the low rough beams above her head, the ceiling lost in dark, a narrow line of windows just below. She noticed the moon, bald and big, a very hot moon bouncing to that painful music. The windows and beams shook. Or was it her being shaken, pounded by him? A seismic shift along her spine crushed into the table so hard felt she might break. Cries slipped from her throat, unforced, natural utterances. Had never been handled with such ferocity, felt so near to ends she became alive. Purpose, passion. She was in love with him, had been all along. That's why she'd broken everything and would again, because he'd broken her.

And then he called, for Foddly.

He burst out, power spilling. Through a blur of falling colours, saw her face turned to him, eyes searching for unison, and twisted it away.

The loss again. Silence, an endless grieving space.

Separating from her, cold as mourning, away, distant, he was gone.

A hard, capable woman, Tezzie believed she was competent in the ways of the body and the heart, shook.

He was lying in the tub, wouldn't look at her. Was she that bad? "Have I contaminated you, Bug?"

"I'm already there. It's your own skin you're thinking of."

"You'll get over her. People do get over . . . lovers." She looked away. "My clothes . . . They're all in shreds."

"My china, it's all in pieces."

She was dressed, a ludicrous bright-pink skirt and top from that optimistic case. A frilly nothing, that's what she was. Should wear those funny trousers like him, and some wellies. It may not be too late for change. "Keep the stuff. I don't want it," she said

"I'll drop it off at the station tomorrow."

"There's no Visi installed here, I can't make my connection, Bug. Is your truck out of the question?"

"Take a bike."

"I don't know how – I've never ridden one."

He dressed without once showing his face. Snatching up a leather coat, left the barn, she following.

The main road came too soon for a woman not used to walking, even with bruises, in shoes that leaked and a skirt that had no leg room.

He took her to the tram depot, the one serving the Factory.

Heart sinking, she glanced at her watch, and saw it was ten. Four hours she'd been with him. All that time, or so little.

The night shift would have come in by now. Would he see her to the tram, past the gates, in case anybody recognised her? Tezzie Beat, travelling on the same tram as the workers? Would never have thought it possible. Something dreadful had happened.

The Factory in view. The depot.

Bug turned back without a word.

*

When Tezzie arrived at the station the following morning, the packages were there for collection, all wrapped with old-fashioned string. No note, knew that because she tore off the paper and searched every inch.

Handing the paintings to her driver. He could do what he liked with them.

Thought she saw the taillights of Bug's truck. Heart swung. She was mistaken.

Bug was miles away, walking, his skin burning, wondering how long he would have to pace out this fire.

Should have touched Foddly that morning, kept her weight and colour on his fingers, the imprint, the language of her face in his hands, its idiom salvaged, a transmigration of form to this silent country. "I can't live like this, but you'll never get rid of me, sweetheart. Just won't happen."

"What am I supposed to do? The whole thing was set up before I was even born – hardly what you'd call a fucking fiefdom. I never had a chance. Not a chance!" Sedge pleaded with the dapper man suffused in smoke before him. In supplication as if to a divine being who could hand down beatification, absolution.

But the man said nothing and the smoke drifted to Sedge, who coughed slightly and wiped his eyes. "They wanted me to carry on the business, Gul. Never uttered a dickie about what it was! We've been in this God-forsaken parish for donkeys' years. Go back . . . I don't know, we go back . . . fifteenth-century, at least."

"Ah! Marauding peasants working the Lord of the Manor – comely wenches falling in and out of the ancestral bed?" suggested the other man at last. "There's nothing noble about going back. You would *not* like to know the length of my curvy lineage. Dark, slithering days, Sedge, blacker than yours now, but nonetheless decisive. Yes," he added with some satisfaction. "It is a comfort that, decision."

"Don't get rampant again – allusions to that devil shit – I can't stand it!" Sedge paced to the French windows, grilles so thick couldn't see out. Then back. "Didn't work, did it?"

"What's that, Sedge?"

"The piano, the looks. This shit's bigger than any of it."

"And the weather, of course," added Gul closely. "Conditions always play a strong part. Mind you, it wasn't until the nineteenth-century the phrase was coined. It had existed but the consciousness hadn't been ready for the coining of it, so to speak." He passed an amiable hand through the air, then proceeded to remove what must have been a strand of tobacco from his tongue, and smiled. "Pathetic fallacy."

"Fallacy?"

"Yes, Sedge. No *phallus*, this time. The crackling of thunder, the roar of storms, bolts of lightning across a leaden sky and then the fatal blow. Wouldn't work on a fine day with a light, westerly breeze. Blame the weather and be done with it – and that was set up long before you were born."

The politician had given up listening and was over by the Visicom. He squatted on a low stool then regretted it – and got to his feet. "The rivers have risen again. It will take one more downpour like January's, and we'll lose another section of coastline. The land isn't recovering and we aren't getting any support from the city."

"Ah, that's because you were prepared to go it alone, Sedge – a proud little boy. The provinces are not going to feed well from their own recourses for long. Not cock of the yard now . . . Marauding peasants, I'm afraid. You do have a comely wench but alas, too young. Mind you . . ." The journalist flicked down his suit. "We haven't finished. It's not over yet. We have a few more hearts to win. Tomorrow we'll have you in that Town." He tittered. "You know, I still have your picture on my wall, and you are a very attractive man. Even now."

Sedge placed himself at a safe distance noting they were the same height. Sure he was the taller. Was he shrinking, or was this sarcastic bastard even gaining on him in inches? And those eyes: cool and blue, jaw almost classical in its definition, short black curls, never a glistening lock out of place – unless he wanted it. The mouth . . . 'Good God! Get a grip, old man,' he told himself. 'He's not a fucking woman!'

Gul must appeal to them as well – they often move both ways. Tezzie had murmured about him. What was his weakness? Did he even have one?

"How *is* your wife?" enquired Gul, picking up a fedora from a porphyry surface.

"I have no idea."

"Not even cock of the bed. Could work that way too. Vulnerable – do 'vulnerable' at the Loyalty store." The journalist waved and left the room.

Sedge rolled his eyes. Loyalty Store? Kissing babies next. Babies? Shit.

Parked in front of her window on one of surveillance stretches, Claudia gleaned the monochrome horizon. She knew all the comings and goings of neighbours. The dumping of cars, computers, household goods; the fights, the fleeing from marital homes and the subsequent re-entry of partners; the Services and sirens as they made their diurnal tour to clear wreckage and waste. Claudia sat and witnessed, soothed by the rhythm, enjoying the entropy. So at the jaunty gait of an alien festooned in flowing cloak and brightly coloured trousers crossing her manor, she was roused to suspicion.

Her son, Speak had noticed too, and tugged at her dress. "What's that, ma? What's that doing here?"

"Get your dad." Dragging her fingers through her lank hair, she straightened her clothes, stuffed her feet into a pair of slippers, left the flat, and thudded down the lobby to the main door. Before crossing the squares of balding lawns she stopped halfway down the path, clinging to the heat of home. Unsure, she called for Tuf.

The big man appeared in the broken doorway, awaiting instructions. Speak at his side.

Claudia approached the cloaked stranger. "Who you looking for?" she called.

He ignored her, producing a bottle from his cloak.

"If you want anybody, we'll tell you where they are," informed the woman, gaining on him, a subtle semaphore twixt her and the distant Tuf. "We know everybody on this estate."

"Good," he replied, uncorking the bottle and putting it to his lips.

He was funny-looking, skin shiny as if he had the damage, a pointy gingery beard, and when he turned, his eyes were filled with hate. She'd never seen so much in anybody. Could be that drink he'd had, but they made her stomach wobble. Maybe he belonged to Gul, and MEJA.

"I have nothing to do with them," he advised her, pausing mid draught.

Claudia couldn't recall saying anything.

"A reconnaissance, madam," he continued, returning the bottle to the crimson folds of his cloak. "Although this place won't be around much longer."

"What you talking like?" Annoyed, she waddled up, her own little eyes burning, and gave her best shot. "I just hope you're not from the Factory. You've got a lot to answer for. This whole Manor's going to the meeting."

"Not from the Factory, or anywhere. I'm just exercising my democratic right to walk where I choose in this repulsive little Town."

"Oh, we're that, are we? Well, look at you! I don't want my kids upset by the looks of you! Get off my Manor, frightening my kids. Now!"

The man grinned. "With you as their mother they should be used to horrors," and laughed, right in her face. Nasty.

"Tuf!" the woman thundered. "Get here . . . this . . ." She couldn't finish, incoherent from the insult of it all.

Tuf ambled heavily over, his brow a hood of sand, face blasted with sand too – a hard man who could wipe out the little freak who upset his Claudia. "What's it you want?"

"And who are you to ask?"

"Kill him, Dad!" Speak was pummelling at his father's legs and kicking up stones from the path.

"Get back in!" Tuf, raised his fist to his son, and turning to the stranger, bore down. "I live here, mate, and you better go."

"I don't think you have any right to tell me what to do." The stranger trawled his gaze across the estate, to the cars ripped open, the concrete buildings disfigured with graffiti, the burnt out windows. "I certainly wouldn't want a child of mine to be raised here," he contemplated mildly. "Still, you don't mind, do you? Only ruin it if was any good. Couldn't trust you with anything. *This* is what you are, and now the authorities have to take it away. Know what it reminds me of?"

Tuf didn't, and was astounded the man had so much time to say these words, but he had. Endless time. He rolled up his sleeves, hands moist, knuckles itching. Beside him, Claudia was panting, hungry for war. Beyond, windows were being opened, a pause, swallowing.

"A dirty protest," the stranger concluded. "What children do when they want attention."

Tuf was looming over him, trembling, trying to sustain the lust for fight. Then the little man looked up at him, and he couldn't think. The eyes – horrible things, didn't want to fight those. More pain in there than he could ever inflict. Why would you want to hit someone like that? They could just turn round and kill you with one look. What was Tuf to do? Everyone was watching. "What is it you want?" he asked once more, the fight draining from his words.

"Just looking. I have a *right,* you know."

Claudia couldn't understand.

Tuf was pale. He gestured to their block.

"Why aren't you protecting Claudia?" she panted. "You're supposed to protect your little girl from nasty people."

Behind them, the stranger was walking away, head bowed, very slowly leaving, cloak flapping.

The couple trudged thoughtfully back to their belligerent son, waiting by the doors

"Who was it then?" demanded the fat boy.

"Something else. There's some people you can't touch." Tuf wondered how he knew this. "They've got so much in 'em whatever you do, don't make no difference." He struggled with the poetry of it all. "Like hitting a brick wall."

Speak was disappointed in his father. "Tuf's a fluff. You're scared of bricks. I'll kill him ma, if dad can't. I ain't standing for my ma being spoke to like that."

His mother delivered a swipe that passed as affection at her well-trained son, and nodded. "Yeah, Tuf, you were. Claudia don't like her big man being scared."

By the time the riotous family had sat down at their kitchen table before a pile of food, Claudia was reflecting quite fondly on the strange man and how he'd held out against her partner. "Where'd he come from, that's what I want to know? You seen him around, Tuf?"

"Sure, I've seen him somewhere."

"He's an alien, a *special* one," confirmed Claudia, a little greed softening her heart. "I like that cape thing, all shimmery and nice. Can't you go and find him and bring him back?" she squirmed.

"Nah, he's the sort what'll only turn up if he wants something. Pleases 'isself." The man stopped, mid bite. "That where I've seen him."

"Where?"

But Tuf had already forgotten what he was going to say.

***

Bright and early, fresh as bullets, their children already caged in a play centre for the day, Claudia and Tuf presented themselves at the Loyalty Store.

The couple had never actually been close to the politician. 'Walking' and meetings had been held, the 'anti' whipped up about the man, but they'd never actually seen him in the flesh. In fact, the pair had not seen anyone who had been in Video Mass or on Visi before, and weren't quite sure how you dealt with them. The famous weren't really human – they'd been somewhere else and come out 'trained'.

It's all very well mouthing-off in the streets, banging a few heads, smashing bottles against privileged doors, but when it comes down to having something cogent to say, some clean bit of jousting, well that's a different matter altogether.

Kite had warned, with all the presage of a soothsayer, that she'd heard regular people talk at these kinds of meetings 'and look quite nice. But when you saw them on the Visi, they were speaking something completely different and looking like a friggin' gorm. Mind what you do in front of MEJA,' she'd uttered onerously. And for a short while, Claudia experienced a genuine respect for the woman, and Tuf acknowledged the yat for being something more than just the one he refused to pay for.

It didn't last. Things never did for Kite.

The Store was packed. Sedge Beat was not the only Law Leader in New Britain, but it certainly seemed as if he had to answer for the folly of the entire party. And, of course, the Factory.

Agitators were outside the front of the building when he arrived, and at the back for when he left. Inside, staff had cleared shelves and set up a rostrum. A photograph of the politician had been posted on the far wall.

Not a bad place, the Loyalty Store now it was empty. With great stained glass windows adorning the vaulted ceiling, it looked like a cathedral, a naked monument to Mammon, and some of the near-destitute and the short-term housed made a note of its generous accommodation for future times. After all, Beat owned this too, and according to his fables, their lot should be in for a kingdom sometime.

The Services rustled around, the military treading softly, frisking here, a spot search there.

Under the steady scrutiny of halogen lights, the audience was subdued, necks straining. Where was the piano? No piano.

Somebody coughed. Eyes turned. With an alacrity that amazed even themselves Tuf and Claudia had forged their way through the crowd, paring bodies like wheat, and in a matter of seconds, were settled demurely at the front.

The public when they are being the *people,* can't help themselves. Even though they hated the man, despised what he had done, found his politics risible, there was a shiver of awe. And they clapped. A flutter of joining palms, becoming louder, applauding the politician as he made his flawless way to the podium.

Maybe he wasn't that bad. He *was* the leader and here were they breathing the same air. Surely that counted for something?

Claudia gripped Tuf's hand proud to be in front of Sedge Beat, the man they'd worked so hard to loathe. Oh, and the way of him! Tall, wasn't he tall? And young. What was he wearing? Silvery suit. Nice the way he was turning down his cuffs like that. A smile, a little cough to that clenched hand, a nod to the other man. Oh, *him.*

"Gul, always around. Runs the Video Mass. Know him personally," someone whispered loudly.

"Where's Beat's other half?"

"Yeah, where's the missus?"

"She's can't make it . . . Ain't got nothing to wear."

"Never bothered 'er before now."

"Ill . . . She's ill. That other bloke said that. Didn't you hear him?" yet another voice spoke up.

Murmurings and breaking words, heavy timber carried on catgut.

"Wife's dead."

"No wonder he looks so thin."

A call from the back. The reply came near the front. Faces turned, jaws protruded and attention leached from the speaking Leader.

"I ain't come 'ere to listen to you, mate, so shut the fuck up!"

A missile, hurled at the platform missed, its target. A child screamed. Bodies heaved. A heckler was carried from the auditorium.

Sedge Beat raised his voice, acknowledging and calming.

Claudia's wasn't interested in talking, and her attention was diverted by the strange antics of a boy a few feet from where they were standing. He must be another alien – they were all over the place, except this one had a face like a girl, blond hair, falling in ringlets on his short cape. Crouched on the floor like that, he looked as if he was about to pick out his prey – aiming an invisible gun and staring up, mad-eyed, at the politician.

"Look." She kicked Tuf. "Over there – the fluff. Why's he getting away with that? They can see what he's doing . . ."

"Because he belongs to the other one, MEJA, knocks it off," came the bald assessment.

"What, Gul? That ain't legal, Tuf. How old?"

"Not legal."

"Mind you, don't look like he'd live that long to enjoy himself."

Sensing the interest the boy had got to his feet, a lovely vision. He blew a kiss at the rostrum, and turning to Claudia, shook his golden curls, a little wave rippling across his fingers.

Claudia leaned forward so far she almost fell over.

The boy was approaching then stopped. Long, willowing body, hands lacing hips. "I'm going to kill him," he mouthed, and sashayed off.

"What'd he say? Who? Who's he gonna kill, Tuf?"

"Nobody. That sort don't do nothing. His dad worked at the Factory. Everybody who's there's gonna kill Beat. They'll never do nothing."

Claudia had had enough of the meeting. It was all under control. The whole event lacked lustre, guts. That boy though. "What's his name, Tuf?"

"Carlos something."

The lights were flickering, then bright snappings, men wheeling around with cameras on their shoulders. Another speaker took the floor. At the end of the rostrum, the loyal or the vigilant gathered to pat and shake.

On the floor, voices blowing like litter among the crowd. Small gatherings dusted into enclaves, then joining, turned to go.

Quietly following the crowd, Claudia's vast bulk emerged into the cool grey of an empty mid-morning, dissatisfied. Taking Tuf's arm she tried to salvage something from the day. "I reckon we've got a find there, big man."

"Who has? What you talking about?"

"That Carlos, he's damaged, isn't he? And if he's with Gul, doesn't that make a difficulty for *somebody*?"

Tuf couldn't understand. "It don't work like that, girl. They keep everything separate. Politicians, MEJA – they can do what they want. They don't mix it up."

A car went past. A few protestors banged on the window. A woman grabbed a wing mirror and wrenched it off. "Get out your motor, you jammy bastard! We all have to walk, so why don't you?"

"What went on in there is nothing real." Claudia observed phlegmatically.

A man in a tight-cut, dark suit slid past, walking briskly ahead, the boy Carlos by his side,

Claudia couldn't help it, just blurted out: "We're with you, Carlos! The damaged!" she screeched. "We're together, boy!"

Gul shot a look, his face summoned to an iron fist, eyes like gimlets.

The woman was taken aback. She could say what she liked. Free country. Then realised the journalist wasn't directing his venom at her, but to someone beside her. She hadn't even seen him: the little man who'd come to the estate. How long had he been standing there, smiling, at that Carlos? Claudia noted that too. Wasn't bothered by anybody. Didn't care.

The boy had rushed forward, all gush and tears. "Bug! Did you see me? I hate him. Just tell me when."

"Just be careful, Carlos," cautioned the man. "So long."

A small cameo, yet bursting with information. Bug, eh? Claudia was about to have another look at the stranger with the long cloak, but he'd vanished.

Carlos, she could take or leave, she decided, but this Bug – must have him! What Claudia Shell could do, with a special one like him?

When Foddly arrived at the Villa that evening, Sedge was already drunk.

He peered at her through swimming eyes. "I'm a shit aren't I? You can see why they want me hanging from a gibbet." Patting the couch, his hand slipped then he followed suit, eyes crossing. "I've been pissed since eleven, lovely girl. There is a point beyond which you cannot become any more pissed, and I reached that, fucking hours ago. . ." His eyes slid to her swollen profile in the doorway. "Jesus Christ! Did I do *that*?"

Face slithering back into view, hands clasping his mouth. "Why didn't we sort it out years ago, Fod? All this bollocks wouldn't have happened. You and me, making nice easy babies and . . . Instead of which I've got people wanting to kill me." His eyes rolled. "Do you want to kill me, sugar, for what I've done? Jeesus! I should have just fucked you in that house, that Gothick horror, years ago. That's what I wanted. I followed you there . . . on your little boneshaker, arse like a peach. Had my eye on that succulent little . . . Does *he* know that? Course he does . . . and I am a shit." He swerved up. "But you have to admit," he pointed out, finger wobbling. "No. Not even an honourable one."

Flopped back, hand over brow. "My wife, Fod. My wife, *Tezzie,* not Fod. D'you know what she's done? Apart from taking *my* paintings. You know what . . ?" He struggled and tried to keep the woman in focus. "Do you mind me swearing?"

Foddly was over on a stool, looking at her feet. This was dreadful, worse than she'd anticipated. "There're people waiting outside, Sedge. I had to sneak in the back way."

"There's always people. Always have been, always will be . . . *Prōles*."

"Sedge, they're waiting!"

"For what? You go and speak to them. Go on! Do it! You're part of the fucking dynasty, now. *Speak* to them!"

“I haven’t anything to say.” Foddly was frightened. He was out of control. Everything out of control, fear, men, nothing was safe, nowhere to go from threat, revenge. Her pulse battering the tips of her fingers.

“Sorry, Fod, I’m . . . pissed. Tezzie screwed your boyfriend . . . she really enjoyed telling me that, you know.”

In the hallway, nausea had overtaken fear. Foddly sat next to the cloakroom her legs in an uncontrollable tremor.

“Glastonbury! Glastonbury, please . . . Dad, why aren’t you here? I need you. Somebody please help me!”

A brick, she guessed, was hurled at the window, madness breaking in from outside. Then what chance did hers have of escaping?

Staggering up the stairs, she heard Sedge begin to sing. Another missile, sounds of sirens. She found Saprah’s room, all silk and softness on the bed, the scent of a child unsullied by this. Or perhaps no one escapes unharmed. “Glastonbury, please help me. I’m no good at this. Dad went and then . . . Now there’s no one but you.” She focused on a clock, an old-fashioned one with big numbers round the face, a foolishly benign face. Curling up, she snatched the pillow, folded it, and hugged it against her chest. “Actually, apart from . . . Bug, there’s only been you, Glastonbury. It was he who made me see you. Let me stay with you, come home. I think it was meant to be.”

A flutter of the inside shape. A kick from her stomach. Then another. The quick and the dead.

The summer was cool. Even at the end of July the sun had not embraced the season. Muggy days came, an easterly wind, cloudy skies. The hill that rolled down to the spinney had never warmed, its grass damp and chill.

A wicket gate led to the secret glade where the fairies were supposed to hide. Tumbling down one would have to take great care not to disturb them.

Today was not for tumbling, Foddly's belly too curved. It was a secret visit though, and she skidded on the muddy slope, hanging onto Glastonbury's arm. "You do love me?" she asked.

He nodded.

"More than anyone else?"

"Is that a fair question?"

"I don't want to share you with anyone."

"I see. Have to share yourself soon, give up these exclusive walks with old men . . ."

"No I won't. Nothing will make me give up these, not even a baby. That won't stand in my way."

Glastonbury stroked his chin thoughtfully and guided her into the glade, the leaves above their head, a mosaic of light.

"This is a palace I'll always return to." She rested against a tree and plucked a leaf. The branch sprang back, quivering. "When I was little, Glastonbury, I had the most wonderful pair of shoes. They looked like chestnuts all polished and shiny. I remember, one day looking at my legs all tanned, my white socks and those shoes stuck on the end. I was so happy; I decided I would never forget it, that moment, the way the world looked with my legs sticking out. I haven't and I won't. I'll always have that memory."

"A diamond view?" suggested the man.

"You understand most things, Glastonbury . . . But I don't think you know . . . how I really am. If you did, I don't think you'd like me at all. I don't have one – a '*me*' to like. Just fooled everybody. A bit of a fraud."

Glastonbury was walking between the trees, snapping back the hogweed. He wore that old coat, a silk scarf around his neck, hands always . . . well, never really clean. Fingers soiled from recent toil, gardening, painting, living and working in the life. And eyes, forever green – didn't match him, the rest of him.

Then motionless – a second illuminated, ancient eyes, skin like muslin, transparent and so fragile it seemed as if he could blow right away. Or maybe he hadn't been there either – a vaporous thought transposed upon solid form, coming from a dream so strong, a need so imperative she'd made him real. Could one fraud blame another?

It was a simple thing like a child testing a daydream and letting the words out to see if they might fly. "Marry me, Glastonbury, so we can be real. I don't care how old you are. The Abbess will understand. We live together anyway. We can have a *pure* marriage, not consummated, although . . ." Foddly studied her own hands, smooth white skin, her round stomach beneath the cotton shirt. "We wouldn't need to but if you . . . I would find you beautiful, because it is that." Right next to him now, close to his face, looking upwards. A sliver of blue light through the trees – arches numinous with light, like going to church. A hymn of light. Had that with Bug. Placing her head on the lapel of his coat, felt his hand stroking her hair. "I can't manage on my own, Glastonbury. It's too hard."

Silence. A sky filled with blue silence.

"I've seen a whole load of blackberries over the other side." He pulled off his scarf. "Help me collect some.

Scrambling up the hill, the two found the brambles, fingers stained with juice, they picked the fruit, talking all the while with no further mention of marriage or dreams that wouldn't fly.

* * *

"She hasn't taken to it well. Some don't, you know, Glastonbury. Clearly inherited her grandmother's frailty. I expect it will be down to me to arrange everything." Sonjia tinkered about in the chaotic basement at Coolton Ascent. "Oh, and do not say: 'I told you so!'" she warned, shaking a damp edition of *Pilgrim's Progress* at her friend.

"That girl's not equipped, and whether you like it or not, you knew the risks," replied the man wearily.

"We did it together, Glastonbury. The boy was orphaned in death, had the same needs as any other child . . . he was cast adrift."

"And what about his reception in this life?"

"We can't be responsible for that. Maybe it's never going to be the right condition for this poor soul to return, he'll always have to struggle."

"Have you ever thought, Sonjia? Stopped to wonder . . . ?"

"Glastonbury, my dear, before you pontificate, tell me, why do you to stay down here in the crypt, cellar or whatever it is? There are perfectly good rooms upstairs. Your paintings and books are crinkling. Let some light in."

"I'll be going home soon."

"Pity. We have so much work to do. There are more out there who haven't made the transition from flesh to spirit, hoverers, ones reluctant to leave, or waiting to be reborn. . . " She scraped back her hair until the moon-face pecked by decades of madness was a globe of wobbling silver. "I used to hear him calling after she went. A kind of howling, haunting – I cannot describe the pain."

"You'll have plenty of opportunity."

"We couldn't leave him out there. . . This will be his kingdom. There's a place for him here, in our Palace of Souls."

"There are so many tragic endings which never really finish, Sonjia. Unendings waiting for completion. Beginnings. He may already be here."

"Are you suggesting a mother does not sense her own child? I *know,* and this is the way it will be."

"Sonjia, he is not *your* child, no one's child. This is the trouble. We have nowhere for him to go if this fails."

The woman gathering up a loose silk gown got to her feet and made ready to leave. "You can't deny me this, like you denied me everything else. It was an idea I had when you were still *James,* or whatever name it was. You don't talk about the past – where *you've* been. Maybe you also wish to abandon it." She traced a finger over the embroidered rose on her sleeve. "I heard the girl and her 'proposal' but you and I will always be connected by this. We won't look back. I won't allow it – spoiling the future with their miserable history."

And as if already dignified by some future victory, she bent down and briefly touched his cheek with her lips. His face was cold, marble-white from cold. "Come back for me, Glastonbury when my time comes, because I'm afraid that for now, we are going to part good company."

Glastonbury did not stir as she left. He sat contemplating the shadows in the caliginous view. No long visions. After a while, he roused himself and made his way to a small kitchen.

Sawdust on the quarry tiles, planks of wood in the sink.

He returned to the living room and picked up his old coat, then dropped it back on the chair. In the alcove he lifted the lid of a leather trunk and drew out a long cloak.

Slamming his door he clattered up the steps, past the porch and crossed the grounds. He swept though the gates, down the hill, his cloak billowing, hair in a plait bobbing on the hood. A man of how many years, walking with such speed?

By the Factory, then the Town.

Another man approached Glastonbury as he arrived at the coast, following as he strode along the beach.

Rill waved and caught up with him.

The two spoke silently and stared at the sea.

"You've lived here a long time, Rill."

"Since the trouble in my own place, sir. I'm here because my folks came. I miss the land though. The man in the ships says he'll take me back."

"Tor? Don't believe everything that rogue says," Glastonbury grinned.

"He's making plans like the end already happened. He says it's going to be a colony and all them lot'll be sending the bad ones to him, to train."

"As long as they don't send them to us, eh, Rill?"

"He has the skill though, knows the language. May be of some help later . . . But he's a man who travels both ways and I ain't that certain he couldn't fall on the other side."

"Any of us can do that."

A shadow crept across Rill's face. "*Any* of us?"

"Have you seen Bug of late?"

"I help his friend, Carlos." The aborigine wiped a weathered hand across his mouth. Screwing up his face he scratched his head, uncomfortable next to an awkward truth. "There's something uneven about that young boy. Like moulting inside. His skin changes colour, now he keeps *other* company. Yep, Carlos could fall on the inside."

"We'll have to watch for that. And Bug. How do you feel about him?"

"That's your business, sir."

"I thought we shared, Rill?"

"He don't always see. He loves without seeing."

The early moon, a half in the indigo sky.

"Would any of us, if we saw?" Glastonbury began to pace the beach, calling across the sand. "The moon's like a sixpence falling out of a sailor's pocket tonight,"

Rill laughed. "I told *you* that!"

"And where does it fall?"

"In the sea. Swims there for a while, then gets caught so it can show itself again." Rill was leaving the shore, the wind behind him. "A blue-moon's a long time, sir. Surprised you let it happen."

Woad

September came with an Indian summer, its generosity, greater by far than August. The autumn flames were highest in October, and Foddly's day passed without word from Bug.

Bronzes and crimsons, where did the leaves come from? Foddly hadn't even noticed the trees had been so full, and here they were all fallen. Even in November the skies were blue, colours rising from the ground in mists, a halo about the world. The apple trees Glastonbury had planted years ago had blossomed this year, their fruit still thudding to earth.

She walked near the barn. Glastonbury had gone away and guessed it was to Bug. Didn't get too close, just enough to know she'd been there and imagine it was still her home.

The villa lay empty for a while. Sedge had gone on a nationwide expedition – a harvest for some.

In Town, people enjoyed the sun. No walking or meetings but they gathered, harvesting their own yields – subdued muted anger, breaths of golden death on the veins of a leaf. A drifting discontent landing with the softest fall.

A secret season.

Some time in November – no one can remember when, Foddly gave the call.

Screaming for him.

So he came. In his way.

They both did.

Glastonbury was there with Sonjia, efficient nurse, coaxing and eager.

Foddly hung onto Bug as if he were her last breath of life.

Couldn't push, it hurt too much.

"Don't make me push! I hate you!" she shouted at everyone. "I fucking, fucking hate you all. Let me out. I'm leaving. Put it back. I'm going home!"

"The head's showing . . . Hold on, sweetheart," urged Bug. "Baby's still in the caul. Hold on."

So she pushed.

"Push!"

So she held on.

Sonjia eased out the head, loosening the cord.

"Push!" Glastonbury shouted.

A sack leaking. Membrane. A tiny boy finding breath inside the sea.

"The fishermen think it's lucky – to arrive in the packaging is a rare thing," Sonjia heard herself say. "Where's Rill? He may like the sack." Kneeling, she fell to Glastonbury, eyes swollen with sea themselves. "Hold your little baby, Foddly," she whispered. "Your lovely baby." And cut the cord.

They all watched how Foddly took the child.

Cautiously, as if it were a doll.

"Let him rest on your skin," said Bug. "He wants to get to know you."

"What will you call him?" asked Sonjia as she inspected the placenta.

"Nothing. I don't know what to call him."

In the tiny cottage, unnamed baby lay sleeping, wrapped in layers of muslin and soft wool. A blanket was settled in a large drawer, a sheepskin on top.

"Let him stay on you as long as possible," Bug told her. "It's important the baby keeps close to your scent. Sleep when he does then he can suckle."

"Will you sleep with me as well?"

A couch was pulled over next to the thin bed, and Bug lay next to mother and son.

"I'm going to cut my hair off," she informed him miserably.

"Why?"

"So I won't recognise myself."

"He'll always know who you are, sweetheart. And so will I."

"But you won't come back. I wish he were ours and then you would."

Bug helped guide her nipple to the wriggling mouth.

"There's no milk coming," she said. "It's just tickling."

"He's getting something, there's enough. You'll have it by the truckload tomorrow, spurting it at the ceiling."

"How come you know so much?"

"I've made it my business."

Foddly tended her son letting him stay on her breast, although couldn't really understand what he was doing there. She watched Bug sleep, his clothes still on. He looked young and old all at once.

She was too tired to think. A baby in her arms. Too much feeling to have to think. All night the child cried, ripping her from comfort.

In the morning, Bug made some food and put the tray on the bed.

From his battered leather armchair, Glastonbury grinned up at her. "Warm now – our first fire of the season last night. How's the little lad?"

Foddly ignored him while she struggled with her shirt. "He doesn't seem to do anything but bleat."

"Hungry, I expect. Needs to feel welcome," said the old man mildly.

"You're another one who knows everything. Where's Bug gone?"

Glastonbury was holding her hand. Eyes steady and gentle, they calmed her for a while.

"Bug. Where is he? How long have you been here?"

"All night. I've been with you all night, you and your baby," he whispered. "Look, Sonjia's over on the couch. Rill's tucked up in the parlour, and I've brought you some nice breakfast."

She glanced to her side. "Bug? Wasn't he . . . here? Did I *imagine* him?"

Saw the infant in arms she didn't recognise as hers.

The Abbess was awake. She was standing, a peculiar shape on her already odd face, Glastonbury beside her, a curious expression too. Who were they, these crazy people? And what was this bundle on her stomach . . . screaming for something she couldn't give?

Maybe none of this was real either, and she'd wake up and start again.

*

Despite his visit, Glastonbury had not been able to persuade Bug to go back with him to the cottage to see Foddly, and he remained in the dark, dreams marching before him. But he spoke to her.

He saw the child come and his colour distressed him, a stranger in his own life – mother and child, strangers. They had no belonging, no connection, borrowing a reluctant love. Foddly wasn't the earth yet, given time, could have found some foundation. Not a resting place because she had nowhere to rest herself. "So this is your game, Glastonbury, using a vessel like her."

Leaving the barn that evening he walked a little distance in the woods talking to her all the while, but couldn't make it to her side. Just couldn't do it.

How easy it is when one has power, to use it. Yet to move away, draw back, may offer the greater influence, the longer view. One moment taken in pride or pain can make the distance from forgiveness incalculable, a journey to darkness from which some may never recover.

So near to bowing, to going back and catching the inner dream, to sliding next to her and gathering up the whole. But he couldn't bend. He'd loved her since he could remember loving, yet couldn't bend. Then he would have to break.

So close to ends beginnings are. But until an end is acknowledged, another season cannot arrive.

2016

Madder

Tiny cries in winter woods subsided, evened out. The space between demands lengthened and became a rhythm. Now winter had a colour. It was red.

Not a January known and relied upon, it seemed to seep from somewhere else, an unannounced disparate climate. It was warm. A mild, soft wind, disturbingly alluring tangled the branches around Coolton Ascent.

Like a treacherous lover preparing sweetness only to push the betrothed from their peak of bliss, January wooed and promised. Buds popped, rampant for beginnings, erect, brimming to burst with song. Unwitting idlers basking in the clement days remarked upon the sudden spring. The scent – it deceived too. A pervasion of ductile fronts, flesh in the air, longing and response, a subliminal chorus singing and receiving applause.

Overcoats were left at home, cyclists smoothed the curves of parks and lanes soft with sun. But even strollers in crocuses and daffodils did not convince the cautious. This year had grown too soon.

It had.

One night in early February, the tempest struck.

Slow at first, a low humming.

Cows in a field, moving in a sudden heave. Dogs barking. The night came down in day.

Workers leaving the afternoon shift from the Factory noted the change. "It is winter, mate. What d'you expect?"

Rain – drops then needles. Splash, splash.

In the distance, wherever distance may be, thunder rolled. Temperature dropped. Those standing talking rushed mid-flow promising fulfilment at some other time.

Gales came, whipping the trees. Roofs were lifted, chimneys toppled.

On the coast, waves swallowed the beach, lashing at sandbags and consumed defences.

Deep in the country, trees fell and lightning seared the tops of branches.

In barn, Bug stared and watched the narrative unfold across the windows.

At cottage, suckling baby suckled – the constant shadow of Glastonbury at the door.

On top of hill, shrubs were wrenched up and scaffolding torn down. Sonjia stood in the torrent, and shouted at the sky, defying it to touch another brick.

In Town, storms sped through streets. Across concrete wilderness a judgment of rain engulfed the graffiti, bad end and good.

The rivers burst their banks.

For days it rained. An onslaught.

Rain, rain. Never so much water.

The Great Floods had come, and for a while, all anyone could do was survive.

Quinacridone Red

It was worse than 2015, more devastating than any of the other storms. Sedge Beat was away. The people noticed.

There was a nationwide alert. The small stretch of coastline became famous overnight and asked for help.

Support was strong, initially. Military, Services – everyone concentrated on the task at hand. The homeless were given temporary shelter, strangers from the conurbations opened their hearts and homes to the dispossessed, and, under the spotlight, compassion flourished, the community thrived, witness to a new humanity borne of disaster.

The press from other areas hoped to learn from this and gave lavish coverage. These floods must be taken seriously, and here, in this small Town, hadn't people coped? Bonded?

Gul was right. Amazing what a bit of weather can do.

Sedge came back. New Britain. Born again. Renaissance.

The press left – moved their cameras like conscience, away.

Actions when not recorded, players when not performing, rapidly revert to private scripts. Support shrank away as a smile withers on the face when it realises no one else is smiling, and self-interest took over where selflessness left off.

Visicom links stayed down, communications halted. Neighbours once allies were now the foe and after *their* food. There wasn't much left. It belonged to them. They had more mouths to feed.

Food trucks were diverted. Certain people found them and named their price. No one could agree. So a little murder here, a lynching there. Barter. Democracy.

MEJA found out, and turned up at the crucial time. The wicked entrepreneurs had their pictures taken, and unless they made other arrangements, their photographs would hang in the Town. And so would they.

The rain stopped, rivers subsided but community was gone.

Another kind of damage emerged: exclusion, genuine hunger, genuine anger.

Then the sewers: effluent rising, disease, fevers, more blisters, a new plague rising from the filth of ages, an unclean spirit abroad. Homes were lost in the turmoil, families unmoored – the certainty of generations slipped from grasp. Once again, the Services couldn't meet the needs. People coped as best they could. And if they couldn't . . ?

Along the Coast once elegant villas had been inundated, their owners fled. Museums, civic centres submerged, records of lives consumed in the chaos, waters drifting in, history floating out, and some folks were beginning to doubt their heritage. If you don't have a past, don't understand your place in it, how will you know how to treat the future? A little clue, at least, would help.

On the hill all was secure, as if protected by the gods. Deep country remained safe too and was left alone.

The fire in the little cottage flickered throughout the day, but the fuel was going and soon there would be nothing dry left.

One night, Bug collected the three of them in his truck, and installed them in the barn for a few days. Glastonbury took a chair, Foddly and her son the bed. It was so warm no one could speak. – not that there was much to say anyway – and Bug stayed awake for two nights, drinking Blujah flickering with a new malice at the old man.

Spring came. Willing heat lifted the skin off abandoned interiors, the bones of lives bleaching in an early sun.

Foddly and her son survived, cared for by cottage and allotments, by years of someone else's foresight and frugality.

Bug thrived by scavenging, taking what he saw, trading away the spoils of devastation.

Coolton Ascent did well. Rare books and prints slipped into its possession. Fine furniture and paintings arriving in truckloads – conservation, it was agreed, was not theft. Who else would look after these treasures? So the House became a cache, bestowing upon itself the choice pickings from catastrophe, while the Town, bereft of opportunity, sank into destitution. No one from down there came up and no one from the hill invited them.

Sedge Beat could almost be described as moral amongst such skulduggery, and for some hallowed time he was – giving direction, strong, clear guidance. As if being visited by conscience, he was seeing beyond the material to another dimension, a duty of care, to some at least.

Even the Policy Makers were becoming useful at last, sorting out the squabbles in the Town, agencies keeping tabs on the unruly, the wily Gul collecting names for future reference.

By the summer the Services were back and some communications restored. Everything really did now balance on that mythical knife-edge Sedge had told Foddly of, all those years before. He was the one walking the line. The merest quiver of breath carried on an unfavourable wind, the faintest doubt and he could fall.

Don't look down. Don't look at all.

Saprah returned, once more installed in the villa.

Sedge had not attempted to see his son. He had been informed of his arrival via Carlos Dean's mordant exchanges, and elected to leave that problem unattended for now. It was not going to leak as yet. Anyway, people were far too preoccupied with drains and sewers and having a roof over their heads to be concerned by a detail like that.

It happens, as it so often does, without warning. The Law Leader should have taken note, listened and when he had the chance, got out, cut and run. MEJA had caught the story. The Factory had started back. The land was poisoned, everybody knew, and Carlos Dean had begun to die.

***

Gul lay with his lover, his hand fanning the boy's stomach. Blond. Perfect.

Carlos stared up at the ceiling of the office, its tiny spotlights flickering. "Are we going to make beautiful pictures, baby?"

They rolled together in icy vapour, barely touching, searching out feeling as though in pursuit of pleasure yet not quite attaining it. Faces never registering ecstasy, passion transferred, stored up in another life. Experience deferred to later.

All that afternoon they played, a bright sun lapping up the remains of the summer in the top room of that squalid building.

"You're a star," murmured Gul, "and now you'll live forever. What more can this servant do for his Golden Prince?"

Carlos lowered his glassy stare. "My lord Bug . . ."

"Your *lord* now, is it? I never ceased to be amazed by your preoccupation with that man! He's a dwarf in comparison to you. We mustn't squander our limited recourses on feeble returns. No, Bug is not your man, I can assure you." And kissed him.

Closing his eyes, a sudden grey engulfed Carlos. He sat upright, rigid, clutching his stomach.

Gul watched with interest. The boy leapt from the bed and a stream of vomit hit the wall. Another followed.

"I'd say that was a good three metres," estimated the man. "Feeling better now?"

Carlos lay back down, breathless. "I'm going to kill him for what he's done to Bug and to me."

Gul handed him a glass of water and a towel. "I have an idea, prince, when we've cleared away your beautiful insides."

"So do me. Does yours involve medicine?"

"Powerful medicine, sweet Apollo! I can't believe I went to his party."

Laughing, Carlos shook his head, hair falling in burnished ringlets, August yellow in his eyes. "You'll do it for me?"

Gul breathed softly, plucked a cigarette from a silver case and lit it. "Blow it all away in a puff of smoke, Carlos."

Claudia was going to do very well out of all this. She'd decided.

Hadn't done badly already.

She and her family were among the few who had secured reasonable accommodation, their names now firmly registered for new housing by the old guard, who had come into their own once more. And she sat, strategically demure, on the ground-floor offices of the Town's new Clinic.

Good old establishment.

"Don't remember me, do you, Claudia?"

No she didn't.

"Well, I remember you when you were a little girl! Things don't change, do they? What happened to your mother?"

"She went overseas," supplied Claudia, then realised she'd missed a trick, and let her quivering lower lip droop. "Actually she died – sudden. Tuf . . ." No, the gorm had seen him with the kids. Stick to the gone.

The old guard, a distant memory rekindling, made a note. "It's a hard time for everyone. We'll do our best, Mrs Shell. You have how many?"

"Just the five. But I'll need special requirements . . . My size," she said coyly.

The official glanced down at the woman's bloated stomach, the rolls of material upholstered with flesh, and resisting judgment, nodded.

Status established, Claudia left her seat and giving a sly wink at Kite in the queue, padded out of the clinic.

Outside in a meagre sun, Tuf was over by a half-demolished wall, a morose eye on his brood. He was talking to someone. It was the fluff that ran the Video Mass.

When Gul saw the fat woman, he withdrew and drifted off.

"What's *he* want?" she demanded.

Tuf seemed worried. "Nothing much. He wants me to do something."

"What's he got on you?"

"Nothing much."

"So you'll have to do it then. Where?"

"The Factory."

Claudia's button eyes lit up. "Big man this is Rumpus! Can I come?"

Tuf scratched his sandpaper chin. "I don't know, little girl. If it don't work out we could lose a lot."

"What you talking like? We've got nothing more to lose. What did that journalist bloke say?"

"Said we can protest. They'll let us. But he ain't Law."

Claudia tapped her partner's arm. "Look who's coming."

In the distance, the languid Carlos Dean willowed towards them. "You'll be there?" he enquired, a dazzling smile *en passant.*

"Course we will, Carlos. What about your friend – Bug?" prodded Claudia. "Will he be going?"

"Everyone will be going but not all will be leaving," he promised with a wriggle of his curls, and sashayed on.

"Everybody. See, Tuf?"

"You've let them down, I'm afraid, sir. The weather, turned bad again. Elements, you see, Mr Beat. Just remember John Ruskin and learn to read the omens."

The villa had taken a battering itself during the storms, mainly from human assault. Personal and public. The lounge had less furniture and thick blinds were down at the window, a Visicom flickered in the corner.

"What about my daughter?" the politician asked quietly. "Where can she go?"

"To her mother, I would have thought," replied Gul.

"I have no idea where she is."

"Good for her. Always had her head screwed . . . You know, the Victorians were very strong on morality, and repression, of course. Superb hypocrites. For instance, this fellow, John Ruskin, couldn't stand pubic hair – well, not on his wife – and yet he was a prurient . . ."

Sedge swung round in a fit of clarity. "What the fuck are you raving about? I don't give a shit about pubic hair on Victorians or anybody else! Why do you play with me? You have played with me. All these years you've been working up to something else. What?"

The journalist lowered the cerulean stare and snaked his tongue around glistening lips. Reaching for his pocket he tugged, then, producing a silver case drew from it a long cigarette.

Sedge, despite his fury, was noticing things about that cigarette case. Remembering, just flashes, rapid sequences, subliminal messages from other, similar actions the man had performed. Always had the same cigarettes. Why hadn't he realised it before? Always five, even if he took one out, and always secured by that purple ribbon. But how could he see? Gul used to slip them out slyly, light them before he could say: "Get the fuck out of here, you evil bastard!" Yet he had seen them every time; had known how many there were and how many were always going to be left. The message had simply never registered, until now.

"What are you, Gul?" he asked, almost without caring. "Where did you come from? I don't know what it all means but I have nothing to thank you for."

Gul lit the cigarette, and Sedge noticed that too. It just lit. A cloud of smoke instantaneous. What happened next didn't surprise him either. His life was not his own. Since Gul had appeared he had lost authority.

"Never did have any of that, Sedge – authority," Gul assured his thoughts.

Sedge sat heavily on a chair.

Twisting the cigarette in his fingers, coils of smoke engulfing the face, the body, Gul moved the silver case around in the other hand. "I collected this little memento some time ago, long before you could have been blamed for anything. Unfortunately possessions, the chattels of a lifetime, often outlive that personal history. In fact it is exceptional if they don't because how would we *inherit* . . . anything?"

The politician wanted to speak but couldn't find the words.

"However," continued the ball of smoke. "Objects may retain that life, be imbued with certain of its aspects – did you know that? Oh yes, Sedge. Quite extraordinary what history you could recover from such a small document as a silver cigarette case. An account, a record of an entire wasted existence, perhaps. Abandonment. Rejection . . ?"

On the chair, Sedge began to shake. Why he didn't know. Struggling to his feet, he staggered to the sofa and lay down, eyes closed, listening to the narrator. Gul was that, a madman in possession of a fucking fable, in possession of him. He heard the journalist begin to pace beside him, the smoke acrid in his nostrils. Felt sick.

"Sedge, if an object can preserve such information imagine what a soul can do."

The politician was on his feet. "Now don't you come out with that abstruse shit! I don't go for it. You know me by now, old boy. So don't even try that!"

"What will that child inherit, I wonder? The one . . ." Gul mused out loud.

"Oh, *that's* it? So all this is about that little bastard? Well how do you know it's mine? You don't! I can easily say it's not mine. She'd been screwing somebody else, you know – before me. That midget. Oh yes! Where's he? Go and torture him."

"He does a good job of that by himself, and you do know it can't be his. Inheritance, Sedge. A little hand-me-down from your father to his. End of the line, so to speak." The smoke had cleared and Gul was radiant once more. Perfect teeth, suit immaculate, not a hair out of place even the eyebrows plucked to perfection. Lifting a small silk handkerchief from a top pocket, he patted his mouth and held the silk in his hand.

At this point, Sedge expected a dove to appear.

"You have to face your responsibilities in this life, you know," rebuked the journalist, returning the silk to his pocket. "Or they may come back to haunt your children. Sins of the fathers and all. Don't you care what may happen to your offspring, Mr Beat?"

Did he? Of course! Saprah. Yes. Remembered her curls, that tremulous look, clutching onto words. Break your heart. Nothing, given her nothing. He wanted to cry. Hadn't done that since his first days at school. Jesus! This was fucking crazy.

"Things don't always work out, Sedge," consoled the dapper man. "Had my own disappointments. All I have now is a cigarette case. Not much of a legacy is it? I would have much preferred . . . But they don't always work out. Fathers have a lot to answer for."

Sedge, snatching at any sign of the mortal in the man, was reassured. "Was that your father's? I can see if it belonged to your . . ."

"Missed the point, Sedge. Solipsism – there is only *one* director."

"God! You do talk utter bollocks."

The journalist exhaled noisily, the final gasp of summer. "But your boy – I would have dearly loved . . . Terrible burden, consciousness."

There was something sinister about this. "What do you want me to do, Gul? Shout it from the remaining fucking rooftops? It'll destroy Saprah. No, I can't do it. I can't have my life . . . It's already out of control. My wife, my daughter – I don't want this. I'm no use to them. What can I do?"

Gul was strolling to the door about to make his inimitable exit. "Winter's approaching. I suggest you visit the Factory."

"That place? Why?"

"*The sin of hubris.* You have a lot of history to sort out, Sedge. I want you there. It'll be the last thing I ask you to do." He paused. "Best not let Saprah know. I'll have a chat with that dumpling." And disappeared.

* * *

"Hello, Angel. Glad you could make it. How are things at home?"

"I lost my mother, Gul."

The journalist allowed the pained surprise to float across otherwise marble-still features. With a sigh, he dropped back in his black leather chair and folded his hands respectfully. "I'm very sorry. Sit, Angel. When did . . ?"

Angel sniffed, and sat on a red plastic petal-shaped creation with spindly legs. "A couple months ago. It was a small affair – the funeral. I'm glad the floods didn't interfere . . . Sounds selfish."

"Don't be so hard on yourself. How are you feeling now?"

"Wretched. Haven't been in touch with anyone much. It was a relief." Her chin trembled. "A bit surprised that . . ."

Gul cocked his head to one side, arching his eyebrows. "Yes?"

"Sedge. I invited him, and Foddly. You'd think after all the help . . ." Angel blew her nose on a large handkerchief.

Gul nodded at the desk, eyes wide yet barely encompassing the breadth of human frailty. "He's had a hell of a time."

"Oh, I know, I know. I'm being completely selfish." Tears cascading down her pale plump cheeks, her nose dribbling. Handkerchief out again.

"I would say you were behaving like any normal devoted daughter," wooed the journalist, "who, after years of supporting her, has lost the invalid parent. Life must feel like a void to you at the moment."

How nice, thought the young woman. You'd never think he had it in him. A void. That's exactly how she felt. Empty.

Gul fanned his finger on the desk at the top floor office. It was the only room in the clinic to have been refurbished, and was decorated in the late twentieth-century style, although Angel didn't appreciate that. Just looked very bare and white to her. He sat in front of that tall window reaching from floor to ceiling, looking so kindly at her. Gorgeous eyes. Absolutely stunning.

"Angel, you may not like me for saying this, but what I suggest you need is a project."

"Yes, I suppose I do. To fill . . ."

"Could you forgive Sedge – for his neglect?"

"I don't hate him! I was just surprised."

"Foddly?"

"Not around. I keep hearing about this boyfriend trouble. I don't get involved, and she wouldn't tell me anyway. I sometimes think people don't really like me except when I can be useful. I never seem to get invited to places. Even at the House, I just stay in the background. Bull knows all sorts of stuff I don't. I mean, Gul," she oozed, "they could be living in a different world."

"Oh, indeed. But we mustn't become embittered, Angel. Goodness is its own reward, and the time we are feeling the least loved, is the time to do the most loving."

Quite extraordinary.

How mean-spirited Angel had become, without even realising it. She had a home, a certain amount of independent wealth and here, all around her, people were suffering.

The journalist rested his chin on a lectern of fingers. "I want to share something with you, and I do not want it to go any further."

A glow of pride suffused her skin. Tingly belonging.

"Sedge is . . . Well, I'm concerned. The reason he didn't attend your . . . The threats . . ."

Angel, sienna eyes wide, lashes wet, hand on her little mouth.

"Had to deal with virtual insurrection," he continued carefully. "How he's managed to calm the passions, I have no idea. That man has followed through his principles to the last degree. You know, Angel he still fights for the people, even now."

The woman shook her head, deeply shamed.

Gul sighed. "Talking of mothers – poor Saprah. So sad. When you think about how you are affected by loss . . ."

"What loss? What do you mean?"

"Sedge would never say of course. Pride. A very private, proud man."

"She didn't actually leave? That woman! Oh, I'm sorry. Tezzie's actually gone?"

Gul nodded gravely.

Angel bent forward suddenly, dropping in an attitude of penance. "Look, tell him . . . No, that wouldn't be right. They do say to stay with one parent. Normally, I'd let Saprah come to me – I've got the smallholding, but all this to-ing and fro-ing is no good for the girl."

"Neither is the pressure her father's under. He won't ask, of course, but I know if you were to offer, it would be *thankfully* received," drifted the man.

Smoothing down her skirt, Angel saw the world anew. She loved Sedge, as blind to his faults as she was to the journalist's iniquity. And there was nobody else to adore. Saprah was the nearest to him she would get. "Of course. I'll do whatever I can."

"Thank you, Angel. I think if we say the weekend? It'll give Saprah time to adjust." The man stood in his spotless office. Tall, commanding in that tight-cut black suit, he made an impeccable if exaggerated circumference of the desk, and gestured to the door.

Angel trod across the soft carpet, noting the paintings on the wall. They seemed vaguely familiar.

"There is one more thing I'd like you to do. For me, that is," the journalist added. "Sedge has no input in this whatsoever. I just feel it needs to be said. Don't want him losing any more friends. There's a meeting, and I'd like Foddly to at least offer him her support."

"What can *I* do?"

"Leave a message at that place, Coolton Ascent, for Foddly. Just a line. Tell her that Sedge is very sorry he hasn't been in touch, but could she please understand etc . . . Pressure. . . I'll tell you what to say." He tapped his chin. "Better still, do you have any paper? We don't keep it here."

Angel rummaged. Why? Knew she hadn't. "No."

"Ah! Now look at this. Can you believe it, Angel, an old postcard? Miracle. That's Carlos for you. Collects all the old stuff – shame about the subject."

At the desk, Gul and Angel intimately bent over the card, rather like newlyweds about to sign the register. She felt peculiar when she saw the picture: a couple holding hands. The woman's stomach looked swollen. Very odd costumes: the man in a wide-brimmed hat and fur gown and the woman in a long dress. "Oh yes," she murmured. "Haven't seen one like that for years. Who's the artist?"

"Van Eyke. People always assume she's pregnant, but apparently not. It's just a record of a well-to-do marriage. And in that mirror – see . . . the artist is the witness. And now us! Clever stuff, eh?"

Angel didn't know anything about that, and wrote what she was told.

Stationery surprisingly well stocked now, Gul gave her an envelope. Hadn't seen one like that for a long while either.

On the way to the door, he put a finger to his lips.

She agreed, complete confidence, and left the office feeling certain she'd done well, made up for bad thoughts. Least loved must give most loving. Foddly must have been neglected too.

It wasn't really from Sedge, though, the postcard. Why couldn't he say it? It was a shame she couldn't hand it to Foddly personally.

*

Angel went to the House straightway. No one was about. She placed the envelope, clearly addressed to Foddly, on a consul table in the hallway and went to prepare for the weekend.

It was Bug who saw the envelope first. Maybe that was supposed to happen. He opened it without hesitation and read the message. Carefully re-sealing the envelope he returned it to the table.

In his room, he gathered a few belongings including a small pistol, and leaving Coolton Ascent made his way to the barn.

*

When Angel arrived at the villa the following Saturday, Saprah was at the door. She looked pale and tired, more grown up.

"How are we going, Angel, to your house?"

"How we normally go, in that nice car you like."

"It's gone. We don't have any cars now."

Angel's heart fluttered. Queasy, almost dare not ask. "Sedge – is he. . ?

"He's given me some money and stuff, pictures of me and him." Saprah's eyes unlit forests, expressionless face.

A heart without a rhythm.

Angel would never see because she couldn't bear to, any more than others, who were able, would change their path.

It was a strange day, a strange time.

It can happen like that. Sometimes things don't work out.

It was a good excuse. Bull hadn't been to the woods for months. Yes, must be well over a year. He had no idea when he'd see Foddly, the girl had disappeared off the scene – with family no doubt, and as Glastonbury was her main contact, he took the opportunity to pay a call.

A copper tinge to the air as he crunched his way through leaves, bits of sky poking through naked branches. The morning had the edge of winter about it. "What a year," he mused. "Nothing would amaze me now, the way things are going. If the earth caught fire . . . Purgatory, that's what we're in ruddy . . ."

Was he surprised? It didn't fit that's for sure, the image of the cottage that day. Didn't recognise the place. Too light, lines of small flags outside. Were they flags? The outhouses had gone. Piles of wood everywhere. Storm, obviously. Had he come to the wrong place? No, of course it was Glastonbury's. That garden, and they weren't flags, they were tiny clothes. Babies stuff, sheets and suchlike.

Approaching the door he heard crying. Couldn't think straight. None of this matched, a jarring counterpoint to his knowledge of Glastonbury – a man undomestic in this sense.

He cast around to make certain he should carry on, thought of the Town, emergency housing for the homeless? The man had said nothing to him.

He knocked, and waited. Silence. Rapped again. This had the feeling of the clandestine. Stomach similar to when uncovering little workings of the likes of Shell and Daley. Tight. Nervous. Heard footsteps. Place wasn't big enough to take this long.

Foddly's face. Should have expected that but not the way it appeared. Confused, annoyed even. "Fod! I presumed you were . . . away. Haven't seen you for an age."

She seemed to struggle with cloud, a fog. It was in her eyes. Dull, miserable. Yes, Foddly emanated misery. A trenchant desolation and his was an unwelcome intrusion. Like the weather, just had to accept it.

She glanced behind her. "Glastonbury's not . . . I won't invite you in. Sorry, Bull, up to my eyes . . ."

Yes, that sounds right, thought the man wryly. Then remembered why he'd come. "Glad it's you, Foddly because I've brought something. A rare thing," he added brightly and proffered the envelope.

The woman, a sideways look, almost met his eyes, and took the note. "Who from?"

"Open it and see," he said, wanting to see himself.

She scrabbled with the paper and pulled out a card then quickly pushed it back, changed. "Shame you've missed Glastonbury. I'm looking after . . ." Face glacial, eyes clear reached his, a little push to see how far, how much. Seeing through his eyes. "I'm doing my bit." Her skin reddened, a scarlet blush, a giggle, hair russet and shiny again that little pixie chin. Old Fod. "And I hate it, Bull. I'm just no good at it." She waved her hand to the line of clothes.

"Taking in washing?" suggested the man obtusely.

A cry tugged at the silence behind.

He frowned.

"More than that," said Foddly in a hurry. "We . . . I decided to take in one of . . . Emergency housing. There're so many families who have nothing. A young girl lost her home – already had two little ones, then this new . . . So she's here. *He's* here."

"He or she, Fod?" the man enquired, almost amused. "Surely you can't be that bad!"

"He, Bull – a little boy. I do my best, but to be honest, I'll be glad when the . . . girl has been helped. You . . ." A sudden clarity. A step too far, perhaps. Backtrack.

"Who is she, the mother?" he asked, a little heat in the violet eyes. "I may be of help. This is exactly the sort of situation I want to hear about. If you feel it's too much, then we need to help the lass – another way."

Alarmed, hand flying to her mouth. "I can't say. It's a confidence. Couldn't break that. She'd feel exposed."

"We have the transfer system, Fod."

"Transfer?"

"Yes. We transfer the responsibility for a child from parent to a suitable agency. And if your young lady is in agreement, we can find . . ."

"Agency?" she interrupted. "Sounds a bit remote."

"Except they have protectors who must report back to the mother. We never lose touch with her."

"Even if she doesn't want . . ?"

Bull shook his head. "Sounds desperate. How much trouble is she in? The child, is he ill?"

"No, but *she* is. Very ill. I'll think about what you said . . . It's really lovely to see you, Bull. I've missed you. How's Angel?"

The baby crying again, filling the air.

"Her mother died."

"Oh, dear. I ought to see her. I haven't spoken to anyone much. Since the flood I can't seem to think straight."

"No, we're all suffering in one way or another. But thanks for helping out. You better see to his lordship. I'll come back when Glastonbury's here, if that's all right. Take some details."

"What details?"

"This mother and her child – a vulnerable, Foddly! Two at least, if not the whole family. Some wretches are gobbling up the whole ruddy cake and here we have a genuine case for support. There are still *some* decent types out there."

"But I don't want you to, Bull. Please, as my friend. No details."

Why didn't he see? Was this woman so securely embedded in his stubborn outlook, he couldn't shift her? Or was the lie so vital he let it stay? "What's the poor soul's name? The mother must have given him a name, Fod?"

She turned into the small parlour. Bull curious to look.

In the corner a large basket. Soft sweet smell.

Foddly lifted the bundle, her back to him. "No, she didn't. I feel as if he's been stolen. There's a war going on and he's been stolen."

The man in the tiny doorway, shadows swelling, gorging on the meagre light. She was telling him things. Bull Somerset, dull yet holy in some way, a sacred niche in his tedious façade. "Well," he said, scratching his beard. "Not my idea of spoils, Fod. Lost would be a better description. But if what you're feeling is right, then we ought to find a way of giving him back."

He left, troubled but pledged to secrecy. Glastonbury had clearly sanctioned it and he, Bull, would be there if either of them needed him.

"How many times have you vomited like this?" Bug connected a small hose to the tap and began spraying down the barn wall.

Carlos, prostrate his skin a lake of sweat and fought for words. "Sorry . . . I couldn't stop it."

"I'm not blaming you," assured the man. "But you must get some serious help if this is becoming a regular thing."

"Can't remember. I had my first one about two years ago."

"What triggers it?"

"Don't know, Bug. It just comes on."

"Are you on your own when it happens?"

"Er . . . no. It's only happened with Gul. And now you," he added with smile.

"So it's when you get excited with Gul. Before or after?"

Carlos, colour reviving, sat up and straightened out his clothes. "Very candid. Aren't you disapproving?"

"Why should I be? It's your life, Carlos. Your body."

The boy gave a little stagy sulk. "Thought you cared. I must be excited by you; don't you feel responsible?"

Bug shook his head. "Stop your impression of a lily, and get up and help me."

"I'm gutless, you know. No guts, baby! If I had I'd do so many things." Carlos wrung out a cloth and cleared away the hose. "Will you touch me like Rill, when he heals my stomach? I can show you where to make your hands burn!"

"Good try, but no. There won't be anything of you left to heal. Glastonbury can take over."

"You hate him now, don't you?" Carlos swung upon the table and crossed his legs, crimson mouth brimming with rumour. "Who do you hate most, Beat or Glastonbury?"

Bug was over by the dais, opening the cupboard beneath the steps. He rustled amongst some paper.

Carlos caught a glimpse. "Wow! Hey, baby, what is *that*?" He leapt from the table, ran over and flinging himself on the bed, leaned over Bug's shoulder.

"A khanjar, a pistol-grip dagger," returned his friend. "Could collect your entrails in one deft sweep. Eighteenth-century watered steel blade. Exceptionally fine."

"Those are rubies! Can I hold it?"

"They are, and you can't. You're far too delicate a flower to handle such a thing of destiny."

Carlos shrieked with glee. "What else have you got there? Hah! Trying to cover up the old man's pistol? You haven't seen me scrap." He tilted his head and tried to catch his eye. "Do you want to see me fight, Bug? I can use a gun."

"No thanks. What I do want to know is what you have planned for the Factory."

Switching up the boy got to his feet and left the dais. "Nothing. Beat has killed my life and yours. He's a thief. Taken things. Precious things."

"That doesn't mean you have to be the one who takes them back."

"You don't know how much he's harmed you. Foddly was just the beginning! And I know about . . ."

"You can't act for me, so don't try." Eyes glinting, Bug started to move towards the boy, a slow threat of a walk.

Carlos couldn't meet the stare and felt the strength drain from his stomach again. "I'm sorry, I shouldn't have mentioned, her. I'm not going to say anything. Promise. But I can't stop it now."

"What?"

"We aren't the only ones. You just can't see it. You know, Bug, sometimes you just can't . . . see."

Flesh Tint.

When he opened the door of the office, Gul was at the window, his back to him.

Neither spoke for a while.

Bug sank into a long, sleek chair of chrome and leather. Stretching out his legs, he folded his arms, a swift appraisal of the room.

"Make yourself at home," murmured the journalist from the window. "But I'd like to keep the Pollock."

"Welcome to it – our Tezzie does get around . . ."

"Just a little hand me down, Mr Itin, from his wall to mine – slightly more elevated than a table."

"*Context* is everything. Chair's a fake too."

"What are you sitting on, thin air?" Gul reached for his pocket.

"Wouldn't surprise me – it's what you live on. But keep it thin, if you don't mind. No obfuscations."

Gul let his hand hover. "You certainly make up in verbiage what you lack in inches. What is it you want?" He gave the vertical blinds a little flick. They wriggled, teeth of light combing the room.

Bug squinted. "I don't think I *want* anything. Can have too much, and a man is never free if his heart desires. I'm trying abstemious. I've come to see how you do it – live on nothing."

The journalist didn't move, his back firm, clad in his dark suit. A vignette. "*Why,* might be the better approach. That tantalising glimpse of content, you had that once, but it's all evanescent pleasure, fleeting hope. I exist through others, their emptiness. Give it direction."

Spreading his fingers, Bug watched the tremble and smiled. "Vacant possession . . ."

"If that's an offer, I'm not interested," Gul returned swiftly.

"It isn't, all my mansions are all full. Not so with Carlos. Your occupation is making him sick."

"He's dying because of Beat, the land, the Factory. You should know. And we have our remedy of sorts."

"I don't want him involved."

Gul waved an irritable hand. "For an ascetic, you're full of wants. He'll be going to the Factory – to support you, as it happens. It's all for *you.* Yes, you seem to occupy him far more than I."

Slipping from the chair, Bug crossed to the desk. Drawing a small pistol from his coat pocket he inspected it. "Glastonbury's, this. Ought to return it, but as he has something that belonged to me. . . By the way, you can leave *her* out of this as well – keep away from Foddly."

Gul brushed down his jacket and folded his arms. "Ah, those possessions again. That is where *tenacity* could have paid. You go for the wrong kind of return – pride won't get you anywhere, except falling." He began to rotate, so slow his revolution it was almost beneath perception.

Bug kept to him like a shadow, carefully avoiding his face, the pistol pointed. An impossible slow dance, choreographed silence. He was pressed against the window now, Gul by the desk. "Sit," he directed softly.

The journalist sat, a contained rage in the azure eyes. "Aren't we the little acrobat?"

"Have you thought what will happen to that child?"

"Have you? I presume we are talking of the *little bastard*, as Sedge so fondly calls it. A missed opportunity for us both."

"I don't quite see it in those terms."

"Don't do the spiritual aristocrat for me. Fancy yourself as a collector, eh? You and that Glastonbury fellow should have a long chat. Sort out a bit of that provenance you seem so obsessed by. I make copy, Mr Itin, record events. Communication is my trade, I merely pass on the message."

Bug was tired. He fought but languor thickened his thoughts, as red does the precision of white. "We've met before," he muttered, through the sleep. "A long time before this."

"You're fading fast," Gul assessed coolly. "Maybe we bid against each other at some provincial sale. I think you should leave the important ones to Glastonbury. He's the one who knows and we do go back an awfully long way; be quite amazed at *our* provenance."

Bug slid the pistol back into his coat. It wouldn't have had any affect anyway, like trying to kill the sky with a rock.

Outside the clinic, he peered up at the top floor. What was happening? Weakened, overpowered by something. But his enmity to Glastonbury was still young. Pride. He couldn't go to him. So fell back on himself.

But if the journalist had been planning Bug's demise, he would have to wait.

Magenta

Like a man who knows his hour has come, Sedge Beat had projected himself beyond the vagaries of time. A new perspective tailored to fit, minutiae examined, detail occupying and commanding the greatest attention. Each crease and crack he visited around his life, each hairline fissure led to this almighty chasm, and it was marvellous to see at last how everything seemed to connect. Even the trees shivering beyond the grille, their naked branches waving to suggest that nature itself was in communion with this derisory game.

He had taken care though, chose the mustard tweed suit today – good colour – a narrow magenta tie drawing a startling line down a cream cotton shirt. Sported the old Italian shoes. Had them years. Still excellent.

Couldn't make up his mind whether to take a drink. Bourbon, perhaps? He cast around. Nothing much left. Arranged all that. Piano? Yes. Scriabin, or Prokofiev. Was this the time? There was no other.

He sat in front of the Broadwood and lifted the lid.

Could have been standing there for ages because he hadn't seen her arrive. And how did she get in?

She was on her own. A halo of autumn. Good God! Poetry, at this hour. Standing abject. Utterly desolate. What could he do? What the fuck could he do?

She was wearing a long skirt – like something out of the Wild-West – fringed jacket and boots. A twenty-first century cowgirl. Staring. Had something in her hand. Jeesus! What? Oh, a paper or something. What did she want? Him to sign a fucking birth certificate? Now? Irony, oh sweet irony.

A lifetime could have passed in those moments, and in some ways, it did.

Sedge was surprisingly buoyant, eloquent, found himself very amusing. Fluctuating clarity. The absurdity of seeing the way things are at the end. One spends one's entire life, twisting and embroidering to avoid the lucidity and . . . bang! The bastard's there anyway. He wasn't taking much notice of Foddly in her effete distractions. He had some talking to do, explaining.

"Shuttup!"

What did she say? Only one person . . . He could hit her for that. Quite within his rights. Comes in here, without invitation and tells him to fucking shuttup. The little . . .

"They're going to kill you!"

At least it stopped him, but he'd never have struck her anyway. "Don't be so bloody. . . silly."

Her face smeared with misery, eyes like the leaves he'd seen hanging by a thread this morning, the ones he'd crunched underfoot. Golden sadness crumbling.

He was blubbing. Sedge Beat, a precious boy, a famous man who could play the piano so well, squeezing that urchin face, tears over those eyes. "Fod, I'm so sorry. I'm just no good. After everything, I'm no good. You know that. You do. You've always known what I'm like."

"Well at least you didn't ask me to trust you," she said, without humour.

"Remember when we were kids, Fod?"

"No."

"We went to the Gothick horror."

"We weren't children."

He drew a line around her face then cupped it in efficient hands. "Go back to him, Fod."

"Who? Bug doesn't want *me*. He won't have me!"

"Bastard!"

"What?"

"He should help you."

"You really are so . . . This is *ours*, yours and mine. We made this . . . thing happen. We can't undo it."

"Oh, Fod, I know. If I could, don't you think I'd be unknitting all the fucking shit I've got to face at the Factory? By the way, where is . . ? "

"A friend."

"I hope it's no one . . . That place."

"They won't be saying anything at the House, and don't worry about your daughter – Angel is as blind as a bat. She won't ever see. Even after years with Bug, some people still think I'm icy, like a nun. They'd never believe I was a mother. *I* don't actually believe it."

But Sedge was seeing. It was an obverse view. He hadn't time for this and wished he had. That weakened him most of all. A plea to the unlistening. An opportunity indefinitely postponed. "I've got to do some talking, Fod. I can't help you or . . ." He relented. "What's the . . . his name?"

"Nothing. I don't want to call him anything, it might taint him further."

"You are a strange one, Foddly. I should never have got involved. Kept you as some private fantasy when Tezzie went screwing. Now here you are, more doomed than me, yet I'm the bastard without a future."

"If they find out, our son won't have one either."

Sedge didn't want to think anymore. "What have you there, in your hand?"

Foddly showed him the card.

"Ah, I know this. The *Arnolfini* marriage thing." He narrowed his eyes. "What are you trying to say?"

"Nothing. It came from you . . ."

"From the devil more like. This has to be Gul. Have to admit, he never ceases to amaze."

"So, you didn't apologise? Didn't think the thoughts written here?"

Taking the card he read. Pointless curiosity. "No. Not me. And if you've come here today because of a ruse, I'm sorry but that really isn't my fault."

"Is there nothing, Sedge, that's your fault?" Foddly, a path of light. Yes, even there, in the darkest moment, a difference he could make.

"I'm not very kind to you, any of you. A man of straw. You must understand that, Fod. Always be a disappointment. And now I really have to go."

"I'll come with you."

"Grow up! A maudlin little you won't benefit from this. Won't come out with her man all shining and brave. I'm not going to make it all better, for anybody." He wandered over to the Visicom and keyed in a few numbers. The screen flared blue a line of text following. "That was close, Fod. For a minute, thought I might need to borrow your boneshaker." He grinned, a desperate grinning skull. Involuntary humour – the oldest joke.

Patting down the brilliant tie he swept back his hair, still thick and glossy for man past forty.

Before he left he went to the piano and closed the lid. "Saprah will have this. I've made arrangements."

A buzz, and he was at the door, in the portico. Dusk in his eyes and not yet midday.

She hadn't known him as long as Bug, yet he too had been a landscape.

He turned sharply, face a graph. Clicking his fingers he summoned her to the drive. "Move it," he said, pointing to the bike. "I hope to God I never see that fucking thing again."

A black car drew up and he slid inside.

* * *

"I wanna pee. I always wanna pee when I get excited." Kite jumped up and down on the mud, beyond the Factory. "When we getting in there, then?"

"When we get the order," Claudia informed swiftly. She hadn't time for distractions, the whole of her solid mass concentrated upon the task at hand. They were waiting for the others to arrive, about twenty in all. Her big man would be bringing them. She loved it when Tuf was like this, organising, silently arranging things. When people said nothing it had more meaning somehow, but now they were stuck in this field, until they were called.

Taciturn herself this was the beginning of their time. It demanded reverence.

*

Sedge called by at the Clinic offices. Gul had left. That wasn't right. He should be here.

The driver said nothing when Sedge spoke to him. They waited for a while and then proceeded to the Factory.

The gates were open.

"What a hole. Can see why people hate this God-forsaken place," the politician muttered. He had a metal case in his hand, a few tapes inside. Didn't know why, never used them. Swinging open the car door, he looked round. Italian leather soles made contact with the tarmac. And slammed the door.

The car, a long crunch fading to silence.

A firm hand on his arm. "Top level, Mr Beat. Right to the top today, sir."

Sedge couldn't believe it. Gul, clad in alpaca coat and trilby, was smoking that perpetual bloody cigarette. Yes! Got to be the same one. Born with it, if he was ever born. Never lit it or put the thing out – everlasting fucking puff. He laughed inwardly, then realised it wasn't funny. Far from it. "And where were you, Gul?" he enquired, as if it mattered anymore.

"Here. We're all waiting."

"For what?" Sedge looked beyond the journalist. MEJA were setting up, cameras, cables like slithering tails. Sure there were others too, familiar faces from the Town. What was going on? Why bother with pretence at this stage of the game? "What the fuck are you doing, Gul? You've set up this debacle. A little bit of theatre for the boys?"

"Thought you liked attention, Mr Beat. I'll make sure your best side is showing . . . Maybe that's been the problem all along – we couldn't decide which was your best side."

The politician could see them clearly now, straggling in the airstrip beyond the Factory, their shivering bulks like reluctant parents at a rugby match. Had his parents ever come to watch him play? Of course not. He hadn't gone in for the savagery, wanted to keep his teeth. And after all that vigilance . . .

Then someone else, a shadow behind him then sulphur, blood, the taste of salt. A crack on his head.

Which came first was difficult to tell.

*

Foddly arrived at the Factory. Couldn't see anyone. No guards or military. She'd never been in there before, and slipping through the gates, was fascinated by both the space and the enclosure.

Stillness. A quiet Sunday afternoon. Light fading. She crossed the concourse. Silence. A hard, desperate place, the clock tower, the red bricks and wide entrance. To the side, a smaller door.

Propping her bike against a wall, she approached the building, a searchlight picking out her journey.

The door was open. Up the stairs, stone, narrow. Dark blue paint then green then mustard. Flight after flight of different dirty paint. On each level she passed saw inner windowed doors that led to the work areas.

The smell of diesel of iron. Close sweat and concentration. A bang and a screech Hinges whining, shutters opening, lifts humming, but on which floor was impossible to determine, a ubiquitous noise. Machinery grinding, an arsenal of sound travelling so quickly and now all in the colour brown.

Someone was talking. On this floor? Lost count. A door swung open then banged to. Smoke. Strong smell of oil. More voices, outside this time.

Pressed against the wall, Foddly breathed fast, clothes sticking to her skin. Someone was climbing the stairs. More than one. Coming nearer. But she was at the top! Shoving the door, she entered a vast room. Right over in the far corner was another door, an oblong slot of light. A fire escape. Her feet clipped the silence. She stopped.

Emptiness, void. Breasts tingling with milk, she thought of her son lying in his basket, Glastonbury beside him.

Laughter stifled. Below or to the side or even above.

Crouching down she saw a lift, blocks of things piled on it, windows caged in wire.

Slippery wooden floors. Oil spilled.

A figure, over where she had been standing near the stairs, a flash of light, a quick sliver of white. It was the moon. Night comes so sudden. Smoke all around her now. That oil had become a seam of fire.

A man appeared with a torch in his hand another man to the side. Didn't know if they'd seen her. Squeezing to a window, Foddly saw the gathering below. That was sudden too. The ground, the barbed wire all illuminated by lanterns and more torches. The noise dense with anger. Calling for him. "Beat! Beat!" Insensate.

Why? Had he really been that bad?

Sedge, a heap under a workbench, covered in mud and grease. She was here. Why?

A firework was thrown into the room. From where?

Sheets of flame rising from all sorts of unexpected places. Shots at the window.

Didn't seem to care. For once she was looking beyond herself.

"Get out, Sedge! Come on, the place is alight."

His shaking was so violent he couldn't speak. He clung onto her arm, his face drained of any of himself – a squealing, petrified child. "Help me! Help me! Oh, God! I don't want to die. Please. I can't do it. I'm not fit to do it!"

"Just get up! The fire escape might be open."

It was shut firm.

He crawled out, crumbling in his tweed suit, and, grabbing the edge of the bench, staggered towards the door.

The crescent moon ablaze.

"Break the fucking window!"

"We can't get through the window, Sedge."

More shots and chanting. Burning, thick, black smoke now, the bench on fire. Sedge pushed past her, seizing what looked like an iron bar and smashed at the wood.

He stood for a moment, framed in sky

Foddly couldn't move or breathe, saw him topple. Air burnt, the smell of gunfire. Hatred. Everywhere people screaming and shouting.

She crawled to the fire escape. From her strange vantage point of slipping down oil and iron, she could see Sedge on the ground. By the barbed wire now. Did they know it was him? He might get away . . .

Some people were clattering up the steps but the person next her was booting them away. "Bug? Why are you . . ?"

"Get down Foddly! Just get down! Don't bother with him!"

Then another face she knew amidst all the others. A tranquil face, smiling up at her, past her. He had a rifle, and swung it round, and aimed.

"Carlos . . . Don't!"

Did she say that? No, it was Bug who was shouting. He'd thrown her to the ground and was running, his shirt on fire.

It was a long way down. From the fire escape, Sedge noted, the world was moving so slowly. He had fallen yet it was still taking too long to get out of the moment. They were waiting for him and his legs weren't working. Why had she bothered to come? They were waiting for him. All right, he'd go and greet the ungrateful shits. If that's what they wanted, he'd give it to them – nothing more to lose. But the world was so fucking big. All that unused space. Pathetic. Or maybe that was him. So who'd notice if he wasn't here?

The smell was like bonfire night. A bloody party out there, all for his benefit, a heaving cake of worms with torches for candles. Surely he could slip down these steps and leave? No one would bother to stop him.

On the tarmac he wanted to apologise although it wasn't really his fault. Whatever he'd done it wasn't really him. But he was here and no one else was going to carry the can.

Something fell upon him, a great fat creature, then more started pulling at his face, his arms, wrenching the rings from his fingers, his watch. Dragging him over to the barbed wire with its little patch of grass, they shoved him face down in the mud. "Eat your own shit, Beat!"

Very nice, he thought wryly. But it's all yours. Imagine that, a joke.

Off with his jacket. Sleeve ripped clean off, then trousers. He was being plucked like a chicken. A boot in the shin. Funny, how he could bear that pain. Thick fingers clawing at his mouth. Inside. Fist. Steel. After something. What? Teeth. "Not my teeth!"

Smell of ends so close. Suit, shirt. Take the fucking lot – all bollocks. The whole thing's frippery, I realise that now. Oh, God why did I come? I should never have listened to Gul.

Head wrenched back. Sky filled with untimely dawn, flashbulbs bursting, a giant spotlight and him so small. Just a kid. I'm still only a . . . "No! Not now! Please . . Mother!"

Carlos Dean at very close range.

Too near not to be deliverance. A gift.

A cheer so loud it stopped the world.

Sedge Beat burst open, head broken, a bit of his face left, not much, so drenched in magenta, but it was he. Could tell. Even now.

Carlos jumping and shrieking, demented. He rushed over to Bug who was rolling over and over in the mud.

On the top floor of the Factory windows shattered and flames spewed.

The people on the ground were moving in one toxic heave towards the doors.

Foddly inched away. A torch was thrown at her.

"She's with the him, the fucking bitch! Sure I've seen her."

A hand steered Foddly backwards. Leather-gloved, hard grip. A severe outline: Safe. Soldier, sergeant, friend.

"You're a friggin' bad penny, d'you know that, Foddly Shaw!" The soldier lowered her gun, eyes quick with light, face like a flag. Crumpled "Get out! For Chrissake, get out!" and shoved. "*Go*, you silly cow!" A brooch was crackling on her lapel. "Got the main man down," she told it. "The bastards are torching everything in sight . . . Armed! We need more . . ."

Foddly backing towards the gates her legs like vapour. A clear run and she was free. Couldn't leave. Heard another low-grade sound behind, near some bushes.

"Run, Foddly!"

Another shot. A heavy figure fell. Soldier, sergeant, friend.

Foddly ran.

And ran.

* * *

The windows at the top of the Victorian building were blown out, skeletal wire swinging in the easterly wind, bricks blackened. The scorched entrance was smeared with paint. Within the Factory the lower levels were reasonably intact but the lift hung on iron sinews, a dark bird threatening to swoop. The building was hammered shut and the gates closed. A forbidden piece of history. No one found out what happened in that place its ineluctable memory sealed stored up for late deliverance.

The riots did nobody any good.

Neither Military nor Services stopped the insurgence, just let them get on with tearing up the Town, their lives. Folks would get tired of it. When they needed food or medical help, they'd come to heel.

But they weren't hungry, didn't feel their wounds, kept on ripping burning and smashing, a whirlwind of destruction propelled by an interior momentum in competition with nature, it seemed.

Days went by and the revolting energy renewed itself with each dawn, stumbling across new insults justifications for revenge.

What stopped it was the weather. Winter. Not pathetic fallacy but an unsuitable signature, snow. Unusual, hadn't had it for years. Snow, a pacifying blanket over bawling streets.

Marauding mobsters crunched and slipped, greeting the new precariousness with delight. Like children, they found the virgin spread irresistible and had to leave their mark.

But it was cold and there is a limit to how many balls of ice even a revolting underdog can make and hurl.

Still, they would take up the theme again. Oh, it wasn't over, not by a long chalk. The people hadn't finished yet. That is not to say they didn't need respite. Warriors are entitled to that, you know – fighting for a cause. So where was it, respite?

The Services were oddly quiet about Sedge Beat. Other agencies had leapt up from nowhere to fill his place. Oleaginous types, slithering to lenience allowing forums to delay inquests and post-mortems, and that House on the top of that hill seemed to pacify, bridge a gap.

No one person paid the price yet everyone expected a bill, and when they didn't receive a demand, became suspicious.

Latitude can be a backhanded reckoning.

News of the politician's demise was absorbed by New Britain like a jab against a minor ailment when a plague is round the corner.

Sedge was taken to the old churchyard where his parents lay and buried next to them. All sins absolved, if not by the dignity of ones own efforts, then by the distinction of heritage.

A tight and severe assembly that afternoon, with notable absences. Tezzie, for instance.

Saprah came, standing very close to Angel, staring beyond the trees. A quick look behind her, almost like a reflex. Was she really expecting someone? Of course. There's always hope. Must be.

*

Foddly stayed in the cottage. Days untouched by consciousness. Hours abandoned in light and dark.

Didn't speak about what she'd seen. Was it her fault? No. Nothing to do with her. She didn't exist. A spectator, that's what she was. Foddly Shaw, empty and inconsequential on the borders of lives, broken lives, yet vacant as she was she'd had an effect.

So burying herself in the void, she watched her baby as he screamed, knelt down and studied his face. "Don't ask for me. I'm not here." Then crept back to nothing.

For weeks she stuck in the gloom while Glastonbury tended the child. Sonjia came, now and then. She didn't speak to her either. No point. Would make no difference. Can't bring back the dead or make the born return. No matter what anyone thinks.

The night Sedge was killed Angel had a dream. Never one for bristling antenna, the woman was amazed her vision so vivid. In it, she saw Sedge. He was speaking very gruffly, not like him at all. He had a jester's hat on, bells and everything. She told him to take it off because it spoiled the look of him. He couldn't. His face kept changing from up to down, smiling then sad, like a mask.

"Take off the hat," she said Then someone came along with a big knife and cut his head right from his shoulders, hat and all. "Happy now?"

When she awoke her nightclothes were soaked in sweat. Tiptoeing past Saprah's room in the small bungalow, she heard girl muttering in her sleep.

In the bathroom, the screech of tyres, the front door being battered.

Bull, glistening white, eyes ablaze. No Foddly, then.

"Who was that, Angel?"

"Bull."

"Where is he?"

"Gone."

"What's the matter with you?"

Angel slouched on the edge of the bed. She could see the outline of another form in her mother's old room. A small hard shape. Wooden, almost. Next, she heard Saprah slide out from under the covers and leave the room, pattering about a bit.

She came and stood in front of Angel. "Why did he go so suddenly? He should've stayed a bit longer than that . . . and it's night!"

Angel wrung her hands pulling at the stubby fingers and rubbed her palms. "He's gone . . . that's all. He went, Saprah."

Up on the wall a picture of sky and hills lots of fluffy clouds, beneath them tiny lambs prancing about in the rolling green. Lower down, on a little cupboard, a framed image of Saprah and her father.

"When things are really so bad, Saprah," she measured. "We have to think of other people. When things are taken from us, we have to think of giving back."

"What can you give back if you don't have anything?"

"There is always something. I know there is always . . . something."

"You're talking rubbish, Angel. You do that when you don't want to get upset. With your mother you did that – and Foddly, when you talked about her. I didn't like her either. She stole Daddy."

Angel, so still, a round pudding, stolid, too densely full to enjoy.

Saprah was over by a wicker chair, banging her feet on the carpet, a little madness in her dark eyes. "Tell me then, Angel, what you think of her?"

"It's nothing to do with Foddly."

Jumping up, Saprah's arms tangling in the air. "What am I doing here? Where are my parents? They should be together with me. We should all be together. This is a wrong place!" and flomped onto the bed. The girl found the difference in Angel's face more alarming. Crying. Tears on that pastry skin. Why was she doing that?

Large hands clasping small ones, folding over the fingers.

The woman lifted them to her lips.

"What's happened to him, to Sedge?" the girl asked. Then, falling back on the covers she let the plump hand drop. "Oh, they've killed him. That's what's happened. I knew they would," she said quietly.

Amazing how quiet these things can be.

"People don't understand how someone as good as him could want to help them. It says so in a book, Angel. They destroy the good." Face brimming with survival, she riveted her eyes on the woman. "You know, don't you, how good he was? I don't understand how they could make such a mistake. They got it all wrong. You can talk rubbish, if you like. I don't mind. Go on, talk!" Into Angel's arms. "He loved me more than anyone . . . Didn't he? He did, I know he did."

"Yes. More than anything, and anyone. You are the . . . future. He said that. I'm certain . . . And I'm going to protect his future."

Saprah swallowed hard. One gulp and she'd gone. A face expressionless, eyes dead. Gone somewhere.

"I'm tired, Angel. I need to talk to myself."

"Can I get you a drink?"

"No."

"Good night. I . . . love you, Saprah. I'll take care of everything."

"Good night."

In the narrow sitting room, Angel Brown, not yet thirty, slumped down on a settee like an old woman besieged by age.

In a thin light, Saprah was standing before her. The girl's nightie was wet, a turmoil of red on the front, the colour dribbling down her legs.

Angel flung off her blanket. "I'll get you something. It never occurred to me it would be that time."

"I've decided, Angel. I'm going to forgive them. That's what he would want. All this blood stuff is a sign."

"No, dear, it's something else. Grown-up girls have that. Brave, grown-up girls. Surely you . . . Hasn't anyone told you?"

New Britain fell. Toppling for so long it should have grown wings.

Conflict fires a sense of cohesion, if nothing else, determining purpose. But it is only temporary, its power marginal. Without structure a hurt community drifts and bleeds. Coagulation, clumps of like-passioned people congeal, but the slightest bump and they separate and bleed again, becoming scars of their shared selves, factions of a common wound. It is much better if the clumps gather and unite against one enemy rather than each other.

In the Town, denizens were uniting. An awareness of the common enemy was taking shape, a reassuring divide. A remedy of sorts.

Coolton Ascent was growing, its strange influence heard abroad. It was said, by those who watched, that there were riches beyond the wildest up there, untold wealth sacked from all sorts of privileged places. An old man and woman, who ran the place, pretended they could bring the dead back. Yes, imagine! See spirits and watch them fly out of the body. Some people could catch them. And if you knew how, you could do it yourself – catch a soul. If you knew how. If you believed it.

The damaged did believe it, and they didn't know how. They just sat in the new units being thrown up, lightless boxes with one window. And who was building these black holes? Who said it had to be like this? Not New Britain anymore. Another enemy.

Things were not working out at all.

Still, the New Town with its new units and new Loyalty Store was grateful for the new focus of enmity.

Coolton Ascent became the Church, had power, which the Town could dispute and despise. But the plateau following the chaos had descended to a desultory scorn. People just couldn't be bothered now. Their time would come – the meek. It was a shame they couldn't read, most of them, because it was all written down, apparently in a big book.

Nonetheless they were getting other things, a little encouragement from the Policy Makers, the Old Guard were seeing to that. And folks were being asked to help out. That made them feel included as well, entrusted. Faith – always a good sign. The misunderstood need to break free from misunderstanding, to be seen anew. There were the needy and what better for those who have needs than to be with those who have needed.

*

Over the months, Bug stayed holed-up in the barn, his burns tended by Rill. The only other visitor was Carlos.

"I did it for you, Bug."

"You shouldn't have, Carlos, it hasn't helped. Me or anybody."

But there was no point in talking to him because the boy was so sick.

One morning Carlos left, the light ejecting from his head in broken spurts, the failing colour a plaintive cry.

Bug cradled him like father would a child, feeding him from a bottle until he came back. But maybe he didn't want to return.

"I love you more than my own mother, Bug," he told him one morning. "Next time, we'll die together, you and me. We can live 'out there' forever."

Carlos would say these things and forget. Still young, a fevered view.

The boy had avoided contact with the journalist since the incident at the Factory. He was confused. Couldn't believe what they had done together.

A jealous Gul persisted, wooing his Golden Prince from a chill distance – promises laced with threats. And as Carlos saw he could never possess the one he craved, fell back on him.

In the following years, life with MEJA became a dress rehearsal, a macabre theatre enacted with people who at this time Carlos barely knew: a young girl locked in her own grieving hollow, creatures from the Town Gul would court with vile images, perfidious agents and dark players as yet unscripted. Innocent ones would feature too, a child who, through no fault of his own, would find himself in the spotlight.

2017

Lamp Black

I wish I could forget it all, go to sleep and . . ."

"Yes? Go to sleep and . . ?"

"Wake up and it's all over. Everything gone."

"A fresh start – is that what you mean?"

"I want none of this to ever have happened, existed, not even him. Is that betrayal?"

In a garden, the grass still damp from rain, a man and a woman talked. A small child sat between them, looking at a lilac tree.

The woman had been talking for a long time, then got up and went into the cottage. When she reappeared, she had a bag in her hand as if she was going somewhere. The child tried to see what she was saying, but her face was in shadow. All about her, the lilacs were blowing, blossom dispersing in the wind.

"Take me away, Glastonbury."
"Where do you want to go?"
"I don't know. Anywhere but here."
"You might miss the way home, Foddly."
"I don't have one."
"What about your son?"
"He doesn't have one, either. I'm not his home. Take me away, like you did Odella. I know you did."

"But she came back. You can't eradicate these things, Foddly. You understand that. We've talked about it."

"I can't live like this. I see nothing except war, and I brought him here. He shouldn't have been made to come back."

"What do you mean by that?"

"I don't know, but it's all wrong. They'll kill him if they find out. You keep him. Hide him. Bull knows people . . . Sonjia, she's always arranging things."

"Your son will always recognise you."

"Bug said that, Glastonbury. *He* doesn't. I don't even recognise myself."

"Foddly!"

The scent of lilacs. Sun in the boy's eyes. Couldn't speak for calling. Glastonbury lifting him up high. In the garden, flowers. Spring.

Both watching.

* * *

"What is your name?"

"*You know . . .*"

"What is your name?"

"Fodellah Shaw."

"Why are you doing this?"

"Because there's nothing left."

"Have you ever seen the light?"

"I may have. Around people . . . there are colours."

"What is the colour around your son?"

"I don't know."

"I'm afraid, Fodellah, I can't help you until you tell me what it is you wish to forget."

The Abbess, dressed in a black gown with lace sleeves, sat with Foddly in the dim of the church vestry. She looked forlornly towards the lectern, then back to Foddly, her eyes slipping in quick-silver, a hazardous splash of mercury on picnic lawns. "I have a book you may wish to peruse. If you intend to become a nun, I suggest you investigate the deeper questions, my dear. We'll try again tomorrow."

* * *

Glastonbury wouldn't face him and sat with his back to the door, huddled in a coat, with his glass and a cut of bread on a plate beside the chair.

In the small damp parlour, the air was saturated with the scent of lilacs.

"I've been developing, Glastonbury."

Yes, so I see, Bug. Happens like that sometimes, in extreme pain – an overview. Of course it was all started long ago when you first left, as an infant. I put your contempt for everything down to that."

"Talking of contempt, are you going to do what she asks?"

"I am."

Bug ran his fingers across the dresser making tracks in the dust. "You've tried it before, on her grandmother – it didn't work out then and you'll still go ahead?"

"I had nothing to do with that. This is a different way, son."

"Amounts to the same thing and you know it. She'll have to face herself, her son, one day."

"You had a chance, Bug. Maybe you could have changed it, for yourself, at least."

"You think so? This is *your* game! I'll find her again but then, of course it will be too late . . . if that apparition, Gul has his way." He moved from the parlour onto the threshold, the sun high. "What you've done – what you're doing is so wrong – unforgivable."

"That's up to you, Bug. We all have our frailty. This is my weakness. Like you, her, I have my limits."

"Another fake. Should have bargained for that. But it's always been Foddly. I knew, as soon as I saw her, Glastonbury. I wanted you to see that too."

"I saw."

"But it made no difference."

"No."

* * *

"I'm ready now, Mother."

"To relinquish your hold, Transition?"

"Yes."

"To die?"

"Yes."

"And be born again?"

"Yes, Mother."

The Abbess knelt before Foddly. Lifting her hands, she stroked the lights encircling the novice. Each one she saw drew to her until she had lined them up outside the young woman.

Straightaway Foddly saw Bug. He was behind her on a bike, spinning round in circles showing off. Then he fell and she was rolling on the grass, laughing.

By the sea next, with her mother, arguing about an ice cream. Then her father – forgotten how silly he looked when he was trying to be cross.

Glastonbury stood before a long window talking to a man in a dark suit. He was the one she'd met that day at Sedge's, years ago. Smirky good-looks – hadn't changed over the years. Ought to give him a name because she knew him.

Glastonbury was remonstrating, becoming very angry. He never did that. The man was smiling as he pulled out a small silver case from his pocket.

"Why has Gul got Grandma's cigarette case?" she enquired.

Glastonbury refused to reply.

"What was that?" the Abbess spoke some miles away. "Have we found Odella? Describe her for me."

"No, I'm not even born yet. How did I know that silver case was hers?"

"See if you can find her."

Foddly struggled with Gul. He was lighting a cigarette or rather it just became alight, smoke, plumes of grey and white covering his face. He should be so much older shouldn't he? Couldn't look the same all the time. She coughed, her breath caught. Couldn't breathe.

"Oh it's shocking, that stuff," sympathised the old woman. "I utterly loathe it. He's not a nice man, my dear. Best avoid him, go right past."

Beyond, a beach trickling gold, so clear, the sea blue and sparkling. Fresh air. Open air. "*We're eating fish and chips in the open air.*" Someone else said that, a voice too young to be her own. Was it her voice? No, more like a boy's.

A hand reached out, fine tapered fingers with polished nails. The hand stroked her face.

Sun was bright even on a cold day. "I won't feel the sun again," she said.

By her side now, the Abbess chuckled. "I do like a pun, Foddly. But you will, of course."

Foddly didn't want to laugh, couldn't understand the joke. It was the arm she saw now, the one connecting the hand – hers, joined to her body. The arm was clad in a chiffon blouse, a gold bracelet on the narrow wrist, its hand moving. A tender gesture.

"Come back out," the Abbess instructed.

"Where is she?"

That was Glastonbury speaking. Brought the lilacs with him. She tried to see him but was trapped by the current pulling her down, an eddy of such force she couldn't move. Wanted to comb her hair, brush it back in all this wind. Down at her feet, ridiculously pointed shoes. How could anyone walk in those? Must have tiny feet. And those heels – you'd fall off! Wouldn't like to be in her shoes.

"Well, don't then – be in her shoes," snapped the Abbess. "You do have a choice."

Foddly didn't and stood. Not in the damp vestry next to Glastonbury and the Abbess, but on that stretch of sand. Someone calling. That young voice again, then Grandma Odella, as clear as day. Eyes wide. So young and pretty. She was plucking a cigarette from that silver case. She lit it, the smoke smothering her face.

"Oh, don't do that, I can't see you properly!" Foddly heard herself say.

Then Odella changed. Her mouth became a wide tear, like the sky, mad with tearing.

No noise came out. A silent film.

Back again and the hand stroking. She snatched it before it could change, and hung on tight. "Don't *you* go," she said. It was her.

"Where, you silly . . ?" *That* was hers too. How many voices did she have? Mother? Child? Can't be both, an impossible fusion.

Now Glastonbury had come back at last.

"Are you angry with me?" she asked.

"Disappointed perhaps, with myself."

"Have you been waiting long?"

"Not really. But watch, Foddly. You may miss something. You have to forget everything, so you must remember it all, first."

That was cruel because Bug was there again. Not very old, and he'd fallen off his bike – always doing that. Hurt his leg. He kicked the front wheel. She didn't laugh this time and sat next to him on the grass. "Have you got the stuff that keeps the pain in?"

"Blood, you mean, Fod. Nothing keeps the pain in. I've got this," and brought out a handkerchief. Blood oozed through the cotton. Placing her hand on his knee, she saw it became red too. She looked at it closely. "I can't feel anything. It's not the same."

Bug fell backwards on the grass, laughing himself. "When we do feel the same thing, it's got to better than this!" He went, evaporated in the air. She stretched out to grab him but he'd gone.

Reversing down a hill, back to the sea then the beach. She passed by Odella's eyes, beside autumn skies. Stopped off to watch a couple embrace before they said goodbye. Picked up a tiny baby and kissed it. Took off his clothes and put the warm belly to her face, and blew. Heard the baby squeal with delight. Sat down and rocked. His face, her world, her breast, his. Tucked up in a corner, years ago, a gracious moment. Shouldn't forget that.

Then a man was there, husband maybe. He looked just like Bug. He bent down and kissed the woman with the baby. A soft swimming kiss.

Foddly could feel that. Wished she could always feel it. Then why . . ?

"Pull it through. Let the colours sew."

Glastonbury, or that funny old man, Rill would say that.

Couldn't really see anything in detail. Faces a mist. Now she was interested in the light that stood outside the vestry door. It was exhausted.

"Leave that until another time, my dear," warned the old woman. "You'll have plenty opportunity for carrying later."

Day after day she met the Abbess with her bizarre costumes and bewildering demands.

"Lift. Fly! Close down."

What did she mean? Yet Foddly did as she was bid without understanding how. Visiting the sea, the House, until they too disappeared for a while.

Then the boy came The one she'd dreamed of – clinging to her, a grip so fierce it was as if he were welded to her skeleton. He wouldn't leave. She tried to shake him off, amputate him, bring down a sword and sever him from her flesh, but there he was still dangling. "Leave me alone, I've got to go . . . I have to."

Until she was him. That was terrible. She kept shouting but no one came. Nothing beyond her toes, the world a terrifying silent void. Couldn't reach out for fear of falling.

Foddly didn't want to be the boy anymore and planned her escape. Another child flew by . . . an infant really. Maybe she could fly with him.

"Leave that thought," instructed the Abbess. "Tried him, already. It didn't work."

Gradually feelings faded altogether. Fear of voids or endless dropping, vanished. Faces were unrecognisable becoming geometric shapes, equations she felt no need to interrogate. Somebody else can work those out, because the only one she needed to know about was the one in front of her: the Abbess.

Images moving so fast they were like the tail of a comet. Then only the finest thread through the eye of a needle. Sew, pull and sew. Cut. Selvedge.

"What is your name?"

"Fodellah."

"May I call you '*Sister* Foddly'?"

"Yes.

"How are you, now?"

"Tired, Mother."

"Close down. Good. We're going to the main house. Your room at the top is being refurbished, Sister. I've put you next to Bug," she informed breezily. "He's brought us some wonderful costumes. An old friend makes them up, apparently. An individual, Bug – some may call him a pariah, but we have a fondness for the outcast here." The old woman nodded to someone behind her and wafted from the vestry, across the gardens.

Foddly followed aware of the tall man walking beside her. The man, she realised had the most wonderful green eyes and she had known him all her life. Almost like a father.

*

The room Foddly had been given had French windows that led onto an ornate balcony and she could see right over the countryside.

The room was an odd shape, didn't seem to have a centre. Well furnished with a few choice pieces. Good rugs. Someone had taken great care. Beautiful marble fireplace – could do with a vase of bright flowers on that mantelpiece.

Over at a small oak desk she turned over a book on its polished surface. "*Gulliver's Travels,* by *Dean Swift,*" she read. "How lovely – look at that later." In the meantime it would be interesting to see what that room next to this was like.

In the hallway, she knocked on the door. No response. A tree scraped against the tall side window. Glancing up saw an odd reflection: a woman in voluminous trousers with cummerbund and embroidered jacket. Didn't recognise herself.

Back at the door, she twisted its porcelain handle, pushed and entered the room. So much colour and scent, a fragrance she couldn't put a name to. Ought to know. A flower of some kind.

Beyond, the massive bay windows were draped with velvet, fine paintings hung on the panelled walls. Lavish and extravagant the room was a little realm all its own. Could easily live here and forget the outside existed.

Her eyes travelled from the ceiling and the shimmering girandole, down across the expanse of floor with its carpets and the bed in the centre, settling on an octagonal table. Next to it a rocking chair, in it, a man cross-legged, was watching as he rocked. He didn't seem at all surprised. Could have been waiting.

"Oh, I'm so sorry . . ." She blushed and turned to leave.

Leaving his seat, he came up to her, right up intimately close. He was small and wiry. His face, marked and stretched tight over high cheekbones, emphasised the slanted eyes. Like a wolf, she thought. And he's wearing these funny clothes too.

The man smiled but it remained as an uncomfortable shape beneath his ginger moustache.

She could tell from his light he was hurt, terribly damaged in some way. Would need healing.

"Could all do with that, Fod," he said.

That was quick. Have to close down.

His long fingers were playing at a small pointed beard. Graceful, eloquent fingers, ones that could pull the colours out . . . make them match. Hadn't realised she knew so much.

All this was happening beneath time. Had no grasp of that. So exhausted.

"You don't mind me calling you Fod, do you, *Sister*?" He spoke very quietly.

"No, of course not."

He was impish, might seem cruel to some. Eyes, like sapphires, had the longest and loneliest gaze and if she could recall what it was he was seeing, might feel lonely too. Yet she liked him. Just did. Tried to place him, capture a memory but failed and so tired.

"Can't remember, Foddly? It'll come back to you, no doubt. You look blown away. Go and sleep. I'll still be here when you wake up."

"What's it look like at the seaside, Serene? Does it look different by the sea?" drawled Claudia, a bloated hand shielding her eyes from the sun.

Her daughter leaned over, a dark shadow falling across the child. "Funny. It looks funny."

"You can get privileges for that," Kite said resentfully, flopping back on the hot sand.

Claudia rolled her eyes. "Oh, you're quick! And you just keep this quiet! I only showed you because of other stuff."

Kite eyed the new boy as he stared at the sea. Not a move. "Thin. Has he got the damage?"

"Clean as a whistle. Not a scratch."

"Why'd they give it then? Where's the mother?"

"Ooh, Kite, you are so suspicious. At least we look after our own. Tuf, do you reckon we could pass Speak off?" she gurgled. "Get more out of the authorities? No one would know . . . the way things are."

But the man wasn't listening.

The yellow beach, a respite from drab Town, was smoothed out like custard before them, the waves frothing on a wobbly horizon.

Serene, a solidly vicious girl, caked in sand was pulling at the child's hair. "Look, it don't make a noise if you do that."

Claudia wasn't interested and lay down herself, stomach defiantly buoyant. "*And* we've got a protector, Kite," she beamed, enjoying her friend's ire. "Bug Itin, from the Hill. We reckon he's been sent direct from the Church. He's a special, does sleep tricks. Worth having the trouble, just for that," she winked.

"I thought protectors was for the transferred kid." Kite mumbled tetchily. "Dunno know how you work it, girl."

"'Cos we're the damaged," supplied Serene.

The group crowded around the small boy, who sat quite passively against the chalk wall, while he was prodded and poked. Didn't respond. It was as if he had left the beach, his own self, for the duration of this scorching scrutiny.

Tuf remained determinedly oblivious to the child and focused on the sky. "Ain't been here for years. Amazing we got any coast left," he muttered to himself.

Another child tottered into view. Lumpy and dripping with sea, he knelt clumsily at the boy's side, shoving Serene away.

She resisted and punched him. "Get off, Wit."

"Mine!" he snarled. "I'm looking after him."

The girl went to tear.

"Give over," advised Claudia, listlessly.

Kite prepared to leave; she had a client at four. Shaking her shoes, she poured the sand in circles as if seasoning a pot of potatoes.

Claudia squinted up. "What d'you call stuff that gets taken in riots, Kite?"

"Food!"

"No! Bigger things. There's a name for it. Anybody can take it."

Kite shook her head. "Dunno. Can't think of nothing – except loot, but that's the decent stuff – *we'd* never get a look in." She took out a mirror from her bag and began to smear a violent orange grease on her mouth. "That lot up the Hill took all the treasures. Anything good, they'd have it."

Satisfied, Claudia heaved her morass of flesh and clothing over to the side where Tuf was still gazing out to the distant waves.

"See them ships with the big masts?" he said pointing. "They've only just turned up. All that lot wasn't here last time. There's a Dutch geezer, called Tor, runs it all. From what I've heard, he's a right . . ."

"Forget them. Look what we've got here." She pointed at the transferred boy. "He's loot, big man. And loot's worth something. Especially when folks want it back."

Wit heard her. He squeezed up to the silent child, placing his freckly face right next to his pale one, and saw the boy had eyes that were oranger than Kite's mouth.

"Don't you worry, Loot," he whispered. "I'll protect you. They ain't gonna get you, I'll make sure of that."

The boy, Loot, spoke, but his words were wrapped in silence.

2039

Coolton Ascent.

Renaissance Gold

Foddly, what is it you have there? Looks like a hundred cigarettes, my dear. That would be a cruel joke, although I may deserve it.

Have I upset everyone, staying so long? I was told, you know, by Glastonbury that I would. Did you ever meet him? Not sure I did. Maybe he didn't really exist, just someone who turned up every now and then. One could never really say one had met Glastonbury. I'd tell him everything – he'd listen, neither condoning nor opposing what I said, as if he were just observing. When I think of it, he revealed nothing of himself . . . Nothing. So it must have been that, I found so compelling. The mind, you know, is different from the soul. Would never escape to nothing, there.

Ah, now there are more of you! All gathering round an old crone – a witch. That's what the nurses would call me here. Yes, I can recall that.

You're lost. So sorry, I can't see any of you clearly. My darkness, I'm afraid – eyesight. You are just fading blurs on the edge of this view.

Oh, don't sing . . . please. I know you don't want to. Something tells me . . . The way your shapes are dwindling.

He's in the corner, Foddly. I can see him, smoking, trying to merge with the other beacons. Blow out the candles and you'll see him too – in his *vestments*! He is a bad man, the way he endures like this.

I really hoped Glastonbury would shoo him away but he never did. What *did* Glastonbury do? Yet he had the most remarkable green eyes, like emeralds. Made one think he would have made a wonderful father.

I wasn't much of a mother, was I? An *un-mother*, let's say. But neither were you. We are selfish, all of us. We must, at some point, move beyond ourselves. Nurture is a way to do that – outliving history. And if we fail, we are locked forever in the interior view.

I had a child, a little boy, once. Someone left him waiting in the sea. It's a very lonely place, waiting. He must have become mixed up with all the others . . . calling. So many and each a grain of sand on the beach. So who would recognise them? A mother, perhaps? But if she too, had gone . . . if she had kept that singular prospect?

Come here, and let me look at your face. I should have taken more notice. A very sad face. Have you been waiting too, my dear?

All of you, been . . . waiting?

1992

A boy went past with his dreams. Eyes so full, he couldn't see.

Aureolin

The two stood before a large house, its gates padlocked, the long driveway covered in gorse and weed.

"How old do you think that house is?"

"Ten, twelve. Older than you, Bug."

The boy grinned, because it was a leading question. "Well I can tell you, Fod, that house hasn't been around as long someone I know. He's lived forever."

"You can't live forever you'd get too tall. And tired. People don't go on like some things . . . " The girl crossed her arms, and concentrated. "The sky, that goes on, but a person. . . Who, Bug?"

"Ah, well, if you don't believe, it's no good me taking you."

"Where?"

"To see him."

"In the sky?"

"The woods. Not far." The boy jerked up the front wheel of his bike. "Go on this, if you want. You can have the seat." He tried not to show the desperation. She didn't like it when he got desperate. "I don't mind one way or the other, but there're very few people who know about him."

"No, I can't. Mommy won't let me."

"Yes she will!" he shouted. Couldn't help it. "Freda asked her. It's O.K. Please, Fod! Please!"

Never again. He'd never plead with her like this again. But it was so important.

The girl was suspicious, saw his face all red and his eyes shiny. "You'll go fast, Bug."

"No I won't. Slow as you like."

"What's his name?"

"Glastonbury. And his eyes are greener than that." He pointed to her emerald coloured dress.

She looked down. Apart from the mud, it was very green. "Is he a human being or a fairy?"

The boy played this one careful "That's why I want you to come, Fod. I need to you to see, tell me what you think."

On the seat, she hung onto him.

"Hold on tight, Fod."

"You're going too fast!"

"We have to get there."

Her face against his back, he could feel her breath through his shirt. "Put your legs straight out!" he yelled. "They'll get in the way of the pedals. And don't let go." He raced on, his hair flying, her gripping tighter.

"You're wicked, Bug Itin!" she shouted. "You're always playing tricks. Does this Glastonbury really exist?"

"You'll soon find out, Fod. Just don't let go!"

The End